WITHDRAWN
No longer the property of the
Boston Public Library.
Sale of this material benefits the Library

Praise for
CODE OF THE WEST

"This book is right out of the Larry McMurtry school of writing . . . The goodness of the heroes, the badness of the villains, and the trademark humor as well . . . Well put together, a real find."

—*The Tampa Tribune*

"A captivating barnburner of romance, adventure, and gruesome frontier justice. Latham . . . carries off this rollicking tale with class and style."

—*Publishers Weekly*

"A magical Texas love story that is rich and haunting and vividly transports you back to the days of the wild west . . . Once again, Mr. Latham shines as a beautiful writer and a master storyteller."

—Patricia Cornwell

"Originality, vitality, old-fashioned entertainment."

—Larry L. King, author of *The Best Little Whorehouse in Texas*

"I couldn't put *Code of the West* down."

—James M. McPherson, author of *Battle Cry of Freedom*

"A stirring saga of the American spirit . . . Nobody knows Texas better than Aaron Latham, and nobody writes the cowboy with more passion, more fire, and more emotion . . . A brilliant and original telling of a classic theme, which entertains and inspires."

—Linda Fairstein, author of *The Deadhouse*

"A haunting parable of innocence and love, betrayal and forgiveness . . . The novel is highly original in its subtle understanding of Native American psychology and how easily humans persuade themselves of another's inhumanity."

—Robert B. MacNeil

"A wonderfully entertaining read . . . I couldn't wait to pick it up again."

—*The Richmond Times-Dispatch*

ALSO BY AARON LATHAM

Code of the West

The Ballad of Gussie and Clyde

The Frozen Leopard: Hunting My Dark Heart in Africa

Perfect Pieces

Urban Cowboy

Orchids for Mother

Crazy Sunday: F. Scott Fitzgerald in Hollywood

THE COWBOY
WITH THE
TIFFANY GUN

AARON LATHAM

FICTION

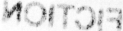

BERKLEY BOOKS, NEW YORK

Most Berkley Books are available at special quantity discounts for bulk
purchases for sales promotions, premiums, fund-raising, or educational use.
Special books, or book excerpts, can also be created to fit specific needs.

For details, write: Special Markets, The Berkley Publishing Group, 375
Hudson Street, New York, New York 10014.

This is a work of fiction. Names, characters,
places, and incidents either are the product of the
author's imagination or are used fictitiously, and any
resemblance to actual persons, living or dead, business
establishments, events, or locales is entirely coincidental.

B

A Berkley Book
Published by The Berkley Publishing Group
A division of Penguin Group (USA) Inc.
375 Hudson Street
New York, New York 10014

Copyright © 2003 by Aaron Latham
Cover design by Honi Werner

This book, or parts thereof, may not be reproduced in any form without permission. The
scanning, uploading, and distribution of this book via the Internet or via any other means
without the permission of the publisher is illegal and punishable by law. Please purchase
only authorized electronic editions, and do not participate in or encourage electronic
piracy of copyrighted materials. Your support of the author's rights is appreciated.

Simon & Schuster hardcover edition: 2003
Berkley trade paperback edition: December 2004

ISBN: 0-425-19841-3

Visit our website at www.penguin.com

The Library of Congress has cataloged the Simon & Schuster hardcover as follows:

Library of Congress Cataloging-in-Publication Data
Latham, Aaron.
The cowboy with the Tiffany gun / Aaron Latham.
p. cm.
1. Arthurian romances—Adaptations. I. Title.
PS3562.A7536C69 2003
813'.54—dc21   2003042848

Printed in the United States of America

10 9 8 7 6 5 4 3 2 1

FICTION

6/05

NOTE

The cowboy is the American knight: the armed man on horseback with a code. Famous knights always had special swords. I gave my American knight a special gun made by Tiffany. Yes, Tiffany really did make silver six-shooters once upon a time. And, yes, what I call the "plagues of Egypt" really did ravage West Texas more or less as described. The town of Quanah was especially hard hit and doubly plagued. And, yes, there really was a Winchester Quarantine.

When I invent a new heroine,
I'm just reinventing Lesley.

THE COWBOY
WITH THE
TIFFANY GUN

CHAPTER 1

BOOM!

Revelie ducked, then crouched. Emotions exploded in her head: She hated the sound of guns. She despised what guns could do. She loathed what she herself had done with a gun, for she had done the worst thing. Now this frightened man-killer found herself crouching at the feet of her son, who stood tall and fearless. Of course *he* wasn't afraid. He had never seen what guns were capable of because she had never allowed guns to come near him. She had carefully shielded him from their violence all his life. The mother understood why she was afraid—while her boy was fearless—but she still felt a little silly.

"Please help me up," said Revelie, extending her hand.

"Okay, Mumsy," said Percy, sounding younger than his seventeen years. Taking her hand, he lifted her gently. "Don't be ascared."

"That's not a word, Percy. It's not in the dictionary. You must always speak correctly. Please."

Soon mother and son were once again promenading along Atlantic Avenue, which skirted the Boston Harbor. They walked south with the water on their left.

"They're just playing," said Percy, "because it's the Fourth." He pointed. "See."

"Percy, don't point," said his mother, who nonetheless looked in the direction he was pointing.

Revelie saw a paddle-wheel steamship with a dozen cannon pointed right at her. Bright American flags with thirty-four stars waved above the ship's crowded decks. All hands had turned out to enjoy the sun and fire the cannon. She told herself that they were surely firing blanks, but she had a hard time believing it. She saw smoke. *BOOM!*

This time she cringed instead of ducking. She told herself that she was making progress.

Revelie—who was still beautiful at forty-three years of age—tried to concentrate on the beauty of the harbor scene. She was slightly taller than average. Her hair was now light brown with rare silver threads running through it. Her ample but tightly laced figure continued to conform to the hourglass ideal. Her legs were concealed under her ankle-length skirt.

The harbor was filled with dozens of other ships with sails or steam engines—even some with both—all flying starry banners. Revelie picked out a favorite, a tall sailing ship with three masts and square sails. Sailors stood shoulder to shoulder on the great crossbars—yardarms—so they looked like birds on a wire. She hoped they wouldn't fall.

Strolling along, they passed wharves, all of which had huge warehouses built on them: great, fat fingers of commerce reaching out into the harbor. First came Lewis Wharf, then Commercial Wharf, T Wharf, and the longest, Long Wharf. Slow horse-drawn wagons piled with goods rolled past them.

BOOM! BOOM! BOOM!

Revelie shuddered. She had always loved Boston because it was so civilized, so insulated from raw violence, ruled by law instead guns. Except on the Fourth, apparently. Guns had won the Revolution and guns were used to celebrate its victory. She understood it, but she didn't have to like it.

"Let's get out of here," said Percy.

"Thank you," said his mother.

At India Wharf, they turned right and walked up India Street where they moved in the shadow of four-story, red-brick buildings. Their cobblestone path bent to the right. None of the streets were straight. They passed the Chamber of Commerce with its pointed roof that looked like a wizard's cap. At the Custom House—a "Roman" temple with six fluted columns and a domed roof—India Street ran into State Street and disappeared. A couple of blocks later, State changed its name to Court Street. These lanes were crooked, changeable things. Now buggies and carriages joined the wagons moving up and down the narrow streets.

"Be careful," said Revelie. "Don't get run over."

Then she regretted her motherly timidity. The guns in the harbor had unnerved her.

"Don't worry," said Percy.

But his mother couldn't help worrying. The world had convinced her a long time ago that it was a dangerous place. She considered it her paramount duty as a mother to defend her child against dangerous weapons, dangerous people, dangerous situations. She had named him Percy in part because it seemed such a safe name. Percys didn't get into fights, did they? Percys didn't go looking for trouble. Percys didn't throw their lives away. Percys wrote poems and obeyed their mothers.

Of course, Revelie sometimes worried that maybe she was too protective: worried that she worried too much. After all, Percy certainly looked like a young man who could take care of himself. He was six feet two inches tall and weighed a thin 175 pounds, more or less. He had dark brown hair, a straight nose, a few freckles, and changeable eyes that sometimes seemed blue and other times looked brown. He wore a black frock coat, snug cream-colored trousers, and a large, loosely tied cravat. He had left his top hat at home. His mother admired his grace: He walked gracefully, turned his head gracefully, moved his hands gracefully. And he had the spontaneity of a child.

On the left loomed the elegant Old State House built of bright red brick. It had a second-floor balcony, a steeple, and a lion and a unicorn on the roof.

"They read the Declaration of Independence from that balcony back in '76," said Revelie.

"Mumsy, you tell me that every Fourth."

"Do I, dear?"

"Why do you think I picked this street?"

"I see. What is our next port of call?"

"The Common. Okay with you?"

"Of course."

"The Common. Then the Garden. Then home."

"Very good."

When they reached Tremont, they turned left and there before them stretched those twin parks: the Boston Common and the Public Garden. They were actually Siamese twins since they were forever joined by a shared fence.

"Oh, no," said Revelie.

"What's the matter?" asked Percy.

She was so rattled that she pointed. Her son followed her aim and saw a dozen great guns lined up in a row on the Parade Ground in the far corner of the Common.

"More cannon," she said. "They're not going to start shooting too, are they?"

"Don't know." Her son smiled.

"I certainly hope not."

Behind the cannon were the troops. A company of blue-clad soldiers were showing off their skill at close-order drilling: slapping their rifles, shouldering their arms, lowering them, lifting them, twirling them like batons. Revelie shivered.

"I hate all these guns, guns, guns," she said. "They're so dangerous."

"Sorry," he said. "Let's go see the Garden."

"Good. Thank you."

They passed through a long, narrow shadow cast by the Army and Navy Monument, which consisted of a single column with a warrior standing on top. Revelie found this shade cold and shivered. Following a well-trodden path, they approached the double gate that connected the Boston Common to the Public Garden.

"I like the Garden better anyway," said Revelie.

"Me, too," said Percy.

"Don't say 'me, too,'" she corrected. "Say, 'So do I.'"

Revelie criticized herself for being so critical, but she had hoped sending him away to Andover Academy would change him. Rid him of what she thought of as "baby talk," but it hadn't. And he was supposed to go to Harvard in the fall. Would he fit in? Would they make fun of him? She hoped her overprotectiveness hadn't contributed to his seeming reluctance to grow up.

Revelie stopped to enjoy the beauty of the Garden's large pond with a fountain in the middle. She preferred the sound of gurgling water to booming fieldpieces. She glanced back over her left shoulder to make sure nobody was lighting any fuses, but trees blocked her view. They crossed the bridge to the other side of the pond, where they found George Washington blocking their way. The father of his country rode a proud horse and wore a three-cornered hat while his bronze eyes stared unblinkingly at the horizon.

"Let's go see what's going on over there," said Percy, pointing.

Chapter 2

"**D**on't point," said his mother.

Turning onto a path that veered off to the left, Revelie and her son bore down on a small carnival that had been set up in the south end of the Garden. American flags flapped and red-white-and-blue banners billowed like sails.

"When did this thing get here?" asked Percy.

"It must be part of the Fourth of July celebration," said Revelie.

"Looks like fun."

He started walking faster, so she quickened her pace to keep up. She glanced again in the direction of the cannon, but still couldn't see them. She felt uneasy. Especially because she heard shots ahead. Or were they? They sounded like shooting and yet they didn't. They weren't loud, but they were disturbing. Then they stopped. Good.

Booths were positioned on both sides of the path. Mother and son strolled past a fortune-teller's stand. Then they passed up a chance to throw darts at a small bull's-eye. But they paused in front of a stall where people were trying to toss wooden rings over the bobbing head of a gray goose swimming in a tub.

"Want to try, Mumsy?" Percy asked.

"No, thank you," she replied, listening hard for gunfire, hearing none. "But be my guest. Feel free to try this sport yourself if it pleases you."

"No, I don't want to make you wait."

Moving on, they crept up on a booth with lots of bunting. Revelie cringed when she saw some strange species of gun lying on its counter. Her son walked faster. In spite of her misgivings, she hurried to catch up.

"What's that?" asked Percy.

"It doesn't look interesting," said Revelie. "Let's keep going."

"But what is it, Mumsy?" he asked, raising his voice.

The keeper of the little booth cleared his throat loudly to attract their attention. "Excuse me," he said. "Allow me to explain."

The curious Percy stepped up to the counter. Revelie hesitated, but then joined her son.

"Tell me," said the boy.

"This thing's what they call an air rifle," said the man behind the counter. "It's brand-new." He picked up the unusual gun and handed it to Percy. "Made entirely of metal, as you can see. Mostly brass."

The boy hefted the weapon that looked like a rifle with a wire stock. How curious. It resembled a gun attached to a wire coat hanger. The word "Daisy" was stamped into the metal just above the trigger.

"Daisy, funny name for a gun," said Percy.

"Yeah, you care to try your luck, son?" asked the proprietor. "A nickel buys you five shots. Lots of fun. You'll like it. Really. If you hit three ducks, you get five more shots free."

"No, thank you," said Revelie.

"How about you?" asked the salesman, addressing Percy. "Make your mother proud."

"I'm already proud," she said. "Let's go."

"Wait," Percy said. "I'd like to try. It's not a real gun. It's just a toy. Can't I do it?"

Revelie thought: He had to know she minded, because he knew how much she hated guns, any kind of guns.

"I don't know," she temporized.

Percy was an only child and therefore Revelie was an indulgent parent. She was accustomed to saying yes to his wishes. Forbidding him guns had always been the one exception to that rule. As he was growing up, she had never let him touch a gun, not even a toy gun, not if she could help it. But now he was almost grown. She couldn't keep him "tied to her apron strings" forever, not that she ever wore one. Her maids wore aprons.

"Be a sport, Mumsy," said Percy.

"How safe is it?" asked Revelie.

"Very safe," said the carnival man. "Uses squeezed-up air instead of gunpowder to fire its little balls. Powerful enough to kill birds but nothing bigger. Nothing dangerous about it. Nothing at all. Unless you're a bird."

"Or you accidentally get shot in the eye," said the mother.

"I'm sure your boy is a better shot than that," said the carnie. "Aren't you, son?"

"I don't know," Percy said. "Never shot a gun before."

"Never shot a gun? A great lad like you. I don't believe it."

"Believe it," said Revelie icily.

"Well, then it's high time he learned how. Every gentleman knows how to shoot."

"I beg to differ," said Revelie.

"Please," said Percy.

"Oh, all right," she said with a sigh, "if you really want to."

"Thank you, Mumsy." He turned to the carnie. "Tell me how."

"I'll load it for you."

Percy handed over the air rifle. The man pried up a lever on top of the gun and inserted a small lead ball. The lever came back down with a click.

"Here you go," said the carnie. "Just line up the sights and pull the trigger. You know what the sights are, don't you?"

"I think so. I've seen guns before. Just never got to shoot one."

"Good luck."

Propping the rifle's coat-hanger stock against his shoulder, Percy stared down the barrel at the ducks. These wildfowl were made of wood and swam on a wooden pond. One followed the other in a never-ending line. He chose one as his target, followed it with the sights, and squeezed the trigger. The wooden duck fell over dead.

"You never shot before?" asked the carnie.

"I would like to hear the answer to that question myself," said Revelie. "Percy, have you been secretly shooting? Where? When?"

"No, never. Cross my heart. I guess I'm lucky."

"Beginner's luck, is it? Give it here. I'll load it again."

He pulled up the lever and dropped in another ball. Then he handed it back.

"Thank you," said Percy.

With growing misgivings, Revelie watched her son raise the rifle once again—and smile. He was obviously having a good time. He pulled the trigger and killed another wooden duck. Then his smile stretched wider and his even white teeth showed through. Oh, no.

"I don't know," said the carnie. "Maybe your more'n a lucky beginner. You ain't tryin' to put one over on me, are you, son?"

"Cross my heart and hope to die."

"Don't say that," said his mother.

Percy missed his third shot. A wooden duck's life was spared. Revelie was relieved. But her son's fourth show was true and knocked over its victim. His mother shook her head. And the fifth shot slammed another poor waterfowl.

"Congratulations," said the carnie. "You win another turn."

Percy fired and hit a duck. He fired, hit. Fired, fired, hit, hit. All hits, no misses.

"You're either lying about being a beginner," said the carnie, "or you're a natural."

"It's fun."

Revelie shivered as if it weren't a hot Fourth of July.

CHAPTER 3

Revelie heard the bell ring and listened for the rustle of the maid's petticoats. Yes, there she went. The door creaked open and then creaked closed again. The girl's footsteps climbed the stairs. She knocked softly on the library door.

"Come in," said Revelie.

The maid entered bearing a telegram on a silver tray. Her mistress lifted the message and then lowered it to her lap.

"Thank you," she said, dismissing the girl.

Revelie sat there studying the yellow envelope apprehensively. She knew news in a hurry was usually bad news. What could have happened? What tragedy awaited her? Hadn't she already endured enough of them? Husband shot dead, mother dead, father dead. Who was next? Fingering the telegram, Revelie stared joylessly out a bay window at Joy Street. She started tearing open the envelope—then stopped. She knew she couldn't put it off forever, but she could put it off for a little while.

Laying the message on an Empire end table, Revelie stood up and walked to her books. Her fingers gently touched the leather backs of old friends. Byron. Keats. Coleridge. Wordsworth. Tennyson. And her favorite, Percy Bysshe Shelley, the poet after whom she had named her son. Of course, she had left out "Bysshe." After much reflection, she had chosen "York" as his middle name because her great-great-grandmother came from that part of England.

Automatically, her hand selected the collected poems of her favorite poet. She carried the green-trimmed volume back to her wooden rocking chair. Opening the book in the middle, she wondered what poem she should read. What would be soothing? She started turning pages, going forward, then back, then forward again. "Ozymandias"?

No. "Ode to the West Wind"? No. "Prometheus Unbound"? Much too long. "To a Skylark"? Maybe, well, no.

When she reached "Adonais," Revelie finally stopped. She stopped in spite of herself. She knew this poem would not cheer anybody up, but for some reason she could not resist it.

> I weep for Adonais—he is dead!

She looked out the window again.

She told herself that she was very likely being silly. The news might not be so bad. Why was she reading a death elegy? But she couldn't stop.

> Oh, weep for Adonais . . . Lost Angel of a ruined Paradise!

She closed the book.

Picking up the telegram, she tore it open. Written in neat cursive script was the news:

Loving shot. Bad.

The message wasn't signed because that would have cost more, but Revelie imagined that Too Short had probably sent it. She folded the piece of paper over and over again until it was a tiny square. Then she unfolded it and read it again. The bad news hadn't changed. She kept expecting to cry, she wanted to cry, but the tears didn't come.

What was she to do? She had once loved Loving, who moved so gracefully. Maybe she loved him still. But that love had cost her—had cost everyone—so much. She could almost see him now, with those deep eyes that were sometimes brown, sometimes seemingly blue.

She had never really explained Loving to her son. She had always told herself that he was too young to understand. But was he still too young? Had he outgrown her excuses? Did she owe it to him to tell him what they had been to each other? No, he still seemed too young, so much younger than his years. She wanted him to grow up, and yet she didn't.

Besides, however old he grew, however grown up, could she ever tell him what had happened and make him understand? Understand from her point of view? Would Percy ever forgive her for loving her husband, Jimmy Goodnight, the greatest of ranchers, while at the same time falling in love with his best friend, Jack Loving, the best of the cowboys? She had ruined an almost legendary friendship and done even worse. If she told him, what would he say to her? What would he feel?

Clutching the telegram, Revelie got up and walked to the window. She sat down in the window seat and watched the buggies passing on Joy Street. She asked herself again: What should she do? With her father and mother gone, she had no one to turn to for advice. Since she had moved back to Boston, she had so many secrets to keep, she had been careful not to get too close to anyone—anyone but her son. Now she had no one to ask but herself: What did she want to do? What did she feel she must do? She couldn't decide. The news was too new. She had not absorbed it yet.

Revelie heard the front door open and close. She recognized the sound of her son's tread upon the stairs.

"Percy," she called.

"Yes, Mother," he answered.

"Could you come into the library? I have something to tell you."

CHAPTER 4

The world rocked gently from side to side. Nothing stood still, everything wobbled. It was an unsteady, uncertain world. Revelie's stomach had been queasy for hundreds of miles. Her mind felt sick, too. Was there a connection? She worried about Loving, but she was also concerned for herself because she was still wanted in Texas for murder.

Just thinking the word—just mind-mumbling "murder"—chilled her even here in this summer-cooked railroad car. The heat reminded her of the fire, the one from which Loving had rescued her, the very hell that she certainly deserved. Because she had broken *the* commandment, hadn't she? Thou shalt not kill. Thou shalt not shoot at your husband and end up killing an innocent cowboy instead. Unfortunately, unlike her son, she couldn't shoot straight. She was probably lucky she hadn't killed two cowboys and the cook. Having cheated the hangman once, she had promised herself she would never return to Texas. Oh, well, she had broken promises before.

Revelie was afraid for herself, for Loving, and for her son whom she was carrying with her into harm's way. She couldn't believe she was doing it, couldn't stand that she was doing it, and yet she was doing it all the same. What sort of world was she about to expose him to? Surely it hadn't changed materially since she had last seen it. It would still be a world of guns. A world of violence. A world where her boy might or might not find a father. She told herself over and over again that she should tell Percy about Loving, but as usual she put it off. Of course, there was still time to do so. There were a thousand miles and more: space to make and remake her decision a thousand times over. She rocked to the left and thought she would tell. She rocked to the right and thought she wouldn't. Leaned left, yes. Leaned right, no.

Left, yes. Right, no. She got dizzier and dizzier. She hoped she wouldn't throw up on her son who rocked beside her. What was he thinking?

"I'm going to walk," said Percy.

"Where are you going to walk to?" asked Revelie.

"Far as I can go. Want to come?"

"No, thank you. I'd fall over. All this rocking."

Watching her son stride gracefully away down the aisle, Revelie promised herself that she would tell him as soon as he returned. Yes, definitely, positively, almost certainly, probably, maybe, no, never. But how would her son feel if he found out from somebody else? Yes, yes, she should, she could, she must. But what if he judged her guilty? What if he thought less of her? What if he looked at her differently? Perhaps she should have told him years and years ago. Well, it was too late now, wasn't it?

Even if she told him about Loving, could she tell him her other secret? Could she admit to her son that his mother had killed someone? Shot a man dead? Mumsy certainly was not who her son thought she was. Would he look at her as if she were a stranger? Would he be horrified?

Revelie looked out the train window at the passing Hudson River Valley, but this time natural beauty failed to comfort her. The great oak trees rocked as if they couldn't make up their minds either. The roadbed of the New York Central & Hudson River Railroad was rougher than she remembered. Would she have any teeth left in her mouth when she reached Texas? Would she have any secrets left in her head?

Yes, when her son returned, she would tell him at last, she decided.

A half dozen states later, Revelie still had not told her son. She was exhausted from carrying her secret for so many hundreds of miles, and there were still hundreds to go.

A Harvey Girl who looked twenty—wearing a black shirtwaist dress, a white apron, and a white cap—handed out menus. Revelie thought her son gave this waitress an especially warm smile, and the young woman returned it. She was too old for him; he was too young for her.

Or was he? Was she? The Harvey Girl hurried off to smile at other customers. Good.

"Mumsy, you look tired," said Percy.

"I am," said Revelie, brushing sticky hair off her moist forehead. "Tired and hot."

"We can stay over," he said. "Sleep in a bed. They have rooms."

"No, I want to get there as soon as possible," she said. "It's important."

"But you don't want to get sick."

"I already telegraphed Too Short to meet us tomorrow in San Angelo. He'll be worried if we're not on the train."

"He'll be more worried if you throw up or drop dead."

Revelie thought: Now he's taking care of me as if he were the parent. Anyway trying to, bless his boyish heart. She told herself her world was upside down. She should be caring for him, protecting him, but she wasn't sure how to go about it. Was an honesty policy really the best? But if she wasn't honest, wouldn't he find out on his own? She was afraid of her own child.

Maybe she should tell him right now. But looking around the restaurant, she felt too hemmed in by other travelers to speak frankly, honestly, of secret things. There were six long tables in the Harvey House dining room, each with seating for ten, and most of the places were occupied. Sitting side by side at the third table from the door, the mother and son had strangers to the left of them, strangers to the right of them, strangers in front of them. It seemed that almost all of the passengers on the train had decided to try the food at the famous Harvey House in Florence, Kansas. There were other Harvey Houses up and down the tracks of the Atchison, Topeka and Santa Fe, but this one was the biggest and supposedly the best.

Studying the menu, Revelie was surprised at some of the offerings. The West had certainly changed since she had left it some seventeen years ago. Not only were there unexpected dishes, but all the men were wearing jackets in spite of the July heat. They had to or eat somewhere else because the Harvey House strictly enforced its "coat rule." Unfortunately, a good half wore hot alpaca coats provided by the restaurant itself. Revelie wished her husband Jimmy Goodnight could see how far his West had come. She felt he was at least partially responsible for helping to civilize this wild and violent land. The "coat rule" was an extension—almost a parody—of his Code.

"Have you folks decided yet?" asked the waitress upon her return.

At first, Revelie thought she meant: Have you decided whether to tell him—or not? But she quickly righted herself and studied the menu more closely.

"Do you really have quail in aspic?" asked Revelie.

"Yes, ma'am," said the waitress. "Says so right there. Never tried it myself."

"And claret?"

"Yes, ma'am. Vintage, like it says right there, which is a real good brand."

"Then that's what I'll have, please: a glass of claret and quail in aspic."

"Thank you, ma'am. And the gentleman?"

Revelie saw them smiling at each other again, her prince from the East and this western Harvey Girl. The mother studied the young woman more closely. She had reddish-brown hair worn in a long plait and bright bluebonnet eyes. But her nose was a little too long, and her pioneer bones were a little too big. Couldn't her son see that he was too good for this waitress? Much too good? Calm down, relax. Why did this serving girl disturb her? She reminded herself that Percy and the Harvey Girl would never see each other again. Tomorrow he wouldn't even remember what she looked like. The strain must really be getting to this weary traveler.

"Miss, what would you order?" asked Percy in a friendly voice, still smiling.

"Me, I just eat a burnt steak," said the pretty Harvey Girl. "But a gentleman like yourself is liable to want somethin' fancier."

"That sounds good. I'll have a burned steak. And whiskey."

"He's kidding about the whiskey," said his mother.

"No, I'm not."

"Yes, you are. He would like a glass of milk, please."

"Do you always do what your mama says?"

"No!" he sputtered. "I don't want milk."

"Yes, you do."

"She wants me to get milk so you'll think I'm too young for you."

His voice sounded particularly young as he voiced his thoughts with childlike perception and candor. "She's afraid you'll flirt with me, and I might want to flirt back."

Percy gave his mother a disapproving look. She was not accustomed to such looks. She didn't like the way this one made her feel. Was he right? Was she intentionally trying to belittle her son in this Harvey Girl's eyes? Was it her fault he always seemed so young? Too young?

"Anything else I can get you folks?" asked the Harvey Girl.

"No, thank you," Revelie said coldly.

"I'll be back in three shakes of a dead lamb's tail," promised the Harvey Girl.

Percy winked! He actually winked at her. Was Revelie's baby boy really growing up? Oh, no. Not now. Not here. Not yet.

"A dead lamb's tail?" said Revelie. "What a charming expression."

The waitress retreated, leaving Revelie and Percy alone in the crowd. The mother felt shy with her son and did not like the sensation. She didn't know what to say to him. She didn't want to talk about the waitress because that subject might invite another look. And she couldn't bring herself to talk openly about Loving because that might provoke a worse look. She sat there tongue-tied.

"I wish I could remember more about the ranch," Percy said at last. "I know there's a canyon and a big house. Horses. Cows. I don't remember buffalo. Will there be buffalo around?"

"Not anymore," Revelie said.

"Too bad."

"Yes."

"There were some new trees. Trees I didn't know. They weren't like the trees in the Public Garden. What kinds of trees were those?"

"Different kinds. Chinaberries. Cottonwoods. Mesquite. Cedar. Your father was very interested in trees. He talked about them a lot. He used to say we all have forests inside us."

Was her voice false as she spoke of his "father"? She hoped not, but she feared that it was.

"Really?" asked Percy. "How come? What'd he mean?"

"I'm not sure." She wanted to change the subject, but couldn't think of one. "But it was a good thing."

"Good."

Revelie wondered why her son was asking so many questions. Was he trying to trick her? To trap her? Did he suspect something? No, she was just tired and upset. And she was hungry. Where was her food anyway? Couldn't that hussy move any faster?

"Here you are, ma'am," said the waitress. She placed the quail in shimmering aspic in front of Revelie. "And you, sir." Smiling, she served Percy a steak that appeared to be burned. "Eat up. I'll be right back with your drinks." And this time *she* winked.

As good as her word, the Harvey Girl soon reappeared carrying a glass of wine and a goblet of milk. She served the mother first, then the son. Good, Revelie could use a drink. Maybe she would feel calmer now. She took a sip as she watched her son cutting into his burned steak. Turning her attention to her own plate, Revelie was surprised to find her meal served on real china.

Then a man in a long black coat with tails suddenly appeared. He bowed and peered at the wineglass, then the goblet. What was going on? Unbending, the man picked up the goblet, studied it more carefully, and then dropped it on the floor. The heavy glass shattered and milk exploded on Percy's well-shined shoes. The crash turned most of the heads in the dining room, which embarrassed Revelie. She disliked being gawked at. She had already suffered more than enough gawking in her life.

"Now clean it up, Miss Swenson," said the dark figure. "That glass had a crack in it. Never ever let that happen again. Do you understand? I'll send you right back where you came from."

"Yes, sir," said the cowed Harvey Girl.

"Now be quick about it."

Revelie felt an unexpected surge of happiness: The girl was getting her comeuppance. Then she regretted the feeling as being somehow unworthy. This young woman had never done her any harm. What right had she to wish her ill?

"Wait a minute," said Percy.

"Yes, sir," said the man in tails. "What can I do for you, sir?"

"Why don't you clean it up yourself?" His tone was calm, friendly. "You dropped it. You broke it. You should clean it up. That's fair and square."

Oh, no, the boy was attempting to come to the aid of this distressed waitress! He was defending her! Revelie had known that girl was going to be trouble.

"Percy, no," she said. She turned to the man in tails: "He didn't mean it."

"Yes, I did so." He looked up at the man. "She's afraid I'm falling in love with your waitress. She thinks I want to come to the aid of a damsel in distress, like in storybooks. Well, maybe I do."

Revelie thought: He is always doing that, reading my mind.

"Sir, I broke the glass because it was cracked already," explained the man in tails. "She should never have given you a cracked glass. We have rules. These rules are meant to assure the dining pleasure of our customers."

"Me, too," Percy said.

"Don't say—" Revelie began but didn't finish.

"I've got rules, too," said the boy, the putative son of a code maker. "One rule's don't mistreat women. Another one's don't spill milk. Especially on shoes. My shoes. That's two good rules. And I got another one for you. Number three. It's clean up your own mess!"

Somebody clapped. Then somebody else. Revelie realized that the crowd was on Percy's side. She just hoped they wouldn't encourage him to do something foolish.

"I don't have time to stand here arguing with you, sir," Tails said. "I have work to do."

The man in black turned and started to walk away, but Percy grabbed one of his long tails. That stopped him.

"Where're you going? You've got work to do right here."

"Please let go of my coat, sir."

"Not till you clean up your mess."

Revelie's feelings changed from embarrassment to fear. What if this repulsive man had a gun under his long-tailed coat? They were out West now. Violence could suddenly rear up without warning.

"I'll clean it up," said the Harvey Girl. "I don't mind. Really."

"Listen to her, Percy," said Revelie, now the ally of the hussy. "We don't want any trouble."

"I'm warning you, sir!" said Tails, turning around to face his teenage foe. "Do you hear me?"

Releasing his grip on the coat tail, Percy stood up out of his seat. He slowly unfolded his six feet two inches and stared down at the little man, who stood about five six. The shorter man instinctively took a step backward.

"No, I'm warning *you*," Percy said, suddenly sounding grown up. Much too grown up. "Do you hear *me*?"

Revelie looked around. She saw that the cook had come out of the kitchen to see what all the fuss was about. He leaned back against the far wall, holding a butcher knife in his right hand. Several waitresses crowded around him as if for protection. The long blade made the mother quite uneasy.

"Be careful," said Revelie. "Be very careful, please."

"I'm not afraid of him," said Percy. "Look at him."

Revelie wondered: What had gotten into him? He wasn't a brawler. He never got in fights. What had come over him? Well, it was obvious, wasn't it? The girl had done it. *She* had changed him. *She* had put him in jeopardy. Why didn't *she* mind her own business?

"Don't insult me, sir," said Tails. "I don't like it."

"I don't care what you like," said Percy. "I don't like milk on me. When you finish cleaning the floor, you can shine my shoes."

"I won't!"

"Yes, you will so!"

Tails reached in his coat pocket and pulled out a Derringer pistol. It had two very short barrels, one on top of the other. The gun was no bigger than the head of a snake.

Revelie thought: Oh, no, it's happening again. And again with a Derringer. Like "father," like "son." She couldn't stand it. She had spent his lifetime trying to keep her son away from guns. And now she was about to lose another loved one—a best-loved one—to a firearm. She couldn't breathe.

Percy reached out casually and swatted the gun as if it were a mosquito. The Derringer flew through the air, hit the floor, and skidded under a table, hiding. Then the boy hit the little man in the face, hard. Tails sprawled on top of the spilled milk and the broken glass.

"Owww!"

Percy reached down, grabbed Tails by the tails, and pulled him through the mess on the floor. The poor man's rear end absorbed more spilled milk and jagged pieces of glass.

"Thanks for cleaning that up." Percy laughed.

"Let's go!" said Revelie.

"But you have to eat," said her son. "You like fancy food."

"I'm not hungry anymore." She saw the cook advancing with his butcher knife. "I'm your mother, in case you've forgotten, and I'm telling you: Let's get out of here!"

He thought it over.

"Okay." Her son shrugged.

"Hurry."

CHAPTER 5

The Harvey Girl followed the mother and son out of the restaurant. Revelie couldn't believe it. What did she want now? Couldn't she ever leave them alone? It didn't help that Percy smiled at her again. He almost seemed pleased that she was pursuing them.

"Where do you think you're going?" asked the mother, irritated.

"Well, shit and shit some more," said the girl who kept following them.

"Watch your language, young lady."

"I ain't no lady and don't wanna be."

"Don't say 'ain't.' And answer my question. Why are you following us?"

"I'm comin' along with you, thank you very much," said the Harvey Girl, hurrying to keep up.

"I beg your pardon?"

"I said I'm comin' with you."

"No, you aren't."

"Yes, I am, 'cause if I stay here, they'll kill me."

"I doubt that very much."

"You got me in trouble. Now you gotta git me outta it. Fair's fair. Fair and square." She touched Percy's elbow. "I sure appreciate what you tried to do, but you just went and made things lots worse. Whole hell of a lot worse."

"She's right," Percy said. "It's my fault. We can't just leave her here. We have to take her with us."

"No, it just won't work," said the mother. "If she has to leave her job, she should go back home. Where are you from, Miss?"

"Missouri," said the Harvey Girl. "But I cain't go back there. I come here because my parents done kicked me out."

"And why was that?"

"I'd rather not say how come."

"Of course."

In spite of the temperature, Revelie walked even faster, making herself all the hotter, but to no avail. The Harvey Girl quickened her pace, too, following the mother and her son. There was no shaking her. The three of them passed beneath leafy shade trees—a brief respite from the heat—on their way to the nearby depot. Their Atchison, Topeka and Santa Fe train waited patiently for them on the tracks.

"You cannot come with us," the mother said over her shoulder. "It is entirely out of the question." Then she thought of a practical argument. "Besides, you aren't packed and the train is about to leave."

"I'm gittin' away with my life. That's better'n baggage. Besides, I ain't got much and won't miss that."

"But you can't travel without clean clothing. You simply cannot."

"You just watch me."

"I'm afraid we'll smell you."

"Mumsy," scolded Percy.

"I'll stink and stink some more," said the Harvey Girl, "just to make you happy."

They walked in silence for a dozen paces. Revelie kept asking herself how she was going to shake off this female tick.

"You're unmarried, I presume," the mother said, trying a new tack.

"Yes, ma'am, I ain't."

"And my son is unmarried, too. How would it look? What would people say? It would damage your reputation just as much as it would my son's, more really. Given your background, perhaps you don't appreciate—"

"I 'preciate they're gonna kill me, ma'am. Maybe have their way with me first and then murder me. I 'preciate that a whole damn lot. And it's your fault."

Revelie thought: not mine, his.

The Harvey Girl seemed somehow cool, immune to the heat, which was another reason to dislike her.

"Mumsy, we can't just go off and leave her," Percy said. "We have to take her with us, really."

"No, we don't," said Revelie. "Think of what you're asking. Now I don't want to hear another word about it. Are you listening to me?"

"Well, Junior, are you gonna listen to your mama?" asked the waitress. "Is she the last word as far's you're concerned? End of story? Good-bye, good luck, and who cares? Is that about it?"

"No," Percy stammered.

"Good," said the hurrying Harvey Girl. "By the way, I'm Jessica Swenson. Call me Jesse, okay?"

Revelie told herself that she would never know this girl well enough to call her by a nickname. And neither would her son.

"My name's Percy Goodnight," said the boy, striding along. "This is my mom, Revelie."

"Glad to know you. Thanks for helping out."

"We aren't helping out," Revelie said sternly.

The uncertain trio made their way down the aisle of the railroad car. Revelie shook her head slowly back and forth as if saying no, no, no, no. How had she acquired this new traveling companion? Of course, she reminded herself, she knew very well how it had come about. Her theory of parenting had always been: Say "yes." Except when it came to guns. Then "no." But maybe, now that her son was seventeen, it was time to add a second exception: girls.

"There's a place," Percy said. "Three of us can squeeze in."

"There'll be no squeezing," announced Jesse. "It's too hot for that. You and your mama sit there. I'll find me a place."

Maybe she did feel the heat, after all.

"No," said Percy.

"Yes," said Revelie.

The mother and son sat down next to each other and watched Jesse make her way on down the aisle. She didn't look back. Revelie hoped she would keep right on going, out of the car, out of the train, out of their lives.

"Thank you, Mumsy," said Percy.

"I still think this is a bad idea," said Revelie. "And expensive."

"Don't worry. She'll pay you back."

"Sure, she will."

"She said so."

"Oh, grow up, Percy."

Jesse found a seat near the front of the car.

Revelie squirmed. She couldn't get comfortable. She closed her eyes and tried to relax, but failed. Tense, she was assailed by questions. What was she going to do with this unwanted girl? Would Loving be alive or dead when they finally reached the ranch? What should she tell her son about the cowboy with the changeable eyes? And what if some ambitious Texas lawman decided to arrest her for murder?

She desperately wanted to sleep, but sleep didn't come on command. Now she wished she had finished her glass of claret. Perhaps a little more wine would have sung a lullaby in her overheated blood.

The train whistled and then began to move, slowly, working the rheumatism out of its wheels and axles, its couplings creaking, but it soon gained confidence and speed. Revelie watched as clapboard buildings and trees slid away to be replaced by nothing. Well, it wasn't actually nothing at all—mustn't be too critical—but it *was* an unrelieved flatness. A fertile flatness. Fields of wheat stirred in the never-ending wind. The horizon was a hard, clear line drawn against a pale, cloudless sky. This line seemed to mark the edge of the earth, the end of the world. Revelie absorbed the inherent loneliness of this place.

Telegraph poles thump, thump, thumped. They reminded Revelie of bars on a cage. She had had enough of bars to know she didn't like them. She knew she didn't want to look out at the world through them again. They wouldn't really arrest her, would they? It had happened so long ago. Seventeen years. The length of her son's whole life. Hadn't everybody forgotten her? But she still remembered it all vividly, so why wouldn't Texas? Having once cheated Texas out of a hanging, she wondered: Was it time to pay that long-owed debt?

It was good to be moving again. Movement stirred and cooled the air. But she was in no hurry for a rendezvous with justice. Moreover, she hated the sense of getting closer and closer to bad news about Loving's health. She wished this journey could go on forever with her destination continually retreating before her.

Then she had a happy thought.

"Maybe the girl can find a job at the next Harvey House down the line," Revelie suggested with a smile. "That would solve the problem."

"Her name's Jesse," Percy said. "And I don't think that's a good idea."

"Why not, pray tell?"

"I'm sure the Harvey Houses talk to each other. They'd find her. She'd be in trouble again, and it'd be all my fault. She might even get murdered."

"Then what in the world are we going to do with her? Tell me that. Do you have a plan?"

"I'm working on it."

"You are?"

"Uh-huh."

"Would you care to share it with me?"

"All right. Maybe she could work at the ranch."

"No, ranches don't need waitresses. Can you imagine a waitress picking up her orders at the chuck wagon and then serving them to the cowboys? It's ridiculous. Completely ridiculous."

"There are other ranch jobs. Jobs she could do. Jobs she'd be good at."

"No, definitely not. They don't need any more hands at the ranch. I'm sure Loving would tell you the same thing. Besides, we can't be telling the ranch who to hire and fire. We've let them run it as they saw fit all these years. And the ranch has been good to us. So we can't start—"

"Yes, I can."

"No, you can't. I forbid it."

"You can't."

"What are you talking about? Of course I can, and I do. I'm your mother."

"You can't forbid me, Mother. Nobody can."

"And just why is that?"

"Because it's my ranch. I own it."

His mother knew she couldn't argue with him there: When his Boston grandmother died, she had left him her share of the ranch. And Revelie had deeded her own share over to him about the same time because she had sworn she would never return to Texas.

"It's yours but—"

"It's mine."

. . .

As the hours rattled by, Revelie dreaded more and more crossing the border into Texas. What if somebody recognized her? She caught herself hunching her shoulders to make herself smaller, less conspicuous. But that wasn't enough. She took out a bright white handkerchief and proceeded to soil it by wiping off her lip gloss. Then she started rubbing at the rouge on her cheeks. She noticed her son studying her.

"Mumsy, is something wrong?" Percy asked.

"No," she said too quickly.

Revelie went on rubbing at her cheeks. Then she switched to her darkened eyebrows. She was tempted to spit on the handkerchief to dampen it, but spitting seemed too unladylike. Oh, hell, she spat.

"Mumsy, you sure you're okay?" he asked with more concern in his voice.

"Yes," she said too loud.

Now the cloth worked better. When she finished with her eyes, she went back and washed her cheeks and lips again. She told herself that she would go on scrubbing until she was so plain she would attract no wandering eyes.

When she had finished, Revelie turned her head and looked out the window, not because she was especially interested in the landscape passing by, but because she wanted to hide her face from the other passengers. Her neck aching from the constant torque, she kept expecting somebody to come up and tap her on the back. And they weren't even to Texas yet.

When they finally crossed the border, night had fallen. Revelie was thankful for the dim car, lit only by a couple of lanterns, but she still couldn't relax. While her son slept beside her, she still kept her head turned to the black window as if watching the unseeable landscape pass by.

CHAPTER 6

Revelie sat on a wooden bench inside a shack with a bay window. It was the depot in San Angelo, Texas. It didn't have a Harvey House, didn't have food, didn't have beds, didn't have much of anything except a bay window. Which reminded Revelie of her Boston parlor. Still feeling hunted, Revelie crouched well back from the light, her eyes never leaving the bright pane of glass. From her dim corner, she was watching for Too Short, but she didn't see him. She hadn't seen him for over an hour. The bench was uncomfortable. The situation was uncomfortable. Percy and Jesse walked up and down, measuring the small room, chatting. Revelie tried to keep an eye on them, too.

"Miz Goodnight, are you all right?" asked the Harvey Girl. "You look pale this mornin'."

"I'm fine," said the un-made-up Revelie, "but where is he?"

"I don't know," said Percy.

"I don't neither," said Jesse.

The mother thought: She is cheeky and ungrammatical. Doesn't he see it? He can't be that blind, can he? Or that deaf?

"Didn't he get my telegram?"

"Don't know."

"Don't neither."

Owww! Shut up. Please just be quiet and let me think. Why hadn't Too Short come? What could be wrong? Maybe Loving was dead already. Perhaps they were holding the funeral right now. They couldn't put it off—couldn't wait for her arrival—because the body was rotting. The body smelled. Loving was teeming with maggots. Tears rolled down her cheeks.

"What's wrong?" asked Percy, coming to her, concerned.

Jesse hung back.

"I'm just worried," said Revelie.

"About Too Short?"

"Too Short?" exclaimed Jesse. "What is he: knee-high to a nail?"

Ignoring the question, the mother said: "Yes, I'm worried about Too Short. Of course."

"But mainly about Loving?" asked her son.

"I'm worried about them both." What did he know?

"I'm sorry, Mumsy. Wish I could do something."

"I know."

"I'll go look outside."

"Good."

"I'll come with you," said Jesse.

Not so good. Revelie would have gone with them to chaperone, but she was sensitive about showing herself outside. What if Texas lawmen already had the little depot surrounded? Were they slowly closing in?

Revelie watched the back of her son—and the Harvey Girl—as they receded from her. She felt abandoned. Maybe she should risk arrest, go outside and walk with them. But it was so hot out there. And it would be so hard trying to make conversation with Jesse. She let them go. Then she couldn't stop staring at them as they promenaded up and down beside the tracks. She saw their lips moving and wondered what they were saying to each other.

Then the mother saw her son motioning her to come out. She mouthed "no" to him. She was fine where she was even though she couldn't stop squirming. But he kept on motioning to her. He was saying something to her, but she couldn't read his lips. He said it over and over.

"Yes," he was saying, "yes, yes, yes . . ."

She mouthed, "No, no, no."

Seemingly irritated, her son turned and charged the door.

"Get out here!" shouted Percy, sticking his head inside. "Someone's coming. Coming fast. Maybe it's Too Short. I don't remember how he looks. You do."

"He looks short," said Revelie, trying not to show her excitement. "That's how he looks."

"Not on a horse, he doesn't," said Percy. "Come look."

Reluctantly, Revelie rose from the wooden bench, but then she hesitated. She had a bad feeling. Bad news was galloping toward her. Was she supposed to hurry out to meet it? Couldn't bad news wait? Slow down. Don't whip the horse. Don't spur it. Don't work it into a lather. Since bad news was always in a hurry, while good news took its own sweet time, she knew to expect the worst. Loving was no more. She had loved him and lost him. Forever this time.

"Mumsy, come on," insisted Percy.

Making a conscious effort, Revelie put one foot in front of the other, mechanically. Bad news might be racing toward her, but she didn't have to run to welcome it. Step, pause, step, pause, like a bride going to meet her groom at the altar. This time, she was a very reluctant bride.

"Mumsy!"

He came to her, took her by the hand, and tugged her out the door. Instinctively, she looked right, then left, half expecting to find a posse waiting for her. Percy pointed north in the direction of the canyon. She almost told him not to point but swallowed it this time. Shading her eyes, she looked north. She saw a rider galloping toward her, closely pursued by two riderless horses.

"It's Too Short," she said in a soft voice.

Now she paced up and down in front of the depot while Jesse and Percy followed behind her. She walked so fast they had to scurry to keep up. It was as if she were running to embrace bad news.

All too soon, Revelie watched Too Short pull up his horse and walk it carefully across the twin tracks. They all scurried to meet him. The short man slid down off the tall horse.

"I'm sorry," Too Short said.

"I knew it," Revelie said.

She sank into a squatting position—the way she had on the Fourth— and looked up at the sawed-off man. She was crying. Glancing at her son, she saw confusion on his face. She could hear his silent questions as if he shouted them: Why is she so upset? What was Loving to her? What was she to him? Unable to sustain eye contact, she looked away. She so wished she were a better actress. She hugged her knees tightly.

"I'm sorry I'm late," said Too Short.

"Is Loving dead?"

"No, ma'am."

"You're sure?"

"I'm sure he was breathin' when I left outta there. I dunno what he's done since I been gone. What I do know is he was powerful deter-mined to hold out till you got there. But we bedder hurry."

Revelie closed her eyes and cried harder than ever. It was a happy cry, but not entirely happy, since Loving was still in danger. She tried to choke down the sobbing sounds but failed. She hugged her knees harder.

When she opened her eyes, she stared directly into the eyes of her son, who was kneeling before her. She saw the questions in his expres-sion. He didn't understand. How could he understand? Was there accusation in his perplexed gaze?

"Let's go," she said. "Come on."

"Looks to me like," Too Short said, "we're gwine to need more horses."

"No, we won't," said Percy. "Jesse can ride with me."

"No, she cannot!" said his mother. "We'll buy another horse. Too Short, can you do that for us?"

"That's li'ble to be expensive," said Jesse. "I don't mind ridin' dou-ble, really."

"Nobody is riding double!" Revelie decreed.

Jesse looked at Percy as if she expected him to contradict his mother. Revelie was pleased to see him look away.

Too Short bought a horse from the livery stable. It wasn't the best horse, but it was something to ride, even if its back bowed. He also pur-chased two mules for the luggage, made heavier by the new books Rev-elie had brought along to read to Loving—if he could still hear her voice.

"Let's move," Revelie said impatiently.

"Mount up," said Too Short.

The mother watched her son swing up onto the back of a handsome gray horse with a black mane and tail.

"What's his name?" asked Percy.

"Smoke," said the little cowboy.

"I like it. That's good."

"Good. That one's named Whiskey." Too Short pointed at the muddy brown horse under Jesse. "Anyhow thass what they said."

"Oh, good, two of the vices: Smoke and Whiskey," said a smiling Revelie. "What's mine called: Opium?"

"No, yores is named Boston, ma'am."

"Boston? You're making that up."

"No, ma'am. Loving named her. Said she was the purdiest filly he ever set eyes on, so he was gonna name her Boston."

Revelie tried not to blush.

As they rode out of San Angelo, Percy bounced in his saddle. Or rather he posted as he had been taught by his Boston riding instructor. He was leveling out the bumps in his horse's gait, coming down when the horse went up, going up when the horse came down, moving in opposition to his mount. But he was the only one. All the others moved with their horses, western style, riding like cowboys. Too Short and Jesse rode western because they were westerners. Although she was an easterner, Revelie didn't bounce because she had learned to ride in the West, taught by her husband, Mr. Goodnight. The mother wondered if her son felt awkward since he was, so to speak, out of step. She hoped not. He shouldn't, since he looked so handsome in his black frock coat, posting away.

Revelie glanced back over her shoulder to see if anybody was following.

CHAPTER 7

P ercy dismounted and stood on the edge of the world, looking down into the void. Feeling a little dizzy, he rocked backward, away from the lip where the earth came to an end. Bending over, he picked up a small, red rock. He straightened up, cocked his arm, and threw the stone as far as he could into empty space. Then he took a step forward, shaded his eyes, and looked into the abyss, following the flight of his missile.

"Don't get too close to the edge," the mother told her son. "Be careful."

"I won't fall in," Percy said. "I promise."

The rock grew smaller and smaller, just a speck. Then it disappeared. Percy never heard it hit. He moved even closer to the edge.

"Percy, you heard me. Get back this instant."

Staying put, the boy gathered all his resources, took a deep breath, and then spat as far as he could out into the abyss. His spittle arched beautifully and then fell and fell and fell, fell, fell. The farther it dropped, the better he felt: his spirits going up as it was going down.

"That's a record," Percy said proudly. "Maybe not a world record but mine anyway. That's great. Anybody else want to try and beat me?"

"Sure," said Jesse, preparing to dismount.

"No!" said Revelie. "Don't dawdle. We're in a hurry."

"With all due respect, ma'am," said the Harvey Girl, "this don't look like a real good place for hurryin'."

"We'll hurry carefully. No more spitting. Let's keep moving."

Percy shrugged and then swung back up onto Smoke. He watched as the pint-sized cowboy led the way riding a spotted Indian pony. The boy tightened his legs around the ribs of his gray-coated mount. Percy, a classics major at Andover, imagined that he was descending into the underworld. A friendly Hades. He loved Greek and Latin in spite of the syntax because he loved the stories. Far far below, he saw a red River Styx.

His mother followed him over the edge. Jesse brought up the rear.

As he passed beneath the lip of the world, crossing from light into shadow, Percy felt a chill. Then he smiled down broadly on this strange new world, which he already owned. But was he worthy of it? A vast place like this—this great red hole—should somehow be deserved. Percy told himself that he might own a fabled ranch, but he wouldn't be a rancher until he could prove he could do the job. He felt a little ashamed of himself for owning so much so young through no effort of his own. How would he be received by the cowboys, who were surely older than he was? He was a boy who had been given a man's toy to play with: How would he do?

"Be careful, Percy," called his mother. "Hold on to the pommel."

"Mind your mama," yelled Jesse.

Percy didn't reach for the horn. He knew a real rancher wouldn't need to hold on. Nor a cowboy either. Glancing back, he saw his mother taking her own advice—hanging on for dear life. She had never been much of a horsewoman. Descending the cliff, she was riding sidesaddle, for God's sake. No wonder she needed something to cling to. But Jesse, last in line, rode astraddle, like a man. She had her skirt tucked up and her legs exposed. She would certainly think less of him if he obeyed his mumsy and grabbed hold of the horn.

"Percy, hold on!"

He tightened his legs around Smoke and speeded up, putting more space between him and his mother. He felt silly—and July-hot—descending into the wilderness wearing a black frock coat as if he were walking into a drawing room. He supposed Too Short and Jesse must be silently laughing at him. He must look silly to them. He couldn't stand it any longer. He had to get out of this thing right now. Like a snake shedding its old skin, he peeled off the drawing-room jacket and hung it on a passing mesquite tree.

"Percy, what are you doing?" asked Revelie.

"I don't need it anymore," Percy said. "Good riddance."

As she was passing the mesquite, Revelie reached out, plucked up the coat, and cradled it in her lap as she descended.

Percy untied his black cravat, pulled it from around his neck, and held it by one end, staring at it. His tie resembled the empty husk of a snake. He draped it over a cedar tree. Shedding custom, shedding civilization, he felt new, invigorated, excited. He sensed the promise of a new life in a new skin.

His mother retrieved the cravat.

CHAPTER 8

Percy watched his mother race up the front porch steps of the big red house that had once been her home. He knew she wasn't a woman who often hurried. She was too dignified to hurry. But she no longer cared about dignity. What was wrong with her? She tripped on her skirts but it didn't slow her. Crossing the porch in three strides, she burst through the heavy front door. Percy scurried to keep up, with Jesse right behind him. He had forgotten how big the living room was. Nor did he remember the deer-horn chandeliers. Nor the fighting deer heads either. The two bucks had been unlucky enough to lock horns in what turned out to be mortal combat. When a hunter appeared, they couldn't run because their horns were inextricably entangled.

"What happened there?" asked Percy, pointing.

"Don't point," said Revelie. "I shot them."

"Don't seem fair," said Jesse.

But his mother didn't take the time to defend herself. She must really be in a hurry.

"Where is he?" she asked in a high, tight voice.

"In your room," said Too Short, who was also having trouble keeping up.

"Oh. Just a moment. I need to freshen up."

Percy didn't understand: Suddenly his mother was no longer in such a hurry. Disappearing into a bathroom that opened off the main hall, she stayed a long time behind the closed door. Well, if you had to go, you had to go, no matter how long it took. Even if you had come two thousand uncomfortable miles to see someone who lay only a few feet away. He waited. They all waited.

When the bathroom door finally opened, Revelie stepped out in full war paint. Gone was the scrubbed face. She had reddened her lips and pinked her cheeks and blackened her eyebrows and lashes. Percy was amazed. What had gotten into his mother?

"You must be feelin' better," Jesse said. "You don't look so pale no more."

Percy didn't say anything. He just stared and wondered.

Brushing past Jesse, Revelie was in a hurry again. She charged down the dim corridor, reminding her son of a burrowing animal dashing down its tunnel in search of safety. She threw open a door halfway down the hallway and plunged through. Next came Too Short, then Percy, then Jesse, who hovered in the doorway. Loving had a bandage around his head that began just above his closed eyes.

"How is he?" asked Revelie in a hushed voice.

She addressed her question to Tin Soldier, who sat in a cane-bottomed chair beside the feather bed. The blacksmith, who cradled his steel hat in his lap, could mold metal to his will, but not the accidents of life.

"Been sleepin' fer a coupla days," answered Tin Soldier with a shake of his head. "Started just after Too Short up and left to git you folks."

"He's in a coma?" asked Revelie, alarmed.

"I dunno about that there, but I cain't wake him up."

Percy watched his mother hurry to Loving's bedside. She fell to her knees so quickly that she must have bruised them. Her son winced for her. He saw her take the sleeping man's hand.

"Wake up!" pleaded Revelie.

Loving didn't stir.

"Please, wake up! Open your eyes. Look at me."

He didn't move. Not even an eyelash. She started crying again.

"Please, please, please."

Percy ached for his mother while wondering why she was in so much pain. What was this sleeping man to her? Was she so upset because Loving had been her husband's best friend? Because he was Percy's father's friend above all others? So seeing him near death reminded her of that other more painful death? Was that it? Her tears watered the feather bed.

"I'm here now," Revelie said. "I came back. Wake up and look at me. Please. It's me, it's me, it's really me."

Seeing her kiss the unconscious hand, Percy frowned. He was so confused. What was happening? Why was it happening?

"I've come back, and if you wake up, I'll stay. I promise. No matter what."

What in the world? Percy moved up and stood beside his kneeling mother at the edge of the bed. She looked up and seemed to remember him for the first time. A look of horror passed over her face. Was she afraid of her own son? Why? She couldn't possibly be. And yet she covered her face with both hands and cried all the harder. The boy felt guilty because he had not meant to bring on his mother's tears.

"I'm sorry," she sobbed. "I'm so sorry."

Percy and Too Short sat next to each other on the front porch steps. Killing time, the boy kept glancing at the six-shooter buckled around Too Short's waist and strapped to his leg. Ever since he had fired the air rifle at the carnival, he had found that guns fascinated him. He wondered if he would be as good with a real gun as he had been with the toy. He knew his mother didn't want him to touch any sort of gun, which made them all the more attractive. When Too Short noticed him staring, Percy looked quickly away, embarrassed.

"Uh, what happened to Loving?" the boy asked. "How'd he get shot?"

"I ain't too sure," Too Short said, screwing up his face. "Some gunfight or other."

"But how did it start?" He could hear his voice thicken. "Why? I don't understand."

"I don't neither. Sorry I cain't help you out there none."

"You sure?" Percy felt something was being kept from him. "Didn't anybody ask?"

"I dunno." Too Short sounded exasperated. "I really dunno. I'm sorry."

They both fell silent, awkwardly silent. Percy found himself staring at Too Short's six-gun once again. He wondered what it would feel like to hold it in his hand. Was it heavy? Would the grip be smooth or coarse against his palm? Then the all-important question: Could he hit anything with such a gun? The pint-size cowboy noticed the boy staring again. Percy quickly turned his head.

"You interested in guns?" Too Short asked.

"No," Percy answered.

"Oh."

"Sort of."

"I see. You a good shot?"

Too Short waited for an answer but didn't get one. "Yore daddy shore was. Not as good as Loving, but good. Loving's the best."

"I don't know if I'm good or not. I never shot a real gun. Shot an air rifle once, but that doesn't count."

"Guess that there comes from growin' up in civ'lization, huh?"

"I suppose."

"Well, you ain't in civ'lization no more. Wanna give it a go? See if'n yore yore daddy's son when it comes to shootin'?"

"I'd like that very much."

"Come on."

Too Short took Percy to a lonely place beside the red-flowing Styx. The water chuckled softly. A red-tailed hawk circled overhead. The boy was excited. His excitement was all the sweeter because he knew his mother would disapprove. He wondered if she would hear the shots inside the thick walls of the stone house and be alarmed.

"Less see," Too Short said. "I figured mebbe we'd see if you can hit one of them there gourds."

He pointed, which pleased Percy.

"Do you mean those melons?"

"They ain't melons. Them there's gourds. Tougher'n melons. Try eatin' one someday. Now lemme show you a coupla things." Too Short drew his pistol from its holster. "Now you thumb back the hammer." The little cowboy used his thumb to cock the gun. The cylinder rotated and clicked. "Then you point it like you was pointin' yore finger. See?"

"Yes," Percy said, pointing his finger as if it were a six-shooter, his thumb cocked.

"Good." Too Short pointed again. "Now see that big gourd over there?"

"Yes."

"See if'n you can shoot it dead."

Too Short lowered the hammer and handed the six-shooter to the boy. Strangely, the weapon felt both awkward and at home in his hand. He rocked it forward and backward, from left to right. Then he held it at his side, pointing down at the red earth.

"Go ahead," said Too Short.

Percy raised the gun, thumbed back the hammer, aimed as if rudely pointing a finger, and squeezed the trigger. The bullet hit the red earth six feet in front of the gourd. The boy recoiled with embarrassment.

"Well, you didn't scare the damn gourd too much that time," said Too Short. "Try it ag'in. Hold yore breath just before you shoot."

"Okay."

Percy held the gun at his side again, raised it again, cocked it again, and shot four feet over the gourd. He shook his head. Shooting had been so much easier in Boston's Public Garden. Maybe he wasn't a natural after all.

"Thass a little better," said Too Short. "Yore gittin' warm now. Try again."

Ashamed, Percy lowered the gun once more, raised it once more, and killed the gourd. It exploded.

"Damn. Nice shootin'."

Percy raised, pointed, and blew up another gourd.

"Yore shore 'nough yore daddy's boy," Too Short said.

CHAPTER 9

As he approached the big red-stone house, striding along happily, warmed by his marksmanship, Percy saw Jesse sitting on the front porch steps. He quickened his pace. Too Short kept up with him.

"Hi," Jesse called. "He woke up."

Too Short started running, Percy was right behind him. They took the steps two at a time, crossed the porch, and burst into the big living room with the fighting deer's heads. They slowed as they reached the dark corridor. Too Short was the first one through the sickroom door. Then he stopped abruptly, causing Percy to run into him from behind.

"Sorry," the boy apologized.

He noticed his mother's face was wet with tears.

"So you finally got tired of playin' possum," Too Short said, "and opened yore damn eyes."

"He wasn't faking," said Revelie, not getting the banter.

"Thass it," said Loving. "I just wanted to see if you boys could run this here place without me. When I seen you couldn't, I figured it was about time to call off the possum act."

"We was doin' just fine without you. Why don't you just go on back to sleep and let us run this here place proper like?"

"Much as I'd like to take you up on that there offer, I cain't do that to this here place. It's suffered enough."

"This isn't funny," protested Revelie.

Silence descended on the sickroom as dusk darkened the air. Percy walked to his seated mother and placed his hand on her shoulder. She looked up at him with a wet face.

"We heard shooting," his mother said. "Very upsetting. What was happening? What was wrong? Do you know?"

Since he knew his mother didn't want him to touch guns, Percy hesitated.

"Just target practice," Too Short said. "Nothin' to worry about." He paused. "The good news is yore son's a crack shot. Anyhow he's got the makin's of one." Another pause, but still nobody said anything. "Shoots like his daddy."

Percy noticed his mother and Loving staring at each other, then both looking away. What was going on? What was he missing?

"I disapprove of shooting," said Revelie. "Consequently I disapprove of marksmanship. Please do not encourage my son to become a gunman."

"But I think he's got a gift," said Too Short. "Might be better'n his daddy."

"Do I have to spell it for you? N-O."

"I can spell, ma'am." Too Short turned and started walking out of the sickroom.

"No!" Revelie said, but in a different tone of voice. "Don't go. Please don't. I'm sorry."

Too Short stopped but didn't turn around.

"Come back, please," she said softly to his back. "You've always been so good to me. So fair to me. And I thank you. You came all that way to meet us at the station. I'm just upset. Forgive me."

Too Short turned back around and faced her. "Sorry, ma'am."

"It's just that I have always tried to protect my son from guns. You of all people know how destructive guns have been to our family. I wanted to spare my boy from gun violence. Gun misery. But you didn't know. How could you?"

"No, ma'am."

"Of course, my son could have told you. He knew." She turned and stared at the boy. "Percy, did you tell Too Short?"

"No, Mumsy."

"Why not?"

"I wanted to shoot a gun."

Revelie clenched her hands into fists.

While Loving rested, Revelie and her son sat in the living room, in front of the great fireplace. It was now an empty hole, dark and dead. Would a warm flame ever burn in it again?

"How could he be sleepy?" Percy asked. "He's been sleeping for days. Wouldn't you think he'd be caught up on sleep?"

"He's very weak," Revelie said sadly. "It's to be expected."

"Mumsy, I was kidding. Anyway trying to."

"Oh. Perhaps my sense of humor is in a coma. I'll try to wake it up."

They sat silently staring at the fire that had gone out a long time ago. Percy was obviously restless, squirming on the dappled cowhide couch.

"Let's do something," he said. "Maybe go exploring."

She considered the matter for a moment. "Well, I know what we should do. We should pay our respects to your father's grave. Would you accompany me on such a mission?"

"Sure. Maybe Jesse would come, too."

"I don't know. She never knew your father. I can't believe his grave would interest her."

"Are you kidding? She'd love to see that tombstone with the ax stuck in it. You don't see something like that every day."

"You remember that?"

"Of course."

"But Jesse's supposed to be helping Coffee prepare dinner."

"Coffee can get along without her." He raised his voice: "Jesse! Where are you, Jesse? We need you."

The young woman appeared with flour on her hands. "Whaddaya want?" she asked. "I'm in the middle of mixin' up a flock of biscuits."

"I've got something to show you," said Percy.

"Let's go," said Jesse.

"What about the biscuits?" asked Revelie.

The three of them walked along the bank of the red river that had dug the red canyon. It seemed too calm and quiet—too lazy—to have done so much. They went upriver against the current.

"We're looking for a hackberry thicket," Revelie said. "Mr. Goodnight liked that thicket."

She did not add: So did I. But she remembered what they had done in that thicket. The memory made her smile.

"What happened to Loving?" Percy asked. "Did he tell you about it?"

"No," Revelie said, seeming to rush her answer.

"I been wonderin' the same thing," Jesse said. "How and how come?"

Revelie gave her a stare that said plainly: Who asked you? "It was some sort of senseless gunfight. There are just too many guns in this country. Guns and gunmen. That's all I know."

Somehow Percy wasn't sure he believed his mother. He felt she knew more than she was willing to share with him. Peeking into the sickroom, he had seen Loving and his mumsy talking in low voices. Wouldn't she have asked him what happened and why? She obviously liked him, so wouldn't she be curious? Maybe she was just reluctant to speak in front of Jesse.

"There it is," said Revelie, starting to point and then stopping herself. "Anyway I think that's it." She nodded in the direction of a thorny thicket. "Let's have a look."

The threesome veered to the left and approached a spiky wall that barred their way.

"The hackberries seem to have grown considerably since I was last here." She looked to the left and to the right. "I'm not sure we can get in." Her head swiveled back and forth. "Maybe this isn't the right place, after all."

"I'll take a look," Percy said.

"I'll help you," said Jesse, who probably didn't want to be left alone with the mother.

Percy moved off to the right and she was right behind him. When he stopped suddenly, she bumped into him.

"'Scuse me," she said.

"I liked it," he said.

"Don't git fresh."

"Sorry."

"Don't be too sorry."

Percy had stopped because he saw a place where somebody had cut a path through the wall of thorns. He supposed Loving or Too Short or one of the other cowboys must have hacked this opening in order to pay his respects. He was glad to find this unexpected entrance.

"Come on," Percy called. "Mumsy, we can get through here. There's a hole."

"Coming," Revelie said.

She soon joined Percy and Jesse at the passage through the thicket. "Jesse, you'll love this," he said, leading the way. "It's amazing."

Passing through the breach in the wall of thorns, Percy stopped suddenly once again. Jesse bumped him again, but neither of them said anything. Then Revelie came up beside them. They all stared at the grave. They all studied the shallow hole in the ground where the tombstone had been. They all wondered where it had gone. Who had taken it? Who and why?

Percy blushed with anger.

CHAPTER 10

"What the hell!" gasped Percy.

Beside the hole lay the shattered handle of an ax. All that was left of the ax that had made Percy's father a Texas legend. It occurred to the boy, standing beside the defaced grave, that his dad had been just seventeen years old when he pulled that ax out of an anvil. The age his father had been then was the age his son was now. Percy couldn't imagine himself organizing a trail drive, moving a herd into an uncharted land, and transforming a secret canyon into the first and most important ranch in this country. How had his young father done it? What had the ax given him that he didn't have before? Well, whatever it was, it had been stolen from the son.

"Shit!" said Jesse. "And shit some more!"

Revelie, who had married the man who pulled out the ax, gave the girl a disapproving look. She opened her mouth to say something harsh, then seemed to change her mind, and said something else entirely: "Right you are." She paused. "But why would anyone want to break that handle? Did they do it just to taunt us? Does somebody hate us that much?"

Then they saw the double "RR." The brand had been scratched in the soft red earth with a sharp-pointed stick, perhaps the shattered handle.

"What in the world?" asked Percy. "What's that supposed to mean?"

"I've seen something like that before," Revelie said at last, but then kept silent.

"Where?" asked her son. "When?"

His mother sighed. "It's the sign of an outlaw organization."

"A gang?"

"Yes, a gang. They call themselves the Robbers' Roost Gang. They used to taunt your father with their signature. They used it to sign their depredations."

"I don't understand."

"They would kill a horse, brand it with their RR, and leave it for your father to find. Or they would murder a prize bull and brand it." She paused and took a deep breath. "Once they even branded a young woman."

"Shit!" said Jesse.

"And shit some more," said Revelie.

L oving was awake again. A small crowd gathered in his sickroom. He was propped on feather pillows in his feather bed. It was a soft throne for a hard man.

"Yeah, sounds like them Robbers' Roost fellers to me," said Loving. "Or somebody who wants us to think it's them. Anyhow."

"Why would they break the ax?" asked Revelie. "Just for spite?"

"Mebbe just pure meanness. But I figure they didn't come to steal the tombstone and all. They was prob'ly just after that damn ax. But it was stuck so tight, they busted the handle tryin' to pull it out. So I s'pose they just give up and decided to steal the whole kit and caboodle, tombstone, ax head, and all."

"Of course," said Revelie.

"What should we do now?" asked Percy.

"Catch 'em," said Loving. "Track 'em, chase 'em, run 'em down, and git what's yores back. Wisht I could go with you."

"We'll be thinking of you," the boy said.

"What do you mean by 'we'?" asked his mother. "You mean 'they,' not 'we.' They will catch them. The cowboys."

"No, I'm going, too."

"No, you aren't."

"It's my duty."

"If you have a duty, it is to stay here with your mother and not worry her to death. First, you go shooting guns behind my back. Now you want to go running after dangerous outlaws. No!"

"Better mind Mama," said Jesse.

"Shut up!" said Revelie. Then she stared at her son: "No!"

. . .

"No!" said Revelie.

"Mumsy, I can't go chase outlaws without a gun," said Percy.

"Then don't go. Good. That's settled."

"You're embarrassing me in front of my cowboys."

"They aren't yours. Cowboys don't belong to anybody. That's their charm. But that's not the point. You're mine. And I'm telling you: You aren't going riding out of here carrying a gun. You don't know what guns can do. I know!"

"Stop."

"No, you stop and think for a moment. You don't know the West. You don't know the dangers. You don't even know how to handle a gun."

"I do, too. I'm good."

"Please." She took a deep breath. "Listen to me, Percy. I do know this country. They have a code, thanks largely to your father's efforts. And it's against that code to shoot an unarmed man. Don't you understand? If you don't carry a gun, you'll be safe. Anyway safer."

"No."

The two of them stood uncomfortably on the wide front porch of the big red-stone house. Too Short and Tin Soldier lounged on the steps, pretending not to listen. Jesse burst from the house, slamming the heavy front door.

"I want to go, too," Jesse said.

"No!!" said Revelie. "Absolutely not. Have you lost your mind? Has everybody?"

Shaking his head, Percy realized he was irritated at his mother, which rarely happened. They had always been staunch allies in their small family of two. But now she was being unreasonable and shrill. The West was having a bad effect on her.

Percy looked up as Coffee came around the corner of the big house carrying something in his hand. He was waving it so it was hard to see what it was. Then the blur resolved itself into a six-gun. The boy smiled and hurried down the steps to meet the cook. He wanted to reach that revolver before his mother did.

"This here's the best I could do," Coffee apologized. "Only spare gun I could find. The front sight's done bent. The grip's held together with balin' wire. Fix anything with balin' wire. It's a .45 and it'll kick. Liable to blow up the first time you shoot it. But it's the only one I could locate, so take it or leave it."

"I'll take it."

"No!"

"Thank you."

Percy extended his open hand and the cook placed the gun in it. The boy saw that the grip was indeed bound up with the fine but tough wire used to hold bales of hay together. The wire went round and round and round a dozen times or more. The gun was also rusty and looked generally pathetic.

"Coffee, you're a traitor," Revelie said.

"How come?"

"You're abetting my son in his defiance of me."

"I ain't bettin'." He sounded hurt. "I don't even play cards, no matter what you heard."

"You're all impossible."

Revelie turned and walked regally back into the house.

"Coffee, rustle up a gun belt," ordered Too Short. "I don't want him stickin' that gun in his pants and shootin' off his dick. I'm sure his mama wants grandkids someday."

CHAPTER 11

Percy, Too Short, and Tin Soldier headed for the corral, where several cowboys were already saddling horses. They might be "his" cowboys, but he didn't know them. They looked tough, making him feel even more like a child. But at least he was a boy with a gun. His hand descending to his gunbelt, he pried out a .45-caliber bullet. Then he started turning it over and over with his thumb and index and middle fingers.

"Too Short, tell me their names, please," Percy said.

"Thass right, you ain't met most of the boys, have you?" said the short acting foreman. "High time you got to know 'em. Some of 'em're pretty fair cowboys."

They walked another twenty yards and stopped at the open gate of the corral. "Hey, listen up, ever'body. Lemme make you used to Percy. He's gonna be ridin' with us. Now y'all step right on up here and meet Mr. Goodnight's baby boy." Nobody moved. "Come on, don't be shy."

Percy self-consciously watched the cowboys step forward to form a semicircle around him.

"Hi," he said.

"Percy, this here worthless cowboy's named Juan Gonzales, but ever'body calls him Vaquero.'"

A Mexican cowboy stepped forward and extended his hand. Percy shifted the bullet to his left hand—but continued turning it—as he reached out with his right. When they shook, the boy felt calluses and was ashamed of his own smooth hand. Vaquero was almost as short as Too Short. He had a black moustache that drooped and black eyes that sparkled. He wore a black cowboy hat and spurs with rowels the size of silver dollars.

"Glad to meet you, Vaquero," said Percy.

"*Sí,*" said the beaming cowboy.

"And this here worthless piece of manure's named George Little, but ever'body just calls him 'Little Dogie.'"

A huge man with a full black beard stepped closer. Nothing little about him. He extended a shovel of a hand and the boy extended his as well. Percy watched his hand disappear inside the huge mitt of the giant.

"Glad to meet you, Little Doggy," he said.

"Now hold your horses," said Too Short. "His name ain't Little Doggy. He ain't no kind of dog. No, his name's Little Dogie, like the song. Rhymes with 'old fogie,' see? When he gits some older, we're gonna start callin' him Little Dogie the Old Fogie, but thass still some few years off yet."

"I'm sorry, Little Dogie," said Percy, getting it right this time, turning the bullet faster. "Pleased to meet you."

"Same," said the giant with a scowl.

"And this here dumb-as-dirt cowboy's named Ivan Pushkinsky or somethin' like that."

"Thass Ivan the Terrible to my friends," said a tall, slender cowboy with blond hair and almost invisible eyebrows. "My daddy come from Russia."

"Glad to meet you, Mr. Terrible."

Ivan nodded.

"And this here cowboy's got some damn Comanche name thass just about almost impossible to say so we done give up tryin'. We just call him 'Custer,' and he don't seem to mind."

Custer, the Comanche, was dressed like all the other cowboys, but his hair was much longer, hanging down his back. He raised his hand, palm outward, rather than offering to shake, but he didn't say *how*.

Percy wondered if he should raise his hand, too, but decided against it. "Glad to meet you, Custer," he said.

"And this here's a fella called Opry. I reckon he picked up that there moniker on accounta he cain't never seem to stop singin'. And many have tried, lemme tell ya. You'll see—uh, hear. Claims he ain't got no real name. Just been Opry as fer back as he can remember. Can you beat that? He's prob'ly hidin' out from somebody fer somethin'."

Opry had a scar at the right corner of his mouth that made him look as if he were always smiling a crooked smile. Or had just hit a high note on the button. He wore leather cuffs, which were stained dark by age and grime. The boy was fascinated because he had never seen such accessories. It being a hot morning, the cowboy brushed his forehead with his forearm to wipe off the sweat. His right cuff was stained darker still.

"Pleased to meet you, Opry. Pleased to meet all of you. Vaquero." He nodded. "Little Dogie." Another nod. "Ivan the Terrible." Nod. "Custer." The boy raised his hand, palm out.

"We all got nicknames," observed Little Dogie. "Thass how it works here. What about you, Mr. Percy? Ain't you got no nickname?"

"No, not really," Percy lied.

He didn't want to tell them what the boys in lower form had called him when he was just a kid. He was embarrassed by his nickname. They got it from his initials. His full name was Percy York Goodnight. Unfortunately, his mother had embroidered his monogram on all his handkerchiefs. PYG. The boys pronounced the *y* like an *i*. They made his nickname sound like a barnyard animal. He had hated it at first, but had gradually gotten used to it. He even grew to like it in a strange way. It was distinctive. It was unforgettable. And it wasn't "Percy." He had never been crazy about his first name. So he became Pyg at school and Percy at home. But he never told his mother and didn't intend to tell these cowboys.

"Not even when you was a little kid?" persisted Little Dogie. "No offense, but I ain't never heard tell of a cowboy named Percy."

The boy shifted the bullet back to his right hand and turned it faster.

"Shut up, Dogie!" ordered Too Short. "Who askt you anyhow? You're just talkin' to hear your head rattle and it ain't a purdy sound."

"No, he's right," said Percy. "He thinks it's a sissy name."

"No, I didn't mean—"

"Yes, you did. And I agree with you. I do." Percy paused to consider. "As a matter of fact, I did have a nickname when I was little." He paused again. "The other boys called me 'Pyg.'"

"I'm sorry," said Little Dogie. "I surely am. When am I gonna learn to keep my big mouth shut?"

"When somebody shuts it permanent," Too Short said irritably.

"Please, don't apologize," said Percy. "I don't mind that name.

Really. They said it P-I-G, but they spelled it P-Y-G. Why's a long story. But I'd be proud if you'd call me 'Pig'—just as long as you think 'P-Y-G' when you say it. Okay?"

"No . . . no . . . no," murmured the cowboys.

"Please. I insist. Just don't let Mumsy hear you call me that."

"You cain't go on the warpath dressed like that there." Custer laughed. "No matter what we calls ya."

Pyg twirled the slug of lead faster than ever. What was the matter with his clothes? Why were they all staring at him? He felt as if he had his fly open and actually looked down to check. No, at least that was all right. Well then, what?

"What's wrong?" the boy asked in a low voice.

"It's them pants," said Little Dogie. "Makes ya look like a sissy. Course you may be partial to that look."

Pyg studied the trousers worn by the cowboys. They were certainly different, what he could see of them peeking out from behind leather chaps. Some faded brown, some washed-out blue. He couldn't tell what they were made of, but it certainly wasn't gabardine. And the cowboys seemed equally puzzled by his choice of wardrobe.

"Whaddaya call them there pants?" asked Little Dogie.

"Jodhpurs," Pyg stammered.

The cowboys all laughed again. The boy checked his fly again. Then he studied the rest of his trousers: They ballooned at the thighs but hugged his calves. The cuffs covered the tops of his polished, low-heel riding boots. He didn't see anything amusing. He had always liked how he looked in riding clothes.

"What's so funny?" asked the boy

"Damned amusin' name fer britches," said Little Dogie. "Whut was it? I didn't quite catch it."

"Jodhpurs," Pyg said slowly, struggling to keep his voice even. "What are *your* trousers called?"

"These here is Strausses," Little Dogie said proudly.

The boy waited for an explanation but none came. "What are Strausses?"

"What're Strausses!" exclaimed Goliath. "Where was you raised? In a damn music box?"

"That'll be about all outta you," interrupted Too Short. Then he faced Pyg and shrugged an apology. "Uh, well, I mean do you really wanna know 'bout Strausses?" He shrugged again.

"Of course," said Pyg.

"Well, they say they was invented by some danged tent-maker. He figured out that out chere folks need pants a lot more'n they need tents. But all he had was tent canvas, so thass whut he made his britches outta. Prob'ly a packa lies."

"That's interesting," said Pyg. "It makes sense in a way." He paused, thinking. "Do you suppose I could borrow a pair of Strausses?"

The cowboys all laughed once again. The boy glanced down once again.

"What's so funny?" Pyg asked.

"None of these cowboys own more'n one paira pants," explained Too Short. "If'n they was to loan you a pair, they'd have to go ridin' in their underwear."

"Oh."

The cowboys stared at Pyg and he stared right back.

"I got an idea," Too Short said at last. "We'll put some chaps on you. That way them jod-things won't stick out quite so bad."

"Thank you," Pyg said rather formally.

There was an extra pair of chaps in the bunkhouse but no extra pants. They were moth-eaten, bat-wing chaps, with tarnished rosettes, but the boy thought they were beautiful.

Now Pyg wished he had a wide-brimmed hat.

CHAPTER 12

As they trotted away from Home Ranch headquarters, Pyg felt intensely self-conscious because he was bouncing. He could see that his posting set him apart from all the other cowboys. It marked him as an easterner. A sissy. A tenderfoot. An outsider. He tried to stop bouncing, but then the saddle relentlessly banged his balls. It seemed that in order to prove his manhood—show he wasn't a sissy—he might have to lose his manhood. How could the cowboys stand it? Why didn't they all have high voices? Pyg went back to posting.

"Kinda jumpy aincha?" chided Little Dogie. "You ride like a damn grasshopper."

"Leave him alone," said Too Short.

"Just makin' conversation," said the giant.

Again Pyg tried to stop bouncing, but the intense pain between his legs launched him into the air once more. He couldn't help it. He had to make a choice: busted balls or bruised ego? He sided with his balls. Little Dogie laughed at him but didn't say any more.

When they reached the soft ground beside the river—the river that had dug the canyon, a red stream cutting through red earth—the horses slowed to a walk, much to the relief of Pyg. Now he could settle down in his saddle without imperiling future generations.

Pyg was feeling so good that he felt sorry for a lone longhorn who looked miserable. The cow stood stone still with its head down and its forefeet thrust slightly forward, bracing itself. Its ears, like everything else about it, drooped. Well, not everybody could be happy, not even in paradise.

Somebody was singing very softly:

"As I was out walking one morning for pleasure,
I saw a cowpuncher riding alone . . ."

Pyg looked around to see who was serenading them. It turned out to be Opry, whose lips were barely moving. He had an impish expression on his weathered face.

> *"His hat was throwed back*
> *And his spurs they were a-jingling,*
> *And as he approached, he was singin' this song . . ."*

Now several of the other cowboys joined in and the tune swelled:

> *"Whoopie ti yi yay, git along little dogies*
> *It's your misfortune and none of my own . . ."*

Pyg flinched as Little Dogie turned angrily in his saddle to see who was making fun of him. His face reddened and his eyes narrowed.

"Oh, it's you," growled the giant. "I mighta knowed. See, Pyg, Opry is under the mis-impression that he can sing. And he's always tryin' to prove it, all encouragement to the contrary notwithstandin'."

But then the big man's expression relaxed and he joined in the singing. His voice, bigger than the others, boomed so loud it echoed in the canyon:

> *"Whoopie ti yi yay, git along Little Dogie . . ."*

He tipped his hat and laughed loudly. The others laughed along with him, relieved by his good humor.

> *"You know that Wyoming will be your new home."*

As the last words of the song were fading, Pyg noticed another sad cow. Motionless, head down, ears drooping. This longhorn looked as if it had died standing up and didn't have the energy to fall over. Had it? No, it picked this moment to take a piss, so it couldn't be dead. But something was strange. It was the color. Red urine flowed down the red riverbank toward the red river. Maybe everything in this canyon was red. Did the longhorns shit red dung? Or was the cow spraying blood?

"That cow's pee looks funny," said Pyg.

"Pee?" said Little Dogie. "We call it 'piss' out here."

"The cow's sick," said Too Short.

"What's wrong with it?" asked Pyg.

"Fever."

"What kind of fever?"

"A bad one."

"It looks so unhappy. I never thought about cows being sad."

"Thass right," said Little Dogie. "That poor critter ain't got a grin left in its system."

They climbed the north face of the red canyon and then rode into the wind. It blew hard and steady. It hummed, then howled, then wailed. It was sometimes lonely, sometimes angry, always resolute. Determined. Relentless. It blew all morning and all afternoon.

"Does the wind always blow like this?" asked Pyg.

"'Fraid so," said Too Short. "Once you up and leave the canyon, this here country's flat for about a million miles. Nothin' to stop the wind from blowin'. Yore daddy used to like to say that if the wind up here ever stopped blowin', all the prairie dogs'd fall over."

Laughing and squinting into the wind, Pyg said: "Be a good place to go sailing."

"What?" asked Too Short, who had probably never seen a body of still water much larger than a puddle.

When they stopped to make camp that night, the wind was still blowing. The wind fanned the campfire and blew the smoke south toward the canyon. All the cowboys sat on the north side of the fire. Pyg noticed and did the same.

Opry serenaded them in a voice that needed a lot of tuning:

> *"Oh, I'll eat when I'm hungry,*
> *I'll drink when I'm dry;*
> *If a horse don't fall on me,*
> *I'll live till I die."*

Pyg laughed.

"Don't encourage him," said Little Dogie.

They had to make do with boiled coffee, cold biscuits, and beef jerky because they had left Coffee the cook behind. He would do his best to look after the ranch while the others were gone.

Too Short's face was stretched by a tall yawn. "Might as well fold up in a blanket and take a chance on tomorrow."

"Hope the critters steer clear of Pyg tonight," said Little Dogie.

"Cut that out," said Too Short.

"Cut what out? I figure my friend Pyg's got a right to know. See, this here country's lousy with some mean critters that come creepin' 'round at night."

"What kind of critters?" asked Pyg.

"I'm warnin' you," said Too Short.

"Pyg wants to know. He asked. Well, we got lots a bitin' critters. We got ants. And we got scorpions. And we got snakes. Rattlesnakes. Diamond-backs. Sidewinders. The occasional coral snake, that's deadliest of all."

Pyg realized he was once again turning a bullet over and over with his thumb and index and middle fingers.

"Don't listen to him," said Too Short.

"Them snakes is cold-blooded sons-a-bitches, so they just loves curlin' up with a cowboy in his nice *warm* bedroll. It's a temptation they just cain't hardly resist. Them snakes is freezin' their damn balls off and—"

"Snakes don't got no balls," said Too Short.

"Here's what's li'ble to happen. You suddenly wakes up. Somethin' hurts. Hurts bad. You figures out you been bit by some damn critter, but you don't know what kind. That's the problem. Was it an ant? Or was it a snake? Or was it a scorpion?"

"Damn yore eyes!" Too Short told the giant.

"And if'n it was a scorpion, was it the kind that kills you? Or was it the kind that hurts you so bad you just wisht you was dead?"

The bullet in Pyg's hand tumbled faster. "How do you tell the difference?"

"Well, you can just say your prayers and wait to see if'n you die. Or if you're real curious, you can look fer the varmint. The big scorpions hurt. The little ones is fatal. Course, if'n you does find him, he'll probably git pissed off and just sting you ag'in."

"How little is little? How big do the little ones get?"

"You're right. Sometimes it's hard to tell the killin' kind from the hurtin' kind. The only sure way is to see if you up and die. Course, maybe it wasn't no scorpion atall. Maybe it was a damn rattler. You'd have a damn chance if'n you was awake, 'cause you'd hear the damn rattles. But not if'n you is asleep . . ."

"Sleep tight," said Custer.

"Not you, too," said Too Short.

"My advice," said Little Dogie, "is sleep with a big ol' rock in yore hand. That way you got a fightin' chance. Now some cowboys like to sleep with a six-gun in their damn hands, but you're li'ble to git excited and shoot yore balls off. So my advice is to go with a rock."

Pyg pulled off his moth-eaten chaps and shiny boots and was ready for bed. He rolled up in a patchwork quilt but couldn't sleep. He twisted and turned on the hard ground, winding this way, then the other, like a tumbleweed in a whirlwind. His body couldn't seem to relax and get comfortable. Nor could his mind. His body wanted to sleep, but his mind kept warning him to remain alert. Keep awake, stay alive. While he didn't sleep, he cradled a fist-sized rock in his hand. Curled up in a quilt, he felt nice and warm, but warmth was dangerous. Warmth was his enemy. Warmth would fill his bed with snakes. So he unrolled, lay on top of his quilt. But the constant wind soon chilled him. He wrapped up again. He told himself he had to sleep, then warned himself he mustn't.

The cowboys seemed to be sleeping fine. Why weren't they worried about scorpions and snakes? Maybe you just got hardened to the dangers. Got as hard as the hard ground on which they lay and snored. He told himself he had to toughen up. Would this night never end?

"Yeeoowww!" Pyg screamed like a stuck pig. "Help!"

Oh, no! He had fallen asleep and a snake had bitten him! He was dying! Now where was that rock? Somehow he had lost it in his sleep, lost it in his bedroll, lost it in the confusion of the night. But was it a snake? Maybe it was a scorpion. But would it kill him or just sting him? Where was it? Now he was searching for both the rock and the varmint. Where in the world . . . ?

Pyg heard laughter. What was going on? Were the cowboys mean enough to laugh at a dying man? Why weren't they helping him? What was wrong with them?

"Help me!" he yelled. "Something bit me."

"You'll l-l-live, boy," said Little Dogie, choking on laughter.

"How do you know? What if it was a snake?"

"It waddn't—no snake."

"Or a scorpion?"

"Waddn't." He tried to stop laughing and catch his breath. "I poked you with a sharp stick." He held up a mesquite twig that he had sharpened with his knife. "See?"

Pyg curled into a fetal position and pulled his bedroll up over his head. Rooting around, he found his rock. He wanted to bash Little Dogie over the head with it, but he was afraid the giant might not even notice.

"Fun's over," said Too Short irritably. "Ever'body go back to poundin' yore damn ears."

An hour or so later—anyway it seemed like an hour—Pyg poked his head from under his blanket and looked up at the stars. He promised himself that no matter what happened, he was never going to scream like that again. Never! Not as long as he lived.

He tossed and turned and squeezed the rock in his right hand. He wished he could trade places with the stone, be as unconscious as it was, as oblivious. Rocks were never embarrassed or angry. Rocks never screamed. Rocks had no trouble sleeping. Rocks were never uncomfortable. Rocks led the good life. Rocks . . .

"YEEOOWWW!!" Pyg screamed louder than ever. "What! Help!"

But this time, as he regained consciousness, he decided to help himself. Gripping the rock tightly, he struck out blindly at his attacker. He didn't bother to check to see whether the attack came from a varmint or from Little Dogie. He didn't care. If he crushed a snake, fine. If he cracked the giant's skull, even better. He felt his weapon connect with bone. The bone broke.

"OOOooowwwww! You shit! You broke my nose! Oh, shit and shit some more."

It was of course a familiar voice. Pyg focused his eyes and his mind. No, he wasn't dreaming. He had really hit her.

"I'm sorry," he gulped.

"You broke my nose."

"I'm really sorry."

As Jesse clutched her face, blood squirted from between her fingers. Pyg wanted to comfort her, but he couldn't think how. He was afraid to try to take her in his arms. He didn't even dare touch her.

"Look!" she said, holding out her bloody hands. "Now I'll be ugly. Shit and shit some more. And some more. And some more, more, more."

Pyg wanted to hide under the covers again, but he didn't want to appear to be either a coward or a baby in her eyes.

"Nice work, Pyg," yelled Little Dogie.

"Who's Pig?" asked Jesse.

As the red sun rose, Pyg tried not to laugh. He shouldn't laugh, mustn't laugh. But she looked so funny. Both Jesse's eyes were black and her nose was swollen the size of her fist. It was also skinned and realigned. Instead of flowing smoothly from north to south, it now had a slight east-to-west crook in it. Pyg bit the inside of his cheek to keep from laughing. Besides, he deserved the pain.

"If you laugh," Jesse threatened, "I'll kill you. I'll kill you dead and dead some more."

"Where did you get those clothes?" Pyg asked, trying to keep a straight face. "They're so becoming."

"Yore damn mama wanted me to wear soma her clothes. Since I didn't bring nona my own. But I said 'no, thanks,' I'd rather borrow from Coffee. So I did." Evidently cooks had larger wardrobes than punchers.

Her outfit made her look even funnier, men's faded blue Strausses that were too big and a man's faded red work shirt with a torn pocket. Her belt was a piece of baling wire. You could fix anything with baling wire. Pyg couldn't help laughing.

"Where's that rock?" Jesse yelled. "I need a rock. You're dead."

Pyg bent over laughing. Jesse slapped his face with her open hand. It hurt. His cheek stung.

"You think I'm kiddin'?"

But Pyg couldn't stop laughing and his laughter was infectious. Soon the cowboys were laughing along with him.

"I'll kill you all!"

Jesse reached inside her borrowed work shirt and pulled out a gun. The laughter stopped. It was a small gun: the little double-barreled Derringer from the Harvey House. So she couldn't really kill them all. Two at the most.

"Fun's over," announced Too Short. "Less saddle up."

Jesse continued to point the little gun at Pyg, who stared at the two huge holes at the end of it, but the other cowboys went to work. They caught their hobbled horses, coaxed bits into their mouths, and threw saddles on their backs. Pyg felt like laughing again but managed to swallow the tickle. He doubted she would shoot him, but he didn't really know her very well.

"You two better head on back to the ranch," Too Short said.

"You *two*," Pyg protested. "No, I'm coming with you."

"She's gotta go back, and it ain't a good idea to have a female travelin' alone. Not out chere. You better take her."

"No, I'm comin', too," said Jesse. "I'm not goin' back. He can if he wants to, but not me."

"Posse ain't no place fer a woman," said Too Short. "You know that."

"No, I don't. I cain't go back to that ranch. No way. If you don't want me comin' along, you better just find some more rocks and stone me to death. Like in the Bible. Finish what this Pig already started."

"What's wrong with the ranch?" asked Pyg.

"Nothin's wrong with the ranch. It's your mama. I cain't spend another hour with that woman."

Pyg smiled for two reasons. First of all, he could imagine how his mumsy and Jesse got along after he left. But more important, the boy had just noticed that the Harvey Girl wasn't wearing any underwear. Not on top anyway. Well, he wasn't sure, but he didn't think she was. Her breasts moved as if they were no longer in bondage. Now that she had left both the Harvey House and Revelie Goodnight behind her, she was free and so were her tits. As far as Pyg was concerned, Jesse was welcome to come along and hunt outlaws with them as long as she brought her breasts along.

CHAPTER 13

They rode into Tascosa, a self-appointed posse that included a bouncing tenderfoot and a Harvey Girl astride a stolen horse. A couple of tumbleweeds escorted them down Main Street. Percy was surprised to see how unsubstantial the town appeared. None of the buildings were made of brick, none of stone. They were all constructed of rickety wood or eroding adobe. The paint had weathered off every building but the saloon, which evidently still had some civic pride.

"Hey, Pyg, see that there stump?" said Too Short. "Thass where your daddy busted them thumbs." They rode a little farther. "And thass where your daddy met your mama when she was strung up by her thumbs. You know the story, doncha?"

"I've heard it a *few* times," Pyg said.

"I ain't," Jesse said through swollen lips. "Sounds to me like this tale's all thumbs, huh?" Amused by her own joke, she looked like a grinning monster. "What happened?"

"You tell it, Too Short," Pyg said. "You were there."

"Please," said Jesse.

"Well, we come ridin' into town one day, and we seen his mama hung up by her damn thumbs. They was big and blue."

"Served her right, I'm sure," said the Harvey Girl.

"Well, his daddy didn't think so. Hangin' a woman up by her thumbs kinda rubbed him the wrong way. So he up and rescued her. And that's how come there got to be a Pyg. Thass about all."

"Now that story's just plain too short," protested Jesse. "Is everything about you too short? Your tales? Your legs? What else? Hmm, I wonder."

The monster grinned again. Evidently she hadn't forgiven Too Short for trying to make her go back to the ranch.

"Thass tellin' him," said Little Dogie.

"What about all them other thumbs?" she asked. "The outlaw thumbs?"

"Oh, yeah, well, we was gonna hang the whole gang, but his daddy said no. The way he figured it, bustin' up their thumbs, well, it'd be more fittin'. Used the blunt end of that damn ax of his, the one we're chasin'."

"Wish I'd been here to see it," Jesse said. "Sounds like quite a show."

"It was, but you waddn't born yet." Too Short paused. "You know, you're kinda bloodthirsty fer a girl."

"But that's a good thing, right?" said Jesse.

The curious posse stopped in front of the Cattle Exchange Saloon. The cowboys, the tenderfoot, and the Harvey Girl dismounted and tied their reins to the hitching rail. Jesse had taken her horse, a sorrel gelding named Boy Howdy, from the Home Ranch remuda without asking permission, so she was technically a horse thief in danger of hanging. Stepping up onto the raised, wooden sidewalk, Pyg noticed that it wandered a decidedly zigzag path, because none of the buildings were lined up with any of the others.

"We'll ask around in here," Too Short said. "See if anybody's heard tell of a stole tombstone."

"Now, Too Short, I don't want you gittin' drunk as a boiled owl ag'in," said Jesse.

"Thass tellin' him," said Little Dogie.

Crossing the wooden sidewalk and passing through the swinging doors, Pyg stopped because he couldn't see. The dark interior felt like a cave. When his vision returned, he noticed that the floor had been scarred by a long line of cowboys dragging their sharp spurs. Advancing to the bar, he felt deliciously naughty. His mother had told him over and over again that he was forbidden to drink until he was twenty-one. But Mumsy wasn't here.

"Whiskey," Pyg told the bartender.

"You sure?" asked Too Short.

"His mama likes him to drink milk," Jesse said.

"Sure I'm sure," said the boy. "Of course."

"Put hair on your chest," said the Harvey Girl, who stood to his right, leaning on the bar.

The whiskey burned his mouth and his tongue, but Pyg tried not to let on. Heat spread through his chest. He didn't like the taste or the burn, but the whiskey gave him a pleasant sense of belonging. He felt grown up, manly.

Soon Pyg found himself staring at an overripe woman who was sitting alone at a small table. She had a shot glass and a bottle in front of her. Now that he had had his first real drink, he began fantasizing about his first woman. He assumed she was for sale. She wore a shiny red dress with lots of breast showing. He was reminded of soft-boiled eggs in egg cups. He told himself he wouldn't mind falling in love for the afternoon. Then he found himself wondering: Could Jesse read his thoughts? Was his hunger obvious? Embarrassed, he hoped not.

Surprised, Pyg saw the woman get up from her table and come toward him. Evidently she had read his mind. What would she say? How would she begin the negotiations? He wished Jesse weren't at his elbow. He felt caught between the two females. Was he blushing? The woman stopped so close he could have reached out and touched her.

"You cain't come in here," said the blowzy woman.

"Why not?" asked Pyg, feeling even younger than seventeen.

"I ain't talkin' to you, sonny boy." She pointed at Jesse. "She cain't come in here. I'm the only one allowed. This here's my damn territory."

"It's a free country," protested Jesse.

"Not in here it ain't. Nothin' in here's free. Includin' yours truly." She winked at Pyg, then scowled at Jesse. "Now git goin'."

"But I ain't no whore. I ain't tryin' to horn in on your territory. I ain't no competition."

"Who're you callin' a whore! Damn yore eyes. I don't appreciate that kinda talk."

"Well, shit and shit some more. I believe in callin' a whore a whore."

The whore picked up Pyg's shot glass and threw the whiskey in Jesse's face. Then Jesse threw her own drink at the other woman, hitting her in the chest. The whore and the Harvey Girl dove at each other. They both crashed to the floor, screaming and pulling each other's hair. The spigot inside Jesse's nose opened and gushed blood.

"You're ruining my dress!" screamed the whore.

"I ain't bleedin' on purpose," said Jesse.

Pyg was excited by the girl fight—and appalled. He didn't know what to do. Should he try to come between them? Instead, he started a bullet doing somersaults in his hand.

"Stop," he said pathetically.

He took a step forward, but a stern hand restrained him.

"Bedder stay out of it," Too Short said. "You're li'ble to git yourself hurt."

Percy retreated a step but felt bad about it. The tumbling bullet picked up speed.

Jesse managed to pull free of the angry whore. She rolled up onto her hands and knees, then got her feet under her and stood up. She had her Derringer in her right hand.

"Keep away from me," Jesse ordered, pointing the little gun at the big whore.

"Gimme that," said the professional as she got slowly to her feet. "I'll have a pin put on it and wear it on my purdy bodice."

"I don't wanna hurt you," said the Harvey Girl.

"Well, we'll just see who gits hurt." The whore had an amused expression on her red face. Red from smeared makeup. Red from exertion. Red from fury. She backed up carefully until her back was against the bar. "Joe, gimme," she said.

The bartender reached behind the bar, pulled out a big silver revolver, and handed it to the whore. She swung the gun up and pointed it at Jesse.

Terrified, the Harvey Girl pulled the trigger. The little gun made a surprisingly big sound. Blood gushed from the whore's left ear. She reached up, touched the wound, then looked at her fingers, which were now bloody.

"You're a dead woman," she said.

Jesse fired again. This time she missed her target completely. She pulled the trigger again and the gun just clicked. The Derringer had fired its two bullets and was now useless. It wasn't even big enough to throw.

"Now it's my turn," said the whore.

She raised her silver revolver, closed one eye, and sighted down the barrel. She took her time, made it last, savored her revenge. Jesse dropped to her knees as if praying for her life. The whore just aimed lower and slowly, carefully, pulled back the hammer.

"Please, no," Jesse said. "I'm sorry."

Pyg dropped the cartwheeling bullet.

"Too late," said the whore, squeezing the trigger.

The deafening roar reminded Pyg of the cannon firing on the Fourth of July.

CHAPTER 14

When she opened her eyes, Jesse had a surprised look on her face. The whore looked surprised, too, as she sat down slowly on the floor and leaned back against the bar. One was surprised to be alive, the other surprised to be dead. Jesse started crying. Her nose ran blood while her eyes ran tears down her face.

Lowering his gun, smoke curling from its muzzle, Pyg kept waiting for the woman in the red dress to get up off the floor and start yelling again. What was wrong? The game was over. It was time to stand up and start another game. The vomit in his mouth surprised him. It was hot and bitter. Throwing up, he felt more like a child than ever. Embarrassed. Bashful. He turned away. But a part of him knew that his nausea had nothing to do with childhood. He was sick because he had committed a sickening adult act. The worst crime. He was a killer. And not just any killer but a woman killer. Realizing he was trembling all over, he stumbled to a chair and sat down in it. He tried to catch his breath.

"Thanks," said Jesse.

"Shut up," said Pyg, wiping his mouth.

Little Dogie lumbered over and looked down at the bleeding whore. He bent over and felt her wrist for a pulse. He shook his head.

"Too dead to skin," said the giant. "Nice shootin'."

"You shut up, too," said Pyg.

"Or what? You'll shoot me?"

"I said shut up."

The giant squatted. He put his hand gently on the whore's cheek and reached up with his huge thumb to close first one eye, then the other. Then he picked up her silver gun and studied it.

"It's a .45. Looks like a nice shootin' iron. Never seen one just like it before." He stood up slowly, still holding the gun. "Reckon it belongs to you now."

Little Dogie walked over to Pyg and placed the revolver on the table in front of him.

"I don't want it."

"Take it. You done good work. You saved your girlfriend's life. That lady waddn't gonna miss."

"She isn't my girlfriend."

Pyg found himself studying the gun, which seemed to glow in the darkness of the saloon. It was indeed a curious weapon, covered with filigrees and curlicues from muzzle to butt. And it looked like real silver. No, that couldn't be, could it? Perhaps it was silver plate like his mother's tea service back in Boston. The elaborate decoration seemed out of place here. It belonged on a tea table at teatime. How could something so beautiful do something so ugly? It occurred to Pyg that he didn't even know the name of the woman he had killed.

"Better take it," said Little Dogie. "If you don't, somebody else will. I don't expect she's got no heirs."

"Besides, it's fittin'," said Ivan the Terrible. "You won that there gun fair 'n' square."

"*Sí,*" said Vaquero.

The bartender raised up from behind the bar—where he had been hiding—and cleared his throat loudly. Everybody looked in his direction.

"You bedder git outta here," the bartender said. "You just killt Big Sal's girl. He ain't gonna be too pleased with y'all."

"Who's Big Sal?" asked Little Dogie. "And how come you figure we oughta give a shit?"

"He's one of them Robbers' Roost boys. That's how come you oughta give a damn."

"Oh, we do, Joe. We sure 'nough do. We gives a great big ol' damn. How 'bout you tell us where we can find this here Big Sal?"

"Sorry. I don't think he'd appreciate that. But he done give Prudence that there silver gun, so you better just leave it on the table and git movin'."

Pyg thought: So that was her name. He started to smile and then felt guilty about the urge. He tried to look solemn.

"Joe, you're gonna scare us to death if'n you ain't careful." Little Dogie smiled, put his foot on the rail, leaned forward, and grabbed the bartender by the neck with one hand. He lifted him over the bar and dumped him on the floor at his big feet. Joe knelt there coughing. "I expect you better start worryin' a little more about how dangerous we are, 'cause we're here and he ain't."

Reaching down, Little Dogie picked the bartender up by his ankles. Poor Joe dangled head down. The giant held one ankle in his left fist, the other in his right.

"Somebody make a wish."

Little Dogie started pulling the barkeep's legs apart as if they were a wishbone. The giant had long arms. Joe, who had short legs, screamed.

"Change your mind? Feel more talkative now?"

"Y-y-yeah."

"Speak right up." Little Dogie lowered the bartender a few inches so he could almost touch the floor with his fingers. "Don't be bashful now."

"Put me down."

"I don't hear nothin' yet. Tell me somethin' and be quick about it. Your face's turnin' all purple."

"I dunno where he is—"

"Really, somebody make a wish."

"I wish I had a last name," said Opry. "How's that?"

Little Dogie spread the bartender's legs even wider. The purple face grimaced in pain.

"No, no," he protested. "S-s-she g-got a l-letter. J-just t'other day. I 'spect it come from him. Now p-put me down."

"You happen to see where that there letter come from?" Little Dogie lifted Joe higher. "Huh?"

"No—"

"Then you ain't doin' us much good, are ya?" The giant spread his victim's legs still wider. "Hey, Custer, it's your turn now. Make a wish."

"You know what I want," said the Comanche. "I want the buffalo back. Thass all."

Pyg watched as Joe's legs threatened to snap.

"I know she k-kept it," sputtered the inverted bartender.

"Where?"

"I dunno."

"Thass the wrong answer," said Little Dogie. "Lemme tell you what you oughta wish, Purple Face. You bedder wish you can learn how to walk on one leg."

"Mebbe it's between her, uh, you know, them things."

"Between her legs!" asked the giant. "She keeps her love letters there? I like a girl like that. Too bad she's plenty dead."

"No, no," stammered Joe. "Between the other things. Where she puts her money and stuff."

"Oh, her tits. Why didn't ya say so?"

Little Dogie dropped the bartender on his head. The little man curled into a ball on the dirty floor. Then they all stood around staring at the dead woman's tits.

"Who's gonna see if'n it's there?" asked Ivan the Terrible.

"You volunteerin'?" asked Too Short.

"No, I was just wonderin'," said the Russian. "Now if'n she was alive, I'd be first in line. But dead? It don't hardly seem fittin'."

"She won't mind none," said Tin Soldier.

"*Sí,*" said Vaquero.

"I just cain't see feelin' up a dead gal," said Ivan.

They all mentally scratched their whiskers. Pyg, who had less of a beard than most, was as stumped as the others. He absently reached out and touched the silver gun on the table in front of him. Then he pulled his fingers away quickly as if they were burned.

"Hey, Joe, you do it," ordered Little Dogie.

"No!" said the bartender as if he were in pain, hugging his knees.

Pyg glanced at Jesse. Slowly, one by one, the other men began looking at her, too. She didn't look happy at the attention.

"Shit and shit some more," she observed. "Okay, I guess I'm elected."

Jesse walked over, taking long strides like a man, and stared down at the dead whore in the red dress. The Harvey Girl knelt.

"There's somethin' in here," said Jesse.

"Yeah, but is they a letter?" asked Little Dogie with a big-man giggle.

Jesse pulled out a soiled envelope and stood up. Quickly she backed up a couple of steps. Her fingers were shaking as she fumbled to open it. Pulling out a scrap of brown paper—it looked like wrapping paper—she unfolded it hurriedly. Then she studied it.

"Who's it from?" asked Too Short.

"Just signed 'Big,'" said Jesse. "Anyhow that's what it looks like."

"Whass it say?"

"Says he's in some place called, I dunno, Q-U-A-N-A-H. That make any sense to y'all?"

"Custer, you tell her."

"Quanah," pronounced the Comanche. "Town named after one of my people, a chief. You ain't never heard of Quanah Parker?"

"Sorry." Jesse shrugged.

The bartender struggled to his feet and ran out of the saloon, leaving the swinging doors flapping.

"Pyg, pick up that there gun and less go," ordered Too Short.

Obeying by reflex, Pyg reached down and took hold of the gun. It felt heavier than his own six-shooter. He followed the others out into the bright sunshine where he blinked and sneezed. The sun always made him sneeze. Was he allergic to the sun, of all things?

"Stick it in your belt and mount up," said Too Short. "We best git goin' before her disappointed customers start showin' up."

"You know, I feel kinda sorry fer them customers," said Tin Soldier with real concern in his voice. "What're they gonna do now?"

"Fall in love with a dadgum heifer," said Little Dogie.

CHAPTER 15

Pyg was still bouncing, but he tried to bounce less. He would go small bounce, small bounce, small bounce, *ouch*, big bounce.

"Hippity hop," said Little Dogie.

Pyg wondered if he would he ever learn.

"That Tascosa is a pretty salty town," observed Opry with a grin. "Kinda place where:

> *They're so tough their skins hurt,*
> *And they wash their ears with dirt—"*

"Stop singin' before I pull out your damn tonsils by the roots!" roared the giant.

Opry took the big man's advice and fell silent.

Nudging his horse to speed up, Pyg caught up with Custer.

"Quanah Parker," the boy said, "that's a funny name for a Comanche chief, isn't it?"

"Half-breed," said Custer. "His daddy was a Comanche chief, but his mama was a white lady name of Parker. Cynthia Anne Parker. You never heard of her?"

"Sorry."

They rode on through a landscape that slowly changed from flat and featureless to broken country. This new panorama was easier on the eyes but harder on the horses. The poor animals dropped down into arroyos and then climbed wearily up the other side. They crossed dry creek beds, traversed draws with crumbling banks, and scared coveys of quail that beat the air with stubby wings. Occasionally a snake scared them.

"God's country, *sí?*" Vaquero said.

"Your god must be one tough hombre," said Little Dogie.

"My god's the same as your god."

"No, he ain't. Your god talks Spanish, and my god talks English."

"Jesus spoke Aramaic," said Pyg.

"What?" asked everybody.

They rode in silence.

"Smells like rain," Jesse said.

"I don't smell nothin'," said Little Dogie.

"You wouldn't, big white man," said Custer. "White folks cain't smell shit." He sniffed the air. "I think she's right. Rain's buildin' up but it won't bust loose till it gits good and ready. Mebbe tonight. Mebbe tomorrow. Mebbe the next day. But it's acomin'." He studied the girl. "You got a good nose, Miss Jesse."

"Not no more," she said. "I think *he* done busted it."

It was swollen.

"But it still works real good," Custer said. "You got a nose like an Indian. You sure you ain't part Comanche?"

"Watch out who you're callin' names!"

"'Comanche' ain't no bad name. It's a damn compliment."

"Well, keep your damn compliments to yourself, okay?"

Pyg thought: She's feisty.

Which of course made him like her more.

That night, as the campfire huffed smoke, Pyg examined his new gun. The silver six-shooter was covered with swirling leaves and blossoms, but these plants had bloomed not in flowerpots but in someone's mind. The boy had never seen their like in the Boston Public or any other garden. He hefted the gun in his hand, rocked it forward, then back, shifted it from one hand to the other. He restrained an urge to try to twirl it on his finger. The butt was especially heavy. It felt like solid metal—but what kind? Steel? Nickel? Brass? Or could it possibly be solid silver?

"Don't shoot your dick off," Little Dogie said.

Ignoring him, Pyg turned the gun upside down and examined the butt more carefully. There were no screws, no seams. It seemed to have been cast as one piece. Squinting in the dim firelight, he noticed writing on the bottom of the butt. Tiny letters had been engraved into the silver. He made out a capital "T," then a small "i," then a capital "H," then an "a," an "n," and a "y." Funny word. What did it mean? Could it be a name? Then he saw his mistake. The "H" was actually an "ff." Now he could read the word. It was the same name that was engraved on his mother's silver tea service: Tiffany. He decided not to share this news with the cowboys, because he wasn't sure how they would take it. He liked tea services, but he doubted that his new "friends" cared much for them.

"I been wonderin'," said Jesse. "You think maybe it shoots silver bullets?"

"Let's see," said Pyg.

The boy broke open the cylinder—a trick Too Short had taught him—and shook out several bullets. He pressed his thumbnail into one of them: It was soft.

"Sorry," Pyg said. "Looks like—feels like—lead to me."

He tossed a bullet to Jesse, who caught it in both hands. She examined the ammunition carefully. She even bit into it.

"Too bad. We'll have to find you some silver bullets."

The next morning, Pyg put his old gun away in a saddlebag. Goodbye baling wire, so long rust. Then he dropped his silver gun in his holster. He liked its substantial weight. It anchored him.

"Could I sorta borrow that old gun of yours?" asked Jesse. "Never can tell, mebbe someday I can shoot somebody for you."

"Of course," said Pyg.

As the day wore on, one weary horseback mile following another, the country began to soften. Mesquites turned into oak trees. Clumps of tough buffalo grass changed into a rolling prairie lawn. But the grass was still brown.

Pyg noticed a fragile-looking house in the distance. It appeared to be made of wood and to have few pretensions.

"I wonder who lives there," he said, pointing.

"Your mama wouldn't like that," said Little Dogie. "Pointin', my, my."

"Farmers," said Too Short. "More and more of them clodhoppers are movin' into the country ever'day, I'm afraid."

When they drew closer, Pyg could see rows of short plants with round leaves. They looked wilted.

"What's that?" he asked.

"Cotton," Too Short said. "Appears like it could use some rain."

"Don't worry," said Little Dogie, "Injun Jess says rain's just 'round the damn corner."

"I ain't no dirty Injun," Jesse protested.

"What?" asked Custer.

"I'm sorry," she said. "But—"

"Maybe I oughta do a rain dance," said the Comanche. "Help these here Writers out."

"Writers?" asked Pyg, hoping to deflect a quarrel with a question.

"Thass what we calls white folks like you," said Custer. "And thass not all. We got a name for Meskins, too. We calls 'em 'Common Writers.'"

"No," protested Vaquero. "We Meskins ain't no common nothin'. Are you kiddin'? We can all speak twice as many languages as any of y'all. Me, I talk a little Nez Perce, Blackfoot, Flathead, English, Spanish, and my favorite, Profane. See, you sons-a-humpin' bitches, I ain't common atall."

Pyg wasn't sure whether Vaquero was really angry or not, but when he heard the others laugh, he began to relax.

"And thanks to this here redskin, I'm even learnin' some Comanche," the Mexican cowboy continued. "Custer, tell these damned palefaces what you call monkeys."

"Oh, yeah, we calls monkeys 'Writers with tails.'"

"Thass tellin' 'em."

"And Chinks, they's 'Writers with Pigtails.' And guess what we call melons?"

"What?" Pyg asked.

"Them's 'round-headed Writers.'"

"Some language," Pyg laughed. "I like it."

He thought about this funny way of talking. He had always imagined that Indian talk was unrelentingly fierce. It was like discovering that wolves have a sense of humor.

"If I'm a Writer, what are you?" Pyg asked.

"A Human Bein'. Course."

"Really?"

"Whaddaya call her?" Little Dogie asked, pointing at Jesse.

"Watch it," she said.

"Her?" said Custer. "Well, this lady, she's looks like a Writer, but she smells like a Human Bein'."

"So you're sayin' she's a stinkin' Injun, huh?" Little Dogie laughed. "Guess it takes one to smell one."

"I mean smells with her nose, not stinks."

"Smells, stinks, it's all Injun to me," said the giant.

"Go fuck yourself," Jesse said. "Nobody else will."

In the distance, Pyg saw peaked roofs rise up out of the waving grass like sails approaching Boston Harbor.

CHAPTER 16

They rode down Main Street past wooden buildings, then a single stone structure, then more wood, until they came to a dugout on the other side of town. Pyg felt sorry for anyone who had to live and work half-in and half-out of the ground. It was like being half-in and half-out of the grave. They all reined in and dismounted.

"Don't hardly look big enough for us all," said Too Short. "Me and Pyg'll go on in. Rest of you sit on your fists and lean back on your thumbs."

"I'm not gonna sit on my fist." Jesse laughed. "I can tell you that right now."

"Good, you come with me 'n' Pyg. Make us look more peaceful like. Don't wanna scare nobody, least not right off." Too Short studied a sign on the front door that said THE CHIEF NEWS followed by COME ON IN. "*Chief,* huh? You better come, too, Custer."

Too Short opened the door. Pyg, Jesse, and Custer followed him inside. At the back of a big, dark room, a fat man with a fat beard sat at a wooden table reading. He looked up.

"Howdy," said Too Short. "I heard tell this here's a newspaper office. Any truth to that there rumor?"

"The truth, that's our business, believe it or not," said the fat man. "My name's W. W. West and I'm supposed to be the editor."

"Thass a whole lotta *W*'s," observed the little cowboy. "We was kinda expectin' an Injun chief."

"Sorry to disappoint you."

"Apology accepted. My name's Too Short, sorta actin' foreman over to the Home Ranch. This here's Pyg, spelled with a 'y.' He's kinda particular about the spellin'. And that there's Jesse. And this fine specimen of an Injun is named Custer."

Venturing a smile, W.W.W. stood up and came toward his visitors. As he passed a large hand-cranked press, he brushed it affectionately with his fingertips. Then he stuck out his hand. They all shook.

"What can I do you for?" asked W.W.W.

"We're lookin' for a feller named Big Sal," said Too Short. "Thought you might know somethin' 'bout him, bein' as how you're in the news business and all."

"Why are you trying to find him?"

"Got some news fer him. See, we're kinda in the news business, too."

"What kind of news? Could be I'd be interested."

"Just a message from his girl."

"Which one?"

"Prudence over to the Exchange Saloon in Tascosa, matter of fact. Got any idea where we might find this here Big Sal?"

"I'm afraid Sal can be kind of touchy. And he isn't particularly partial to strangers."

"We ain't strangers. We're from his girl. We're practic'ly family. See?"

"We don't want any trouble around here. We're peaceful folk. How do I know you're what you say you are? Maybe you come from this Prudence and maybe you come from somebody else."

"Pyg, show him your damn gun."

Startled, the boy blinked, then reached for his fancy revolver. It seemed to leap into his hand of its own accord, clearing the holster quickly, gracefully, with a minimum of motion. Pyg was surprised to see the fat editor raise his hands. The boy felt contrite: He hadn't meant to scare anybody.

"Don't shoot," said W.W.W.

"Don't shoot him," said Too Short, smiling, "yet."

Pyg lowered his bright gun so it pointed at the packed-earth floor. It felt heavy and powerful in his hand. It made him feel powerful. He liked the feeling, but felt guilty about liking it.

"You may put your hands down," said Pyg, proud of himself for remembering the proper grammar that his mother cared so much about.

W.W.W. lowered them slowly, suspiciously.

"You ever seen that there gun before?" asked Too Short.

"I don't think so," said the editor.

"Show it to him up close."

When Pyg took a step forward, W.W.W. stepped backward. The boy held out the gun flat on his palm. The man recoiled.

"Stand still," Too Short ordered.

With the fat man now anchored, Pyg walked up close and held the gun under his nose. The editor sniffed as if he might recognize the gun by its odor.

"No, I've never seen it before," said W.W.W., his voice quivering.

"You ain't an especially gifted liar," Too Short said.

"I'm telling the truth." He trembled. "You've got to believe me."

"You're scared to say anything, aren't you?" Pyg felt sorry for the frightened man. What was he doing out here in the West anyway? But then the boy asked himself the same thing. Hoping to calm the editor's fears, he asked: "Want to hold it?"

"No, I don't like guns," the fat man said, recoiling.

"My mumsy doesn't either."

"But I bet Big Sal likes guns just fine," said Too Short. "And I figure he might just want this one back. Whaddaya think?"

The editor walked warily back to his table and sat down. Maybe his legs felt weak. Being back where he spent so much of his work day, the newspaperman seemed to relax a little.

"Perhaps I should take a closer look at that gun, after all," he said. "If you don't mind."

Pyg walked over and placed the gun on the table in front of him. The editor bowed his head and studied the revolver closely without ever touching it.

"Well?" asked Too Short.

"Well, you're right: I was prevaricating. This does look like Sal's gun. He showed it to me one day. He scared me, too. I guess I scare easy. Anyway he was real proud of this gun and wanted me to write something about it. He said he won it from a gambler in a poker game, but who knows?"

"Did you write about it?" asked Pyg.

"No, not in the end. But I did do some research. I discovered that the gun seemed to resemble several that were exhibited at the Columbian Exhibition held in Chicago last year."

"The what?" asked Too Short. "Come ag'in."

"The Columbian Exhibition. It celebrated the four-hundredth anniversary of Christopher Columbus' discovery of America. You know, 1492–1892."

"That boy Columbus sure did us a big favor," said Custer. "On the reservation, we had us a big ol' party fer him."

"Really?" asked Pyg innocently.

"No," said Custer.

"Nonetheless, the Exhibition seems to have been quite an affair," said the editor. "In spite of your reservation's understandable reservations, many citizens seem to remember Columbus fondly."

"Git back to that there gun," said Too Short.

"Well, it turns out that the Smith and Wesson company commissioned a company called Tiffany to decorate several of their guns for this big show. They made quite an impression at the Exhibition. Many of the handles were made of solid silver. Is it heavy?"

"Yes, sir, it is," said Pyg.

"Yes, I expect it's solid silver."

They all stared at the silver gun on the table. It had just earned more respect.

"That's interesting," said Pyg. "Why didn't you write that story?"

"I was tempted to, of course, but I was afraid I might inadvertently misspell Sal's name—or make some other mistake—and he would come and kill me."

"Good thinkin'," said Too Short.

"Do you still want to return the gun," asked the editor, "now that you know it's valuable?"

"Yes, sir," lied Pyg. The lie made him feel more grown up somehow, which was strange because kids lied all the time. "If it's worth something, that's all the more reason to return it to its rightful owner." He hoped he wasn't spreading it too thick.

"Commendable," muttered the editor, "if not entirely credible."

"Sir, are you calling me a liar?"

"Certainly not." W.W.W. thought for a moment. "Well, perhaps I could suggest someone who just might be able to help you. Of course, I'm not sure she really knows anything, and I'm even less sure she'd want to tell you if she did. But she might."

"Thank you. We'd certainly appreciate it."

"Pull up a chair. Have a seat. All of you."

Pyg sat down in a chair across the table from the editor. Jesse sat to the boy's right, Too Short and Custer to his left. The chairs had cane bottoms. They were ready to play poker, but not with cards anybody could see.

"I have to ask a favor of you," the fat editor said solemnly. "Please don't tell her that I told you about her." He paused. "Do I have your word?"

Jesse, Pyg, Custer, and Too Short all nodded.

"I suppose that's good enough," said the editor. "I'll just have to trust you. You look like men whose word can be relied upon. You, too, ma'am."

Now Pyg wished he hadn't lied to this trusting soul. The three of them nodded again.

"Well, she runs a curious establishment about half a mile out of town. It's part grocery store, part saloon, and part fortune-teller's den."

"Fortune-teller?" said Too Short. "'Fraid I don't set much store by fortune-tellers. We ain't lookin' to git our hands read. We're just lookin' to find this here Big Sal who belongs to that there purdy gun."

"Come on, Too Short," protested Jesse. "It sounds like fun."

"We ain't funnin' on this trip, Miss Jess."

"Sorry."

"She's more than a fortune-teller. Where outlaws are concerned, she's more of a comrade-in-arms. Anyway that's what people say. Seems she got in some trouble up in Kansas, which is why she came down here and changed her name. She could tell you about more than what's written in your palm if she wants to."

The editor stopped to consider. He seemed to be a newspaperman who feared actually spreading any news.

"Come on," said Too Short impatiently. "What's her name and where can we find her?"

"Around here, she goes by the name of Sally Jones, but I don't believe that's what her mother and father called her. They say her real name's Kate Bender–"

"Kate Bender." Too Short whistled. "I heard tell of her. Ain't she s'posed to be some kinda lady killer? I mean killer lady?"

CHAPTER 17

Leaving the rest of the cowboys in town—they deserved some amusement—Too Short, Pyg, and won't-take-no Jesse rode out to Kate Bender's place. It didn't look like much more than a shack hemmed in by mesquite trees and prickly pears. Pyg felt uneasy but at the same time curious to meet a killer woman. They pulled up outside the store and dismounted. The boy gently stroked the heavy silver handle of his fancy six-shooter. A sign over the front door said GROCERIES.

Too Short knocked and waited. He rapped again. Pyg wondered if maybe this Kate Bender had given up on her store and moved on. Perhaps the newspaperman had been lying. There was a lot of that going around.

"Hello," called Too Short. "Anybody home?"

The pint-sized cowboy pushed the door open and walked in. Pyg followed—his fingers now wrapped around the heavy butt—and Jesse brought up the rear. Looking around, the boy saw no killer woman, but he did find a strange interior. The store was divided down the middle by a burlap curtain. He naturally wondered what was hidden on the other side.

"Anybody home?" Too Short called again.

The burlap curtain didn't move. The shack was quiet and felt deserted, but there were still groceries on a couple of warped shelves. Gallon cans of Cawova coffee. Calumet baking powder with an Indian chief in full headdress pictured on the cans. Gallons of A&P sorghum syrup. Tins of tobacco. And on the floor sacks of flour and cornmeal. Who would go off and leave these supplies unguarded?

"Less look around," said Too Short, pulling the burlap curtain aside to reveal the hidden half of the room.

Pyg moved closer so he could see, too, and he sensed Jesse looking over his shoulder. The boy saw dark bottles on another crooked shelf. The booze seemed on the verge of falling to the packed-earth floor. The bar was a plank on sawhorses. And there were a couple of tables and a few rickety chairs.

"Don't mind if I do," said Too Short, as if he had been invited inside. "Come on."

The three explorers pushed past the curtain and studied this poor excuse for a saloon. There was a warped shelf of dirty glasses. Painted on the far wall was the outline of a man. That was the only paint in the shack.

The burlap curtain quivered and a woman with a double-barreled shotgun suddenly appeared. She had copper curls and hazel eyes. She was pretty, which sent a shiver through Pyg—he suspected that the most dangerous women were beauties.

"Make yourselves right at home," said the man killer.

"I'm sorry," Pyg said, staring into the gun's two great eyes. "We didn't think anyone was at home."

"So you figured you'd just come in and help yourselves to whatever you wanted!"

"No, look, we didn't take anything. We sure apologize for intruding."

While still keeping an eye on the shotgun, Pyg also managed to study the woman holding it. He tried to decide if killing so many men had left any mark on her face. He didn't see any.

Glancing at the burlap, he recalled what he had been told about how she murdered: If a stranger came in all alone—and if the store was empty—Kate would seat the loner with his back against the curtain. Her father would be waiting on the other side. When he saw the stranger's head mold the burlap, Pop would slam him with a hammer as hard as he could. Then pretty Kate would lean over and slit the stranger's throat.

But all that blood seemed to have washed over her without leaving a trace. Maybe she wasn't really a killer after all. Pyg reminded himself not to be a fool. He might be young, but not that young. Still . . .

"So, Sonny, whaddaya want?" asked the redhead with a bawdy grin. "Might be we got it in stock."

"Gimme a whiskey," Too Short said.

"Me, too," said Pyg.

Kate laughed.

"What's so funny?" asked the boy.

"Me, too," Jesse said immediately. "But would you mind washin' the glasses first?"

"Yeah, you bet I'd mind. Water's scarcer'n hooch 'round here. It ain't rained in a damn month of coon's age. And I'm talkin' a real healthy coon. The alcohol'll kill the germs. Kill anything."

"Good enough," said Too Short. "We'll take three killer whiskeys in three dirty glasses. How's that there?"

Kate lowered her shotgun and stood it in a corner where it was in easy reach. Then she went to work bartending. She started pouring drinks that barely covered the dirt at the bottom of the glass. Pyg noticed a hunting knife on the bar. He paid particular interest to the weapon since Kate was supposed to be a throat cutter. He stared at the blade but couldn't see any dried blood.

"Like my knife?" asked Kate.

"No!" Pyg said too quickly, too loudly.

"Maybe you heard I was good with a knife?"

"No!"

"Well, I is."

When Kate picked up the knife, Pyg took a quick step backward. Jesse flinched and Too Short just stood his ground. The pretty redhead gripped the point between her thumb and index finger. She cocked her arm, holding the knife behind her ear. Like a coiled rattler striking, she threw her dagger and hit her man squarely in the heart.

CHAPTER 18

The painted cowboy on the far wall was dead for sure. The knife quivered in the wood. Looking more closely, Pyg noticed that the target's chest was considerably torn up. This unfortunate soul had died a thousand deaths.

"Anybody else wanna try?" asked Kate.

Pyg just looked at the dirt floor. He didn't know much about knives because his mother disliked them almost as much as she disliked guns. As a kid, he had secretly tried throwing a pocket knife a couple of times, but he had never been able to make it stick in anything.

"Sure," said Jesse. "I'll give it a whirl."

"You're just one surprise after another, aincha?" Too Short said.

The Harvey Girl reached inside her man's shirt, pulled out her Derringer, and shot the painted cowboy in the stomach.

"Your aim's a little low," said Kate. "When you squeeze the trigger, you're pullin' the gun down."

"No, I hit where I was aimin'," Jesse said. "I like to gut shoot 'em. Want 'em to suffer a little before they die. Matter of taste."

Pyg thought: She *is* one surprise after another. But he doubted that she had really been aiming at the midsection. Having seen her shoot before, in another saloon, he knew she wasn't a very good shot. Of course, she had been under more pressure that time.

"Your turn," Too Short said.

"What?" asked Pyg.

"Show her your gun. And show her you know how to use it."

The boy hesitated, then reached for his Tiffany gun. The silver barrel cleared the holster, he pointed it like a finger, and shot the knife out of the wall. The blade lay in two pieces on the floor. Pyg felt a little safer.

"Hey!" yelled Kate. "You busted my damn knife!"

"Sorry," said Pyg. "I'll buy you a new one."

"You bet you will," she snapped.

"Take a closer look at his gun," said Too Short. "You ever seen a gun like that there before?"

Kate squinted. She could hit a fly on the far wall, but she would have trouble with an enemy right in front of her nose. Maybe that was why she cut their throats. No aim required.

"It's got a solid silver butt," Too Short said.

"Oh," said Kate.

"Thass right."

"Yeah, I seen it before. What's it to ya?"

"We're lookin' to return it to its owner. Fella goes by the name of Big Sal. Thought mebbe you could help us some."

"You wanna give it back?"

"What I said."

"How come?"

"Figured he might want it back. Nice gun. Mebbe he misses it."

"I heard he done give it to some gal over to Tascosa. He figured she had a silver butt, too. What I hear. She git tired of carryin' around that there heavy thing?"

"She got dead."

"Too bad. Ain't too many silver butts around. Used to be two of 'em, and both of 'em belonged to that there lucky lady. Now they's just one. Real shame, ain't it?"

"Yeah, well, she wanted the gun to go back to Sal. Seems like the right thing to do."

"Now here's what let's do. You leave that there gun with me and I'll make sure he gits it back."

"Sorry. Like to give it to him myself. Make sure. I'd feel better about it."

"Why? I don't understand?"

"That lady was a good friend a mine. A real good friend."

"Sure. Well, I'm afraid I cain't help you."

Pyg surprised himself by clearing his throat. They all looked at him. Why had he done such a thing?

"I was just wondering, uh," the boy began uncertainly. He stopped and then started again: "Well, we heard you could tell fortunes."

"Thass right," Kate said proudly. "I got the gift."

"That's what we heard." Pyg paused to try to decide just how to put what he wanted to say. "So I was hoping maybe you could look into the future because you have the gift. And maybe you could see if we are ever going to meet this man named Sal. Could you do that?"

"Course." She smiled broadly. "Cost you two bits."

Pyg fished in his jodhpurs pocket and came up with a quarter. He gave it to the fortune teller, who took it greedily. Then she fished a pair of wire-rimmed glasses out of the cavernous pocket on the right side of her skirt. The lenses were perfectly round. The left one had a crack running right down the middle.

"Gimme your hand."

Kate stared down into Pyg's palm for what seemed a long time.

"Well?" prompted Too Short.

"Yeah, I see it now," said the country soothsayer. "Yep, you meets up with him. You sure do. Now anything else I can do fer ya?"

"Well, I was wondering," Pyg said, "where this meeting takes place. Can you see that?"

"No," she said too quickly, pushing his hand away.

"How disappointing," said the boy. "We heard you were better at your job than that. Maybe you could try again. I know I would have to pay more. How much would it cost to look again?"

"Just be wastin' your money."

"Five dollars?"

"No."

"Ten dollars?"

"I done told you no!"

Pyg felt foolish. He had been proud of himself for coming up with this ploy. He had told himself he might be of some use on this hunt, after all. He had wanted to impress Too Short—and Jesse.

"But mebbe I could see the future some clearer fer twenty."

Pyg extended his hand, palm upward, again. She hesitated, but then took it, holding him by his wrist. She bent down close and studied his hand as if it were a map with roads and trails written on it. She followed one of the roads with the tip of her index finger. It tickled. Pyg tried not to squirm.

"Yeah, there t'is," the palm reader said. "That little fold there." She paused, staring hard. "Could be a canyon, but I think it's more'n likely a cave. A big ol' cave. Mebbe the biggest damn cave in the whole damn world. Thass where it's gonna happen. Right there."

She looked up and took her glasses off.

"Thass shore interestin'," said Too Short, "but it shore ain't worth no twenty bucks."

"Thass twenty plus the knife plus the drinks," she corrected him. "Lemme look some more."

Kate put her cracked glasses back on and bent to her work. She tickled Pyg's palm again. She licked the tip of her finger and then drew a very small "x" on his palm.

"That supposed to mean somethin'?" asked Too Short.

"Mebbe," the fortune teller said. "Looks to me like that there cave's over yonder in New Mex."

"Big place," said the little cowboy.

"That there line," she said, "that looks like the damn Pecos River."

"Long river."

"Big cave. You'll find it. I'll take my money now."

CHAPTER 19

Pyg was being pursued by the very outlaw they were chasing. He couldn't see the face very clearly, but he was big. Huge. Gargantuan. They were running across the bare Staked Plain where there was no place to hide. Sal was a fast runner for a big man.

Pyg had an idea: He turned himself into a prairie dog so he could run down a hole and hide safely below ground. Now all he needed was that hole. Oh, there was one. He scampered down it. But then Big Sal turned himself into a diamond-backed rattlesnake and slithered down the hole right behind him.

Pyg was doomed unless he could think of something. What could he turn himself into now? A lizard? No, snakes ate lizards. A buffalo? Too big for this hole. He thrashed about in his binding sleeping roll trying to escape from this fatal trap.

Then he knew what to do: Pyg turned himself into a black-and-white striped skunk. He hoped the snake was smart enough to realize that biting a skunk in these tight quarters was a bad idea. A skunk above ground in the open air was bad enough. A skunk underground could be fatal. Pyg would stink his enemy to death. The snake slowed its slither. Running as fast as he could, Pyg saw a light up head. This prairie dog burrow had a back door dug for just this purpose. He burst forth into the open air.

Vanity now got the best of Pyg. He didn't enjoy being a skunk. Nobody liked skunks. He didn't even like them. Not wanting to be an outcast, he turned himself into his favorite bird: a cardinal. He flapped his red wings and flew away. Good. Free. Weightless. He loved being a bird—until he saw that the snake had turned itself into a redtailed hawk. The hawk plunged its talons into his right shoulder. He flapped his wings harder trying to get away.

"Calm down," the hawk whispered. "Don't break my nose ag'in."

Pyg stopped struggling and tried to wake up, but it was hard. He once again seemed to be trapped underground, clawing toward the surface.

"What's wr-wr-wrong?" he asked but his mouth didn't work right.

"Shhhh. Nothing. I wanna show you somethin'."

"What?" His mouth worked better now.

"You'll see."

Once again, Pyg was being pursued. Once more, there was no place to hide on the treeless, waterless Staked Plain, but this time Pyg didn't turn himself into another species. He remained a man, and she stayed a woman. That was the problem. He didn't know how to act. When they were a good distance from camp, she stopped him by taking his hand in hers.

"What do you want to show me?" Pyg whispered.

"Me," said Jesse.

"Huh?" he said.

"I'll bet you've never seen a woman before. You're such a mama's boy."

"I have, too." This time the lie didn't make him feel more grown up. He knew he was just a fibbing kid. And she probably knew it, too. Right? "Lots."

"You're a liar." She knew. "But that's all right. I don't mind. Now you won't have to lie next time somebody asks you that question." She smiled. "See, I'm saving your soul. Liars go to hell in a hurry."

The Harvey Girl started unbuttoning her too-big man's shirt. Pyg looked away but quickly looked back. Now he saw that he had been right: She wasn't wearing a bra. Her nipples puckered as if they had tasted something bitter. They were bigger than he had imagined they would be. He had supposed they would be tiny pink primrose buds, but they actually resembled the thumb-sized fruit of the prickly pear. Tumescent. Purple. Cactus pears. Maybe they would hurt him—stick him—if he touched. They looked dangerous and inviting at the same time.

"What do you think?" Jesse asked.

Pyg just shrugged. He was speechless. He didn't know what to say. He didn't know what to do.

"You're supposed to think I'm beautiful," she said.

"Yes," he said.

When she took off her shirt and dropped it on the sandy plain, Pyg could see the full roundness of her breasts. They were the size of big balls of yarn. He wondered if they were as soft. But thoughts of yarn brought thoughts of Mumsy, who knitted. He tried to put her out of his mind, but she stayed there, staring at him sternly.

"You're one silver-tongued devil," said Jesse.

She reached out and started unbuttoning his shirt. He instinctively leaned back away from her.

"Calm down," she said. "I'm not going to hurt you." She laughed. "Just don't tell your mama, okay?"

Pyg tried to relax, but he couldn't, especially when she unbuckled his belt and started unbuttoning his fancy jodhpurs, which doubled as pajamas.

"What are you doing?" asked Pyg, confused.

"You'll find out," the Harvey Girl said.

They were both still standing upright, but she was sinking, slipping down his body, kissing the goose bumps on his chest. How far down was she going?

"What's happening?" he pleaded.

"Don't be afraid," she told him. "You'll be okay. I promise."

Jesse kissed Pyg's belly button. Being ticklish, he laughed and squirmed. He tried to back away, but his feet were bound by the jodhpurs around his ankles. He was hobbled like a horse at night. Their hind legs were tied together so they wouldn't run away. Evidently his had been for the same reason.

"Hold still," she said.

"I can't," he said.

She kept descending, lower, lower. How much lower would she go? Pyg felt foolish, happy, embarrassed, frightened, excited, threatened. He wondered what his mother would say if she could see him now. Would she scream and then fall down dead?

"If your mama could see you now," chuckled Jesse.

He thought she was going to bite him, but all he felt were lips, all he felt was wonderful.

"Why are you doing this?" Pyg gasped.

"You saved my life," Jesse whispered.

"Is that the only reason?"

Oh, no, she stopped.

"No."

When she began again, he told himself to shut up. Let her do her work. Don't interfere. Don't distract her.

"No? What else?"

"I like it."

How could she like it? What was wrong with her?

"Really?"

"Really. Now shut up."

He tried to shut up, but he suddenly found himself speaking some language that had no recognizable words in it. He grunted and squeaked and squealed. He sounded like some animal trying to invent a language.

"Shhh," she cautioned.

But he couldn't shut his mouth or stop the hot stream racing through his body, hurtling toward his groin, getting closer, closer, closer.

"YES, YES, YES—" he screamed.

"Hey, what's wrong! Somebody git hurt? What's going on?"

No, no, no . . .

Mumsy had found them. His worst fears had come true. Would she die now? But that was crazy. His mother wasn't here. But the voice did sound familiar. Pyg saw a short cowboy—dark as a shadow—running, stumbling toward them. Coming to the rescue.

. . . no, no, no!

CHAPTER 20

Sleeping on his right side—pounding his ear, as the cowboys said—Pyg dreamed of Jesse. He was back in her mouth. His excitement kept getting bigger. Soon he would explode. It was getting closer, closer . . .

She touched him, licked his left hand. Was he still dreaming? He wasn't sure. It seemed real. No, it was real. He was awake and happy to find her so near him. He reached out to her, and she bit him on the hand.

"*Owww!*" Pyg yelled. "Jesse!"

Why had she done that? Maybe she hadn't meant to, but she had really hurt him. And she wouldn't let go. This game wasn't fun anymore. She played too rough. He tried to push her away.

"What?" Jesse asked sleepily. "What's wrong?"

But her voice came from too far away. Why was she playing tricks on him? What was her game anyway?

"Stoppit!" he said.

"Stop what?" she asked.

Now Pyg really came awake. He raised his injured hand and looked at it. A rattler was hanging from the meat of his palm. He was going to die. Blinding terror surprised him. His fears had finally come true: This time it really was a snake.

"Help, Mumsy!" he yelled. "A snake! A snake bit me!"

Even though he was dying—had very little time left—he wasted a few seconds wishing he hadn't called out his mother's name. They would think he was a baby.

"Whut?" mumbled Too Short.

"Shut up!" protested Little Dogie. "Tryin' to sleep."

"Really?" asked Jesse. "A snake?"

"A snake! Help me!"

Jesse fought her way out of her bedroll and started running. She was the first one to reach Pyg, but then she didn't know what to do.

"*Help!*" she screamed. "Somebody do somethin'."

Bending over, Jesse tried to grab the snake's tail, but it was flipping this way and that. She couldn't catch up to it. Her cries blended with and overlapped Pyg's own.

"Help!"

  "Help me!"

    "Help him!"

      "Hurry!"

        "Shake yore damn hides!"

Too Short came running and stumbling. Dropping to his knees beside Pyg, the little cowboy already had his hunting knife out. He studied the situation for a moment, wiped his sleepy eyes, then reached out with his left hand and grabbed the snake by the throat. His knife blade flashed in the moonlight and cut off the rattler's head. He threw the scaly body aside and watched it writhe in the dirt as if it were still angrily alive. It didn't know any better. The part of the snake that knew it was dead was still attached to the boy's trembling, twitching hand.

"Hold still," ordered Too Short.

Pyg did the best he could, but his hand still quivered. Too Short took hold of the boy's wrist with his left hand. Then he gripped the snake right behind its deadly jaws. He pressed hard on the submerged jawbone until the dead head slowly opened its mouth wide. Too Short pulled the long fangs out of Pyg's bleeding hand.

"Thanks," said the boy.

"Sure," said Too Short.

"He got me good, didn't he?"

"Sorry."

Too Short shrugged and released the boy's wrist.

"Let me take a look," said Custer, who materialized out of the night.

"Sure thing," said the small cowboy.

The Comanche dropped to the ground beside Too Short. He reached out and tenderly took hold of Pyg's hand with both of his. He turned it palm up. Then he bent down as if to kiss the hand. The boy instinctively pulled back, but the Indian gripped him harder and wouldn't let go. He started sucking blood out of the double wound. Turning aside, he spat dark blood on the dark ground.

Afraid he was growing to throw up, Pyg looked away. He watched the snake's body twist and turn and look for its head. It writhed slower and slower. Too Short picked it up by its tail and studied its rattles closely.

"How many?" asked Custer.

"Just two," Too Short reported.

"A young one," said the Indian.

"Is that good?" asked Pyg.

"Mebbe," said Too Short.

"Cain't hurt," said Custer.

Jesse was crying. Pyg wanted to cry, too, but he didn't want to sound like a baby. He told himself he was too big to cry. Still, he wished his mumsy were here.

"Lemme see what I got in my saddlebag," Custer said. "I just might have somethin' that'll help some." He paused. "Got nothin' to lose."

Pyg was both frightened and encouraged: Maybe the Indian had some medicine that could help him, but what did he mean by having nothing to lose? That didn't sound good. That sounded desperate, didn't it? Was he really dying? Dying a virgin? Hurry, hurry, hurry . . .

When he returned, Custer was carrying a couple of saddlebags. He knelt and rummaged in the bags. Pyg watched him anxiously. Out came a small leather pouch. Custer opened it and sniffed. He smiled. That was a good sign, wasn't it?

"Find something?" Pyg asked in a chocked voice.

"Mebbe," said Custer with a shrug. He raised his voice: "I need somethin' to make a bandage. Anybody got anything they wanta tear up?" He waited. "Don't ever'body talk at oncet."

"I'll git somethin'," Jesse said.

Still sniffling, she hurried away. She came back with the white apron from her Harvey House uniform. Tearing the apron into strips, she seemed to enjoy the sound of the fabric's distress.

"Thanks," said Pyg.

"My pleasure," said Jesse.

Custer took one of the strips, wrapped it around Pyg's wrist, pulled it tight, and tied it. It wasn't a tourniquet—but almost.

"That oughta keep the poison from spreadin' so fast," Custer said. "Thass the idea anyhow."

Then, from the pouch, he removed some kind of dried weed. It had a harsh smell.

"What's that?" Pyg asked.

"Thass called snake leaf. Can you see? The leaves is shaped like forked tongues. We say you gotta use a snake to beat a snake. Unnerstand?"

"You want me to eat that stuff?"

"No, I'm gonna make a kinda poultice. Mebbe it'll suck some more of that ol' poison out."

The makeshift medicine man wrapped a small handful of dry weed in another strip torn from Jesse's apron. He folded it into a packet. Then he tied it over the snakebite. Finished, he shrugged and leaned back on his heels.

"Is he going to be okay?" asked Jesse.

"Dunno," said Custer.

"My hand's getting bigger," said Pyg.

"Look at that," said Little Dogie. "It's swellin' up like a poisoned pup."

"Shut up," said Too Short.

"Prob'ly turn black pretty soon," Custer told Pyg. "Don't you worry too much about that. Time to start worryin' is if'n the swellin' climbs on up your arm."

"We gotta git him to a doctor," said Jesse.

"Cain't move him right now," said Custer. "That'd just stir up his blood and kill him fer sure."

"Then we gotta fetch a *real* doctor here," flared the Harvey Girl. "We gotta! Custer, you ain't no doctor. Thass all Injun mumbo jumbo."

"Thanks," said the Comanche.

Pyg watched the swelling creep sluggishly up his left arm. It was as if he were being eaten very slowly. His distended arm looked like a python, one that wasn't too hungry, one that was content to take its time consuming him. He would look away, but then he would always look back. If a watched pot wouldn't boil, perhaps a watched arm wouldn't blow up and turn black and blue—like his hand. But it wasn't working. Every time he looked, he could see it wasn't working. He watched himself die.

"The doctor'll be here soon," Jesse said again.

She sat on the ground beside his "bed," her arms holding her knees. She had spent most of yesterday hovering near him, then slept within inches of him last night, which would have prompted a lot of kidding under other circumstances.

"I know," Pyg said, but without conviction.

Lying flat on his back, the boy crooked his neck so he could look at the horizon and the rising sun. He squinted and then sun-sneezed as usual. Which hurt. The scrub mesquites waved their branches in the unceasing wind, but they were all that moved. No riders approached. No doctor appeared to save him. But Too Short shuffled over and squatted beside him.

"Uh, the boys wanted me to tell you somethin'," said the little cowboy. "T'other night, when they was joshin' you about snakes in your bedroll, well, they was just joshin'."

"I know," Pyg said.

"Nobody wanted nothin' like this here to happen."

"I know."

"Thass gospel. Nobody figured on nothin' like this here. Not no way. Now they all wisht they'd a kept their damn mouths shut. And they oughta have."

"I know."

"They just wanted you to know."

Too Short stood up and shuffled away. Pyg checked the empty horizon, and then settled in to watch his arm continue to swell. He imagined his whole body puffing up like a sausage. How big would his head get? Custer came over and changed his poultice again.

"Pretty soon, we're gonna run outta apron," said the Indian.

"I got other stuff to tear up," said Jesse.

They waited. Pyg felt hot. His arm ached dully. The sash around his swollen wrist pinched him. These moments, which might be his last, bored him. He yawned.

"He'll be here soon," Jesse said.

"I know."

As always, Pyg pretended to believe her. The swelling had reached his elbow.

"Here they come," said Custer.

Pyg crooked his neck again, but this time he didn't need to squint, because the sun was now directly overhead. He saw two small dust storms on the horizon.

"Is that Vaquero?" Pyg asked weakly.

"Gotta be, the way he's kickin' up dust," said Too Short. "And looks like he's got company. I figured he'd persuade the doc to come along. He's a persuasive fella when he puts his mind to it."

"That hog on his hip prob'ly didn't hurt none neither," said Little Dogie, "if'n his eloquence come up a little short."

"It's nice of him to make a house call," said Pyg.

D r. Samuel Hightower wore khakis, clean farmer's boots, a white shirt with no collar, and a black frock coat. He had gray hair and a trim white beard. He was dusty and looked tired. Carefully removing the bandage from Pyg's hand, the doctor studied the wound and then the poultice.

"What's this?" he asked, his accent eastern, his tone skeptical.

"Why thass good ol' snake leaf," said Custer, who hovered nearby.

The doctor unwrapped the poultice and studied the contents.

"Oh, yes, where I come from, we call it adder's tongue," said Dr. Hightower. "I've never heard of its being used to treat a snakebite. Of course, its name suggests a poetic if not a medical connection."

Custer frowned.

"I told you it was Injun mumbo jumbo," said Jesse.

The doctor examined the wound carefully.

"How does it look?" asked Pyg. Childishly blunt, he wanted to know: "Am I dying, Doctor? You're afraid to tell me, aren't you?"

"The wound looks much better than I expected," Dr. Hightower said. "This Mr. Custer here probably saved your life. He seems to know his business. If he ever gets tired of being a cowboy, he can come and work for me." He paused to consider something. "I believe I'll write a letter to the *New England Journal of Medicine* extolling adder's tongue as a cure for snakebite."

Pyg saw a big grin spread across Custer's ruddy face. The patient knew he was smiling, too.

"Thanks, Custer," Pyg said.

"Aw hell," said the Indian cowboy.

"The swelling should start going down fairly soon," the doctor told Pyg. Then he turned to Custer as if he were the leader of this band: "When that happens, it should be safe to move him. You should bring him to my office in Quanah. I'll—"

"But we're headin' in t'other direction," interrupted Too Short.

"I know, but he's very weak. He's going to need several days—perhaps more—of bed rest. He's got to get his strength back before he'll be able to ride. Tomorrow, I'll send a wagon to fetch him."

"The rest of you, go on," Pyg said. "I'll be okay. I'll catch up."

"No, I reckon we better all stick together," said Too Short. "I don't expect your mama'd much like it if we was to go off and leave you high and dry."

Pyg wished Too Short hadn't brought up his mother. At the same time, he missed her keenly. He wondered what she was doing right now. Was she worrying about him? He told himself he could use some of her nursing. As a boy, he had felt it was worth getting sick just to be nursed by his mother. So cosseted.

CHAPTER 21

The next morning, as the sun was just getting sleepily out of bed, Pyg examined his arm. He was relieved to see that the swelling had gone down considerably. Before the sun got too hot, a buckboard appeared. The cowboys loaded Pyg into the wagon bed. This contraption had primitive springs that did little good. The patient bounced all the way back to Quanah, where the doctor checked him over again. He was told he would probably live, but he still had a tough fight ahead of him.

Pyg was put to bed in a room on the ground floor of the White Hotel, where he slept fitfully most of several days. He wasn't sure how many. Sometimes he couldn't tell if he was awake or dreaming. Whichever it was, Jesse was always there with him. That snake, too. He was in midnightmare when a ringing bell woke him. Or was he still dreaming?

"I'm late," Pyg said groggily.

"Late fer what?" asked Jesse.

"For school. The bell's ringing."

"Slow down, Junior. Thass a Goddamned church bell. Time fer Sunday service. Besides, school's out fer the damn summer. Relax." She studied him. "You mean you're still in school, a big ol' boy like you?"

"I finished prep school last spring. Start college in the fall."

"If'n you're still alive by then. My advice is keep away from snakes and stay outta gunfights from now on. Or that damn college is gonna be short one student."

"I'll try to keep that in mind."

"See you do. 'Bout time you looked alive. I begun to think you might be dead, except I never heard a corpse snore."

"I don't snore," Pyg protested.

She sat in a cane-bottomed rocker next to his bed, moving slowly forward, backward.

"Right, it's more of a snort."

"No."

"Yeah. We even got some complaints from the whorehouse next door. Asked us to keep the noise down over here. Said they couldn't hear themselves—well, they didn't say 'think.'"

"Oh, you're kidding"—he studied her—"aren't you?"

"Yeah, they ain't no whorehouse next door. It's across the way, lucky fer them. You look a little better. How do you feel?"

"Sleepy."

"Still?"

"Where's everybody else?"

"Camped outside of town. They all claimed they wouldn't know how to act in a hotel. Left me here to keep an eye on you. Ain't been too hard since you ain't moved hardly atall."

Pyg started to correct her grammar, but stopped himself. He supposed there were worse things a girl could do than say 'ain't,' and he didn't want to hurt her feelings. Still, she should learn better English if she was ever going to make anything of herself. Maybe he would bring it up someday, but not now.

"Where are you staying?" Pyg asked.

"Room next door," Jesse said. "But don't get no ideas. You gotta rest. If'n you was to try something, it'd probably kill you. Save me the trouble."

Pyg wasn't sure he was the one most prone to get ideas. She had already proved to him that she had quite a few. Not that he minded her ideas. He closed his eyes and imagined future adventures with this Harvey Girl. He was almost asleep, almost dreaming, when a loud clap of thunder shook him awake.

"God's snorin'," said Jesse. "Must be catchin'."

The thunder unleashed torrents of rain. It pounded on the tin roof overhead. The room was a coffee can and God was pounding it with a stick. Then He snored again—or snorted—and the whole town shook.

Pyg hated thunder and lightning. When he was a boy, he used to crawl under the bed during storms. Or he would flee to his mother's bed and she would hold him. He could use some holding now.

"Are you afraid of thunder and lightnin'?" asked Jesse.

"Why do you ask?" Pyg said, wondering if fear was visible on his face. "Of course not."

"Well, I am."

"Me, too."

She took hold of his right hand—the healthy one—and squeezed. He squeezed back and felt a sexual thrill. It didn't take much.

Thunder shook the door. It was trying to break in. It wanted to come inside and scare them up close. No, it wasn't the thunder. It was somebody knocking on the door. Pyg wondered why his visitor didn't just open the door and walk on in. It was unlocked. This wasn't locked-door country. So why stand on ceremony? Then a reason occurred to him: Was somebody worried about walking in on another sex lesson?

"Stagger on in, it's open," Jesse called. "We're decent."

The door opened and cowboys spilled into the small room, making it much smaller. Too Short, Custer, Ivan the Terrible, Opry, Tin Soldier, Vaquero. There wasn't room for Little Dogie, who waited outside in the hall. If he had come in, three other cowboys would have had to leave.

"How you doin'?" asked Too Short.

"Better," said Pyg.

"Don't expect you're feelin' up to goin' next door fer some refreshment at the Whistle?"

"What?"

"Thass the name of the saloon, the Wet Whistle. Don't blame me. Anyhow thass where we're headed. Figured we'd check on you first."

"You sure you cowboys ain't plannin' to visit the girls over yonder?" asked Jesse. "I figure you just made up this here visit to the Wet Whistle to cover up what you're really after."

Pyg smiled but thought: There she goes, saying "ain't" again, like some saddle tramp. He liked her. Maybe he was going to like her a whole lot. But she wouldn't exactly fit in up in Boston saying "ain't" all the time. Boston? No, impossible, don't be silly. But he wished she would cut down on her "ain'ts," that was all.

"No way, not atall," said Too Short.

"Jesse, you done ruined us for them girls over yonder," said Opry. "They'd be a big letdown."

"My, my," said the object of the compliment.

Pyg thought the rain seemed to be letting up some. His single window grew brighter, and the tin roof calmed down. He relaxed, too. Now he was feeling sleepy again.

"Have fun," Pyg said.

The cowboys started to file out of the small room, making it bigger. There went Too Short, then Custer, then Ivan. But Opry stopped in the doorway, turned back, and smiled at Jesse.

"Why don't you come with us?" asked the musical cowboy with no last name. "Seems like he's too weak to be much fun. Figure you'd be better off throwin' in your lot with us. Be more fun all around. Huh?"

"Thanks but I better stay here," she said.

"You ain't scared of saloons now, are you?" he asked. "Cain't let that little dustup in Tascosa throw you."

"Don't call me afraid. I ain't afraid."

"Prove it."

Jesse was clearly tempted to accept the dare, but she hesitated. "I appreciate the invite, but—"

"Why don't you go with them?" Pyg interrupted. "You've been cooped up in here too long. You deserve a break. Besides, I think I'll take another nap. Just can't get over being sleepy."

He didn't want her sitting there listening to him snore. Of course, she might have been kidding about that. Had he really snored and snorted?

"I don't need a break," Jesse said.

"*He* does," said Opry, whose leather cuffs looked lighter. With time on his hands, had he gotten out the saddle soap and cleaned them? "Come on, let the poor boy sleep."

Jesse looked at Pyg, who nodded. She shrugged.

"Okay." She stood up. "See you later. Can I bring you anything?"

"An arm."

"You want that well done or rare?" asked the retired Harvey Girl.

When he was alone, Pyg turned on his right side and closed his eyes. He listened to the rain, which was louder now. It got so loud, he was afraid he wouldn't be able to fall asleep, but soon he was dreaming of thunder and lightning.

He did not wake up until the water was rising in his small room.

CHAPTER 22

Dazed between sleep and waking, Pyg thought he was on a sinking ship. The water was getting deeper and deeper in his stateroom. He had to get out or he would go to the bottom of the ocean and never come back. Maybe he could squeeze out through the dimly lit porthole. No, it was too small. Then he saw the rat: It was swimming, its awful feet churning, trying to flee the sinking ship. The flood was already a foot and a half deep. He hoped the hotel wouldn't capsize. No, no, that was crazy. More awake now, Pyg recognized his hired room, but the water was still rising, and the rat was still swimming. Was the White Hotel sinking?

No, that was impossible. But the rising water was still alarming. It was lapping his mattress now. The rain was so loud on the tin roof he couldn't think. The thunder shook his brain in its pan. And now there were two rats swimming in circles. He hated rats! He was afraid of rats! He cringed and hugged his knees. He had to get out of there, to get away.

Feeling extremely weak—helplessly weak—Pyg sat up in bed very slowly. It was hard work. Carefully, he swung his legs over the side of the bed. The water was cold. He could see his knees shaking. His teeth started chattering. Pushing himself forward, he got his weight under him and stood up. His knees disappeared into the dark water. The bottom of his long nightshirt was soaked. It was made of thick wool and was normally too hot, but it was all the landlord had to spare. Now Pyg appreciated the wool because he was so cold.

As he waded toward the door, the boy was already embarrassed. He imagined people standing around in the lobby staring at him, pointing at him and laughing. Maybe he should just get back in bed and wait. Surely the water would start retreating soon. He kept his eyes on the rats as he continued his long journey across the small room. Perhaps he should try to get dressed before he faced the world, but he wasn't sure he could find his clothes. They had been folded neatly on the floor, but they had long since been drowned by muddy water. Locating them would take time, and he felt he had to get out right now!

Reaching the door, he gripped the knob with his right hand and held on a moment to steady himself. Then he twisted and pulled, but the door refused to give in. He pulled harder. Was he too weak? He set his feet, hunched his shoulders, and pulled again. The door remained stubbornly closed. Was the water somehow holding it shut? Now he gripped the doorknob with both hands—the good one and the poisoned one—and pulled with all his diminished strength. The door wouldn't budge. Had the water caused the wooden door to swell in its frame? He yanked again. No, the door didn't feel stuck. It felt locked. But he never locked his door. This was the open-doored West, not the locked-down East. He had made a point of not locking up. How could it be locked now? Pyg yanked, pulled, jerked, tugged. He was locked in and the water was rising.

He would have to try to break down the door. Retreating a few steps, he charged, but the water bogged him down. Weak as he was, he could hardly walk through this flood, much less run. His shoulder thumped harmlessly against the door. Then he leaned against it, breathing hard. Feeling weaker than ever, Pyg looked back at his bed. He wanted to lie down. The bed was pulling at him the way he was pulling at the door. Only it was strong, and he was feeble. He found himself wading shakily back to bed. Shaky because he was weak and cold and scared of rats and drowning.

He wanted Mumsy. No, don't think that way. If she saw these rats, she would go insane, and then where would they be? He was going to have to solve this problem himself, but he didn't feel much like a problem-solver, not at the moment.

Collapsing onto his bed, Pyg discovered that his mattress had turned into a wet sponge. It was also cold. Good, now he wouldn't nod off and drown in his sleep. The rain seemed to be hammering his tin head. He had echos inside his skull instead of ideas. He felt wet inside and out, up and down, through and through. And his left hand ached. Well, if he died, it would stop hurting. Good, he had a plan now.

One of the rats, out of breath, crawled up on the bed with him. Pyg started kicking his legs up and down to make a racket. The rat was evidently too tired to care. He found himself agreeing with the rodent. The second rat crawled up on the bed to keep the first one company. They hunkered down side by side and watched him with glittering eyes. Were they wondering how he would taste? Pyg wished he had his gun, but it was on the floor, too, under several feet of water. Even if he could find it, the six-shooter probably wouldn't work after its bath.

Pyg found himself studying the small dim window. It was dirty and fogged and almost impossible to see through. Why was it so little? Was glass expensive out here? Who cared? The important question was: How was he going to get out of this deadly bathtub? He had no idea, because that window was definitely too small for him to crawl through. If he were only a rat, then he could . . .

Get up! Don't just lie there! At least try to squeeze through that tiny opening. Don't go down without putting up any fight at all. Come on now.

Wearily, Pyg sat up in bed. The rats stared without blinking. Moving carefully so he wouldn't accidentally kick a sharp-toothed rodent, he managed to maneuver his legs over the side of the mattress. Then he levered himself onto his feet. Wading slowly, he headed for the window. The farther he went, the colder he got. Now the flood was creeping up his skinny thighs. Exhausted, he wanted to turn back to his bed, but it would soon be under water. He kept going.

Unable to see his feet, Pyg moved warily. He was afraid he would trip over something. Perhaps his boots or his gun. His toes felt their way over the bare boards. Ow! He got a splinter. He wished the West were carpeted. Now he limped as he waded through deep water.

When he finally reached the window, it looked even smaller than before. He wiped away some of the fog but the grime remained. This wasn't the kind of window that could be raised and lowered. It was just a pane of glass set in the wall. He wrapped his right hand in the wet tail of his nightshirt and hit the glass. It didn't break. He tried again, putting his weight behind the punch. The window broke, leaving a hole in the wall that looked like a shark's mouth. The shards of glass around the frame would chew him up. He cautiously started picking out the shark teeth.

Then Pyg noticed that his right wrist was bleeding. Examining it more closely, he saw a flap of skin hanging loosely exposing blue veins. Were they cut? Well, they weren't spurting. He went back to picking out shark's teeth and managed to cut the end of his index finger. He was just a mess. Blood stained the pieces of glass he was plucking out.

When he had removed about half of them, Pyg decided to stick his head out and take a look around. Moving very carefully so as not to cut off his ears, he eased his eyes through the opening. He was frightened by what he saw: Main Street was a raging, muddy, debris-choked torrent. He had never seen such a wild river, not even in a riverbed. Now he wasn't sure he wanted to get out even if he could get out. He pulled his head back in and glanced longingly at his bed.

No, Pyg told himself, he couldn't go back to bed. He didn't want to end up just another drowned rat. The water was rising much faster now. Getting busy, he went back to picking out the shark's teeth. Soon his thumb was bleeding, as well. The red dripped in the muddy water, discoloring it. He would soon be drowning in his own blood. He tossed the last sharp tooth out the window into violent water beyond.

Then he prepared to go after it. Sticking his head through the opening again, Pyg saw that the river had almost reached his busted window. When it did, the room would fill even faster. Pressing his elbows tightly to his sides, hunching his shoulders forward, Pyg tried to make himself as thin as possible. Then he attempted to push himself through the small opening. He shoved hard, hurting his shoulders, but it was no good.

He tried turning himself in the hole, lowering his right shoulder, raising his left. Good, better, more room. He pushed again. He could almost get his shoulders through, but not quite. He remembered how babies were born, head first, passing through a narrow opening. If they could get out a hole that small, surely he could force himself through this window. Then he remembered tales of babies who had gotten stuck and died. Sometimes they even killed their mothers. Well, at least she was safe. Stop these crazy thoughts and just push. Push. *Push!*

"Help!" he yelled. "Help! Help!"

But Pyg could barely hear himself over the roar of the water. Certainly nobody else would hear. He told himself to save his breath for pushing. Come on. Almost. Just a little more. Out of breath, Pyg pulled his head back inside. He staggered in the waist-deep water and lost his balance. He took a step backward to try to save himself from falling. His chest was heaving painfully. He had to sit down. If he didn't, he was afraid he would fall down.

Backing up slowly, Pyg kept staring at the window because water was now pouring in from Main Street. Maybe it had been a mistake to break the glass. Reaching back, he felt with his right hand for the bed. Finally his fingers touched the wet mattress. Without looking back, Pyg, so very very tired, started sitting down. Yes, yes, no! What if he sat on a rat! He tried to stop himself, but it was too late. He landed with a squish on the mattress. No rat! He wanted to lie down, but he couldn't: The bed was now under water. He sat in the cold, dirty, bloody water shivering.

Now where were those damned rats? Straining, he looked over his right shoulder, then his left. Where had they gone? How could they have gotten out if he couldn't? Were they smarter than he was? Damn them.

Oh, there they were. Swimming again. But this time, they weren't paddling around in circles. They were headed straight for the window he had broken. One followed the other. Just their nostrils, eyes, and ears were above the flood. Damn, damn, damn, they were going to escape while he remained trapped. He would be the only drowned rat. He hated rats, and he had saved their lives. Pyg wished he had his silver gun, so he could shoot them before they got away. He sighted down his bleeding index finger, pretending. The water was almost up to Pyg's armpits when the rats swam out the busted window to safety and a new life.

Standing on his tiptoes on the waterlogged mattress, Pyg stretched up as tall as he could. He wanted to be tall because he wanted to breathe. His face barely broke the surface of the flood. His big toe hurt, his body was shivering, and his mind seemed frozen. It wouldn't move, wouldn't think, wouldn't save him.

"Help," he whispered as if trying to save his breath. "Help."

With brown water closing in on his nostrils, Pyg hopped up and down. Up, breathe. Down, don't breathe. Up, gasp. Down, choke. He felt desperate and pathetic at the same time. All the jumping made him breathless. He stopped bouncing and couldn't breathe at all. He started swimming—dog paddling—slowly in a circle. Like a rat. He wondered how long he could keep it up. He was weak, exhausted, cold. And even if he could keep paddling, what was he going to do when the awful water reached the ceiling?

"Help."

His voice was getting smaller and smaller. Soon he wouldn't have any voice or any air at all. His brain was already suffocating. All the ideas had died a long time ago.

"Help me."

Deciding not to wait for death, Pyg went to meet it: He stopped paddling and sank. His chest hurt. His ears hurt. He exploded up out of the water and bumped his head on the ceiling. Ouch.

Pyg sank again, but this time it wasn't to die. He had actually had one last living idea. As he descended through the dark water, he grabbed the hem of his long nightshirt and tried to pull it up over his head. It got knotted around his ears. He was drowning in a ridiculous pose. He tried to call for help once more but only achieved bubbles. Jerking free of the gown, he was surprised at how much colder the water felt without it. His body shivered with nakedness. But he was ever so slightly thinner without his thick nightshirt, and much slipperier. Would it be enough? Before he could find out, he ran out of air again. Rocketing up out of the depths, he hit his head on the ceiling. Again.

He took three deep breaths and dived under once again, but he was disoriented. He couldn't see an inch in the muddy water, and didn't know which way to go. He thrashed this way and that until his lungs were killing him. Bursting from the water, Pyg hit his head in the same place he had hit it twice before. Now there was only about an inch of air left above the flood. Lying on his back, he kicked his way to the wall with the window in it. Then he reached down with his feet and felt for the opening. Then he tucked himself into a ball and dove headfirst into the brown. He gripped the window with both hands—forgetting for the moment his snakebite—and pulled. Like a baby being born, his head poked through the opening, but then his shoulders stuck. Heads were easy, but shoulders could be fatal. He turned diagonally in the hole. He was still stuck. He pulled and wiggled and swallowed water.

Realizing he had to breathe, he tried to retreat. He wouldn't mind hitting his head again if he could take a breath.

But he was stuck. He couldn't move backward or forward. What a way to die: naked and stuck in a hole. Oh, how they would all laugh when they found his body. Especially Little Dogie. His laughter would shake the earth. Pyg feared drowning, feared death, but most of all he feared embarrassment. He simply couldn't die this way! Motivated by the picture of Little Dogie laughing, Pyg pulled again, pulled harder. He wiggled again, wiggled harder. And this time he kicked as if he were fleeing a shark, trying to elude the razor-sharp teeth of embarrassment.

His shoulders slipped in the hole. They moved forward a half inch, an inch, an inch and a half. He was dying by inches. He kicked and squirmed and pulled for his dignity.

Pyg popped through.

Naked as the day he was born, naked and screaming like a newborn baby, he entered a strange new world. Born again, he was in danger of drowning. The Main Street took him and tossed him. He was swept away, tumbling, flailing, spitting water. Since it was still raining torrents, there was almost as much water above the surface as there was below.

Something was sticking him in the side. Blinking water out of his eyes, he realized that he was being gored by a drowned longhorn. He kicked away from the sharp horns but soon bumped into a dead wolf. A rocking chair rocked passed him. He saw a barbed-wire fence with wooden posts floating along. When it drew closer, he saw a calf caught on the barbs. He rode the new river with a fiddle, wooden spoons, barrels, boots, and people's whole lives.

Pyg was so tired of swimming that he wanted to fall asleep right there in the flood.

He didn't think he could hold out a moment longer when he heard something that sounded like a runaway train. Looking for the source of this frightening din, Pyg saw a windmill. Its great wheel was spinning so fast it threatened to fly right off its tower. Angling off to the right, Pyg swam wearily toward the tower. When he reached it, he clung to one of its great steel legs. Too dead tired to climb, he simply hung on. His heart was banging much too fast. Which would break first? The windmill or his own pump? The air rasping in his throat felt the way the hammering sucker rod sounded.

Slowly he revived. The windmill was as noisy as ever, but his heart began to quiet down. Breathing hurt less. As he started feeling better, he grew more sensitive about his nakedness. Looking up at the tower, he now felt well enough to try to climb it, but then he would be advertising his missing clothing. The whole town—everybody not drowned, at least—would then point up at him and laugh. Then he would be embarrassed to death.

Well, Pyg couldn't just stay where he was. Something would collide with him—a tree, a barn roof, a dead child—and he would be washed away. Looking around, he didn't see anyone looking or not looking. He didn't see anybody at all. Hoping the heavy rain would help screen him, he mounted the metal rungs leading up the steel leg to the top of the tower. The rungs felt wet and slippery. They hurt his "tenderfoot" feet. As he climbed, he made faces. Every couple of steps, he looked down to make sure nobody was looking up at him. When he was about ten feet up, Pyg stopped to rest, but soon he was climbing again. His balls knocked against his legs as he moved. They started itching. Glancing around, he took a moment to scratch them. Ah, that was better. He hoped no one had seen.

Oh, no, somebody had. On the roof of a Main Street store, a woman was pointing at him. At that distance, he couldn't tell her age, nor could he see if she was laughing, but he suspected her of doing so. At least, she wasn't slapping her knee. Now the man beside her was pointing, too.

Spurred by embarrassment, Pyg tried to climb faster. Now he realized he would have to climb all the way to the top and hide himself on the high platform. There could be no half measures, but his destination still seemed a long way away. Finally stopping again to rest, he promised himself he wouldn't look back, but he couldn't help it. More faces were turned in his direction. He hoped none of them were his cowboys. Time to start again. Worn out, Pyg considered letting go and falling. Then he could rest without hearing any laughter. But he kept climbing.

Ouch! Pyg bumped his head again. This time, he bruised it on the bottom of the platform. He had bumps on top of bumps, hurts on hurts, foolishness compounding foolishness. Would he never learn?

Studying the runaway wheel with its blur of sharp blades, he told himself now was the time to be especially careful. He climbed another couple of rungs, never taking his eye off the spinning knives above him. Then he placed his hands on top of the platform and hoisted himself up. He lay face down on the unpainted boards while his blood and the wheel roared in his ears. He was afraid to look up for fear his head would be cut off and just as afraid to look down.

Pyg wriggled forward on his stomach, like a snake, until he could peek over the edge of the small, square platform. He felt dizzy and was glad he was lying down. But stretched out as he was, he remembered drawings of the French guillotine. He could imagine his severed head falling, falling, and making a muddy splash. Would they laugh then?

Lifting his head very carefully, Pyg looked around, absorbing the larger picture, the flooded town, the low hills, the curtains of rain, parting briefly, then closing again. A couple of buildings on Main Street had collapsed and were feeding lumber into the torrent. The rain pounded his bare back and butt. It hurt. He wasn't used to rain on those cheeks. He wasn't sure, but he thought he could make out two rivers—one north of town, the other south—which seemed to have joined to become one great Amazon. He had always liked geography.

Pyg heard a terrible screeching of metal and a crash. He waited for the blade to fall on his poor neck. The platform shuddered. The world shook before Pyg's eyes. The windmill seemed to pitch like a ship in a storm. The screams of metal tearing metal were terrible. His ears hurt. He felt a sharp blade nick the side of his neck, and he screamed but couldn't hear his own voice. Was his head already gone? Gripping the platform as hard as he could, Pyg watched the spinning blades spiral away. The wheel seemed to be flying. It was a great metal bird with a life of its own. But then it forgot how to fly and plunged into the water below. He had somehow dodged the guillotine.

"Help," he whispered in the wind and rain.

This time he heard his own voice. His world was getting quieter. Looking up, he saw only a stub where the terrible wheel had been. The windmill was headless. He peered over the edge and didn't see anybody pointing up at him. Life was improving, but it was still raining.

Pyg wondered whose idea it was. He was happy to see new clothes mounting the tower, but he was irritated to see who was bringing them. He wondered if Jesse had thought up this stunt on her own—or if it had been suggested to her. Who was the culprit? Little Dogie? Probably. Too Short? No, that couldn't be. Or could it? Maybe it was all of them, and now they were all down there busting a gut laughing at him. Jesse had the rescue clothing roped to her back. Watching her mount higher and higher, Pyg was surprised to feel a smile tugging at his face. He was actually glad to see her.

"Hi," said the Harvey Girl, serving another customer.

"Thanks," said Pyg, trying to sound as offhand as possible.

Scrunching forward on the platform—was that another splinter?—Pyg stretched down for the clothing. To reach the bundle on her back, he had to put his arms around her. He was naked and he was hugging a pretty young woman in front of the whole town. He told himself that the platform was concealing him, but he was still embarrassed. His water-wrinkled fingers found and fumbled with the knots.

"Having a good time?" asked Jesse.

"No," Pyg said.

"Well, I like that. Damn you fer not bein' grateful. Damn you and damn you some more."

The knots finally gave up. When the ropes let go, the clothing tried to get away. Pyg hugged Jesse tighter as he fought to save his replacement pants and shirt.

"Don't have too good a time," Jesse said.

"Sorry."

CHAPTER 23

Pyg was dressed in one of Little Dogie's shirts and a pair of pants borrowed from a local schoolboy. He was happy not to be naked, but he was still self-conscious. His new costume made him look too little on top and too big on the bottom. His naked shins were especially self-conscious. But at least he finally had himself a pair of faded blue Strausses, however small.

Accompanied by Jesse and Too Short, Pyg walked down Main Street on an inspection tour. The general store had collapsed on top of all its drowned goods. The blacksmith shop was fortunately made of sterner stuff. Pyg was surprised at how little damage the hotel had sustained. Crossing the muddy street for a closer look, he kept glancing at one broken window. He was imagining himself, hanging half in and half out of that dark hole, dead, naked, laughed at.

The floor of the lobby was covered with mud. It squished between his toes. Pyg walked barefoot over the muddy floor, paused to study a dead longhorn warming itself in front of a dead fireplace, and headed down a dark corridor in search of his boots and his Tiffany six-gun. He would keep his eyes open for a pair of pants that fit, too. He stumbled over something in the unlighted hall, stubbed his toe, and almost fell down. When his eyes grew more accustomed to the darkness, he saw that he had kicked a dead armadillo. Its armor hadn't been much protection against the flood. Probably sank him like a living rock. Pyg imagined a knight trying to swim a river. He rubbed his sore toe and only succeeded in getting his hand dirty. He grunted.

"Poor critter," said Jesse. "Meanin' him, not you."

"They swim about like a horseshoe," said Too Short. "Thass how come they like this here country. 'Cause most of the time there's more piss than rain."

"Well, piss and piss some more," said the Harvey Girl.

When they reached the door to what had been his sickroom, Pyg grabbed the doorknob, twisted and pushed. It didn't open.

"Locked," Pyg said. "That's what I thought. Why would it be locked? I don't understand."

"You didn't lock it?" asked Too Short.

"No, of course not."

"You sure?"

"I'm sure."

Pyg scratched his head and got mud in his hair. The armadillo was having a better day than he was.

"Jesse, you didn't lock it, did you?" he asked.

"No, why would I?" she said.

"Maybe it's just stuck," said Too Short. "Lemme see."

The small but powerful cowboy stepped forward and leaned heavily against the door. It groaned but didn't give way.

"I'll go get a key," said Jesse. "Unless they all washed away."

Pyg watched her hurry back down the dark corridor and out of sight. Leaning against the wall, he waited and wondered what had happened. Who could have locked his door? Why would anyone have wanted to? To protect him? To lock out danger? Or just the opposite? To lock him in? To expose him to danger? To keep him from escaping? Could anybody possibly dislike him enough to want to kill him? Such thoughts were crazy, weren't they? He wished he could talk these questions over with someone, but he didn't know who. He imagined himself sharing his fears and getting laughed at for his trouble. Would Jesse laugh? Probably.

Here she came, followed by the owner of the hotel, who looked muddy and exhausted. His white shirt was now brown. His usual formal coat was missing. His hands were grimy as he inserted a skeleton passkey in the lock, but it wouldn't turn. Nothing was easy. Mud and rust gummed the tumblers. Finally the lock gave up and the key turned. Since the door was water-swollen, it still resisted, but Jesse gave it a good, hard kick and it swung open.

Pyg brightened when he saw what waited for him in the far corner of the small room. His boots glistened in the semidarkness, still upright, just as he had left them. His clothes were stacked neatly—still folded—on the floor as if nothing had happened. On top of the clothing rested the silver gun. It gleamed.

"I wouldn't try shootin' anybody right off, if I was you," Too Short said. "That there purdy gun might just blow your damn hand off." He spat on the floor, which didn't make it much wetter. "Be a good idea to clean 'er up some before you go and git real mad."

"Everything needs cleaning," complained the hotel keeper. "I don't know where to start. It's terrible. More than a body can take. The hotel. The whole town."

"I been thinkin' on that," said the short cowboy. "Mebbe we could give you folks a hand." He smiled. "Be the least we can do since Pyg here busted yore dang window."

Pyg tried to smile, too, but his lips betrayed a worried quiver.

CHAPTER 24

P yg felt guilty because he wasn't doing more. He tired quickly and had to sit down. Even Jesse had more energy than he did. A lot more. Dressed once more in his own shirt and jodhpurs, he slouched in a still-damp easy chair in the hotel lobby, watching the Harvey Girl shovel mud out the front door. His own shovel rested against the wall beside the fireplace. Yes, he was a big help. When was he ever going to get his strength back? Jesse glanced in his direction. He looked guiltily away.

He knew the other cowboys were scattered around town trying to help other flood victims dry out and put their half-drowned lives back together. The boy wondered if his Boston neighbors would have been as helpful if the same catastrophe happened back home. He wasn't sure. He wished he had the strength to show that an easterner could be as helpful as westerners, but all he could do was sit there breathing hard. What must she think of him? Did she think he was a slacker? A weakling? An eastern sissy?

Pyg's guilt grew as his exhaustion waned. He pulled and pushed himself upright and discovered he wasn't as rested as he thought. Well, time to go back to work anyway. He half shuffled, half waded through the mud.

"What are you doing getting up?" Jesse said. "Sit back down. You'll make yourself sicker. Then I'll have to take care of you. Shit and shit some more."

"I can't just sit and watch you work," said Pyg. "Makes me feel worse than working."

"You heard me," she said. "Sit back down. Right now."

"You're not my mother, you know," he said.

"Good point." She gave him a long appraising look. "Okay, I could use a break. Let's go for a walk. See if we can find something to do besides shovelin' mud. Shovelin' mud just ain't a whole hell of a lot better'n shovelin' shit if you ask me."

They went for a walk down Main Street.

"You don't have to walk so slow," Pyg said. "I'm not crippled."

"Stop complainin'," Jesse said.

But she walked faster and he kept up. They waved across the street at Too Short, who was helping to untangle the wreck that had been the general store. When they reached the spot where the barbershop had been, Pyg was surprised to see the striped barber's pole still standing but the shop itself gone. Only a few boards remained. The barber was busy sawing and hammering those planks into coffins. He had already finished two. Pyg wondered how many he would build before he was through.

"Let's go see that W.W.W. man," Jesse said. "Maybe he could use some help. You oughta be able to lift paper, don't ya think?"

They found W. W. West sitting in the mud under a tree, leaning back against the trunk. Was he resting or had he given up? Publishing a newspaper in an underground office had been a mistake. The dugout was still full of water a couple of feet deep. The press looked like a half-sunk ship. The metal was red from mud and rust. The roof of the building was gone. The adobe walls had tumbled down and were scattered.

"How you doin', W.W.W.?" asked Jesse.

The editor looked up, startled.

"Oh, hello," he said. "I heard you were back in town. I hope your luck's been better than mine."

West got awkwardly to his feet and advanced to shake hands. Then he changed his mind because his fingers were covered with mud. He put his hands behind his back to hide the filth.

"We thought maybe you could use some help," Pyg said. "Looks like we were right."

"Thank you, but it's just too much," said the editor. "It resembles an open grave, doesn't it? Maybe the best thing would be—I don't know—to fill in the hole and just walk away from it. Or run. Give the press a decent burial and be done with it."

"Don't talk like that," Jesse said. "We'll git this place cleaned up and you'll feel better."

"It's no use."

The editor sat back down in the mud, but Jesse and Pyg went to work. Soon they were hanging pieces of blank paper on a makeshift clothesline where they looked like a long row of pillowcases. West finally got up and joined them.

"Thanks," the editor muttered. "But I think that paper's probably ruined."

"Are all news-jockeys this gloomy?" asked Jesse. "You got black ink in your veins or somethin'? Black and depressing, huh?"

"Thank you for all your effort, but I can't print much of a newspaper on wrinkled stock."

"When the paper's dry, we'll iron it."

"God."

They hung out their washing in silence. Pyg liked drying paper a lot more than shoveling mud. Still, his arms felt weak and his left hand was numb. He wondered if it would ever feel normal again.

"Howdy!" a familiar voice called.

Pyg looked around and saw Kate Bender sitting astride a muddy horse trailing a muddy pack mule.

"How do you do?" said West. "How did the water treat you?"

"Better'n you. That might be because I didn't build my store in a hole in the ground, whaddaya think?"

"Did you come to town just to make fun of me?"

"Don't be so touchy. I come to town because the town ain't gonna come to me. Not with the roads in this shape. But I figure a lotta folks are gonna need a lotta stuff. And I'm just the girl can sell it to 'em. Sure too bad about what happened to that there general store, ain't it?"

"That ain't nice," said Jesse.

"I'm surprised you didn't see this flood coming," Pyg said.

"Who says I didn't?"

"Well, you didn't mention it to us. Did you warn anybody else?"

"Maybe I didn't, but I can tell you right now what's gonna happen next. It's right there in the Big Book. The fire next time. That oughta be right good for bizness, too. Mebbe even better. Fire don't leave much. It ain't as forgivin' as water."

"Shit and shit some more," said Jesse. "Well, ain't you the Christian soul. Just make sure you don't start it 'cause I'm comin' after you."

CHAPTER 25

"I wish it'd rain," said Loving. "It's drier'n an old maid's—"

"Excuse me!" said Revelie.

"I waddn't gonna say it," he said. "But I sure do wish it'd pour. Grass is dyin'. Cows're dyin'. Whole country's dyin'."

"How do you know?" she asked. "You never leave this room."

"I can smell it." He frowned at her. "Smell the death." Then he smiled. "That and Coffee keeps me up to date." He frowned again. "Ol' Noah thought he had it bad, but he oughta try it t'other way round. No rain for forty days and forty nights. See how he'd like that there."

"Has it really been that long?"

"Longer. Oh, mebbe we had a speckle or two. But we ain't had no real rain for goin' on two months."

"I wish I could do a rain dance, but I don't know how. My husband would have known just what to do. I'm sure the Comanches taught him what to say to the clouds to coax the rain to fall. But he never told me. Weather and illness—they both make me feel so helpless. So useless."

"Now don't go talkin' like that there. I'm sorry I brung it up."

They lapsed into silence in the large, hot, dry room that had become their mutual prison. His wound chained him to his bed, and her love chained her to him. She sometimes wondered if he would have hovered if she had been the one shot in the head. She knew hovering wasn't a masculine speciality, but he might have. She really thought he might.

"Should I read some more?" asked Revelie.

Reading was a good way to pass the many idle hours they spent together. It helped them both escape their cell, flee to another land, another time, other personalities. She read to him every day and enjoyed it.

"Good," said Loving.

She picked up the large brown book—one she had brought from Boston—and opened it on her lap. It was really too big to hold comfortably in her hands alone. Opening it at the bookmark—a thin strip of rolled gold, a gift from her father—she scanned down the page until she found where they had left off. When she started reading, she couldn't tell if Loving was paying attention or not, which irritated her.

She tried to keep the irritation out of her voice as she read: "'Then I went over to the great arms factory and learned my real trade . . . guns, revolvers, cannon . . . all sorts of labor-saving machinery.'"

Loving laughed out loud, which startled her, because she had not heard him laugh for seventeen years. His laughter made her cry.

"I'm sorry I laughed," said Loving. "I know how much you hate guns. It waddn't funny. Don't cry. I'm real—"

"No, no," Revelie said. "I love the sound of your laughter."

When she finally closed the book almost an hour later, Revelie asked: "Do you think they'll find that ax?"

"Hard to say," Loving said.

"I'm not sure I want them to." Revelie collected her thoughts as she studied her knees. Then she looked up and into the eyes that were blue today. "After all that Percy's heard about how his father pulled that ax out of the anvil"—she put a little too much emphasis on *father*—"well, I'm afraid he might want to try it, too."

"More power to him. I know I tried it a coupla times. Never had much luck. Don't expect he'll do much better. The ax'll be fine."

Was he intentionally misunderstanding her?

"I'm not worried about the ax," Revelie said a little too sharply. "I'm worried about my son. What if he tries to pull the ax out of the stone and can't? What will he think then?"

"Lots of folks couldn't pull out that there ax, me included, like I said. Didn't ruin my life none. Don't s'pose it'll ruin his."

"But you didn't think you were the son of a man who could pull it out," Revelie said, shaking her head.

She watched as Loving stared up at the ceiling for a long time. Now his eyes looked brown.

"So that's it," he said at last.

"That's it," she said.

Revelie looked up when she heard boots in the hallway. Then she smiled stiffly at the cook as he entered.

"Company come," said Coffee.

"What?" asked Revelie.

"Company," Coffee said.

"Oh, ask them to come in," she said anxiously. "Offer them refreshments. I'll be there in a minute."

"They ain't that kinda company," said the cook.

"Excuse me?"

"Nesters, that's who they is."

Revelie stared blankly: What was going on? Who were the Nestors? Neighbors she hadn't met yet?

"What an interesting name. You know there's an old Greek named Nestor in the *Iliad*." She smiled at an amusing thought. "Maybe these are distant relatives? Do they come from Greece?"

"They's from outsida Tascosa, ma'am," said a confused Coffee. "And they's mad enough to bite a rattler."

"What are they mad about?"

"They won't say. Not to a damn cook anyhow. They wanna talk to Loving here."

"Didn't you tell them that he was ill?"

"Course, but they don't believe me."

Revelie turned to Loving. "Jack, do you know the Nestors?" she asked. "What sort of family are they?"

"They ain't no fam'ly," Loving said, a smile twitching. "They's squatters. Homesteaders. Sodbusters. You know, farmers. We call 'em nesters. Like they was chickens buildin' nests all over the damn place."

"Oh, I feel so stupid." Embarrassed, she hoped she wasn't blushing. "I am stupid."

"That ain't it. You're just too smart. Thass all."

"But why are these nest people so irate?"

"Dunno. We just ain't too popular with each other."

"I'd better go see what is on their mind." She turned to the cook. "Coffee, show them in. Give them something to eat or drink. And I'll be there in a moment."

Loving cleared his throat. "No, you ain't gonna talk to nobody."

Revelie flared inside. She didn't really want to talk to these nesters, but she didn't like being told what *not* to do.

"I really think I should talk to them," Revelie said as calmly as she could. "You think just because I'm a woman—"

"You're a *wanted* woman," Loving said, "and these people don't like us. They're li'ble to turn you in."

"There weren't any nesters around when it happened," she said, standing her ground, but more concerned than she admitted. "I'm sure they've never heard of me."

"I wouldn't be too sure. Why take the chance?"

"We don't want to make them more angry than they already are. Then they would be even more apt to cause trouble."

"Coffee can handle it."

"But they won't talk to him. I'll be right back."

A fter freshening up in front of her mirror, Revelie went out to meet the nesters. She found four big, red-faced men in her great living room. She noticed that their boots laced up and had low heels. Otherwise they looked a lot like cowboys, at least to her. The visitors were all standing, but Coffee slouched on a couch upholstered with fabric from a Comanche blanket.

"Good afternoon," Revelie said with forced cheerfulness, "I'm Revelie Goodnight." She searched the faces of her visitors for any sign that they had recognized her name. She didn't detect any. "Coffee, would you mind introducing me to these gentlemen?"

"I wouldn't mind," said the cook, "but I don't know hide ner hair of 'em. I reckon we don't b'long to the same church."

"Oh, I see. Well, perhaps they wouldn't mind introducing themselves."

Revelie waited but none of the farmers said a word.

"Don't all jabber at once," said Coffee.

Another wait.

"Uh, I'm John Cozby," said a chunky nester, "and these here are my brothers. That's David. That's Lewis. That's Kenneth."

Revelie shook all their calloused hands. These nesters all had extremely square faces, so their heads reminded her of boxes. She could feel disapproval, jealousy, and anger radiating from their bodies as if they had a fever. She forced herself not to recoil from the heat.

"Won't all of you sit down?" she said.

The nesters looked at each other. They seemed to be trying to decide if they would be undercutting their position if they took seats.

"Please," said Revelie, sitting down in an overstuffed chair. "I dislike talking standing up."

Somewhat reluctantly, the nesters lowered themselves onto similar chairs and a second couch, this one done in cowhide. Good, at least now they didn't tower over her. A couple of them kept glancing up at the elaborate deer-antler chandelier as if they were afraid it might fall on them. They didn't take off their tired straw hats.

"Didn't Coffee offer you anything to drink?" Revelie asked.

"I shore did, but they wouldn't take nothin'," said the cook.

"To what do I owe the pleasure of this visit?" Revelie asked at last.

She realized that she was trying to cow them with her manners, for she was confident that hers were better than theirs. But did they know enough to realize her advantage?

"Well, this ain't no social call," said John Cozby, who appeared to be the oldest of the brothers. He was about thirty-five years old and about six feet tall. "We was hopin' to talk to somebody in charge."

"I'm in charge," she said firmly, and hoped she wasn't blushing. "I'm Mr. Goodnight's widow. Mr. Loving, our foreman, is seriously ill. The other cowboys are away temporarily, except for Coffee here, whom you've already spoken to. So what can I do for you?"

"It don't seem right complainin' to a woman," John Cozby said, studying his thumbs. "It just don't."

"Then don't complain. Have some coffee and we'll all be the best of friends. Coffee's coffee has gotten better over the years. You really should try it."

"But it ain't right."

"What *isn't* right?"

"What this here ranch—and all them other big ranches—been doin' to us. We gotta complain. Somebody's gotta make it right. We're bein' ruined."

"Excuse me. I'm afraid I don't follow you. Would you like something else besides coffee?"

"We want our cows back. That's what we want."

"Has someone stolen them?"

"No, they're dead. They're just about all dead or dyin'."

"You don't supposed that I could raise the dead, do you?"

"Don't make funna me, ma'am. I ain't in the mood. I know you cain't bring 'em back to life all right, but you could sure as hell pay for 'em. That's what we're askin'. Just payment for our losses."

"What has caused those losses? Is it the drought? I assure you, I would make it rain if I could. I can't do that either."

"Ma'am, the drought's bad enough, but that ain't it. No, it's the fever. They're all catchin' it. They stop eatin'. Stop drinkin'. Just stand there with their heads down not movin'."

"And they piss blood," said sandy-haired Kenneth Cozby, who appeared to be the youngest of the brothers.

"Kenny, don't talk like that in mixed company," said big brother John. "I warned you before."

"Sorry."

They wasted a moment being embarrassed all around.

"I'm sorry, too," said Revelie. "But I still don't quite understand you."

"I'm speakin' English!" exploded John Cozby. "A plain man's English. I don't know what highfalutin language you talk. Lemme make it simple. You made our cows sick! You gotta pay for 'em! Understand?"

Revelie told herself to remain composed. She had, after all, dealt with worse accusations. At least, he wasn't charging her with murdering people, just cattle. She would stand up to him, but do it sitting down. She could see John Cozby clenching his fists. She folded her hands in her lap.

"You can't possibly believe we would do such a thing," Revelie protested. "Why would we? How could we?" She could feel herself getting angrier. Now she had caught the fever. "We're not gods who can rain down pestilence to destroy our enemies."

"You ain't gods," said irrepressible Kenneth. "You're devils."

"Be quiet, Kenny," said John Cozby. "Now, ma'am, I'll tell you how you done it. Maybe not you yourself, but the fellers in charge. You brung up sick cows from South Texas, and you run 'em through our land. And them there sick cows done give their sickness to our cows. And now they're all dyin'."

"What possible reason could we have for infecting your cattle?"

"To break us. To drive us off our land. So you can have it all the way you used to."

"It's greed," said Kenny. "And that's one of them seven deadlies, ya know."

"Kenny, I ain't gonna tell you ag'in."

Revelie told herself that she had to learn more about the ranch and its operations. It was very well to say she was in charge, but she wouldn't really be in charge until she knew more. This man's accusations couldn't possibly be true, she assured herself, but she didn't know enough to mount a convincing rebuttal.

"Coffee, do you have any idea what he's talking about?" asked Revelie.

"Miss Revelie, it's a pack a lies," said the cook. "We done lost hundreds a cows ourselves. Mebbe thousands. That'd just be cuttin' off our noses to spite our ugly pusses. We done lost way more'n these here nesters have. Cost us a hell of a lot more'n 'em."

"But you can afford it," said John Cozby. "You got millions of cows, so you don't give a damn if some of 'em dies off. But we just got a few cows and cain't afford to lose none of 'em. Ever' one that dies is a real blow. No milk. No butter. No meat on the table. You're tryin' to starve us out."

"That makes you worse'n murderers."

"Kenny!"

"Sorry, Johnny."

Hearing shuffling footsteps, Revelie looked toward the hallway. Loving came limping into the huge living room. She got up to go to him, but then she saw his gun. She just stood paralyzed, a well-meaning statue.

"This lady ain't no murderer," Loving almost shouted. "Now y'all git on outta here and leave her alone. You hear me!"

The four Cozby brothers stood up and stared at the sick man with the gun. Loving looked as if he was about to fall down. He cocked his six-shooter. Loving fired and broke a window.

"Less go, boys," said John Cozby. "But this ain't over."

As the brothers filed out of the living room, Revelie stood there dumbly, feeling as if she had failed as a hostess.

CHAPTER 26

As soon as the nesters slammed the door behind them, Loving went down on one knee. Revelie rushed to him. He was hot and slick with sweat. She helped him to his feet and they limped back into the bedroom. He collapsed on the bed and lay there as if dead. She sat on the bed beside him. She held his limp hand and felt his pulse to reassure herself that he was still alive.

Eventually, much as she loved him, Revelie got bored watching Loving sleep. She stood up, paced the bedroom for a few minutes, and then went looking for Coffee. She found him in the cookhouse where he belonged. The shack had a lonely and abandoned feeling since all the cowboys were gone. The cook was sitting on a tall stool in the big kitchen. He started to get up, but she motioned him not to bother.

"Coffee, thanks for helping me with the nesters," Revelie said.

"I waddn't much help," said the cook.

"You were really," she said. "I want to know more about this fever epidemic. I had no idea . . ."

"Well, it's like them damn clodhoppers said. The cows just stand there waitin' to die, and toward the end they start smellin' like they's already dead, even though they ain't yet. It's like they's rottin' standin' up."

"How terrible."

"Yup."

Revelie pulled up a second stool and perched on it.

"What can we do?" she asked.

"Nothin'," he said.

"There must be something."

"Not s'far as I know."

"Something must cause it."

"Some folks figure it's somethin' they ate. You know, always blame the food. That's what happens around here whenever a cowboy gits sick. They blame the cook ever' time. But I ain't so sure."

"What do you think is to blame?"

"I dunno. Some folks say Gawd."

"I suppose Mr. Goodnight would say the Great Mystery."

"I s'pose. But I ain't so sure about that neither. Plain fact is I just don't know, and don't nobody else know neither."

"Well, thanks again, Coffee."

Feeling frustrated, Revelie got up and walked slowly out of the cookhouse. She didn't know how to help the sick cattle. She didn't know how to help Loving. She didn't know where her son was or what he was doing. She wasn't sure whether or not there was a God.

When she re-entered the sick room, Revelie found Loving awake. She sat down on the bed beside him.

"Sorry they give you such a rough time," said Loving.

"They weren't so bad," Revelie said. "Don't worry about me. Just worry about getting well." She thought for a moment. "What is bad is this cattle fever. I wish there was something we could do."

Lying on his back, Loving shrugged his shoulders.

"Well, we've got to do something," she said. "Anyway we've got to try. I want to see some sick cows. I need to examine them."

"Don't be too hasty," he said. "You might catch what they got. Wouldn't want you gittin' sick, too."

"Has anyone caught the fever from the cattle?"

"Not s'far's I know. But you better be careful. Please. You never know."

Revelie could sense Loving's frustration. He wanted to protect her, but he was too weak to protect anything. He wanted to take care of her, but he couldn't even take care of himself.

"I'm going to do something," she promised herself out loud. "I don't know what. But something."

He took her hand, but that was all he could do.

While Loving slept, Revelie read *Tom Jones* by the light of a kerosene lamp that turned the pages yellow. She needed a book of her own to read while he was sleeping. She had found this one—a relic of her marriage—in a box in what used to be her sewing room. She smiled at a turn of a phrase while Loving snored softly a few feet away. She had read the book before and so already knew who Tom's father was, but she didn't mind. She was enjoying her return trip to a familiar landscape. Loving snorted and opened his eyes.

"Hello," Revelie greeted him.

"Hi," Loving said groggily.

She turned a page. He shook his head in an attempt to clear it. She smiled at him. He grinned back. She went back to reading. When she looked up again, he was frowning.

"What's the matter?" Revelie asked softly.

"I was just wondering . . ." Loving trailed off.

"What?" she said.

"Do you think he ever suspected?" he said.

"Percy?"

"Yeah. He ever ask questions?"

"I can't say that he has."

Lowering her eyes to *Tom Jones,* Revelie attempted to signal that she did not want to continue this conversation. But she had trouble concentrating because she could feel him continuing to question her with his eyes. She looked up.

"No, really, he has never seemed suspicious," Revelie said. "Honest."

"How'd you explain what happened?" Loving asked. "I mean the shooting."

"I didn't," she said flatly.

"Oh."

Revelie tried to go back to reading, but of course she couldn't. She raised her eyes again.

"No, I did not tell my son that his mother is a murderer," she said. "I couldn't." She waited. "What was I supposed to say? Clean up your room or I'll kill you? I know how because I've done it before."

"Don't git mad," Loving said.

"What do you want from me?"

"You ain't the only one that worries about him. I worry, too."

"I know. I'd like to read now."

"Read to me."

"But this isn't our book."

Fielding's phrases no longer seemed quite so amusing. She glared down at poor Tom Jones as if he had misbehaved. Well, actually, he had. He was always misbehaving.

Loving cleared his throat.

"Leave me alone," Revelie said.

"I didn't say nothin'," Loving protested.

"But you want to," she accused.

"I want lotsa things," he said.

Revelie closed her book and laid it on her lap. She had been backed into a corner by a man who could barely get out of bed.

"Go ahead," she said. "I'm listening."

Loving gathered himself as if about to do his first physical work in weeks. He straightened himself on his pillows. He wet his dry lips. He studied the covers. Then he defensively crossed his arms over his chest. Revelie couldn't help feeling sorry for him.

"I can see why you ain't said nothin'," Loving said at last. "Because you was way off in Boston and all. Most likely nobody knows in Boston. But you're in Texas now. Differ'nt story. Lotsa people know here."

"I know."

"I'm just afraid if you don't tell him—if we don't—somebody else is li'ble to."

CHAPTER 27

Ten days after the flood, Quanah was beginning to look like a town again. New buildings had gone back up fast for the same reason they had come down fast: simple, minimal construction. Nothing here was going to outlast the ages, but then nothing took ages to construct either. There weren't any pharaohs in Quanah, so they weren't going to build any pyramids.

Pyg and the cowboys could have ridden on, but they hadn't. People needed help and cowpokes were helpful people. It was part of their code and their bargain with the future: Someday they would need help. Besides, everybody said Pyg needed more time to get his strength back, so they stayed, and they worked.

At night, Pyg bedded down with the other cowboys—and the lone Harvey Girl—under the open sky. When the hotel reopened, there was some talk of Pyg moving back in order to continue his convalescence, but he didn't want to. He knew it would make him look like a sissy. Besides, he kept hoping that some night Jesse would creep over, roll him out of his bedroll, and lead him into another sexual adventure. Next time he would be quieter. Next time nobody would hear a thing. Next time he would finish what she had started. But next time kept receding before him. Night after night, he waited for her touch in the dark, but she stayed away. Had she changed her mind about him? Did she no longer feel grateful? Had he disappointed her? Or did she think he was still too weak for such strenuous work? Was she babying him? Of course, he could have slipped over in the night and touched her, but he didn't have the nerve. He could kill a woman—and had—but he wasn't too sure he could love one.

After another disappointing night on the ground, Pyg rode into town with the others. He dismounted in front of the general store.

Jesse got down beside him. Like the town, she was beginning to look better: The black around her eyes had faded to a motley green. The other cowboys rode on down Main Street where they would find real men's work to do: lifting, sawing, hammering. Jesse and Pyg would paint. It was woman's work, but the boy would have to be satisfied with it. Yesterday, they had painted everything they could reach from the ground. Today they would need to rise above the earth—go higher, paint more loftily—but they had just one ladder. As it turned out, ladders were very prone to washing away. Someday Quanah's ladders would probably reach the Gulf of Mexico and go for a ride on the high seas. Which was nice for the ladders but hard on the town. There was a ladder shortage and a general disinclination to use much-needed wood to make more.

Jesse and Pyg would have to share a ladder. She wanted to be on top, and he let her have her way. She climbed up the ladder and he mounted behind her. They went to work painting the rebuilt general store's false front a bright shade of red. Soon she was dropping paint on him. A glob of red splattered against his cheek.

"Ow, you hit me again," Pyg complained.

"Sorry," said Jesse, but she didn't sound as if she meant it.

"That's why you wanted to be on top."

"I ain't never claimed to be real dumb. It ain't my fault if you cain't say the same."

He was really irritated now. "You say 'ain't' too much," Pyg struck out at her. Here she was calling him a dummy, and she couldn't even speak proper English.

"Your problem," she said, "is you just got a bad case of ingrown education."

"I'm serious," he raised his voice. "With you it's always 'ain't' and 'cain't.' Those aren't words. They're not in the dictionary, for your information." He was still mad. "They make you sound ignorant."

Jesse didn't say anything, but he knew she was mad, too. She worked faster and dropped more red paint than ever on him. He looked as if he had been shot dozens of times.

"You don't even say you're sorry anymore," Pyg said.

"That's 'cause I *ain't* sorry," Jesse said. "Maybe my grammar ain't perfect, but I bet I know some things you don't know."

"Like what, sex?" he said, realizing full well that she knew a word-less language that he had never spoken at all. His inferiority made him defensive. "So you know a lot about sex. What does that make you?"

"You callin' me a whore?" Now she seemed angrier than he was. "Don't nobody call me a whore." She paused to catch her breath. He could see her trembling. She was so mad she was shaking the ladder. "I'll tell you who's a whore. Your mama's a whore."

"That's crazy. That's like kids yelling names on the playground. Your mother's this. Your mother's that. So what if I say your mother's a whore, too?"

"You don't know nothin' 'bout my mama, but I know 'bout yours. I sure as hell do. Everybody does. That's all the cowboys talk about when you ain't around."

"You're crazy. What are you talking about?"

"Your mama fucked Loving. That's what. Everybody says you look just like him. And you don't even know it. Fool's heaven."

"Shut up!"

Pyg reached up, grabbed Jesse's arm and yanked. He had to make her stop talking. She shoved back. They both fell off the ladder and wrestled in the red mud and redder paint.

Rolled in his blanket on the ground, Pyg couldn't sleep. The Harvey Girl was keeping him awake once again. Now he wondered—not if she would come to him in the night—but why she had lied to him. What had he ever done to her? Well, he had broken her nose and blacked both her eyes, but it wasn't his fault. Why did she hate him? After all, he had killed for her, hadn't he? He had saved her life. Why did she want to ruin his? He had completely misjudged her. His mother was right.

She touched him. When he felt her light tap on his shoulder, Pyg jumped. Where was a rock? Where was his gun? Now he wanted to break more than her nose. He recoiled from her touch.

"Leave me alone," Pyg whispered. "Keep your hands to yourself." He realized too late how childish he sounded, so he added sternly: "I'm not going anyplace with you."

"Who asked you to?" she whispered defensively. "I didn't come over here to suck on you." She took a deep breath. "I come to say I'm sorry. I'm just sorry and sorry some more."

"Then why did you?" Pyg asked accusingly.

"I guess I'm sorta sensitive 'cause I ain't had much schoolin'. Oops, I keep sayin' 'ain't,' don't I? I'm sorry. But when you up and criticized how I talk, well, I got so damn mad my brain just boiled over."

Pyg didn't say anything as he tried +to study her face in the darkness.

"Well, say something," Jesse whispered. "Please."

"So you admit you lied to me, right?"

"What?"

"You heard me. You admit you're a liar. That's why you came to apologize, isn't it? For lying?"

"I'm apologizin' for hurtin' your feelin's, that's why."

"It was your lies that hurt my feelings. That's the point." Pyg paused because he heard one of the cowboys turning over. He continued more softly: "If you admit to me that you were lying, then my feelings won't be hurt anymore. You admit it, don't you?"

"Well—"

"Well, what?"

He waited for what seemed a long time. He heard something running out there in the dark. Another cowboy turned over. Or was it the same one?

"Sure, I'm a liar," Jesse said at last. "I'm just a dirty liar. Shit and shit some more." She paused. "Are your feelin's feelin' better yet?"

"Are you telling the truth now?" asked Pyg.

"What? Are you callin' me a liar ag'in? That ain't nice. Oops, sorry about that there 'ain't'—"

"I don't care about your grammar. I just care about whether you're telling the truth this time or not."

"If you don't give a damn how I talk, then you don't give a damn about me—"

"That's not the point. Just tell me—"

"I'm a liar, I'm a liar, I'm a liar, liar, liar, liar. Cross my heart and hope to lie."

Pyg heard rustling in camp again.

"Hey, you dang kids," said a sleepy voice that sounded like Little

Dogie. "If you wanna mouth on each other, crawl off in the bushes somewheres. I wanna sleep."

Jesse withdrew immediately and almost silently into the darkness. Pyg just lay there with his mind screaming questions at him. Was his mother Loving's whore? Was Goodnight really his father?

Was Little Dogie the one who locked his door?

CHAPTER 28

"Pyg, stop lookin' like a damn preacher," said Little Dogie. "If this place is too much fun for you, go someplace else. This ain't no place for a baby boy nohow."

"Leave me alone," said Pyg.

The cowboys were lounging in the big downstairs room at an establishment that called itself the Squaw House. It employed just about every variety of woman except squaws. There was a black, a couple of Mexicans, one Chinese, and assorted Writers. Their strong perfume almost overpowered the lingering scent of mildew and sex.

This whorehouse party was supposed to celebrate the cowboys' last night in town. The cost of the evening's entertainment—women included—was to be borne by the town fathers. It was the town's way of thanking the cowboys for all their help in reconstructing Quanah. The Squaw House was one of many building the cowpokes had helped to rebuild. But the job was now done, and this posse would be leaving in the morning, hangovers or the clap notwithstanding.

"Ever'body's been upstairs but you," Little Dogie persisted. "Come on, it's your turn now."

Pyg felt even more uncomfortable now. All the cowboys were staring at him. They were resting after their first trips upstairs, lounging, recovering, refilling. Soon they would be ready for their second trips. And Pyg hadn't even gone once. He seemed to read their minds: Was there something wrong with him?

"I'll go when I get good and ready," Pyg said. "Don't tell me what to do and when to do it." He almost said: You're not my mother, but he stopped himself just in time. Still he felt he had to say more, come up with some excuse: "I haven't been tempted yet."

"Pyg, now don't stick your nose up at nothin' you ain't never tried,"

Little Dogie kept at it. "You're like a blind man criticizing the damn sunset."

"Who says I've never tried it?" Pyg attempted to defend himself.

"Well, less see. Yore mama told me she wouldn't let you. And Jesse here done told me you didn't know how. And—"

"Shut up!"

Pyg glanced at Jesse and then looked quickly away. What was she doing here anyway? In a whorehouse? What self-respecting woman . . .? Yet she didn't seem to feel out of place. He felt more uncomfortable here than she did. Didn't she know she didn't belong? Not in this house. Not with this posse. Why didn't she just go home and leave him alone? Why didn't everyone leave him alone?

"Go on, pick one," encouraged Vaquero. "Don't worry if you don't *sabe* what to do. She *sabes* enough for both of ya, and she'll show ya, step by fuckin' step."

Was he trying to be helpful? Or was he too making fun?

"I got two dollars here says Jesse'll jump one of these here girls before Little Lord Font'roy does." Little Dogie laughed. "I figure she's more of a man than he is."

Pyg hated them both: Little Dogie and Jesse.

"I'll take that bet," the boy said, getting up off the couch.

Pyg walked over to a big redheaded woman with large breasts who wore a bright red, low-slung dress. She was sitting on the floor, since the couches were for customers. Looking down at her—down her cavernous cleavage—he realized he didn't know what to say. How did you ask a whore to take you to bed? Was it like asking a girl to dance? Tongue-tied, he simply reached out his hand. She reached up and took it. Pulling her to her feet, he realized she didn't have much of a waistline: She was the same width all the way down. Gripping his hand tightly—as if he might get away—she led him toward the newly rebuilt stairs.

"Get your money ready," Pyg called to Little Dogie. "I don't take IOUs."

"Don't hurt him," the big man yelled. "I done promised his mama I'd take care of him."

. . .

S he followed him into the room, closed the door, and turned the key with a click. Pyg sensed something wrong, but what was it? Why was he so uneasy? Was it because he didn't know how to behave, had never learned proper whorehouse etiquette? Or was it something more?

"Did somebody steal your window?" Pyg asked at last.

"No." The big-breasted woman laughed.

"You need a window." He was glad to have something to talk about besides the business at hand. "Really. They shouldn't make you work without a window."

"I know, but they done run outta glass before they got to this floor." She laughed a sexy laugh. "Say, cowboy, you ain't lookin' for a way out, are ya?"

"No, ma'am."

"Ma'am? I like that. Well, there's more glass ordered from back East or wherever glass comes from. They done promised to cut me a winder whenever the glass gits here."

"Good."

"But if winders is what you like, mister, lemme tell ya: I got a winder thass much more interestin' than that one's ever gonna be. And I'm gonna open it wide open just for you."

Pyg inadvertently made a face.

"Whass the matter?" chuckled the whore.

"Nothing," he lied.

"Good. My name's Ginger. Whass yours?"

"Pyg."

"Pig? You wouldn't kid a girl?"

"Well, it's really Percy York Goodnight. I go by my initials."

"If you say so. The customer's always right. How you want it?"

"What?" Was there more than one way?

"I git it. They waddn't kiddin' down there, was they? You are a baby when it comes to women, aincha? Well, I'm gonna take care of you, like your friend said. You ain't never gonna fergit tonight. See if I ain't right."

Pyg was afraid she might be. Was she really the one he wanted to remember forever? The holy first one? He was surprised to see her turn her back. Had she somehow read his mind? Was she offended?

"Unbutton my dress, hon," Ginger said.

Pyg reached out with fingers that wouldn't stop trembling. He fumbled with her buttons, but they still came undone easily from plenty of practice. The skin beneath was a milky, sickly white. Under the red dress, she wasn't wearing any underwear, which saved washing it over and over. The whore shrugged out of her red dress and let it fall in a wreath around her feet. Then she turned around and nearly slapped Pyg with her flopping breasts. He took a reflex step backward.

"Now don't rattle yore hocks," said Ginger. "You'll hurt my feelin's."

"Sorry," gulped Pyg.

Stepping forward, she lifted her arms and laced her fingers around the back of his neck. She pressed her naked body against him. Feeling her more than seeing her, he decided that she was prettier than he had at first imagined.

"Now it's your turn," Ginger said lightly.

Releasing him, she started unbuttoning his white shirt. She peeled it back over his shoulders and dropped it on the floor behind him. He knew his mother wouldn't approve of his clothing being treated this way. When Ginger began unbuckling his gun belt, he took another step backward.

"Easy, boy," the whore said, as if quieting a horse. "You're skittish, aincha?"

"Sorry."

"I reckon it's a good thing we ain't got no winder. I'm afeared you'd jump outta it and break your good-lookin' neck."

"Sorry."

"See, you ain't gonna need this here big ol' gun," Ginger said, "because I done give up. Anyhow you got another gun I like better. And I'm gonna show you just where to aim it."

He wished she wouldn't talk. Her patter embarrassed him.

"That thing's sure heavy," said Ginger, lowering the gun and belt gently to the floor. "Whass it made out of? Pure gold?"

"Something like that," said Pyg.

Dropping to her knees, Ginger began unbuckling his bat-wing chaps. She started at the bottom and worked her way up his legs, which trembled faster and faster the higher she reached. The chaps fell away, another barrier gone, revealing his riding pants.

"Whut's this here?" demanded the whore.

"Jodhpurs," said Pyg. "Please don't ask."

Ginger eased them down his shivering legs. She lifted his left foot—as if she were shoeing a horse—and pulled off one eastern riding boot. Then she lifted his right foot and removed the other. When she peeled his jodhpurs off, the boy didn't miss them, not at all, rid of them at last. But then she grabbed his undershorts and pulled them down in one motion. Stepping out of them, Pyg got tangled up and felt himself falling on top of his whore. She hugged his legs to steady him and saved him from tumbling.

"Thanks. Sorry."

Still gripping his legs, Ginger pressed her face against his crotch and blew on his balls. Every kinky hair seemed to straighten out and stand up straight. Her breath tickled and hurt him. He almost collapsed on top of her again.

"Relax," Ginger instructed.

Sure. He felt her kissing him. His hair wasn't the only thing standing on end. He wished she would stop. He was afraid she might. Stop! Don't stop! Please, yes. Please, no.

Pyg's heart hammered loudly in his poor chest. Was he having a heart attack? No, somebody was pounding on the door. But why? Was his time up? No, please, let him finish.

"Fire! Fire! Open the door! Fire!"

CHAPTER 29

Pyg recognized Jesse's voice. Why couldn't she leave him alone? Now she was deliberately spoiling his fun.

"Unlock the door!" Jesse yelled, still pounding. "Get out of there! Fire! Do you hear me? Hurry!"

"Leave me alone!" shouted Pyg. "Go away!"

He heard her trying to turn the doorknob, attempting to break in, but luckily the door was locked.

"Pyg, listen to me. You've got to get out of there. This place is on fire."

"I don't believe you. Little Dogie put you up to this, didn't he?"

"No, I promise." She was kicking the door now.

"It's a trick and you're a liar."

"No!"

"You wouldn't know the truth if it—"

"What? Hit me in the face? Busted my nose? Give me two black eyes?"

So that was it: She was getting back at him for hitting her. It was almost as if she had been peeking through the keyhole and had known the exact moment to start yelling "Fire!" Was she watching the whole time?

"I'll never believe you again."

"Don't say that." She sounded hurt. "I'm sorry about your mama and all. I'm tryin' to make it up to you. Just believe me and git outta there. Cain't you smell smoke?"

Feeling foolish—as if he were giving in to the joke—Pyg sniffed the air. Did he smell smoke? Or had she just put the idea in his head? He tried to concentrate on the business at hand: getting his erection back.

"Pyg, please, don't you smell the smoke?"

"Very funny. No, I don't."

"I'm gittin' outta here. If you wanna burn down, thass your business."

Pyg heard running footsteps in the hall. Good, she was gone. Now he could get back to his whore. He reached down and gently touched her hair. This time, she pulled away from him.

"I smell smoke," Ginger said.

Pyg thought: Not you, too. Women, my God. They get you to a certain unstoppable point, and then yell "Fire!" His balls were going to be blue for the rest of his life.

"She's just trying to make trouble," Pyg said. "Don't listen to her."

"But I really smell smoke," said Ginger. "Oh, my God."

"I'm telling you—"

But then he smelled the smoke. Maybe Jesse wasn't a liar, after all. Or rather she wasn't a liar this time.

"We gotta git outta here!" Ginger interrupted his thoughts. "Less go."

Getting up off her knees, she ran naked for the door. Pyg tarried long enough to grab his jodhpurs. He wasn't going to get caught out buck-naked again. Skipping his undershorts, he hastily pulled on his riding britches. Then he ran, slipped on Ginger's red dress, and fell hard on his hands and knees. Not bothering to waste time getting to his feet, Pyg started crawling toward the door.

"Come on," urged Ginger, her trembling fingers struggling with the key in the lock. "Hurry."

Finally throwing open the door, she rushed nude into the hall. She didn't seem to mind: She was wearing her work clothes. Still on his hands and knees—as if his name were actually Pig—he was right behind her. In the corridor, Pyg stood up and looked around. To his right, he saw a thick cloud of smoke lit from inside by leaping flames.

"What're you gonna do with that there thing?" asked Ginger.

Now Pyg realized he was clutching his silver gun. Where had that come from? He didn't remember picking it up.

"You gonna shoot the damn fire?" asked the whore.

Pyg was impressed by Ginger's coolness. Her whorehouse might be burning down, but she hadn't lost her sense of humor. Wasn't laughing at danger the very definition of bravery? He was determined to match her cool for cool, laugh for laugh, even if he wasn't laughing inside.

"You don't think that'll work?" he asked. "How disappointing." He smiled. "I know it won't help much, but it makes me feel better. This gun's like my balls: I don't use them all the time, but it's always good to have them along."

"You're some kinda philosopher, aincha? Well, think on this: How the hell are we gonna git outta here?"

Looking around, Pyg felt his would-be-brave sense of humor beginning to fade. He now realized that they couldn't run down the stairs because they were on fire. They couldn't jump out a window because there weren't any. Pyg started coughing and couldn't stop. He couldn't catch his breath. Was he drowning again, this time in fire? Feeling a hot ball of panic growing inside him, he felt ashamed of his lost bravery. She was as cool as ever, but he shook inside and out, from coughing, from fear, from mama-wanting despair. Giving in to his terror, he turned and ran from the smoke and flames. Ginger followed him but at a slower pace. Looking back, Pyg couldn't help noticing—in spite of his panic—that her breasts danced on her chest. But it was a stately dance. Was she trying to show him the correct way to comport oneself—out here in the Wild West—when your life was in danger? Pyg wanted to slow down, but he couldn't. When he crashed into the wall at the end of the corridor, he told himself how stupid he had been. Of course, there was no way out: just a deadly dead end.

"Do any of the other rooms have windows?" Pyg coughed and sputtered and screamed.

"No," Ginger said all too calmly.

But then a flying ember caught in her pretty red hair. As if she were a human match, her red head burst into flames. Now she was afraid. Now she started screaming in a language that went back before words, howling primeval terrors. Pyg slapped her flames with his bare hands. Ow, that hurt. He felt guilty because he knew boys weren't supposed to hit girls, but he had to. While she kept on howling, he kept pounding the fire, her hair, her head, unmercifully. And as he did so, he began to calm down. He seemed to realize that only one of them could afford to go crazy at a time. He had had his turn. Now it was hers. He felt calmer still when the prairie fire on her red head started to retreat. He was beating it to death.

"You're okay," he tried to calm her. "The fire's out." An exaggeration. "You're all right." A white lie. "Everything's going to be all right." A black lie. "Take a deep breath."

The fire started to roar in Pyg's ears so loud he couldn't hear his runaway heart anymore. It was coming to get them.

"We gotta git outta here!" Ginger screamed above the screaming flames. "I don't wanna burn up!" She grabbed his arm and squeezed it hard. "It'll hurt." She was shaking his arm. "It'll hurt bad. I cain't stand it. Git me outta here. Please!"

Now he would welcome a flood. Come on, rain. Come on, torrents. But the only storm was a fire tornado. He was still coughing and felt light-headed. Think. Please, think. His mind was already on fire and refused to work properly. He took a deep breath—his brain needed oxygen—and coughed all the harder. Ginger started pounding on the wall at the end of the hall, adding to the terrible racket. Bedlam. It was too loud to think. Pyg had to find someplace quieter.

"Let's go back to the room," Pyg yelled.

"No," Ginger protested, "the fire's down there." She kept trying to beat down the wall. "We cain't go back."

"We have to," he said as calmly and sternly as he could. "Come on."

"No!"

Pyg grabbed one of her wrists and pulled her away from the wall. "We'll close the door, and then we'll figure out what to do."

"We'll never make it."

"Come on."

Still holding her wrist tightly, Pyg dragged her back down the hallway toward the heat and flames and smoke. She fought him, but he discovered that he could be strong in an emergency.

"Come on, hurry. You're just making it worse."

"Damn you! Damn you to hell!"

Pyg turned around, picked up the naked woman, who was now flushed smoldering red, and threw her over his shoulder. She beat on his back as he carried her back into the room, the room with no windows.

"Now we're trapped," cried Ginger. "This here room's our damn coffin. Nice goin'."

Pyg threw the naked whore down on the bed. Then he kicked the door shut and locked it. What was he thinking? Did he really believe fire cared about locks? He looked around and then stooped to grab Ginger's red dress. He stuffed it into the crack at the bottom of the door.

"My dress," complained Ginger. "You're ruinin' my good dress."

"Sorry. Maybe it'll keep the smoke out for a little while."

"You coulda used somethin' else." Complaining seemed to help her regain some of her composure. "What about the sheet?"

"Too late now."

Pyg searched the room for a tool that might save them. Perhaps some sort of battering ram. If there wasn't a window, maybe they could make one. But what to use? There wasn't any furniture except the bed. Should he take it apart and use the pieces to try to knock a hole in the wall? The fire roared right outside the door. He had to find something, had to do something, before it broke through.

Then he saw his battering ram. It hung there in his hand, useless until this moment. Sneezing, Pyg lifted his silver gun and pointed it point-blank at the wall, the exterior wall where the window should have been. He planned to correct that oversight as soon as possible. As he tightened his finger on the trigger, he felt a powerful explosion build to a climax in the cavity behind his nose and between his eyes. He fired and sneezed at the same time. The bullet hit the floor a couple of paces in front of him.

"Nice shootin'," said Ginger. "You done killed the damn floor. Feel better now?"

Pyg wondered if it was a panic sneeze or a smoke sneeze. Wiping his nose with the back of his left hand, Pyg found it hard to believe he couldn't hit the broad side of a bedroom wall. He took a deep breath to calm himself and almost sneezed again because of the smoke. Raising his Tiffany pistol again—and fighting the urge to cough—Pyg pointed and fired. That was better. From a distance of seven feet, he had managed to hit the wall.

"Bravo," said Ginger. "Now you done killed the damn wall. What's next? The ceiling?"

Now Pyg was ready to try a harder shot. He pointed his gun like a silver finger and fired: He hit the wall a half inch below the first bullet hole.

"Missed the ceiling," Ginger pointed out.

Pyg shot again and added a third hole a half inch below the second. Three in a row marching down the wall. Feeling calmer with each shot, he fired again and again. The holes continued to stitch their way down the boards. Pyg stopped to reload.

"I git it now," said Ginger. "Nice goin'." She laughed. "Maybe you ain't plum crazy, after all. And it looks to me like you kin hit the broad side of a barn if'n you want to bad enough."

While he sneezed again, Pyg's peripheral vision picked up the flash of a gun in Ginger's hand. He flinched.

"Where'd that come from?" he asked, startled.

Ginger was as naked as the day she was born but considerably better armed. It was just a little Derringer, but where had she kept it? She certainly hadn't pulled it from up her sleeve. What was her secret? Was she some kind of magician?

"Never you mind," said Ginger. "A girl's gotta keep some of her mystery."

She pointed her little gun and fired. She hit the wall some six inches below and four to the right of the place where she was aiming. It didn't remotely line up with Pyg's bullet holes.

"Don't say a damn word," said Ginger. "I'm gonna creep up on it." She stepped nearer the wall and sneezed at the same time. "Now don't shoot me. You be careful now."

From a distance of two feet, the redheaded whore fired a second shot from her double-barreled Derringer. She hit the wall about an inch and a half below Pyg's last shot.

"Not bad," said Pyg. "I'll close up the gap."

He fired and hit the wall exactly halfway between her bullet hole and his.

"Showoff," said Ginger.

Retreating quickly, she got down on her hands and knees and fished a box of bullets from under her work bed. Pyg went on shooting. Dark spots continued to descend the wall like ants on the march.

"Watch out now," Ginger said. "I'm comin' back."

"I won't hit you," Pyg said.

"Not less'n you sneeze," she said.

"Achew," he said.

"Very funny."

Ginger walked up to the wall, put her gun a couple of inches from it, and delivered two quick coups de grace. Then it was his turn. Then hers. He fired boom, boom, boom, boom, boom, boom. Sneeze, sneeze. She fired boom, boom. Sneeze. Soon the line of bullet holes was a foot long, the width of three boards.

"Let's do the other side now," Pyg said.

"Whatever you say, mister," said Ginger.

Shifting his aim a couple of feet to the left, Pyg started firing again. Six quick holes appeared in a line parallel to the first line. Ginger took a side step to the left, then another, put the muzzle of her gun against the wood, and shot once, twice. She had ceased giving the wall a sporting chance.

"This is kinda fun," said Ginger. "Sorta sexual."

They kept shooting until the second line was as long as the first. It was as if they had drawn a dot picture of a window on the blank wall. Actually they had only drawn the sides of the window. The top and bottom were drawn by the seams between the boards.

"Is this gonna work?" asked Ginger.

"We'll see," said Pyg.

Turning his pistol around, he gripped it by the hot barrel. "Ouch!" He stepped up to the wall and cocked his arm to deliver a heavy blow.

"No, don't!" Ginger said. "Don't hurt that gun. That's the purdiest damn gun I ever seen in my whole life. Wait."

Pyg obeyed while the whore got down on her hands and knees and fished under her work bed again. She pulled out a baseball bat.

"What?" coughed Pyg.

"Some of the boys need some settlin' down," Ginger said. "Comes in handy. Here, take it."

Remembering what he had learned on the playgrounds of Boston, Pyg stepped into the blow and swung from his backbone. When he hit his target, the bat hurt his hands but it hurt the wall worse. His bones remained intact, but he heard wood splintering. Studying the damage, he saw that one board had cracked along the line of bullet holes. Just as it was supposed to. The target practice had weakened the lumber like lead termites. He was feeling proud of himself, but then—

"Strike one," said Ginger.

Pyg glared at her, but she was right. He had cracked some wood, but there still wasn't a window in the room, and smoke was seeping under the door.

"I was just kiddin'," Ginger coughed an apology. "I didn't know you were so damn sensitive. Hit it again."

Swinging for the ballpark fence, Pyg heard another crack and felt the bottom board give way. A chunk of wood popped out and fell into the night. Pyg swung again and again. His hands were killing him. He saw smoke blowing out his small window into the darkness beyond. He kept swinging and dislodged another board. Then he had to pause to cough. When he had coughed himself out, he squared up again and went back to punishing the wall. The third piece of battered board flew—like an ugly ball—out into the void.

They had a window.

"Home run," cheered Ginger. "Mister, you sure 'nough know how to show a girl a good time."

"Ladies first."

"You got a way with words, cowboy."

CHAPTER 30

P yg could only see Ginger's legs and business end. She was stuck half in and half out of the room. The "window"—the one they had literally shot out—wasn't quite wide enough. The whore was having trouble fitting her hips through.

"Want me to push?" coughed Pyg.

"Go ahead," yelled Ginger.

Pyg hesitated.

"Don't be shy now," she coaxed.

But where exactly should he put his hands? What was he likely to touch? He hadn't expected his first exploration of the nether regions of a woman's body to happen this way. Well, she had certainly been right about one thing: He never was going to forget this night as long as he lived. Which should be a long time if he could only "open" his new window.

"Hurry up," yelled Ginger. "You ain't gonna touch nothin' that ain't never been touched before."

Taking a deep breath, Pyg coughed and went to work. He tucked his silver gun into the hip pocket of his jodhpurs. Then he put one hand on each loaf—careful to keep his thumbs tucked in—and shoved. He was afraid to push too hard because he might hurt her. The rough ends of the boards were scratching her skin.

"Harder! Harder! Harder!"

Pyg could hear cheers and laughter coming from a crowd outside. What was so funny? Why were they laughing? As so often, he wasn't in on the joke. Pushing harder, Pyg popped Ginger through the hole in the wall.

"Help! Don't let me fall. Don't let go."

Managing to grab her ankles, Pyg kept Ginger from making a head-first dive onto the hard ground. He peeked through his "window" and saw eager hands reaching up for the naked woman who hung upside-down in the moon and fire light. Pyg managed to lower her gently to the waiting arms below.

A cheer went up.

Then Pyg popped himself through the hole, scrambled, grasped the window sill from the outside, lowered himself feet first, and dropped to the ground. Nobody was interested in catching *him*.

Then Jesse appeared at his side. She touched him lightly on his bare back. He flinched. He had no sooner escaped from one box than he found himself in another one.

"You okay?" Jesse asked.

"Sure," Pyg said defensively.

"Well, I'm glad you're okay."

He didn't say anything.

"You didn't mean those things you said to me, didja?"

"Leave me alone."

"Why're you tryin' to hurt my feelin's?"

"I don't want to hurt anything. I just want to sit down and catch my breath. Is that okay with you?"

"No."

"What?"

What was the matter with her? He didn't need her permission to sit down and take a breather, did he? She wasn't his mother, was she?

"You cain't sit down 'cause the whole town's on fire," Jesse told him. "We gotta git outta here right now."

"You're lying."

"Don't say that no more. I don't like it when you say that about me. Look around. See for yourself."

Looking, Pyg noticed that all the people had evaporated. They had blown away like smoke. Even Ginger, who hadn't stayed around to say "thank you," was gone.

"Where'd everybody go?"

"I done told you. They're all running for their good-fer-nothin' lives. I'm tellin' ya, this town's done burnin' down."

"It can't be."

"Why not?"

"We just finished rebuilding it."

. . .

Jesse held tightly to his hand and pulled him after her down Main Street. She tried to run, but he slowed her down, stumbling along after her as best he could. He felt dazed, angry, lost.

"Hurry," said Jesse.

Pyg tried to move faster, but then his bare foot stepped on a sticker. It felt like a "goathead" with two tiny sharp horns. When he stopped to pull it out—yes, it was a goathead—she almost pulled him off his feet.

"Wait," he said. "Ouch."

They were moving once more, faster now.

"Ouch!" he yelled again, stopping again.

"What is it this time?" she asked, exasperated.

"Ember," he said, brushing it off the sole of his foot.

"You about ready?"

They loped faster and faster down a crowded Main Street. Many of the towns' citizens were still dressed in their night clothes. Pyg and Jesse ran and stumbled past people carrying silverware and plates and photographs and baskets of eggs. One poor woman, dressed in a white flannel gown, was struggling to save an iron and an ironing board. What was she going to press? Jesse and Pyg dodged around a sewing machine abandoned in the middle of Main Street. They hurried past a woman carrying a parrot in a cage. Then they almost collided with an upright piano that had been left to fend for itself. The town was giving up, was leaving behind its hidden treasures: woman-saving machines, soul-saving musical instruments, and hope.

"Excuse me," Pyg said, brushing past people. "Pardon me, excuse me . . ."

He noticed an elderly man—dressed in pajamas and a frock coat—carrying a bundle of clothes in one hand and a bird cage in the other. He did not seem to have noticed that the bottom of the cage had fallen out and the bird had flown. Then he got a glimpse of something familiar. Something that belonged in Boston, not on the landlocked plains of West Texas. Where was he anyway? Was he hallucinating? An old man in a nightcap was carrying a model ship with three masts and flapping sails.

"Come on."

Pyg hadn't realized he wasn't moving. He told himself to stop day-dreaming about sailing ships. It was time to abandon ship. The thought woke him up. He was no longer dazed and lost. He started running after Jesse, caught up with her, passed her, and then started pulling her.

"Come on."

She laughed. Looking back, Pyg saw Jesse smiling, saw a street on fire, saw men and women, boys and girls, cats and dogs, horses and cows—all fleeing. He stepped on more goatheads and embers, but he didn't stop. Pyg didn't even slow down until he had dragged Jesse a hundred yards beyond the last building. Then they slowed to a trot, then a walk, both breathing hard.

When they were a half mile out of town, Pyg and Jesse stopped. They joined a large group of refugees who were watching their town, their businesses, their homes, burn down. Looking around, he was still amused at what people had chosen to save. There was a woman holding a bird cage with kittens inside. Another woman was dressed in a white flannel nightgown and a black hat with ostrich feathers.

"Shit and shit some more," said Jesse. "It's like them dang plagues a Egypt. First the flood, then the fire. When the hell's them damned frogs gonna show up? The frogs and the locusts and the boils?" She scratched the end of her hose. "I think I feel one a them thangs comin' on right now."

She laughed and he joined in her laughter. The town was burning down and they were laughing. He felt a little guilty because he should be crying.

Then Pyg noticed something: Nobody was crying. He listened closely to be sure. Not even kids. They were all quiet. Silent. Resigned.

He knew what they were going to do.

CHAPTER 31

Revelie had decided what she was going to do, but she was in no hurry to get started. She had spent so many hours, so many days, in this half-dark sickroom that she both hated it and was afraid to leave it. She felt as if the larger world would somehow overwhelm her, so she just sat there on Loving's bed and occasionally stroked the back of his hand. She felt a duty calling, but she procrastinated.

"What's the matter?" asked Loving, ever attentive to her moods.

"Nothing," Revelie said.

"You're worried about something."

"I'm worried about a lot of things."

"Something in particular."

"I suppose it's that cattle fever."

"Worryin' won't help none. Nothin' you can do about it. Really."

Revelie picked up the big brown book and opened it to the rolled gold bookmark. Maybe fiction would calm her down.

"'Yes, Guinevere was beautiful, it is true,'" she read, "'but take her all around she was pretty slack.'"

Loving laughed again, which was good to hear, so she kept on reading although she liked the book less and less. At the beginning, every line had been funny, but now the laughs were considerably more sparse. Miles between smiles. Still she kept soldiering on, her voice growing tireder and less expressive as she read. Her monotone did not change until she came to a scene where the king was attempting to heal the sick.

Then Revelie refocused and described with animation a "scrofu-lous" throng of "eight hundred sick people" who had come to Camelot seeking cures. "'The king stroked the ulcers,'" she read. "'Finally, the patient graduated and got his nickel—the king hanging it around his neck himself—and was dismissed. Would you think that that would cure? It certainly did.'"

"It was the nickel," interrupted Loving, chuckling dryly. "That dang king paid 'em to get well."

With a serious expression, Revelie closed the big brown book and said: "I'm thinking of taking a look at the cows."

"No! Because of what you just read to me? That's crazy. That there writer was makin' funna healin' the sick. Much less healin' the cows."

She was surprised by his vehemence. "I want to help," Revelie said at last. "Maybe there's something I can do. Probably not, but maybe. What can it hurt?"

"You, that's who," Loving said. "You'll git hurt. Or you'll git sick."

"No, I won't," she said, a little too forcefully. "I'm not helpless. I can take care of myself."

"You think you can, but you cain't. Cattle's unpredictable. You dunno cows. Not range cows. They can turn mean."

In the middle of their quarrel, Revelie suddenly needed to pee. Her emotions had gone directly to her bladder. "I'll take Coffee with me. He knows cattle."

"Coffee?" scoffed Loving. "He's even a worse cowboy than he is a cook."

"He's not as bad as all that," she protested, her bladder hurting her. "You and the boys have the habit of making fun of him. That's all." She took a step sideways, trying to find a more comfortable position. "He'll do fine."

"Coffee don't know one end of the cow from t'other, whether he's cookin', or whether he's cowboyin'. In case of trouble, he wouldn't be no help atall. Just make matters worse."

"You're being unfair," Revelie scolded.

The pain in her bladder made her shriller and more emotional. So that was how it worked: Her emotions made her want to pee, which in turn made her mad. Surely men never felt this way. Loving didn't need to pee. He just lay there comfortably criticizing. It was so unfair.

"Please, let's don't argue," Loving said. "My head hurts."

Revelie felt a brief flash of irritation: She resented that his headache trumped her aching bladder.

"I'm sorry," she said.

Moving quickly, Revelie headed for the door. She had to go right now.

"Don't go!" Loving called after her. "Come back." He took a loud breath. "Don't go near them cows!"

Revelie threw open the sickroom door and hurried down the hall. She realized he thought she was running away from him, but she felt she couldn't explain. She knew him well enough to make love to him—or had once upon a time anyway—but not well enough to be immodest in front of him.

Rushing into the bathroom, the pain seemingly unendurable now, Revelie wanted to cry "unfair" again. For she had to fight her way out of so many layers of feminine clothing. A man would already be peeing by now. She was still hurting.

Ahhh, at last, that was better. The pain and tension and irritation flowed down and out of her. If only all hurts were so easily cured. She felt herself smiling in the bathroom.

When she returned to the sickroom, Revelie saw an unhappy Loving. He looked forlorn and abandoned.

"I'll make a deal with you," she said lightly, feeling much better now. "How about it?"

"What deal?" he asked suspiciously.

"You tell me what that gunfight was about, and I'll leave your precious cows alone."

"No. Don't ask me ag'in."

Suddenly she was irritated all over again. More than irritated. Angry. She had come back from the bathroom in such a good mood, and he had ruined it.

"I'm going for a ride."

CHAPTER 32

Wearing a black skirt, Revelie Goodnight rode sidesaddle through the cattle. She felt guilty as she checked the herd for sick cows. She should be looking after her human patient, not worrying about diseased longhorns. But in this country the fates of men and cows were inextricably twined. In helping the one, if she could, she would be helping the other. But such thoughts did not keep her from feeling that she was being unfaithful to Loving.

Revelie was accompanied by Coffee, who was mounted on a mule. Her horse was her favorite, a pretty white-faced mare, the one Loving had named Boston. Coffee's gray mule was called Halfbreed. Of course, as she rode, Revelie remembered when her husband had made this saddle for her. She naturally thought of him more out here than she had back in Boston. The sun beating down on her bare head made her uncomfortable. She hoped she wasn't getting sunburned, and wished she had a cowboy hat. But she must ignore such distractions and concentrate on her task. She had to find a—

Wait a minute, was that one sick? Up ahead and to her left, Revelie saw a longhorn with a lowered head and drooping ears.

"That one looks sick, doesn't it?" Revelie asked, pointing, which she didn't do very often, considering it impolite.

"It don't look too frisky," Coffee agreed.

With her left heel, she gently urged Boston to go faster. When she got closer, she sniffed the air. Did she smell death? Her nose scented something sweet but at the same time putrid. She wanted to turn her horse and ride away. It was a frightening smell. She hated the thought of it clinging to her clothes, to her body. Then she would smell like death, too. She shuddered, but she kept riding directly into the foul odor. Coffee followed reluctantly.

As they rode through the herd, the other cattle moved away from them, but the head-down longhorn didn't even twitch. It looked and acted as if it were already dead and just waiting for somebody to come along and push it over.

"Move, cow," Revelie raised her voice. "Go, run."

But the longhorn didn't seem to hear her. She rode around the unmoving animal in smaller and smaller circles. The smell of death kept getting worse. Since she didn't know what she was looking for, she doubted she would find it, but she kept searching anyway. What caused this devastation? Was it something the cattle ate? She stared down at the buffalo grass but couldn't see anything wrong with it. Of course, she reminded herself, she didn't know much about grass. This grass could be as sick as a dog—sick as a fever-ridden cow—and she probably wouldn't see the problem. But she kept on looking anyway.

When her circles had spiraled down to where she was almost touching the immobile longhorn, she stopped Boston and slid to the ground. Still it didn't move. She stepped even closer. Still nothing. She stooped and looked underneath. Oh, it was a steer. Poor thing.

At that moment, the seemingly dead animal startled Revelie by pissing. Except it didn't look like piss. It looked like blood. And some of the bloody urine splashed on the would-be animal doctor. Revelie recoiled backward and bumped into Boston. The horse shied, but the steer just stood there pissing away its life's blood. Revelie looked down and saw that she had bloody spots on her skirt and eastern walking boots. She started to brush the spots away, but stopped because she didn't want to get blood on her hands. Then she realized that Coffee, still mounted on his mule, was laughing. Spinning around, she burned him with her eyes.

"Sorry, ma'am," said the cook, but he couldn't suppress a chuckle.

"This is no laughing matter," Revelie upbraided him.

"Real sorry, ma'am. Don't know what got into me. I surely don't."

"I don't either. Go home if you can't keep a straight face."

"Won't happen again."

But then it did. A burst of laughter shook the cook. Then he looked miserable. His expression made Revelie laugh. Which made him laugh again. Which made her laugh louder. They were victims of a laughter epidemic, each one infecting and reinfecting the other.

"We really shouldn't laugh," sputtered Revelie, who couldn't stop.

"No, ma'am," said Coffee, who kept on shaking.

Revelie turned her back on the cook, which helped a little. The laugh spasms slowly began to subside. That was better. When she turned back around, Coffee had stopped laughing, too. They smiled at each other.

"What must this poor animal think of us?" Revelie said. "We should really apologize to it. It's not nice to laugh in a sickroom."

"You're right, Miss Revelie," Coffee said sternly. "But it's kinda like laughin' at a wake. I dunno about where you come from, but where I come from, that always happens. Fittin' or not. Releases the tension somehow. But you're right, ma'am, we shouldn't oughta laugh."

His attempt at a serious tone almost set Revelie laughing again, but she fought down the impulse.

"Do you see anything wrong with the grass?" she asked.

"No, ma'am," he said. "It's just grass."

Revelie once again approached the longhorn, which had by now stopped pissing blood. Reaching out to touch it, she felt timid, even frightened. What if this steer suddenly turned and raked her with its sharp horns? Not only did she not want to get hurt; she didn't want to have to admit to Loving that he had been right. She couldn't go back to him and confess that she had gotten gored doing just what he had warned her not to do. Of course, rationally, she doubted the steer had the strength to hurt her, but irrationally she felt like a matador daring fate. Or what if she caught something from touching the diseased animal? Supposedly people didn't catch the fever, but she suddenly wasn't so sure.

The steer's hairy hide was warm to the touch, too warm. The fever heated her fingers. Still the longhorn did not move. She was glad it hadn't hooked her, but she wished it had shown some sign of life. She rested her palm on the animal's back and felt its backbone through the hot skin. Now she realized that the steer was far too thin. All its bones were trying to poke through its hide, attempting to escape from this death-ridden body. When it got sick, it had obviously stopped eating.

"Poor thing," Revelie cooed as if speaking to a sick child. "You're just skin and bones, aren't you?" She began to stroke its mottled hide.

"What made you sick?" She used the same voice that had talked Percy through so many childhood illnesses. "Was it something you ate? Was it something you drank? Were you just keeping bad company?" It occurred to her that this probably wasn't a sexually transmitted disease since this was a steer. "Poor thing."

"You talk to animals just like Mr. Goodnight did," Coffee observed.

"Not really," Revelie said. "The Indians taught him, so he knew how to go about it. I'm just babbling, I'm afraid."

She wondered if even now disease was racing up her arm to invade her body. Would she turn listless? Would she pee blood?

Moving forward, she scratched the longhorn between its high shoulders. Did her touch comfort it? The steer gave no sign. Was she irritating it? She couldn't tell. The steer's skin felt very dry. It seemed ready to crack open.

Then she saw the flies and her stomach lurched. They were clustered around its eyes. They swarmed over its nostrils. They buzzed inside its ears. She wanted to retreat, but she wouldn't go back on her boast that she was up to this task that she had set herself.

She held her ground and wondered: Could these flies be the devils that were infecting the cattle? She knew that flies fed on death, that maggots devoured dead bodies, but could they also cause death? Did they kill and then eat? She stared hatred at the small buzzing demons with demonic eyes.

Revelie picked a handful of long buffalo grass and started trying to shoo the flies away. They were reluctant to move, so she swatted harder. The longhorn didn't seem to notice. The flies angrily began to buzz away, but they didn't go far. She could hear them complaining all around her.

Remembering that dogs liked to be scratched behind their ears, she decided to do the same for the longhorn. Maybe this great beast was just an overgrown collie at heart. Bending over, she reached down and started to scratch, but then she recoiled. She jerked her hand back because she had touched something slimy. What was it? She wanted to turn away, get back on her horse, and ride off. But she also wanted to ease the animal's suffering if possible. But was she doing so? Was she doing any good at all? What had possessed her to come out here and play with a dying animal?

Still, much as she did not want to do so, Revelie bent once again and reached behind the steer's drooping left ear. She scratched again and felt the slime again. This time she examined what felt like a small, greasy ball. She wanted to pull away, but she didn't. Now she thought she knew what she had found. Dogs often had them. Deer had them. She gave the disgusting ball a tug. It didn't want to let go. She pulled harder and it released with a faint plop. Holding it up, she recognized a blood-gorged tick. She suddenly couldn't drop it fast enough. Then she crushed it with her eastern walking boot.

"You okay?" asked Coffee from the back of his mule.

"I found a tick," Revelie said.

"Ain't surprised."

Riding back to the ranch house, Revelie felt she had wasted her time and strength. Now she had to decide: Would she tell Loving? It would just upset him. But how would she explain her absence? She could just say she was taking a nap. That would be best. But she already felt like she was keeping a secret lover. And what a lover indeed: a diseased, fly-ridden, tick-infested, castrated cow.

CHAPTER 33

When she entered Loving's sickroom, Revelie was relieved to find him asleep. Sleep was good for him and sleep asked no questions. She sat down in a chair and watched him sleep. He moved restlessly on the bed as if worried about something. She wished she could give him peace, but didn't know how. Afraid her very watching would wake him, Revelie closed her eyes for a moment. She dozed.

"Welcome back," Loving's voice roused her.

"Oh, hello," Revelie said.

Getting up, she moved to the bed and sat beside him. She reached for his hand, but he pulled it away. She could hear him sniffing the air.

"You smell like a cow," Loving said.

"I'm sorry," Revelie said. "I didn't realize."

"Were you gonna tell me?" he asked.

"If you asked me," she said.

They stared at each other, she from above, he from below.

"I don't like it when you disobey me," Loving said.

"Disobey you?" Revelie was suddenly angry. "What are you talking about? I'm not yours to command. You make me sound like a disobedient child. Or a bad wife. I am neither. I don't mean to upset you when you are sick, but—"

"Don't get your damn dander up."

"I don't appreciate your language and even less your implications."

"Whatever that means?"

"It means I am your equal." Trying to calm herself down, she thought about just how to say what she wanted to say. "That was always a part of Mr. Goodnight's Code. An important part. Equality." She was remembering writing out that Code with her husband. "A man isn't higher than a woman. A white man isn't better than a Comanche.

A chicken has as much right to live as an eagle. And you can't boss me around!"

He reached for her hand, but now she pulled away. His eyes—sometimes blue, sometimes brown—were red now. He glared.

"I'm the boss if'n I know more about somethin' than you do," Loving said. "And I know a hell of a lot more'n you about them damn cows."

"Do you know how to cure the sick ones?" Revelie asked.

"No, course not, but—"

"Then it appears you don't know more than I do. We both know the same. Nothing at all. And that sounds pretty equal to me."

"But I know how dangerous them critters can be."

"Please. The sick ones couldn't hurt a fly. They don't even have the strength to shoo the flies away. You can walk right up to them, and they don't even twitch an ear."

"You walked up to them?"

"Yes I did. One of them anyway. It just stood there. Dangerous indeed."

"How close did you get?"

"Very close."

"Did you touch it?"

"As a matter of fact, I did."

"When you git sick, you tell me if them cows're dangerous or not. When you're burnin' up with fever, mebbe you'll change your mind."

"I won't get sick."

"I'm tellin' you—"

"You may be telling, but I'm not listening."

Revelie got up off the bed and headed for the door. Glancing back over her shoulder, she saw Loving trying to rise. But then he fell back on the bed and stayed there. She went on out of the room.

Well, she hoped she was satisfied with herself. She hadn't helped the sick cows and she had made a sick man sicker.

Revelie walked along the red river where once she had strolled with the young Jimmy Goodnight. Here he had taught her how the Comanches declared their love: *My mind cries for you.* Now her mind cried for Loving, but she still couldn't mold herself to his will. Why not? If she loved him? He was sick. He was actually helpless. She knew he needed to feel he could still assert himself. Still protect her, still take care of her. Why couldn't she let him? What had she accomplished by opposing him? She would go back to the sickroom and be softer this time. But she didn't feel soft. Was this hard land making her harder?

Looking up, Revelie noticed the peak that Goodnight had named Sad Monkey Mountain. The rock formation at the top did look like a frowning ape. She felt her own lips aping its expression. The entire canyon seemed sad. The thirsty plants had drooping leaves. Even the grass slouched. Revelie felt her shoulders hunch as she slumped along. The heavy canyon walls seemed to sag in upon her.

Revelie saw a longhorn emerge from a grove of cedars on the other side of the river. Good, it was moving. The mottled animal ambled down to the water and lowered its head. Good, it was drinking. The fever had so far spared this one. It was healthy. It was lucky.

And so was she. Healthy. Fortunate. Nobody had shot her. Nothing had infected her. She was the whole one, the strong one. Wasn't she strong enough to appear weak? Of course she was. Wasn't she? She wasn't sure. She would find out.

Turning by the river, Revelie headed back toward the red sandstone ranch house. She walked slowly. She tried to be quiet. She attempted not to think. She wanted to be like the Sad Monkey but without the frown. Calm. Utterly still. Mind empty. Thinking hurt.

Revelie was still unsure as she mounted the front porch steps. What should she say? What would she say? Could they make up? She envied the Sad Monkey who never had to say anything. Crossing the big living room, she felt herself stiffening. Moving down the hall, she clenched her fists, then relaxed them, then clenched again. She didn't want to give in, didn't feel malleable, couldn't imagine being ruled by anybody. Was she unfeminine?

When she opened the sickroom door, Revelie let out a little scream. Then she ran to the bed. Loving was purple. He lay on his back, his head turned a little to the right, a river of vomit running from his handsome mouth. It trickled down his face and off onto the bed. Was he breathing? Stooping, Revelie pressed her ear to his nose. Her cheek touched the vomit clinging to his lips. Wanting to pull away, she didn't. She didn't hear anything. No, no, what had she done? She had upset him and now he wasn't breathing. Had she killed him? She tried to listen harder. Nothing. Was his face growing darker?

And she had been intending to renew the argument. What had she been thinking? What was wrong with her?

Realizing he was choking on his own vomit, Revelie started clawing at Loving's mouth. Digging out half-digested food. Trying to clear a passageway for air. Her fingernails raked his tongue. Now she wanted to throw up, too. Worse, he still wasn't breathing.

Revelie started trying to turn him over, but his "dead weight" resisted her. She braced herself and pushed hard. He finally rolled partway. She pushed harder. This was hard work. Now she couldn't catch *her* breath. He gave up and tumbled onto his stomach. She climbed onto his back, riding him. Placing her hands just beneath his shoulder blades, she pressed down hard. She was performing artificial respiration as if he were a drowning victim. More vomit poured out of him. Was she making matters worse? Not knowing what else to do, she pressed down harder.

Loving coughed.

Thank God. Thank god. She pumped harder. He coughed again. Yes. And again. He was breathing.

Revelie turned Loving on his side. Now she realized she was covered with vomit, but she didn't care. She kissed his filthy mouth. He coughed in the middle of the kiss. Now she was coughing. She kissed him again, but he didn't kiss back. She kissed harder, but he didn't respond. It was like kissing a dead man.

Why wouldn't he wake up?

CHAPTER 34

Riding southwest, Pyg had the rising sun over his left shoulder. Quanah was behind him, too. He and the cowboys had decided not to stick around for the second rebuilding of the town. They hated to leave the townspeople to their troubles, but it was either move on or move to Quanah and set up housekeeping. This second rebuilding was going to take longer than the first, because fire destroyed much more completely than water. Very little lumber had survived this time. Most of the town was living in tents until shipments of new boards arrived. The town folk had given them a warm farewell, and now they were bound for New Mexico. Still in search of the ax.

As they rode along, Opry sang:

> *"Oh, this trail's mighty long,*
> *But the trail's always shorter*
> *When I'm singing my song."*

"Yore damn song makes it seem a hellava lot longer to me," shouted Little Dogie. "Shut your mouth or I'll plant daisies in it."

They rode through a green countryside spotted by shallow lakes, but the fields weren't green with crops. The flood had washed away most of the cotton and wheat. Now weeds ruled the pastures.

"Pyg, boy, you shore must be some hot lover," Little Dogie chided. "I hear you done set that whore's bed on fire. And you didn't stop there, no siree bob. Waddn't satisfied till you burned down the whole damn town. Guess my mama was right: Little boys ain't supposed to play with fire. Mebbe you better stay outta whorehouses till you grows up."

Listening to the big man, Pyg's anger smoldered. He wanted to strike back in some way. He needed to stand up for himself.

"I've been wondering," Pyg said at last, "where were you when the fire started?"

"Now whass that supposed to mean?" Little Dogie flared. "I was just funnin' with ya, and now you sound all serious."

"I'm not funning," Pyg said. "Where were you?"

He glanced at Jesse to check her reaction to the confrontation. She was frowning. He couldn't tell whose side she was on.

"I'll tell you what I was doin'," Little Dogie said. "I was takin' bets you couldn't get it up, thass what. Givin' good odds, too."

"Then you'd better pay up," Pyg said. Turning to Jesse, he asked: "Did you see him? Was he with you and the others?"

Looking embarrassed, she took her time recalling. "Ever'thing happened so fast," she finally said. "It's hard to remember."

"Try hard," he said.

"I ain't sure," she said.

He scowled at her reluctance, but she misinterpreted.

"Sorry if my sayin' 'ain't' hurts your tender ears."

"Please."

"I ain't sure," she began, and then lowered her voice, "but, well, no, I don't remember seein' him." She thought over her testimony. "And he's too big to fergit, ain't he?"

Pyg smiled, and he thought her face brightened slightly. He was still mad at her because of what she had said about his mother, but she wasn't all bad.

"Now you shut up," said a suspicious Little Dogie. "You don't know nothin'. What was you doin' in that there cathouse anyhow? A whorehouse ain't no place fer a girl."

"There were some few of 'em there," Jesse said coolly.

"Too Short, what about you?" Pyg said. "Was he with you when it started?"

"That's enough," said Too Short.

They rode on in silence. Pyg kept wondering why the fire had broken out when he was the only cowboy upstairs. Was he just unlucky? Or did somebody mean him harm? Of course, he also recalled the locked door that had imprisoned him during the flood. Was there a connection?

Not stopping for lunch, they rode on into the afternoon facing a fierce sun. Pyg felt his face warming and reddening. He continued hot inside as well. He was still angry at Little Dogie for continually making fun of him and maybe trying to kill him. What had he ever done to the big man?

As the sun started to redden—as if it, too, were sunburned—Pyg's thoughts turned from the past to the immediate future. Soon it would be night, time for camp, time for sleep for some, perhaps time for something else for others. He imagined approaching Jesse's bedroll under cover of darkness. Did he want to creep up to her? Yes, he did. But she had called his mother a whore. That was unforgivable. He was furious at her. But he was weary of his virginity. He was tired of being made fun of because he didn't know anything about fucking.

What did he care about more: sex or anger? Did he want to punish Jesse or make love to her? Pyg listened to the sounds of camp as it fell asleep. It got quieter and quieter as the cowboys dozed off. Then it got louder as Little Dogie started to snore. Pyg noticed the Harvey Girl moving restlessly inside her rolled quilt. What did her restlessness mean? Was she asleep yet? Would she mind if he woke her up? How much?

The stars were many and close overhead. Pyg tried to concentrate on them and their grand and infinite mystery, but his mind kept backsliding into questions about mysteries closer at hand. But not less perplexing. Tired from the day's ride, he suddenly felt unequal to solving much of anything. He dozed.

Pyg dreamed of undressing Jesse. Of lying down with her. Which was where his dreams always stopped. He didn't really know enough about what was supposed to happen next to dream about it. Waking, he wondered if more knowledge would lead to more fulfilling dreams.

Little Dogie clicked and sputtered and snored in his sleep.

Now Pyg was wide awake, and he had an erection. Snores assaulted him from without and his blood pounded within. He hoped his libeled mother would forgive him for what he was about to do. Or try to do.

Rolling as silently as he could, Pyg loosened the quilt that was wound around him. Then he quietly pushed himself up onto his hands and knees. He crawled like a baby. He stopped and listened. He crawled again. His knee came down on a sharp rock and he almost cried out.

When he reached Jesse's bedroll, Pyg hesitated. What if he touched her and she cried out? He didn't want to wake the cowboys. He didn't want to be laughed at. Again. He told himself that he should turn around and crawl back to his bed. Nobody would ever know he had come this far and lost his nerve. Making up his mind, he started backing up on his knees.

"Where are you goin'?" whispered Jesse.

"What!" Pyg said a little too loud.

Little Dogie stopped snoring. Too Short coughed. Vaquero turned over noisily. Did somebody laugh?

"Where are you goin'?" Jesse repeated a little louder.

"Shh, I don't know," Pyg said lamely.

"You wanna go somewhere?" she asked.

He started to repeat that he didn't know but stopped himself. He told himself to get hold of himself. Calm down. Act like a man.

"Yes," Pyg said in a shaky whisper. "Let's go somewhere and talk."

"You want to talk?" she whispered. "It's pretty late fer talkin'. You sure you just wanna talk?"

"Come on." He tried to sound forceful without being loud. "Please."

"I don't wanta talk about your mama, you hear?"

"I don't either."

He felt disloyal.

T hey reclined in a dry creek bed. It wasn't as soft as it had looked. A lot of gravel was mixed in with the sand. The flood seemed not to have touched this sometime stream. Dry granules stuck to his moist skin. She still had all her clothes on, but his jodhpurs were missing. He lay on his back while she knelt between his legs making slurping sounds. He thought he was about to explode when she stopped.

"Don't stop," Pyg moaned.

"It's your turn now," Jesse said. "Or rather it's my turn."

"What?" he asked.

"I did you," she said. "Now you do me."

"I don't understand."

"You do to me what I did to you, see? We take turns. Thass just good manners. Time about is fair play and all that. Ain't that right? Didn't your mama teach you good manners?"

Pyg was surprised, confused, embarrassed. This mystery was even harder to understand than the stars in the heavens. He wished one would fall on him.

"I can't," Pyg said.

"You cain't?" Jesse asked. "You ain't a damned Boston Puritan, are ya? Whaddaya mean you cain't?"

"You don't have what I have." Now he was really embarrassed. "How, uh, how can I do to you what you did to me?"

"You *are* a baby, aincha? You mean you really don't know how?"

Now he felt very small. His erection had shrunk along with his self-esteem.

"Don't I know what?" Pyg mumbled.

"How to mouth a girl," Jesse said.

"What?"

"Don't worry. I'll show you."

Jesse stood up, unbuckled her belt, and dropped her trousers. Then she shook the pants off her ankles. Now they were dressed alike. She lay down beside him on the coarse sand.

"Hi," Jesse said.

"Hi," Pyg said warily.

"I'll guide you, okay?"

"Okay."

Jesse reached out and gripped Pyg by the hair at the back of his head. She pulled him toward her. He couldn't believe what she was doing to him. He found himself staring at the black jungle between her legs, which kept getting closer and closer. It did not look like an especially clean place. Life was so much more complicated and dirtier than he had ever imagined.

"Relax, you're fightin' me," Jesse said.

"Okay," Pyg said without conviction.

He had always wanted to see what girls had between their legs, but now he realized: He hadn't wanted to see it quite this near. She peed out of there. He thought he smelled urine. No, it was just his imagination. Or was it? He felt his neck stiffening again.

"Relax, you won't catch nothin'."

How reassuring. Pyg closed his eyes and, oh, no, dove nose first into the teeming vines. He smelled or imagined that he smelled all sorts of odors. Piss? Damp hair? Beans? Horse? Mackerel?

"Don't just sniff," Jesse whispered sweetly. "Get to work."

Pyg really had no idea what work she expected him to do. He told himself he would have been happy to suck her as she had sucked him, but she didn't have anything to suck.

"What?" he asked, getting hair in his mouth.

"My God, you really 'n' truly are a baby," said the Harvey Girl. "Your mama never told you about nothin' like this here, did she?"

"Don't talk about my—"

"I was nice to you. Be nice to me. Taste me."

Pyg cautiously put out his tongue—half expecting something to bite it. When he tasted something dark and salty, he felt his stomach constricting. This was sex? This was what he had waited for all his life? All he wanted to do was throw up.

"Yes," whispered the Harvey Girl, and she started moaning softly.

Something hot and unpleasant was rising from his stomach and forcing its way up into his throat. He tried to clamp his throat tightly closed. Then he couldn't breathe.

"Don't stop," Jesse gasped.

Taking a breath, Pyg felt the lava in his throat rise higher. He tasted salt and vomit. He desperately tried to hold it down.

"Yes, yes." And she moaned louder.

No, no, Pyg told himself. Don't do it. Hold on. Don't embarrass yourself. Think of Little Dogie screaming with laughter. Imagine him telling the story far and wide. Please, please, please, don't do it!

"How could you do that!" Jesse yelled. "How could you do it to *me!*" Now she would wake up everybody. Now they would all know. Now they would laugh at him. Especially Little Dogie, who had probably tried to kill him. Of course, there was one person who wasn't laughing: Jesse.

"It was an accident," Pyg said lamely. "Shhh."

"I hate you!" Jesse shouted.

"I didn't mean to."

He felt sick with embarrassment and shame—and still sick to his stomach at the same time.

"Go to hell!" she told him. "I'll never forgive you for this."

"I'm sorry."

"What's wrong with you?"

"I guess I'm sick."

"I made you sick. How do you think that makes me feel? I'll never ever forgive you. Never ever."

"You already said that."

"Shut up!"

Now Pyg heard the cowboys coming noisily awake. Why did she have to shout? This was bad enough without getting the whole posse mixed up in it.

"Yeah, shut up!" yelled Little Dogie, his voice big in spite of the distance. "Or I'm gonna shut you up."

"*Caramba!*" swore Vaquero. "*Madre de Dios!*"

"*ЧЕРТ ВОЗЬМИ!*" bellowed Ivan the Terrible.

"Writers!" groaned Custer.

"What's wrong?" called Too Short.

Pyg flopped on his back and stared up at the cold, accusing stars. He wanted to drown himself in the Big Dipper. He could hear cowboys crawling grumpily from their bedrolls. They would be here soon and his life would be over.

"If you tell anybody what happened," Jesse hissed, "I'll kill you. I mean it."

Pyg saw her small Derringer in her hand. Where had that come from? He thought he had had his hands all over her.

"If you tell anybody," Pyg said, "I'll kill you, too. I'll kill you dead and dead some more."

"Shut up."

Pyg watched the Harvey Girl stand up and brush off the filth. He wondered if he would ever see her naked again, and he felt an irreparable sense of loss. She pulled on her pants. He got awkwardly to his feet and pulled up his.

"Wipe your mouth," Jesse ordered coldly.

While he cleaned his face, she took off running back toward camp. He went after her, but he walked. He was in no hurry. Not anymore.

When the tardy Pyg reached the others, they were all laughing. He wondered what sort of tale Jesse had spun them. He was pretty sure it didn't make him look like a hero.

"Still ain't popped your cherry, huh, Baby Boy," Little Dogie said.

Knowing he was making a big mistake, Pyg took a swing at the giant's smart mouth. The blow glanced off the big man's smile. Little Dogie threw one punch. Pyg dodged so it didn't knock his head off. It only broke his clavicle. He fell hard on his back and looked up at the unsympathetic stars. Pyg thought he could get up again, but when he tried, an unbearable pain ground in his shoulder. He collapsed once more. Now he stared up at Jesse's eyes, which were just as uncaring as the stars.

"Git up," Little Dogie ordered.

"I can't," Pyg admitted. "I, uh, think something might be broken."

"What're you made outta?" the giant taunted. "Glass?"

"No, crystal," said Jesse.

Oh, great, thought Pyg. He felt as if he were indeed made out of glass and the broken pieces inside were grating against each other. Wanting to run away, to hide, he did the best he could: He tried to roll onto his stomach, but it was too painful.

"Oww," Pyg moaned in spite of himself. "My shoulder."

Too Short approached, bent over, and gently touched the shoulder.

"Oww," Pyg repeated.

"Custer, you better come take a look at him," Too Short said.

Once again, the Comanche cowboy was called upon to play medicine man. He squatted and studied his patient in the dark light. Then he touched the injured shoulder very very gently.

"Oh," Pyg complained.

"Sorry," Custer said.

The Indian's slender fingers played over Pyg's bones as if they were a musical instrument. He played very very softly.

"Oh, oh, oh, oh," said Pyg.

Custer leaned back on his heels.

"How bad?" asked Too Short.

"Busted collarbone," said Custer.

"Pyg, you're as accident-prone as a sword swallower with hiccups," said Opry dryly.

As the boy groaned inwardly, he saw all the cowboys and the one cowgirl come and stand in a circle around him. Their motive seemed more curiosity than sympathy.

"I wouldn't move him tonight," Custer said. "Somebody fetch his roll."

Tin Soldier hurried off to get Pyg's blanket. Then he spread it over the patient without moving him.

"Git some sleep," Too Short told them all.

The cowboys headed back to their bedrolls.

"Custer, ain't you gonna set the bone?" asked Jesse, slightly more sympathetic now. "You cain't just turn your back on him and do nothin'."

"Thass just what I'm gonna do," Custer said.

"How come?" she asked. "You're his friend. Sorta."

"'Cause our people, we got a sayin' 'bout broke collarbones: If'n the two ends're in the same tepee, they'll find each other and grow back together."

"Sure," said the Harvey Girl.

Pyg was also troubled by the lack of activity on his behalf. He was fairly sure broken bones were supposed to be set and casts applied. Back in Boston, he had signed the casts of school friends who had broken various limbs. Maybe the latest in medical practices had not yet reached this frontier. Perhaps this Stone Age medicine man had missed more than a few classes at Harvard Medical School. What if Pyg were maimed for life—out of ignorance—out here in the uneducated West?

"You keep away from him tonight," Too Short told Jesse. "We're goin' home in the mornin'. This here manhunt is done over."

"No," said Pyg.

Despite his protest, he knew that he needed—much as he didn't want—to return to the ranch. He had to have time to heal. And he had a question he was eventually going to have to ask his mother. Was she a slut?

CHAPTER 35

Loving was too sick to fuck, but he did what he could. He lay with his head between Revelie's legs. She realized all over again how good he was at this sort of work. She yelled, she screamed, she howled out all her demons. For the moment at least. When she finished thrashing, she took him in her arms and held him to her breast.

"Ouch," Loving muttered.

"I'm sorry," Revelie apologized.

He squirmed in her arms, trying to find a more comfortable position, not having much luck. It was a hot afternoon and their bodies were sticky. They lay naked without covers. She tenderly touched his neck.

"Ouch."

"I'm sorry."

"Reminds me of somethin' my daddy once told me. Funny, he never talked about bed until he got old. Then somethin' opened up and he did."

"You really talked about that sort of thing with your father?"

"Yes, ma'am. But like I say, not till he got real old. Him and Mama, too. One day he up and tells me they was goin' at it last night. And it went like this here: He'd say, 'Ouch, my knee hurts.' And then she'd say, 'Ouch, my neck hurts.' And he'd say, 'Move a little. My arm's done gone to sleep.' And she'd say, 'My leg's asleep.' And finally they'd both get exhausted and just pass out."

"Oh, that's such a sad story."

"Wait. The next morning, accordin' to Daddy, they both woke up with smiles on their faces like it was Christmas mornin'. And they looked into each other's damn eyes. And they said, 'Waddn't we great last night!'"

"I love you."

"Ouch."

Revelie and Loving were soon dozing. She dreamed a wet dream.

When they woke up an hour or so later, they smiled at each other.
"Weren't we great this afternoon!" Revelie said.

"Yeah," Loving said, "Waddn't we?"

They savored their triumph for several minutes in silence. Revelie told herself to get up and do something useful. Clean up around the place or find a cure for Texas fever. Help out. But she didn't move. It was too hot to move and she was too languid from sex. Beginning to doze off again, she thought she heard voices. Who could it be? Was Coffee talking to himself?

"What's that?" Revelie asked. "Did you hear something?"

"Sounds like the posse done come on home," Loving said casually. "Wonder if they found that there damn ax."

"Oh, no!" she said.

"Don't worry," he said. "I figure that ax is gone fer good."

But Revelie was worried about more than the ax. At the moment, she had a more pressing concern. Jumping out of bed, the beautiful naked woman started racing around the room picking up her clothes. She heard footsteps in the hall. They were light steps that she knew well. No, no, no, no.

"Mumsy!" a familiar voice called out.

The door was closed but not locked. It didn't have a lock. Would he knock? Or would he walk right in? Looking around desperately, she wondered: Had she picked up all her clothes? Where could she hide? Her son stopped and knocked on the door. His mother was glad he was being so polite but wondered why. What did he imagine? What suspect?

"Mumsy," Percy said through the door, "I've got something to show you."

As she scrambled—like a surprised insect looking for a dark place to hide—she was tormented by questions: Where could she run to? What had he found? Had he located the ax after all? Of course, she reminded herself, if he walked in right now, it wouldn't matter much. He wouldn't need the ax to tell him that his mother loved Loving, had loved him, maybe always would love him. And he was old enough to draw his own conclusions.

"Mother!" Percy said louder.

Like a despised roach, Revelie Goodnight scooted under the bed.

"Mother, are you in there?"

She withdrew deeper into under-bed darkness. Revelie felt like dough trapped in a waffle iron. Loving and the bedsprings pressed down from above while the floor seemed to press up from below. Meanwhile, she was exploding from the inside. She could feel Loving up there straightening the bed in which he lay.

"No, she ain't," Loving drawled in what sounded like a pretend sleepy voice. "Come on in."

Hearing the door open, Revelie watched as her son's feet entered the room. She couldn't help noticing that his boots were dusty and scuffed. The bottoms of his chaps were filthy. She had to make a conscious effort to restrain herself from telling him so.

"I'm sorry," Percy said. "I was looking for my mother."

"Ain't seen hide nor hair of her this afternoon," Loving said. "Say, Percy, what happened to you?"

Now Revelie was doubly torn: She wanted to see her son—to discover what was wrong with him—but of course she didn't want *him* to see *her.*

"Just a little scrape," said the boy. "Uh, would you mind not calling me 'Percy' anymore? I've got a nickname now. 'Pyg.'"

Oh, no, thought Revelie. What is he talking about? What has that young woman done to him?

"Pig?" asked Loving. "Like you love mud?"

His mother could see by his chaps and boots that the nickname was apt, but she still hated it. She promised herself that she would never call her son *Pig.*

"Sounds like 'Pig,'" the boy admitted. "But I spell it with a 'y.'"

"Well, Pyg, what happened to your shoulder?" Loving asked.

"Broke my collarbone. Hurts when I move it. That's what the sling's for."

Revelie longed to see her boy, to gently examine his injury, to nurse him, but she stayed put in the waffle iron. She felt the bed's sagging springs imprinting their pattern on her body.

"How'd it happen?"

"Horse kicked me."

"Sorry. I dunno where your mama is. She's gittin' more and more independent ever' day. Won't listen to me. Goes off wherever she likes. Even if'n it's dangerous."

Under the bed, Revelie wanted to punch Loving through the mattress. She imagined herself giving him a good poke in a kidney. The idea so ticked her that she started to laugh and had to fight down the impulse. She tried to concentrate on how uncomfortable she was. It was even hotter under the bed than it was on top of it. She was a cooking waffle.

"Dangerous?" asked Percy.

"She likes to go off and pester the poor sick cows. Prob'ly where she is now. See if'n you cain't break her of that habit. No tellin' what she might catch."

"But Coffee said she was in here."

"Coffee's got beans fer brains and naps in the afternoon."

"Should I be worried about her?"

CHAPTER 36

Pyg felt useless. In his condition, there was only one job on the ranch he was fit for: getting better. He sat in the big living room concentrating on growing his bones back together. He wished he could be out riding with the cowboys, catching up on chores long left undone, making repairs, fixing up, checking the herd. Instead, he sat in the house trying to visualize his bones knitting together—and wondering about his mother and Loving. Perhaps he should just head back home where Harvard awaited him. School would be starting in less than a month.

"What are you thinking about?" Revelie asked, entering the room.

"Nothing," Pyg said.

"You look like you're in pain," his mother said. "Does it hurt?"

"Not unless I move it."

"That mean old horse."

"What?"

"That mean horse that kicked you."

"Oh, yes. He was a mean one all right."

They lapsed into a silence, which was nothing unusual. But it was an uncomfortable silence, which was new. Pyg told himself that he should just ask her. Get it over with. But how should he put it? He couldn't just inquire of his mumsy: Are you a loose woman? He wanted to ask, but he didn't want to accuse. He puzzled over how to put an impolite question politely. He searched for an appropriate vocabulary and couldn't find it. He wanted to ask but he wasn't sure he wanted to know the answer.

"What's the matter?" she asked.

"Nothing," he lied.

Hearing somebody in a hurry, Pyg looked at the door just as it sprang open. The Harvey Girl was out of breath.

"We got trouble!" Jesse said.

"We?" asked Revelie.

"What?" asked Pyg.

"Somebody's been shootin' cows," Jesse said. "We found a dozen so far just this mornin'."

Pyg heard more people coming, bad-news reinforcements. Soon Too Short entered, followed by Tin Soldier and Custer.

"What is going on?" asked Revelie.

"Somebody's been usin' our cows fer target practice," Too Short said.

"Why?" asked Pyg.

"Meanness," said Jesse.

"Prob'ly," said Too Short, "but some of 'em was sick. Looked like anyhow. Fever more'n likely. Harder to tell after they're dead, but they looked pretty bad. Starved. Ugly."

Pyg noticed a new look on his mother's face: She was serious but animated. It was a strangely attractive expression. She was engaged.

"Do you believe," Revelie asked, "they were shot *because* they were sick?"

"Could be," Too Short said.

"Perhaps someone wanted to put them out of their misery," she said. "Or perhaps somebody is attempting to cure the epidemic by exterminating the infected animals." She smiled unexpectedly. "A bullet makes an interesting pill, doesn't it?"

Pyg couldn't help being impressed by his mother's dispassionate grasp of the situation.

"Could be," Too Short repeated.

"Do you have any idea who the executioner could be?" Revelie asked.

Too Short nodded at Custer.

"I done looked for tracks," said the ranch's most gifted tracker. "Found some, too. Low heels. Clodhopper tracks."

"Really," said Revelie, but she didn't seem surprised. "So you suspect our friends the nesters, do you?"

They were all looking at her, differently.

CHAPTER 37

"This is a damned godsend," said Old Will Lee. "Gives us an excuse to wipe out the nesters once and fer all."

"Will, hold your horses," said Loving, who was propped up in bed. "You're always wantin' to wipe somethin' out. Who elected you Gawd anyhow?"

"Nobody, but a buncha people done elected me president of this dad-blamed outfit. Mebbe you don't like it much, but they did."

The Panhandle Cattlemen's Association—originally founded by Jimmy Goodnight—was holding an emergency meeting in Loving's sickroom. The group normally met in Tascosa, but the best cowboy in these parts could no longer fork a horse, so the others came to him. There was Jim Cator of the Diamond K. Jim Evans of the Spade Ranch. Jules Gunter of the T-Anchor. John Dunhill, Jr., of the Matador. Members of the rising generation were also present. There was young Jim Bob Hays, who had taken over the Springer Ranch after the death of his father in a blizzard last winter. And there sat Little Reb Dunhill, whose father had survived Shiloh only to fall in the same gunfight that claimed the life of Jimmy Goodnight. The newest member of the group was, of course, Percy, who felt foolish wearing his arm in a sling.

"Loving, you sound like another damned Goodnight," Will sputtered. "What's wrong with this here ranch? Turns all the men into women."

Listening in the hallway, just out of sight, *the* woman of the Home Ranch was incensed. How dare Will Lee call her cowboys women! And what was wrong with being a woman anyway! She knew her thinking was contradictory, but she didn't bother to sort it out. She contented herself with simply hating Will Lee, who had been her late husband's rival and enemy. She knew Lee bore her no love either. When she had broken out of jail—on the night before she was to have been hanged—

there had been a gunfight and a couple of Lee's men had been killed. Well, she hadn't shot them. They probably shot each other while they were trying to shoot her. But she didn't want to have that argument now. Bearing his grudges, Will Lee would probably try to arrest her if he knew she was back in Texas. So she stayed out of sight.

Revelie was proud of the way Loving was resisting Lee's baiting. She only hoped he could keep it up. In his weakened condition, he was more vulnerable than ever to verbal assaults on his manhood. But he knew she was listening, and she knew he wanted to please her, so she had faith he would say what she wanted him to say. They had gone over the script for this meeting carefully before the others arrived and she disappeared. Since she had to remain invisible, he had agreed to put her plan forward for her. Revelie felt a twinge of guilt: Was she unmanning her man?

"Less be civil," Loving said in a tired voice. "The real enemy here ain't the nesters. The real enemy's the fever. So we oughta—"

"Fevers come and go," Lee said, "but if'n we don't git ridda these nesters, they're gonna be here forever. They're chokin' us out."

Hidden in the hallway, Revelie kept wishing her son would speak up, defy this Will Lee, turn the tide of the argument. But so far she had not heard his voice even once.

"This country ain't no good for farmin'," Loving said. "Even them dumb clodhoppers're gonna figure that out one a these days and go on home."

"You're dreamin'," said Lee. "I say we gotta—"

"Shut up and let me say my piece."

Good, Revelie thought. Shout him down. Tell him the plan. Shifting her weight, she heard the floor squeak. Did anyone else hear? Were they looking her way? She heard moving around inside the room and started to flee, but she couldn't make herself go.

"Let Loving talk," said Little Reb Dunhill. "Will, you ain't God and you ain't General Lee, so just pipe down fer a minute."

Lee glared.

"Thanks, Li'l Reb," said Loving. "We all know where this here fever comes from. Them ranches down on the Rio Grande. They drives their cows through here and our cows git sick and die. So mebbe they shouldn't oughta come this way no more."

"What?" asked Lee.

Listening, Revelie mouthed the word "quarantine," but Loving didn't say it. Perhaps it was too much of a mouthful for a cowboy. As she had explained to him, she had gotten the idea because she had grown up in the port city of Boston. When ships arrived with some-one—or something—sick onboard, they weren't allowed to dock and unload. They were quarantined. Why wouldn't the same concept work here?

"It's like when a ship comes along fulla sick folks," Loving told the ranchers. "They don't let 'em off the damn boat. What's that two-bit word?"

"Quarantine," said Percy, making his mother proud.

"Yeah, they do that to 'em. See?"

"No, I don't see," said Lee. "I ain't never seen a ship in my whole damn life. Whadda I care about ships? I don't give a damn about no ships."

"They ain't no ships 'round here," said Loving, "but they is cattle drives. And they's like sick ships. Why don't we just tell 'em no, thanks, keep out?"

"Could lead to a disagreement. What if they didn't wanna keep out?"

"We'd make 'em."

"I don't like it."

"Now who's soundin' like a nervous girl?"

While the argument went on and on, Pyg squirmed on his cane-bottomed chair. He kept wanting to do more—to ride to the rescue of the embattled Loving—but he kept hesitating. He would be about to say something when he would suddenly change his mind. Or he would open his mouth when somebody else would butt in ahead of him. He felt more and more like an eternal boy and less and less like a cowboy.

"What you're suggestin' would mean puttin' out a picket line a hundred miles long," said Little Reb Dunhill, sounding very much like his dad. "Mebbe more. How else you gonna keep out all them there southern cows?"

"But—" said Pyg.

"We could do that," said Loving, "but we'd hafta work together."

"I dunno," said Little Reb. "You're li'ble to start another civil war. An' lemme tell you, one's enough."

"B—" Pyg began.

"That's right," Will Lee interrupted. "Southern ranchers against northern ranchers. We'd have ranchers fightin' ranchers when the real enemy's them damn nesters. Thass just crazy as all git out."

"B—"

"Less vote," interrupted Lee. "We done talked this thing to death."

"Yeah, second the motion," said weathered old Jim Cator of the Diamond K, mumbling through his long moustache. "I got work to do."

"B—"

"All in favor of startin' another damn civil war, say so," Lee said.

"You cain't say it that way," Loving protested.

"I'll count that as a vote in favor of a range war. Thass one. Anybody else?"

"But you aren't being fair," Pyg said at last.

"Thass two. You lose. Meetin's over. Less go."

After the ranchers had left, Pyg sat alone in the bedroom with Loving. He couldn't help studying the wounded man suspiciously. Why had he so readily agreed to put forward his mother's plan? Was it because he thought her idea would work? Or was it rather because they had a past together? Had they made love? Had they been in love? Were they still? Was—?

"How are you?" Revelie asked Loving as she entered the room. "Are you tired? Could I get you something?"

Pyg felt as if he weren't even in the room. His mother had not noticed him at all.

"I'm fine," said Loving. "I don't need nothin' 'cept a new head." He smiled wearily. "Sorry I let you down."

"No, you didn't," Revelie said with forced cheerfulness.

"Guess I didn't explain it too good."

"They just didn't want to listen. They're fools."

Pyg watched his mother walk over and sit down on the bed next to the propped-up Loving. She leaned toward him and smiled at him warmly. Her hand crept across the covers toward the cowboy's. Were they going to hold hands right there in front of him? Had she really forgotten all about her son? But then her hand stopped, hesitated, and retreated a few inches. Pyg was relieved.

"Thanks for your help, Percy," Revelie said.

So she had remembered him at last, but was she making fun of him. He hadn't done anything.

"But—" he began.

"But they didn't understand. They didn't want to understand. I wish I could have talked to them, but I don't suppose they would have listened to a woman. Oh, well."

Revelie stood up and paced up and down the room.

"Don't worry," she said at last. "I have another idea."

"What?" Loving asked wearily.

"Nesters—"

"No."

Pyg watched as his mother walked back over and sat down on the bed. Her son wondered if she intended to use her woman's tricks to help persuade her "lover." Was Loving really guilty of such a name? Was she? Was Pyg being fair to his mumsy? He shook his head and wished he could stop asking questions. He wanted his innocence back. His and his mother's, too.

"Well, if the ranchers won't help us with our quarantine," Revelie said in her I'm-being-reasonable voice, "maybe the nesters will."

"No," Loving repeated.

Pyg felt himself siding with the wounded cowboy, but he wasn't sure why. Was he being disloyal to his mother? Well, it served her right. She hadn't always been loyal, had she? He told himself firmly: Shut up!

"Everyone seems to agree," his mother said, "the nesters have more to lose from this fever than the ranchers do. That's because they have so little. So why wouldn't they be willing to help us fight the fever?"

"That'd be like a dog tryin' to organized a buncha cats," Loving said weakly. "Dogs and cats is natural enemies. Ranchers and nesters is, too. Fergit it." Then he added: "Please."

Revelie touched Loving's hand. Pyg flinched. His mother noticed and her hand retreated but remained in the neighborhood. Then she turned a blazing smile on her son.

"Percy, what do you think? You'll help your old mother, won't you?"

"I don't know," Pyg mumbled. "I don't really understand."

"It's simple. We don't have enough cowboys to patrol a vast area, so we need help. For their own selfish reasons, the other ranchers won't help us staff our checkpoints. So who else is there? Who else might help? Why not ask the nesters, who would be highly motivated defenders of this country? The worst that could happen is that they would say 'no, thank you.'"

"No," said Loving, "the worst that could happen is the Texas Rangers could ride in here and arrest you."

"Be quiet," hissed Revelie.

"What for?" asked Pyg. He actually pointed at his mother, defying the gods of politeness. "Why would they arrest you?"

"Because—" began Loving.

"Don't say another word," ordered Revelie. "This discussion is over. Percy, I'm going to change his bandage. Please leave us for a moment."

Pyg hesitated. He studied Loving's impassive face and Revelie's determined expression. Then the boy obeyed his mother: He got up and walked out of the room. Outside in the hallway, Pyg felt sorry for Loving, who was certainly being scolded about something. But what exactly?

Chapter 38

Revelie welcomed the box-headed Cozby boys back into her vast living room. They were the first. Soon other nesters began to arrive, their lace-up boots loud on the front porch steps. Farmers walked more heavily than cowboys, as if weighed down by their tribulations. The great hall was filling up. Coffee and Jesse passed through the crowd offering cups of coffee. The clodhoppers looked around suspiciously, jealously, even grudgingly at the grandeur. Revelie felt a little like a queen surveying her subjects, but she was all too aware that she couldn't issue any orders this evening. Since she couldn't command them, she would have to convince them, which wasn't going to be easy, judging by the look of them.

"Thank you all for coming," Revelie raised her voice. "Why don't you all try to find seats and we'll get started."

The milling mob began to look for places to come to rest. Some found comfortable seats on the room's two couches. A few collapsed into overstuffed armchairs. Others lowered themselves onto mismatched chairs and stools collected from all over the house. The least fortunate wound up on benches carried in from the cook shack. When the commotion finally quieted down, Revelie found some thirty men and big boys staring at her with undisguised hostility. Standing before them, she felt like a despised schoolmarm about to address a very unwilling class.

Needing the support of a friendly face, the mother searched for her son, finding him at the very back, sitting on the floor, leaning back against the wall. What was he doing way back there? A few feet away from him, Jesse, too, sat on the floor. Revelie watched for any interaction between the two young ones, but didn't see any, thankfully. Too Short, the only cowboy present, squatted at the back. Revelie had her enemies in her face and her friends far away. Loving was hiding in his room, taking cover behind his wounds, not up to taking part. Although her heart was still beating too fast, she told herself it was time to commence.

"Let me thank you once again for coming," said Revelie. "I know some of you have come a long way."

There was a collective grumbled response as if the room were clearing its throat.

"Welcome, neighbors," she said, "for that is what we are. Even though we haven't always acted neighborly toward each other."

The room cleared its throat again.

"Now we are faced with a crisis," said Revelie, feeling like a politician making a speech. It wasn't a good feeling, but wasn't entirely bad either. "Now our cattle are threatened by this fever. Now we must work together."

The room cleared its throat more loudly, more threateningly, this time. Revelie recoiled and trembled slightly. Was this the moment when someone would stand up and denounce her as an escaped murderer? Had she been foolish to call this public meeting?

"Please, just hear me out," Revelie raised her voice. "I have a proposal to make."

"It's a trick," interrupted Kenny Cozby, the youngest of the brothers. "Don't trust her."

"Please, let me explain my 'trick' before you call it a 'trick.'" She was warming to her work now. "Would that be all right with you?"

"Kenny, let her talk," said John Cozby, the oldest of the box heads. "Give her enough rope . . ."

"Thank you," Revelie said through a dry mouth. "You all know that this fever is carried by cattle herds driven up from the south."

The room tried to clear its throat but choked, coughed, and sputtered. Some of the nesters still clearly believed the ranchers had deliberately started the fever outbreak. They saw it not as a plague but as a plot.

"Nobody did this deliberately," she said. "At any rate I don't believe they did. But that's not the point. The point is that sick cattle from the south have spread this disease to our healthy herds. It seems to me that the solution is simple: Keep out the southern cows."

Revelie thought she saw Percy nodding agreement in the back of the room. Good, thank you. She could use all the support she could get, silent and distant as it might be.

"Just how you plannin' to do that?" asked John Cozby.

"With your help—and with firearms if necessary."

P yg was surprised: He couldn't believe that his mumsy was endorsing guns. The same guns that she had always hated with a religious fervor. What had happened to her? What had Loving done to her?

"It's a trick," Kenny Cozby yelled.

There was a hubbub. Raised voices. Even curses. Low-heeled boots stamping on the floor. They all sounded and looked ugly.

Pyg felt sorry for his mother. They were never going to listen to her: First of all, she was a woman. Second, she was a rancher. Third, she was an easterner. Didn't she know how hopeless it was? Why didn't she just give up? Didn't she see that she was becoming ridiculous? Wasn't she embarrassed? Then he felt ashamed for thinking these thoughts. She was his mother and therefore neither embarrassing nor ridiculous. She didn't need his doubts or his pity. She needed his help. He felt cowardly for hiding at the back of the room, but what could he do? He was just a kid. They wouldn't listen to a kid any more than they would listen to a woman.

Surprising himself, Pyg lurched awkwardly to his feet. Once he was moving, everything seemed a little easier. He could think more clearly. Slouching toward the front of the room, he decided what he would say to these rude nesters. His mother looked surprised to see him bearing down on her, but she smiled a welcome. He stopped beside her and stood facing the hostile mob.

"This is my son, Percy Goodnight," Revelie told the nesters. "He—"

"Pyg," he said. "Everybody calls me Pyg." He took a deep breath, which didn't help much. The room waited. "You're as bad as the ranchers," he said at last. "When we asked them to help, right here in this room, they acted just like you're actin' now. They said they wouldn't try because it might be dangerous." His heart was a barking dog in his chest. "They said somebody might get hurt." He took a break for another deep breath and heart bark. "They were scared." Another breath and bark. "They were cowards." Breath, bark. "Like you."

The room protested. Since they were all talking at once, Pyg couldn't tell what anybody was saying, but he still understood. They were telling him they didn't appreciate being called names. They were claiming they were as brave as the next man and braver than ranchers. They were threatening to show him with their fists just how brave they were. His plan was certainly going well so far.

"Of course, with the ranchers, it wasn't just because they were cowards," Pyg raised his voice above the others. "It was also because they were cunning. They told us straight out that they didn't want to keep out the fever because it was driving out the nesters. That's you."

Pyg listened to all of them talking at once. He waited until they began to quiet down.

"Now you're helping them with their plan. You're afraid to fight this sickness, and that's just what *they* want. You're scared and that's just what *they* expect."

Did he feel a little hypocritical emphasizing *they* when he was one of *them,* one of the biggest ranchers of them all? A little bit, but he would worry about it later.

"I'm tellin' you," Kenny Cozby said, "he's trying to trick you."

Well, he did have a point, but it was a good trick, wasn't it?

"Be quiet," said big brother John. "Let me think."

The eldest Cozby closed his eyes and lowered his head as if he were praying. Probably he was. All the other eyes in the room were wide open, watching him. The room grew quieter and quieter until it was as quiet as church. The praying man looked up.

"You asked the ranchers first?" asked John Cozby.

"Yes, yes," Revelie and Pyg answered at the same time.

"You ain't lyin' to us?"

"No, no."

"You swear before God almighty?"

"Yes, yes."

"Say it: You swear before almighty God."

Pyg looked at his mother, who smiled at him. He smiled, too.

"One at a time," said John Cozby.

The son nodded to his mumsy to go first.

"I'm telling you the truth. I swear before almighty God."

"Me, too. I swear before god almighty."

Pyg wasn't sure whether he believed in a big-G God or not, but he didn't mind using him/Him.

"We ain't afraid," said John Cozby. "Farmers ain't cowards. Who're you callin' cowards? Them there's fightin' words."

Pyg stopped being afraid and began to relax.

CHAPTER 39

"No," Revelie said.

"Mom, I'll be fine," Pyg said. "Don't worry. Somebody has to go to the meeting and I'm the logical choice."

They were all eating breakfast in the cook shack. Coffee flipped flapjacks as fast as he could and the Harvey Girl ferried them to the long table. She didn't look happy about her assignment.

"Too Short, you go with him," Revelie said.

"He's needed here," the boy said. "There's so much work to do with the quarantine and all–"

"Don't say 'and all.' That's just lazy sentence construction. That's–"

"Mother, I'm goin' alone"–he deliberately dropped the 'g'–"and that's all there is to it."

"He don't have to go by hisself," said Jesse. "I'll go with him."

"*No!*" said Revelie.

Pyg was lonely. Yes, it was definitely lonesome out here on the god-forsaken Staked Plains, but at least this flat earth was no longer a trackless plain. Thousands of trips to the distant town had finally worn a faint trace in hard land. All he had to do was follow the path. (What would Old Coronado have given for such a trail through this wilderness?) Yes, he could have used a little company, but he told himself that he had been right to come alone. With the quarantine to be organized, none of the cowboys could be spared, much less Too Short, the acting foreman. The boy informed himself he would be fine.

When he started this trip, Pyg had been in no hurry to reach his destination. He wasn't looking forward to the task that lay ahead of him, so didn't spur his gray horse Smoke. He took his time. But eventually

the journey developed an imperative of its own. He grew tired of riding. He was bored with the sameness of this flatland. He wanted to get
there. He was ready to get there. But would he ever get there? What if
he was following the wrong track? No, he was fine.

Pyg didn't entirely believe his own reassurances until he saw Tascosa rising like a flotilla in the distance. Ships rose sails first; the town
first showed its roofs, a reminder that the Staked Plains might be flat,
but the earth was still round.

His first stop was the McCormick Livery Stable, where he left
Smoke. Carrying his saddlebags over his shoulder, Pyg marched on
down Main Street to the Exchange Hotel, where he stabled himself.

He had been right and his mother had been wrong: He had managed fine all by himself.

P yg made a point of entering the big dining room of the Exchange a
few minutes late. By doing so, he hoped to avoid milling and chatting
with the other members of the Panhandle Cattlemen's Association. He
already knew that many of them considered him and his ranch to be trai-
tors. Some thought him little better than a nester himself, since his
Home Ranch had made a pact with the hated homesteaders.

They were all seated around the long table when he walked in. All
talking ceased. He stumbled, but then he regained his balance and continued to an empty seat near the bottom of the table. No one greeted
him. He smiled at them all, out of tension rather than friendliness. He
didn't notice anybody smiling back.

"You asked fer this here meetin'," Will Lee said accusingly. He
added curtly: "Whaddaya want?"

Surprised by the bluntness of the question, Pyg blurted: "A quarantine. I'm here to make one last appeal. I mean—"

"To help who?" Lee interrupted.

"All of us, everybody." Pyg realized he was turning a bullet over and
over with his fingers and thumb. He hoped he wouldn't drop it and
wished it were silver.

"Ever'body? Nesters, too?"

"It's in all of our interest."

"We was just talkin' 'bout that before you come in—late." Will Lee paused. "Mebbe you can answer us a question we been debatin': Whose damn side're you on?"

Pyg hadn't known the question would come so soon, but he had anticipated that some version of it would eventually be asked. And he had done his best to come up with an answer.

"We're on the side that's against the fever," he said in a barely audible voice. "I hope that means we're all on the same side, but I'm not sure. Please enlighten me."

"'Enlighten'?" said Lee. "You hear that, boys? Hear how he talks. Thinks he's too good fer the likes of us. Ain't he grand?"

Pyg got up and walked out of the room. He was alone again.

Returning to his hotel room, Pyg lay down on his hard single bed. He thought about taking off his boots, but that seemed too much trouble. He even kept his silver gun snug in its holster. It was too early to go to sleep but not too soon to rest his eyes. He wasn't comfortable on his back, so he turned onto his side. He kept asking himself what he could—what he should—have done differently and came up with dozens of possibilities. He was counting second thoughts instead of sheep.

When he woke up again, Pyg tugged out his pocket watch and could barely read it by the faint moonlight seeping through the window. It was a little after 10:00 P.M. He had slept for two hours. Should he get undressed and really go to bed? No, he didn't feel sleepy anymore. He wished he had something to read, but he hadn't brought anything. Pushing himself up into a sitting position, he ran his fingers through his hair. Why not visit the saloon?

Pyg lit the kerosene lamp by his bed. Then he poured water from a metal pitcher into a metal wash basin. He splashed his face and ran wet fingers through his hair. He looked in a small, pock-marked mirror and decided he was presentable. Blowing out the lamp, he got moving.

When he entered the Exchange Saloon, everybody seemed to turn and stare at him. He recognized several of the ranchers from the meeting. He shook his head before he realized he was doing so. At least Will Lee wasn't there. Thanks for small blessings. But, no, he had congratulated himself on his good fortune too soon. There was Lee toward the back of the big, noisy room. The bully actually tipped his hat to him and then fell to talking to a couple of his LS cowboys. Pyg felt a gust of ill will trying to blow him right back out the swinging doors. He wanted to retreat, but he was determined not to give Lee the satisfaction. Hunching his shoulders as if walking into a strong wind, the boy headed for the long bar.

"You drinkin'?" asked the bartender, whose red face suggested that he wasn't above hoisting several himself.

"Rye," Pyg said, trying to say it the way he had heard the Home Ranch cowboys order drinks.

He was afraid the bartender might say he was too young, but not at all. The red-faced man didn't seem to give a damn if the boy went to hell or not. He plunked down an empty shot glass and a half-full bottle of rye whiskey.

"Help yourself," said the bartender.

Pyg wished the man had poured the drink for him because his hands were trembling. He didn't want to spill rye whiskey in front of this hostile audience. His hand did shake, but he only spilled a couple of drops. Maybe they wouldn't notice. Sure. Then why were they laughing?

Coming in here had clearly been a mistake, but Pyg was determined not to run. He took a small sip of rye, his hand still unsteady, and tried not to make a face at the taste. They were laughing again. He decided to stare down the room, but soon gave up the idea. He stared at his drink instead. He took another sip but it didn't make him feel any braver. Now he wished he weren't so alone. Unable to stand the stares anymore, Pyg decided to down the rest of the drink in one gulp and go to bed. He took a deep breath, held his breath, and gulped the rest of the rye. Then he coughed. Now they really laughed.

Pyg put a coin on the bar and headed for the flapping doors. He wanted to hurry—to run—but managed to saunter. Rapidly. And there was Will Lee tipping his hat again, smiling broadly, but now he sat alone.

Outside in the fresh air, Pyg didn't feel much better. He decided to try to walk off his nerves and disappointment in himself. He turned left on Main Street and hiked toward the edge of town. He wanted to get away from everybody. He was tired of stares. He couldn't wait to be alone.

Walking beside the creek that forced Main Street to jog to the right, Pyg heard horses' hooves. He turned just in time to see the rope—striking like a snake—flying toward him. He had not been as alone as he had imagined.

CHAPTER 40

Pyg was a fish flopping at the end of a line. Dragged behind a running horse, he fought to free himself, but he was caught good. The rope cut into his ribs. He had trouble getting his breath. His mouth opened and closed, opened and closed, but he didn't have enough air to scream. He was a fish trying to scream under water. Main Street scraped and scratched and burned him. He was confused and angry and afraid his collarbone would separate again. He kicked helplessly and clawed uselessly. A clod of dirt hit him in the right eye, gravel pelted his cheeks, and dust filled his nose and mouth. He tasted mud and blood. The dragging horse opened its bowels and pulled Pyg through the shit. Then the boy heard the laughter, which hurt worse than the pain.

He tried to think, but his thoughts thrashed about like his flailing limbs. He couldn't get a grip on anything. What was happening to him? And why? Who wanted to hurt him? Then his mind did finally find something to hang on to: the memory of Will Lee tipping his hat. He could feel blood running down his face and hate flooding his brain.

Pyg felt like a calf on its way to a branding—or worse. Where were they taking him? What were they going to do to him when they got there? He tried to hunch into a fetal curl to protect future generations. He certainly didn't want to get his pecker dragged off before he ever managed to put it in anything more important than Jesse's mouth.

Still fighting the rope, he plowed his way past the blacksmith shop. As the horse speeded up at the edge of town, the pain got worse, and his struggles grew weaker. Most of the fight had been knocked out of him by the time they reached the river's edge.

Then Pyg saw the fire. As the flames came closer, the horse slowed down. Finally. Good. But on second thought, was it? He kept remembering what he had heard about what happened to male calves when they reached the fire.

P yg could smell a foul brew bubbling in the big cook pots. Tending to the cooking were a half dozen cowboys wearing flour sacks over their heads with eyes cut out. Over the sacks, they wore their cowboy hats. The effect was to make them look like life-sized, cloth-faced dolls. But these dolls weren't playing. They obviously had big plans.

"What are you going to do to me?" Pyg asked again.

"Shut up," said a cloth face.

"You'll find out soon enough," said an especially dirty cloth face.

Pyg was tied standing up to a slender cottonwood sapling perched on the river's edge. His hands had been pulled behind him and tied on the other side of the tree trunk. The severe angle made his shoulders hurt. A rope around his waist also bound him to the cottonwood. He squirmed but didn't expect it to do him any good. It didn't.

"What do you want?"

"Shut up!"

"You'll see."

That was what Pyg was afraid of. Surely they weren't going to cook and eat him, but what did they have in mind? He hated to admit it, even in the privacy of his own head, but his mumsy had been right. He should never have come alone. He clearly couldn't take care of himself. That hurt.

"What—?"

"Shut up!!"

The biggest cloth face walked up to him and stood there staring at him. Trying to be brave, Pyg stared back. The big man reached out, grabbed his shirt with both hands, and ripped it open, scattering buttons like tossed coins. Pyg gasped for air. The big cowboy proceeded to rip the shirt apart along the seams. He tore it to shreds and dropped the pieces at the boy's feet. The night was suddenly cool and he was afraid: Pyg could feel his nipples stiffen.

No! Big Cloth Face reached for the boy's belt and unfastened it. No! No! The cloth cowboy unbuttoned his jodhpurs and pulled them down to his ankles. Then Pyg's underwear slid down his goosebump legs. What was happening to him? Pyg bucked hard against the cottonwood tree. Was he about to be turned into a steer? He bucked harder and harder. He wanted his mumsy, but he was glad she couldn't see him now.

"I reckon he's ready," drawled the mouth behind the blank cloth. "Come on."

Staring moon-eyed, a terrified Pyg watched the steaming pots bearing down on him.

"You're so all-fired interested in what's gonna happen to you," said Big Cloth Face. "I reckon I'll just tell ya. You ever hear of tar-and-featherin', boy? Thass what we do to undesirables in these parts."

"Please," Pyg said. "What did I ever do to you?"

"This tar-and-feather thing, it's worse'n most folks figure. Can be anyhow. Many a weak heart's done give out, lemme tell ya. It's a real shock to the system, doncha know? And there's bad burns and infections. And here's the best part. Yore pecker ain't gonna be much good after it's been boiled in tar. Too bad. Young man like you. You ain't gonna be worth much to no kinda woman after this here."

"Please," Pyg said again, his voice trembling.

"Okay, boys. Git to it."

They poured the bubbling tar over his naked body. Pyg screamed and bucked and writhed and tried to pass out. None of it did any good. The tar spilled down over his face like lava. He closed his eyes just in time. His eyelids burned. His nose blistered. His lips were on fire. The rolling tar hurt everywhere but especially where his skin had been scraped raw from dragging. The unbearable burn slithered down his neck and rolled onto his chest. He thought the hairs on his chest would burst into flames. His nipples felt as if they were burning candles. The blood in his veins seemed to bubble. Just beneath the tar, his heart boiled. Why were they torturing him? What did they have against him? He didn't deserve this. It seemed so unfair.

"Fetch the next pot."

Pyg wanted to open his eyes to see what was happening, but he warned himself not to. If he got hot tar on his eyeballs, he might be blinded for life. Squeezing his eyelids tighter shut than ever, he listened hard: He heard appalling footsteps approaching.

Once again, the blind Pyg was baptized with hot tar. He could feel it burning down his arms, scalding over his belly, rolling slowly toward his manhood. He tried to buck off the tar, but it rode him tight, rode him hard.

"No!" he screamed and got hot tar in his mouth.

Pyg could feel his burned tongue swelling. He opened his mouth to scream again, but only managed to gurgle. He choked and coughed and tried not to swallow any tar. He attempted to spit out the black heat but no luck. More tar got in. He told himself he wouldn't try that again. Then he couldn't help trying to yell and ate another searing mouthful.

"How you like the taste?" The voice sounded like Dirty Face. "Hot enough fer ya?"

Pyg hated the laughter. He hated them all. He hated the hurt.

"Git another'n!" the voice ordered.

The terrible pain tickled its way down his pecker. The tar held his balls with burning hands. Pyg felt sure the warning had been correct. His sex life was over before it had started. An unendurable ache flowed from his crotch up into his stomach and down his legs. He tried to buck, but he had no strength. He was broken. He just hung there wanting to die.

"You don't fit in 'round here," a different voice muttered. "Why doncha just go on back where you belong."

Who was threatening him? Who hated him enough to do this to him? Again he remembered the tip of the hat. Pyg burned inside as well as out. Molten hatred sloshed about inside his blackened head. He was so furious he had to remind himself to breathe. The fury and the pain came together like two lava flows, each making the other hotter. Now he wanted to live because he wanted to strike back. He promised himself vengeance.

"Ready for some more?"

No!

A new load of lava was thrown directly onto his crotch. He felt the stab of unforgiving pain and couldn't bear it any longer. His lamp blew out and all was nothing.

CHAPTER 41

When he woke up, Pyg didn't hear anyone. He listened but only heard the wind in the cottonwood leaves above and the ripple of the river below. Were the others asleep? Or was he alone? Was he st-, st-, st—his mind stuttered—sterile? At least he wasn't tied any longer. He lay in a heap on the ground.

He was sore all over, some places worse than others, especially down there. He tried to open his eyes, but they were sealed shut by the tar. Did he dare risk moving? He waited. His burns ached and itched. He waited. He had to scratch. He waited. He scratched his nose. But it didn't do any good, not with his fingers covered with tar, not with his nose tar-coated, too.

Nobody shot him. Nobody said anything. Nobody snored. Maybe they had gone. He had to find out. With his tar-blackened hands, Pyg started clawing at his eyes. Then he paused to listen. Nothing. He clawed some more. His eyes were still welded shut. Maybe he was blind. He clawed so hard he was in danger of ripping an eye out. His eyelids strained to lift the heavy weight lying on top of them. He thought he saw a sliver of dim moonlight but wasn't sure. His clawing fingers blotted out the light. He kept digging until he could see dim dark shapes through painful eyes. He dug some more and saw not only tar but feathers. He was covered with feathers and looked stupid.

While he continued to excavate his eyes, Pyg tried to think: What should he do now? He told himself he had to change his appearance before the whole town started waking up and laughing at him. He hated being laughed at. Especially out here in this country. He wanted to be taken seriously out here. He wanted to help.

Maybe Pyg could find some way to scrub and scrape the tar off if he could somehow make it back into town, but he would probably have to hurry. What time was it anyway? Pyg awkwardly began gathering up the scraps of his clothing. He found his boots but couldn't put them on over the tar and feathers. He located his silver gun and holster hanging from a broken branch. He had been sure they had taken it, but evidently, whatever else they were, they weren't thieves. Or maybe they just didn't recognize the silver.

Carrying his burden, Pyg started limping back toward Tascosa. With every step he lost another feather. He left a Hansel-and-Gretel trail.

When he finally reached Main Street, Pyg staggered toward the horse trough in front of the Exchange Saloon. It would be his bathtub. He wasn't sure the tar would wash off, but he told himself he had to try. He dragged himself the last few exhausting yards and stared down into the dark, dirty water, but he was even dirtier. As he was climbing into the trough, he slipped and splashed down hard. He expected the water to be cold, but he could only feel it a couple of places that the tar had somehow missed. Several feathers floated on the surface. It felt good to be off his feet. He relaxed for a moment as if he were lazing in a warm bath back home in Boston.

Then he started washing. He managed to dislodge some feathers, but the tar clung tightly to his skin. He scrubbed harder. The tar stuck tighter. He couldn't give up. He scrubbed so hard he hurt his hide—as the cowboys would say—but didn't do any damage to the tar. There were more feathers floating in the trough, but he was just as black and sticky as he had ever been.

He could already hear people calling him by his new nickname: Tar Baby. Wouldn't Little Dogie love it? Wouldn't they all laugh until they hurt? And he would hurt, too.

Pyg saw a faint white line along the flat horizon. The light was coming. He had to do something and he had to do it now! He kept on scrubbing the tar while he scoured his brain for a better plan. What would take it off?

Kerosene! He should have thought of it sooner. But where could he find kerosene without exposing himself to townspeople and ridicule? Maybe he could locate a kerosene lantern in the livery stable. Now he had a plan. All he had to do was—

Oh, no! Pyg couldn't get out of the trough. He was stuck. The trough was wider at the top and narrower at the bottom, tapering down into a blunt "V." He was wedged into the bottom and the tar was stuck to the sides. He pushed as hard as he could, but he couldn't lift himself out of the water. He rested a moment. Then once again, he strained with all his might, with all his fear, with all his dread. He was still stuck. Pyg tried rocking back and forth. He made waves in the trough but nothing more. He twisted first one way and then the other. Nothing. He kicked as best he could. Nothing. He fought until he was tired beyond tired. Still nothing at all. He wanted to drown himself.

Trying to catch his breath, he imagined the whole town standing around him laughing. The line on the horizon grew brighter. In frustration, he started hitting his head on the side of the trough. Luckily the tar dulled the blows. Trapped, now he had time to do what he had been putting off: worry about whether he would ever be able to get it up again. And even if he could, would it do any good: Were his balls cooked to sterility? Mourning his lost children, he wished he could play with himself to see if he could at least get an erection, but the tar stopped him there, too. He even wondered: If his balls were now worthless, would he be man enough to wreak vengeance on his enemies?

He heard horses approaching, crunching down Main Street, and closed his eyes tight.

That was how they found him, taking his bath in the horse trough, naked except for a second skin of black tar. The horses wanted to drink, but the early-rising riders kept them back. Pyg just bowed his head and let the laughter wash over him. It hurt almost as much as the tar.

"What happened to you?" a cheerful voice asked. "Are you s'posed to be the Tar Baby or somethin'?"

Pyg didn't look up, didn't answer.

"He's hurt," said a deeper voice. "We better git him outta there. Come on."

"Not me. You touch him, you'll stick to him. Ain't you never heard the story of that there Tar Baby."

"I'll Tar-Baby you. Git down here and help me."

"I was just funnin', Papa."

Pyg peeked to see who these people were. He saw slouch hats. He saw lace-up boots. He saw nesters. But he didn't see any faces that he knew. The older man was probably in his forties. A black-and-white beard framed a red face. His son was about Pyg's own age, with shaggy brown hair and freckles.

"Who did this to you?" asked the father.

"Mmmm," mumbled Pyg, who still had tar in his mouth.

"We'll git you outta there in a jiffy. Fix you up. Come on, Alvin, you git the other side."

The older man took Pyg's right arm, the younger his left.

"One, two, three."

They both pulled, but Pyg didn't budge. Resting a moment, the nesters pulled free of the Tar Baby and stepped back. One of the horses edged forward and started drinking from the trough. The gelding stared at Pyg with a big, puzzled brown eye. When it raised its head, feathers stuck to its mouth. The nesters stepped forward to try again.

"One, two, three."

Pyg stayed stuck.

"We're gonna need more help," Papa said.

Oh, no, Pyg thought, don't get anyone else. Let's just keep this our secret. But the secret was already out. Pyg was horrified to hear more voices. Other early risers had noticed that something was amiss. Several laughed.

"This ain't no laughin' matter," said Papa. "Y'all git over here and help us git him outta this here tight spot."

The laughter subsided to chuckles and several gawkers hurried to help out. A shopkeeper in a white apron. The man who ran the livery stable. A big fellow who wore a blacksmith's leather apron. And two women! Oh, no, he was naked. His clothes lay in the dirt beside the trough. Get the women out of here.

"You there, try to fish out his feet," said Papa. "Alvin and I'll git this end."

The blacksmith reached into the dirty, feathery water and pulled up a foot. The shopkeeper dove in and located the other. The man from the livery stable grabbed hold of Pyg's left calf and a *woman* grabbed his right. She looked to be in her thirties and wore a flowered apron.

The other woman, younger and prettier, went behind him and reached under his armpits. Now the naked Pyg didn't know if he wanted to come up out of the dirty water or not.

"One, two, three."

Pyg popped up out of the water, making a great splash, soaking all the Good Samaritans. He felt completely exposed even though he had actually never been so covered up in his life.

"Now what?" asked a panting Alvin.

"He needs a doctor," said the older woman. "Jenny, go fetch Doctor Bob. Hurry up."

"Bring him in the store," said the man in the white apron. "We'll put him on the counter till Doc gits here."

"Hope he don't stick," said the older woman.

CHAPTER 42

"You can't go," his mother said. "Harvard will start classes in a couple of weeks. You should be packing right now."

"No, Mother," Pyg said, "school can wait. The quarantine can't."

"Percy, you can't drop out of school. Really, you can't. I understand how you feel, but your whole future is at stake, not just the lives of some cows."

They were in Loving's sickroom. Studying his mother, Pyg wondered how firm she was prepared to be. Unfortunately, she looked resolute.

"But it's my ranch," the boy said. "Mr. Goodnight left it to me." He had consciously not used the word *father*. "I have to defend it. Besides, the quarantine's your idea. You want it to work, don't you?"

She nodded. "Of course."

"Well, I can help make it work. I'll go to Harvard later."

He braced himself for a lecture.

"Do you promise?" was all she said.

"Of course," vowed a surprised Pyg. "Cross my heart. No, I swear on the Bible." He paused. "No, I swear on my mother's life."

He noticed a slight shudder and then a shrug.

"Don't make me regret this," his mother said. "I'll never forgive you—or myself—if you make me rue this day."

"I promise. I mean it. I do."

The room was silent for what seemed a long, long time.

"I hear you're pretty good with a handgun," Loving said at long last. "But for this here job you're gonna need a long gun. Need all the firepower you can git your hands on."

"I hate talk of guns." Revelie shuddered. "Remember, a gun didn't keep those men from doing that to him."

"If'n you feel that way, then mebbe you better go off and do some sewin' or somethin'," said the sick man. "Because we are gonna talk firearms." He paused. "But be careful and don't stick your finger with a needle. We don't want no senseless bloodshed."

"Don't worry. I won't stick myself because I'm not going. I suppose I can stand a little gun talk. Go ahead if you must."

Again his mother surprised him. She had been surprising him ever since he had come home burned all over by hot tar. She had been upset by his burns, but she hadn't lectured. Hadn't preached. Hadn't told him so. She just treated his injuries with vinegar and soda and lots of motherly sympathy. What was happening to her? He wondered if Loving was responsible for the change in her.

"I don't s'pose you picked up a rifle on your travels," asked the sick cowboy.

"No," Pyg said.

"Thass what I figured," Loving said. "We got some extras in that there."

He pointed to a cedar chest at the foot of his bed.

"That chest once held my trousseau," said Revelie.

"I'm afraid it's come down some in the world since then."

"It certainly has if it holds guns."

Pyg stepped closer and knelt in front of the chest. He smelled the cedar. Finding a key in the lock, he turned it. When he lifted the lid, the smell of cedar grew stronger. He saw a half dozen rifles arranged neatly on top of some old clothes.

"Ain't none of 'em silver," said Loving. "Sorry 'bout that. Figure you can make do with a workin' man's gun?"

"Those clothes—they look like mine," Revelie said.

She stared at Loving. He didn't say anything.

"Well, I reckon they are," he admitted at last.

"You kept them all this time?"

"More like I didn't throw 'em out."

"How—" she began but stopped.

This exchange made Pyg uneasy, so he got busy pulling guns out of his mom's old hope chest. There were five rifles.

"Put 'em on the bed," Loving said. "I sorta collect these things."

"Everybody needs a hobby," Revelie said, "but I can't say much for yours. And you put them in with my clothes."

Loving didn't say anything.

Pyg lined up the guns on the covers beside the sick cowboy. Loving touched them as if they were old friends whom he had missed during his sick days. He picked out one and handed it to the boy stock first. It was metal from beginning to end. Good thing it wasn't silver, Pyg thought, because he wouldn't be able to lift it. The steel stock reminded him of the air rifle he had fired on the Fourth of July, which now seemed a long time ago.

"Less start at the beginnin'," said Loving. "That there's the oldest. Called a Henry rifle. Forty-four caliber. It'll hold fifteen bullets plus another one in the chamber. It was sure a wonder when it first come along. White folks called it, 'The gun you load on Sunday and shoot all week.' The Injuns called it, 'The spirit gun of many shots.' Yore daddy done told me that one."

Lifting the rifle to his shoulder, Pyg noticed Loving and his mother exchanging a look. The boy sighted down the barrel.

"Feels good," said Pyg.

"Yeah, but I don't recommend it," Loving said. "It was good in its day, but there's better now. Gimme."

Pyg handed back the rifle and accepted another in its place. This one had a wooden stock and an octagonal barrel. Otherwise it looked much like the Henry.

"This here's a Winchester 66," Loving continued. "Called a Yellow Belly 'cause it's got a brass frame. It ain't silver, but it's the best we could do." He laughed alone. "Holds seventeen shots."

"What caliber?" asked Revelie, surprising the men in her life.

"Uses .44-caliber bullets with twenty-eight grains of powder. Packs a wallop but there's others what wallop worse."

"Then we want more wallop," she said.

Pyg stared at her, but she didn't seem to notice.

"I'm gittin' there," Loving said, handing the boy another rifle. "This here's the Winchester 73. Iron frame. It's a .44, too, but with forty grains of powder. Has a kick. Just holds sixteen bullets, but its lighter'n the other one."

Hefting it, Pyg couldn't tell the difference, but it felt less strange, since it had a round barrel.

"Is that the wallopiest?" asked Revelie.

"No, not hardly," said Loving, picking up another gun. "That'd be this one here, the Winchester 76 or Centennial Model. See, they call it that on accounta it come out on the country's hunnerth birthday. Now this fella's a .45 with seventy-five grains. Packs a real wallop and has a real kick. I wouldn't advise it for you, ma'am."

"Me? I never touch firearms."

"But your boy might like it."

Pyg had the impression that Loving was showing off for his mother. Demonstrating that he knew a few things about a few things. It seemed a strange courtship that revolved around something Mumsy detested.

"Pyg, look there on the barrel," Loving said. "Can you see what it says?"

"His name is Percy," Revelie said.

Pyg squinted at a line of small engraved letters.

"What does it say?" asked his mother.

"Looks like it says 'one of one thousand,'" the boy said with a shrug.

"What does that mean?" asked Revelie.

"I ain't exactly sure, to tell the truth," admitted Loving. "I reckon they tried real hard when they was makin' the first thousand, and then sorta slacked off after that. Anyhow them one-in-a-thousand ones cost more. That's all I know fer sure."

Laying down the 76, Pyg picked up a rifle with an extremely large barrel. The hole in the end was a big as his eye.

"What's this?" the boy asked.

"Winchester 85," Loving said. "Fifty caliber. And lemme tell you, it sure kicks. It'll knock you clear back two generations. But you won't need nothin' like that there less'n Goliath shows up on the other side."

Pyg naturally thought of using it on Little Dogie one of these days, but he kept the thought to himself.

"Which one would you recommend for *Percy*?" asked Revelie.

"Pyg, what one do you like?" asked Loving.

Not wanting to make a hasty decision, Pyg picked up each rifle in turn, checked their feel, their weight, how much he liked holding each one. The Winchester 73 felt the best in his hand, but he couldn't forget the small print on the 76. He held the 73 in his right hand and the 76 in his left. He raised one, then the other.

"Take the good one," said his mother.

"That's what I'm trying to do," Pyg said. "But which one's that? That's what I'm trying to decide."

"The one where they tried harder," his mother said.

Pyg couldn't believe his mumsy was actually recommending a gun to him. She hated guns. She despised guns. She had dreaded guns all his life. And here she was selecting one for him. The least he could do was listen to her.

"This one," Pyg said. "One in a thousand."

"Better practice some," said Loving. "I don't want you disappointin' my gun."

CHAPTER 43

Pyg noticed that all the cowboys rode with Winchesters while the nesters brought along all kinds of long guns. He recognized several old Henrys with their metal stocks. There was a gun called the Volcanic. There were .22-caliber rifles that wouldn't stop a charging wasp. There were shotguns of all gauges from irritating (410) to deadly (10). There were smoothbore Rebel muskets, left over from the Civil War, that fired tumbling bullets. And there were guns that no longer worked at all but still looked menacing. Carrying his one-in-a-thousand on his saddle, Pyg felt a little smug.

Like a large posse, thirty-four riders rode south from the Home Ranch headquarters. Working together, Revelie and Loving had mapped out where the line should be drawn across the plains: this far and no farther. She had wanted to come along, but had eventually been talked into staying behind. Her son figured his mother stayed back because she wanted to be near Loving. Well, he did need someone to nurse him. But was nursing the only reason she stayed? Pyg didn't know what to think or what to feel. Jesse had stayed back too, on orders from Revelie, but Pyg expected her to show up before too long anyway. He vowed not to break her nose this time.

As they jogged along, the cowboys talked to cowboys, the nesters to nesters. The cowboys talked about rain. The nesters talked about rain.

And leather-cuffed Opry sang a song:

> *"Old Bill was a puncher, and you'll all agree*
> *That a puncher's a man of low mentality."*

The farmers all laughed. Then a sodbuster, one whose name Pyg had forgotten, was moved to sing a song in reply. The singer was a young man, probably still in his twenties, with a red beard. He sang even worse than Opry:

> *"I don't need no brains,*
> *Don't come in when it rains,*
> *Clodhoppin's the life for me."*

Now all the cowboys laughed.

L ate in the afternoon, after they had ridden almost thirty miles, the posse halted in the middle of the trackless plain.

"We'll split up here," said Too Short. "Tin Soldier, you pick out ten farmers and head southeast. Opry, you pick ten more of 'em and ride due south. And—"

"You mean like choosin' up sides in a damn schoolyard?" asked the ever-suspicious Kenny Cozby. "This ain't no game."

"I know it ain't," Too Short said, "but we got three cattle trails to block, so we gotta divide up somehow. And I don't wanna draw straws, if that's okay with you. We're burnin' sun. Start pickin'. Opry, you go first."

"You mean I gotta just pick nesters?" asked the singing cowboy. "I cain't pick no punchers?"

"Thass right," said the littlest cowboy.

"How come?" asked Opry.

"Yeah, how come?" echoed Tin Soldier.

"Because you two are gonna be blockin' a coupla little ol' trails," Too Short explained impatiently. "I'm takin' mosta the cowboys with me 'cause we're gonna be shuttin' down the Goddamned Western Trail. The biggest, the busiest, and li'ble to be the meanest. Thass how come. We're gonna git more cows, so we're gonna need more cowboys. Okay?"

"Him," said Opry, pointing, picking a red-faced farm boy.

"That one," said Tin Soldier, pointing.

"You there."

"Thissun."

As if in a schoolyard, they chose the biggest first, the smallest last.

.   .   .

When the picking was done, Too Short spurred his horse and galloped off to the southwest. The others on his team hurried to catch up. Pyg counted a half dozen cowpokes and six sodbusters: Was this army big enough to shut down half a state?

Too Short's posse still hadn't reached its assigned trail when night fell suddenly as it did on the plains. They stopped to make camp. The cowboys made one campfire and squatted around it. The farmers made their own fire and squatted around it. The cowboys ate beans. The farmers ate beans.

In the night, Pyg kept expecting Jesse to show up. Over and over, he sensed her nearby, woke up with a start, but found no Harvey Girl. He wished she would stop disturbing his much-needed rest. Damn her.

When Pyg awoke in the morning, Jesse was sleeping beside him.

"So how come you showed up?" Little Dogie asked as he sipped his morning cowboy coffee. Boiled in a pot, it had grounds in every sip. "Was it 'cause you cain't stand bein' away from your boyfriend? Or 'cause you cain't stand bein' *with* his mama that he loves so much?"

"Little Dogie, it's 'cause your mama done begged me to come take care of you," Jesse said. "She said you ain't got enough brains to grease a needle. Or sense enough to come in when its rainin' bullets. So I done promised her I'd do what I could to protect her idiot child."

Late in the afternoon, Pyg's posse finally reached its destination, a water hole where northbound cattle drives stopped to let their cows drink their fill. It didn't look like much: just a depression in the plain that formed a small, shallow lake. The grass was higher around the water, which helped to mark the site. Otherwise it would have been almost invisible in the general flatness.

"Now we're agoin' to wait," said Too Short. "Check your weapons. Hobble your horses. And wait. Ain't nothin' else to do fer now."

"That's gonna be hard on us farmers," said Kenny Cozby, "because we don't know how to just sit on our asses. You cowboys better show us how it's done. I bet you're good at loafin'. Had lots of practice and all."

"Eat a prickly pear and die," said Little Dogie. "The only work your breed ever done is stealin' our damn cows."

"Shut up," said Pyg, surprising himself.

"You—" began Little Dogie.

"Shut up!" said Too Short. "Just nod your head if'n you hear me. Don't say nothin'. Nothin' atall. Unnerstand?"

Little Dogie nodded.

They waited three days. After careful study, Pyg decided that neither the farmers nor the cowboys were any good at doing nothing. To pass the time, the two camps argued with each other. There were literally two camps. The six cowboys—Pyg, Too Short, Custer, Vaquero, Ivan the Terrible, and Little Dogie—slept around one campfire. Along with one Harvey Girl. A half dozen nesters slumbered around their own fire. Neither camp posted a watch because they didn't believe three thousand cows could slip up on them.

On the third day, they saw a cloud of dust bearing down on them. Pyg was relieved to have something to do at last. He was excited, apprehensive, ready, not sure he was ready . . .

"Less go out to meet 'em," Too Short said. "Git up off your lazy asses and saddle up."

The nesters all looked at Kenny Cozby to see if they should obey cowboy orders. He nodded. Everybody saddled up.

"Now take it easy," Too Short said. "We ain't the cavalry and they ain't the Injuns."

"How." Custer laughed.

"We'll just ride up slow and peaceful and tell 'em the bad news."

As they cantered along, Pyg was determined not to bounce, and he was doing pretty well. He pretended his ass was nailed to the saddle and couldn't leave it even a quarter inch. His balls still got banged around, but not as much, or so he tried to convince himself. Tried hard. Tried gritting his teeth.

"Hippity hop," sang out Little Dogie. "There goes Peter Cottontail, hippity hoppin' down the cattle trail."

Jesse laughed.

Oh, hell, why did Pyg even try? Ouch.

. . .

When they got close—about twenty yards from the cowboy riding point—Too Short raised his hand.

"Hold up," said the little cowboy. "I'll go talk to him."

The others reined in while their leader trotted forward to meet the point rider. Pyg was glad for the rest. His balls were even gladder. They ached fiercely. He wanted to rub them. No, he mustn't. He had to rub them. No! His hand involuntarily moved to his crotch.

"How you doin'?" asked Jesse.

Pyg jumped. "Good," he blurted out too loud. His hand shot up to his hat.

"Just try to relax in the saddle," she said. "Like you're dancin'. You know how to dance, doncha?"

"Sure," he said too forcefully. He fiddled with his hat to keep himself from rubbing his balls.

"The horse is the boy and you're the girl. Up to a point, see? You let the horse lead. It moves. You go with it. Not that I'm callin' you a girl or nothing. Unnerstand what I'm talkin' about?"

"Sure," Pyg said again, hoping he wouldn't be a girl when this adventure was over.

"I'm sorry I laughed."

"I—" Pyg began but then couldn't decide what to say. Great, he couldn't ride and he couldn't talk. Not western anyway.

Jesse evidently sensed that Pyg wanted to change the subject. "What's gonna happen now?" she asked. "Looks like they're arguin', don't it?"

"Yeah," said Pyg, grateful for the change.

They both fell silent and watched Too Short and the point rider quarreling with their hands. The point man's hands flapped about more than Too Short's.

"Mebbe we shoulda waited till they watered their cows," Jesse said.

"You've got advice for everyone, don't you?" Pyg snapped.

"I'm sorry I laughed," she repeated.

"Never mind," he snapped again.

Too Short and the point rider parted company, galloping in opposite directions. As Pyg watched, the one got larger, the other smaller.

"He doesn't look happy," Pyg said.

"You oughta see the other guy," Jesse said. "Bet he looks worse."

Pyg felt himself frowning, too, because now they would probably be on the move again. His right hand dove in the direction of his crotch, but he caught it halfway and examined a button on his shirt.

Too Short rode frowning back into their midst.

"Turns out I know the point rider who's also the trail boss," said the little cowboy. "Name's Ransome. Some folks call him Rapid Ransome 'cause he ain't. Some call him Rabid Ransome 'cause he is sometimes. Today he's Rabid. I shoulda waited till he watered his cows. Be a lot calmer then."

Jesse smiled at Pyg.

"What're we s'posed to do now?" Little Dogie asked.

"Wait," said Too Short.

Happy to be seated on the ground, Pyg watched the thirsty cattle drinking their fill. They fought each other, butted each other, mounted each other, humped each other, all trying to crowd in at the same time. The cows wore a brand that looked like a cross between an "R" and a rocking chair: an "R" sitting on top of a curved rocker.

Pyg sat with the cowboys, who formed a small clump in the grass. A dozen yards away, the farmers made their own clump. The nesters, most of whom didn't have handguns, cradled rifles. Little Dogie had his long gun, too, balanced precariously on his knees. They all waited.

"Think they're gonna fight us?" Jesse whispered to Pyg.

"Do you mean you don't know?" he whispered back. "I thought you knew everything?"

"Yeah, they're gonna fight," she said.

Pyg's legs grew stiff and his ass started to hurt from sitting so long on the ground. How long were they going to wait? He shifted his weight from one cheek to the other, but it didn't help much. That cheek was tired, too. Before long, he shifted back. Then he forgot his discomfort because several Rocking-R cowboys were approaching. They all looked mean unhappy.

"Here they come," Too Short said.

He got to his feet. Slowly the other cowboys followed his lead. They groaned as they stood up. The Harvey Girl groaned, too. They were all stiff. Cowboys didn't belong on the ground. Leave the earth to the sodbusters. Pyg noticed that the farmers got up, too, but they didn't come any closer.

"Now what's this about this here trail bein' closed!" Ransome bellowed while he was still a dozen feet away.

He was a tall man, maybe six foot seven or eight, with a drooping black moustache. He was skinny as a rifle.

"We're tryin' to fight the fever," yelled Too Short. "Cows from the south bring it in, so we're keepin' southern cows out. That's all."

"That ain't all. That ain't all atall. What're we s'posed to do with our cows? Just shoot 'em?"

The Rocking-R gang kept coming.

"No, you can go around our range or just go on home. Whichever. Wait'll this fever blows over."

"How far around?"

"Hundred miles or so, but I suggest goin' home."

"A hundred miles! You been out in the sun too long."

Now Pyg could see a round scar just below his cheekbone. It was about the size of a bullet. He had obviously seen trouble before and didn't appear to be afraid of looking at it again. Pyg's hand moved to the heavy butt of his silver gun.

"We're serious about stoppin' this here fever," Too Short said calmly. "Gotta be. What we got here's a quarantine. Sorry."

The Rocking-R kept on coming.

"Sorry! Quarantine! What the hell're you talkin' about? You got any authority here?"

And coming.

"Whaddaya mean?"

"Are you the damn law? Lemme see your badges. Who says you can tell us what the hell to do?"

"We do."

And coming.

"Lemme get this straight. You ain't the law. We ain't breakin' no law. This ain't no official kinda quarantine. You're just talkin' outta your ass. You ain't got no authority atall. Git outta our way."

They came faster.

Pyg tried to stand a little taller, to look threatening, but he didn't feel very intimidating. He wished he were as imposing as Little Dogie, who took two steps forward.

"We got authority," said the giant. "This here." He held up his rifle. "This here's what you call a Winchester Quarantine."

The Rocking-R stopped coming.

CHAPTER 44

"We'll see about that," said the Rabid trail boss. "Lemme make you a promise: I ain't goin' around and I ain't goin' home."

"Lemme make *you* a promise," Too Short said. "If you try to drive your cows through here, you're personally gonna die. I don't mean to talk rough, but that's just a fact. Because we got a cowboy assigned to you personally. And he's the best damn shot you ever seed or you're ever gonna see."

"Sure."

"Show him, Pyg."

Caught by surprise, the boy didn't know what to do. How was he supposed to demonstrate his ability? What could he shoot? He looked around for an impressive target, but didn't see any on the griddle landscape.

"Go ahead, show him."

With a disgusted wave of his hand, the Rocking-R boss shook his head. He had heard enough and he wasn't impressed. When Ransome turned to go, the sun glinted off one of his spurs. Pyg found his target. Like a rattler striking, he pulled the silver gun and fired. The spur exploded and the rowel went spinning through the air like a tiny saw.

"I don't want to shoot anybody," Pyg complained after the Rocking-R bunch had departed.

"Mebbe you won't have to," Too Short said. "I figure you scared him off."

But Too Short was wrong this time. An hour or so later, the whole Rocking-R herd bore down on the quarantine line. The Rocking-R trail boss still rode point to prove he wasn't afraid.

"Damn," said Too Short.

"I don't want to kill him," Pyg said.

"It ain't fair," said Jesse. "He's just a boy."

"No, I'm not," the boy said.

"So now you wanna kill him?" she asked.

"No, but that doesn't mean . . ."

The herd kept coming. Their twelve thousand hooves stirred an ominous cloud. A terrible storm bore down on the quarantine line.

"I'm not going to shoot him," Pyg said.

"Shoot his hat off," said Too Short.

Pyg went to his gray horse and pulled his Winchester rifle, the one in a thousand, from its scabbard. He was glad he had taken Loving's advice and practiced with it before leaving "home." He had shot up targets for days, prickly pears, chinaberries high in trees, flies, and wasps. Returning to Too Short, the boy shrugged. The acting foreman nodded. Pyg raised the rifle.

"Use me," said Jesse. "I'll be your rifle rest. Put it on my shoulder."

The Harvey Girl took up a position directly in front of Pyg but facing away from him. He lowered the rifle onto her right shoulder. His target was still a couple of hundred yards away. A long way, a very long shot.

"Tell me when you're gonna shoot," Jesse said, "and I'll stop breathin'."

Pyg sighted down the barrel. Ransome's hat seemed to get bigger as he aimed at it. His vision always seemed to improve as he was about to shoot. Through the barrel of the rifle, he could feel Jesse breathing in and breathing out, her shoulder rising and falling.

"Now," Pyg said.

Jesse's shoulder stopped moving up and down. He held his breath too, gently squeezed the trigger, and was not too surprised to see the trail boss's hat fly off his head and land in the red dust. The nesters, standing a little way off, laughed.

"Nice shootin'," said Jesse, breathing again.

But the trail boss and his herd kept coming. Another cowboy dismounted and fetched his hat for him. Ransome put it back on his head and kicked his horse in the ribs. He seemed unimpressed and unafraid.

"Shoot off his horse's ear," Too Short said.

"I don't want to hurt his horse," Pyg whined.

"Then shoot *his* ear off."

"No, he never did anything to me."

"Then do like I tell you: Shoot the damn horse's ear."

"Use me," said Jesse.

Shaking his head, Pyg braced his rifle on her shoulder once again. Sighting down the barrel, he saw that this shot was going to be even harder than he had imagined. He would have to be careful to miss the rider when he shot the horse. He told himself he should be a man and defy Too Short, but he didn't have much practice at defiance. Besides, if he didn't frighten this man off, he was afraid he was really going to have to kill him. He took his time and let the man get a little closer.

"Now," Pyg said.

Jesse stopped breathing and he did, too. The whole world seemed to stand still and the air grew clearer. Hating himself, Pyg pulled the trigger. The horse flicked its right ear as if shooing off a fly, and blood spurted. Pyg hadn't shot the ear off—hadn't intended to—but he had punched a .45-caliber hole through it. He also missed the man. Pyg felt proud and bad at the same time.

The farmers didn't laugh this time. The trail boss kept coming. He was a hard man to frighten or impress. Pyg's shoulders sagged. He told himself he wasn't a killer even though he had killed.

"Kill his horse," said Too Short.

"No," said Pyg.

"Then kill *him*."

"No."

"You gotta stop him. He's the first. If he gets through, then we'll have a hell of a time stoppin' any of the other herds. But we stop him, word spreads."

"No."

"I'd shoot him myself, but I'd miss and kill a cow, and I don't wanna do that."

Jesse laughed, but Pyg didn't even smile. The trail boss and his herd kept coming. They were 150 yards away. Getting bigger. One hundred yards. Getting a lot dustier. Seventy-five yards. Getting smellier.

The trail boss reined his horse to a stop. Good. They were quitting. Ransome pulled his rifle from its scabbard. Not so good. He dismounted, stared at Pyg, sank down on one knee and braced his rifle on the other knee. Bad. He pointed it at Pyg.

"Git down!" Too Short ordered.

But he needn't have bothered. All the cowboys were already on their bellies in the red dirt, the farmers, too, as flat as the flat earth. Too Short dropped and Jesse flopped.

Pyg sank down on one knee like the man across from him. He, too, braced his rifle on his other knee. He had an arrogant, audacious idea. It wasn't really a plan because it was too unlikely, too impossible. It was just a notion. He knew he should be afraid, should be hurrying, but he wasn't, not really. Sighting down his one-in-a-thousand Winchester, he drew a bead on the black hole at the end of the other man's rifle. Looking down the barrel of an angry man's gun, he aimed down that barrel. The gun had a big mouth, maybe .50 caliber. It looked huge. As he stared at it, aimed at it, the big hole seemed to get bigger and bigger. His targets always seemed to behave that way when he really concentrated. It no longer looked like an impossible hit. Pyg squeezed the trigger.

Trail boss Ransome's .50-caliber buffalo gun exploded in his hands. It blew up like a bomb. His face was bleeding.

Too Short clapped Pyg on the shoulder again as they watched the Rocking-R herd grow smaller and smaller. The trail boss rode in the disappearing chuck wagon.

"It's better to be lucky than good," Jesse said. "That was some shot. Right down the barrel of his gun."

Evidently she believed what they all believed, that the boy had been shooting at the man instead of the gun. Nobody would try to shoot down the barrel of another man's gun. Nobody would be that conceited or foolish.

"Can I tell you a secret?" asked Pyg, his voice shaking. "Do you promise not to tell?"

"Sure."

"It wasn't luck."

CHAPTER 45

Too Short sent scouts out every day. They reported back that a couple of herds had decided to turn back on their own without challenging the Winchester Quarantine or its uncanny marksman. Pyg's hope of keeping his ability a secret wasn't working out. The news had spread. The keepers of the quarantine did so little business that the only danger they suffered was boredom.

Bored, Pyg went off riding by himself. Since everywhere he looked the landscape was the same, he used the sun as a compass to keep track of his direction. He had been warned over and over not to get lost. You could die of thirst out here while circling a water hole. He had been bored back at camp but now the landscape bored him more. Was there no escape from boredom?

Just as he was about to turn back, second thoughts overtook him in the form of Jesse, who came riding out of the sameness. When he recognized her, he rode to meet her. Two dust plumes converged on the trackless plain.

"I thought maybe you could use some company," Jesse said.

"It's getting boring out here," Pyg said. "I was just about to go back. There's really nothing so see."

"Maybe I can change that," she said.

Pyg didn't know what to say, so he rode in silence. He was happy to see her, but she made him wary out here all alone.

"Less git a little farther from camp," Jesse said. "I don't wanna be interrupted ag'in. Do you?"

Pyg didn't answer. They continued to head west, away from camp. The sun shown in their faces. He pulled his hat lower to shade his eyes. Occasionally he sneezed. She didn't seem to mind the sun as it sank slowly before her.

"This oughta be far enough," Jesse said. "What say we stop?"

"All right," Pyg said, a bullet tumbling in his right hand while his left held the reins.

They both pulled up their horses. She got off first, as if she were the more eager, but appearances were probably deceiving. He was certainly eager, too, just less experienced and less sure of himself. When they were both standing on the flat spinning earth, they faced each other from a few feet away.

"I don't need much foreplay," Jesse said.

"Excuse me," said Pyg. "What did you say?"

"Foreplay. You ain't never heard of foreplay? Well, that don't much matter since I don't need much anyhow. Take off yore bottom half."

"What?"

"You heard me. Git at it."

He just stood there paralyzed—surprised rather than reluctant.

"Okay, I'll show you how," Jesse said. She unbuckled her belt, unbuttoned her Strausses, and started pushing them down. "See, it's easy. Think you can do it?"

With trembling, hurried hands, Pyg unbuckled his bat-wing chaps, shook himself out of them, then attacked his jodhpurs, unbuckling, unbuttoning, shoving them down.

"Less lay down," said Jesse.

They lay together on the flat spinning earth. She kissed him. He kissed back. She started to moan. He unbuttoned her flannel shirt. She wore no underwear. Her breasts fell into his hands like ripe peaches. Big peaches. Now she moaned louder. He was so excited he hardly knew what to do next.

Her moans kept getting louder. Louder and deeper. She was so excited, she didn't even sound like herself. Who was she anyway? Really? Did he deeply know her? He couldn't believe he was distracted by her moans, but he was. Their pitch was all wrong. Too deep! He felt as if he were about to make love to a man. She sounded like a combination of woman and man. Did all women sound like men when they grew passionate? He didn't know.

"What's that sound?" moaned Jesse.

"What?" asked a breathless Pyg.

"I hear somebody moanin'."

"What?"

"I said I hear somebody moanin' and groanin'."

"I thought that was you."

"Part of it was me. The other part's kinda worryin' me. Listen."

They listened and heard a distinctive moaning sound coming from not far away.

"Sounds like somebody's hurt," Pyg said.

"Could be a trick," Jesse said.

"Get dressed," he said.

"Race you," she said. "Last one with their pants off is a rotten egg."

They both hurried into their clothing. To Pyg's utter astonishment, Jesse beat him. In his whole life, he had never known a woman to dress faster than a man. Jesse was something special, but he wasn't sure whether it was especially good or especially something else.

"We have to take a look," Pyg said reluctantly, very.

"Yeah, we gotta," Jesse agreed.

"But be careful."

"I'll watch my hide."

"Walk behind me."

"Are you kiddin'?"

Side by side, they crept toward the disturbing moans. Slowly, the sound grew louder. Pyg's eyes swept from horizon to horizon searching for an ambush. All he saw was flat. Flat here. Flat there. Nothing anywhere. As the moans got bigger, it actually began to sound familiar. But who? Then the moaning stopped. Pyg felt somehow abandoned and a little alarmed. The siren sound had enticed him on and now . . . what? The attack? The shot fired from cover? The end? Jesse gripped Pyg's arm. The moaning started up again and sounded even more familiar. Who did it sound like? Pyg's ears strained. Maddening. Frightening. Frustrating. They trudged warily toward what sounded like real pain.

"Could it be Custer?" Pyg asked at last.

She stopped, so he stopped. They both listened hard.

"I think you're right," Jesse said.

They both walked faster toward the hurt. As the moaning got louder and louder, it sounded more and more like the Comanche cowboy. They started to run. It had to be Custer. They ran.

"Oh, no," gasped Jesse.

Custer lay moaning on his back in the tall grass. A trail of crushed blades and stems stretched behind him. He had evidently dragged himself until he had grown too weak. Now he was a beetle on its back.

"Custer," Jesse yelled and raced as if to attack him.

Not knowing what else to do, Pyg took out his silver gun and started firing in the air. It was as if he wanted to kill the thin useless clouds that never produced any rain. When his gun was empty, he reloaded and started firing again. Each shot screamed: HELP! He didn't know what to do for the gravely wounded Custer, but perhaps his firing could attract the attention of someone who knew more. Surely the others would hear and come galloping.

"You're gonna be all right," Jesse said, kneeling in the dirt beside him. "You're gonna be fine. We're here now. Don't worry."

Don't worry! Pyg wondered if he could have ever said those words, that lie. Today it was a gift to be able to lie so convincingly, but was it always so? What about when she accused his mother? Was that another convincing lie? Yet Pyg was glad Jesse was lying now. Telling a gut-shot man he was fine. Saying just the right thing. Something he wouldn't–couldn't–have said.

"What happened?" Pyg asked, not knowing what to say, wanting to say something.

"Wlllleeee," gurgled Custer.

"Will Lee?" asked Pyg.

The Comanche nodded. "Willee shot me."

"Will Lee?"

The Indian was wriggling back and forth on the ground, like a dying alligator.

Pyg dropped to his knees beside Jesse. He wanted to comfort Custer, but how? He felt he should reach out, touch him, make a physical connection, maybe pat him or stroke him. But his whole being rebelled at putting his hands on so much pain and suffering. It was as if he felt pain could be passed, like an electrical charge, from one body to another. Pyg just knelt there on the flat world with his hands pressed firmly together as if he were praying, but he wasn't. He didn't know what he was doing. Telling himself he had to do better, Pyg steeled himself to reach out literally to another human being who needed his comfort. Choking down his repulsion, he forced himself to unclasp his hands. He ordered himself to extend a helping hand. His trembling fingers touched the wounded man's shoulder.

"Don't touch me!" gasped Custer, flinching, gaining strength.

Pyg pulled his hand back from the hot stove of rejection. He had tried so hard, had wanted to help so badly, had overcome so much, and all for nothing, even less. He hadn't helped but hurt. He felt cheated, but he didn't know by whom.

"We've got to stop the bleeding," Jesse said.

She started unbuttoning her shirt. She evidently planned to fashion a faded flannel bandage.

"No, don't," Custer hissed. "Isss too late."

Blood trickled from the corner of his mouth. He knew he wasn't going to be all right, wasn't fine. Jesse stopped unbuttoning and started buttoning again.

"They're plannin'," Custer whispered through the blood, "to go 'round the water hole."

Pyg and Jesse both leaned down closer, being careful not to touch the dying cowboy.

"Will and a coupla cowboys was scoutin' out a new trail. But I seen some dust, and I come for a look-see."

Custer stopped talking and his body contorted with pain. He twisted to the left, to the right, but the pain followed him wherever he went.

"Can I—?" Pyg began.

"No, wait," Custer whispered. "I rode up and told him I knew what he was up to. And he called me a 'nester-lovin' red nigger' and shot me right in the middle of me. Damn."

Jesse sighed deeply. "Custer, I know I ain't always been too friendly," she said. "I'm real sorry 'bout that. Really, I am. Really really am. But I had my reasons." She paused. "They was bad reasons. I know that now. Like I said, I'm so sorry. And I'm not just sayin' that 'cause—"

"I'm not sure he can hear you," said Pyg.

"Oh, no, I wanted him to hear me. I wanted to tell him—"

"I know."

"No, you don't know. How could you know? *You?* You of all people. You with your . . . oh, go to hell."

Pyg was stunned, stunned by the tragedy before him, stunned by Jesse's emotion, stunned by her hostility, stunned almost to emotional paralysis, almost but not quite, unfortunately.

The others arrived too late. Not that they could have done anything anyway. All the cowboys stood around Custer's body not knowing what to do or say except to hate. The nesters had stayed back at the water hole to stand guard and weren't represented. The cowboys cursed under their breath. That was the best eulogy they could muster.

"Looks like he crawled a good ways before he died," Too Short said. "Vaquero, you mind backtrackin' him? See if'n you find anything worthwhile. I got no idea what."

"Be right back," said the Mexican cowboy.

He mounted up and rode off following a trail of crushed and crumpled grass that led more or less due west.

"He won't be back soon as he thinks," said Too Short. "That Indian coulda crawled for miles. Hate to think on it."

"We have to arrest Will Lee for murder," Pyg said, more loudly than he had intended. "He has to be brought to justice."

"Justice," scoffed Little Dogie. "Out here."

"Shut up!" said Pyg.

They were both surprised when the giant didn't say anything else.

Vaquero didn't get back for over an hour.

CHAPTER 46

"That there's a Comanche moon if'n I ever seen one," Too Short said as they rode out of camp.

"What's that?" asked Pyg.

"Means a full moon," said Too Short. "The Comanches used to like to raid when there was a big moon so they could see to git away. Liked to ride most all night afterward, see? So that there's a Comanche moon, and ain't that fittin'?"

"Except they may see us coming," said the boy.

"Don't go lookin' on the dark side. Look on the bright side."

"That's the problem. Perhaps it's too bright."

"Tell you what, if'n they see us, you'll just shoot their eyes out. They won't see too good after that, will they, huh?"

Under cover of semidarkness the cowboys and the farmers were riding toward Will Lee's camp. It was about ten o'clock at night. The cowpokes rode to the left, the nesters to the right. Pyg had been surprised to learn that the Lee family owned another ranch down by the Rio Grande, which was run by Will's little brother Mason. Big brother Will must have ridden down to join the drive when he realized there might be trouble. He was probably looking forward to it.

Pyg's band planned to slip up on a sleeping camp and spirit Will away before anybody was awake enough to do anything about it. But there was that worrisome but undeniably appropriate Comanche moon. They rode southwest as quietly as they could, quieter and quieter the farther they went.

They left Jesse behind to guard the camp, but she showed up before they had gone much more than a mile. She didn't say anything, just cantered up and fell in with the other riders. Nobody told her to go back. Everybody knew it wouldn't do any good. Soon the Harvey Girl was riding beside Pyg. Neither of them said anything. He was some-how embarrassed by her presence and glad to see her at the same time.

"No nooky tonight," said Little Dogie. "We got bizness to—"

"No talkin'," hissed Too Short.

"That's right," the boy said. "Keep quiet."

"That goes for you, too," Too Short whispered sternly.

Chagrined, Pyg worried that Will Lee and his gang might have heard all the chattering. He hated Little Dogie for making so much noise and wasn't much happier with himself. He silently swore he wouldn't say another word, no matter how provoked. He would be as silent as the moon.

When he wasn't worrying about what Will Lee might hear, Pyg wor-ried about what he and the other cowboys might *not* see. What if they failed to find the Lee herd, rode right past it in the dark? He told him-self that a cattle drive was too big to miss, especially with a Comanche moon to light their way, but he was not entirely reassured. He kept star-ing intently into the thin darkness, but he didn't see anything but flat earth stretching away to a flat horizon.

"What if we cain't find 'em?" whispered Jesse.

"Don't worry," the moon whispered back.

"No talkin'," Little Dogie lectured. "You hear me?"

Too Short just shook his head.

Ever so faintly came snatches of words, borne by dark winds. "*. . . Yore misfortune . . .*" Had Pyg heard it, or hadn't he? Maybe it was a sound mirage. Was there such a thing? He strained and thought he heard: "*Git along . . .*"

"Little Dogie, he's singin' to you," Jesse whispered. "Sounds like some kinda love song."

"Shut up!" Little Dogie bellowed in a whisper.

"*You* shut up!" an angry Pyg bellow-whispered even louder, coming to the defense of the Harvey Girl.

"Might as well blow a damn bugle," Too Short lamented softly.

Some lone cowboy was calming his cows with a song as old as trail drives. Making a slight course adjustment, Too Short turned a few degrees to the south and rode toward this musical beacon.

. . .

Too Short held up his hand and all the cowboys reined in their horses. Then he dismounted and motioned for the others to join him on the ground. The creaking saddle leathers seeming to scream in the quiet night. Too Short approached Vaquero and whispered something in his ear.

"No!" Vaquero whispered back too loud.

"Shhh!" whispered Too Short.

"Make her do it?" whispered the Mexican.

"No, I don't wanna," whispered Jesse, who had no idea what they were talking about.

"Shhhhhh!" whispered Too Short. "Vaquero, you're the best we got with horses, so you're gonna stay back here with 'em. Or else I'm gonna have Pyg shoot your damn balls off."

The boy laughed. He couldn't help himself. The other cowboys laughed, too. All but Vaquero. It was a flash flood of noisy glee.

"Shhhhhhhhh!!" ordered Too Short.

Hiding in the tall prairie grass, Pyg, trembling slightly, rose up enough to study the camp. About one hundred yards away, the sleeping trail drivers lay in a semicircle, all on the north side of a smoldering cow-chip campfire. (After all, there was no wood out here.) By now, the boy knew that the wind almost always blew from the north, pushing smoke to the south, which explained the configuration of the camp. He was surprised at the number of bedrolls. Twenty or more. Will Lee had evidently brought some of his own LS cowboys to reinforce his brother Mason's cowhands. Pyg's posse was outnumbered and surely outgunned. Absorbing this news, the boy twitched, then looked around to see if anybody had noticed. He found Little Dogie smiling at him. He twitched again.

"There's a lot more'n I figured," whispered Too Short.

"Yeah, they got a couple dozen to our eight," whispered Little Dogie.

"You can't even count," whispered Pyg. "We've got thirteen."

"Naw, lemme show ya," whispered Dogie. "First off, girls don't count. So subtract one, makes twelve of us."

"Shhh," shushed Jesse.

"Second, Vaquero's back there nurse-maidin' the horses, so he don't count neither. Subtract another'n, makes eleven. And third, well, ever'body knows a farmer's only half a man. So take away three more makes eight, like I said. Count 'em yourself."

Overhearing, several farmers clenched their fists and advanced on Little Dogie. A part of Pyg hoped they would gang up on the giant and beat him bloody, but a more sensible part held its breath.

"Damn you!" hissed Kenny Cozby. "But we'll settle this later." He held up both hands to halt the other farmers. "You can count on it." Kenny stepped up and stared the big man in the face. "When we git finished with you, you ain't even gonna be a man atall."

"Shhhh," Too Short ordered. Then he whispered: "We gotta make a new plan. We cain't just rush in and arrest the bastard. They's too numerous. Lemme think."

Pyg tried to think, too. Maybe they should . . . No, that was too complicated . . . Maybe they could . . . No, that wouldn't work either . . . Or perhaps . . . no, no, no . . .

"Less git a little closer," whispered Too Short. "Mebbe if'n we can see better, we'll think better." He glared at them all. "Now if'n anybody says a damn word, Pyg's gonna shoot their damn tongue out. I swear."

Too Short motioned his small band to follow him. Crawling through the tall grass, they tried to be quiet, but without much success. Little Dogie made more racket than three other men. Occasionally Too Short would pause, rise up, look, and then crawl some more. They kept going on hands and knees until they were only about sixty yards from the camp. Now they all looked.

"Thass him on this enda the line," whispered Little Dogie. "Thass Old Will."

"You're blind," whispered Ivan the Terrible. "That's Mason. Will's the next one over."

"You're bat blind and foreign to boot. If that's Mason, I'm a damn Pygmy."

"You're nuts. If that there's Will, I'm—I dunno, lessee—Kate the Damn Great."

"Then I guess what I heard about you's true, huh? You fuck horses, doncha? Must be a Russian kinda thang."

Terrible actually reached for his gun.

"Cut it out," Too Short whisper-ordered.

Staring at the two Will Lees, Pyg saw his enemies multiplying. While one Will slept soundly, the other Lee shrugged his shoulders and bicycled his legs. He raised his head, shook it, and seemed to stare right at the invaders. Then the head nestled back down on a saddle.

"Less grab 'em both," whispered Ivan. "We can sort 'em out later."

"Sudden like, you ain't so sure, huh?" whispered Little Dogie. "Besides, thass twice the work."

Too Short shook his head and glared. Then he turned to Pyg: "You got the youngest eyes. Whadda you think? Which one's which?"

"I wish there were two Comanche moons," whispered Pyg, using the subjunctive, as he had been painstakingly taught to do. "I can't tell. I think it's . . . No, I don't know."

"We don't know who's who or what's what," whispered Too Short, "and we still ain't got no plan. Damn."

Pyg felt a planning failure.

Once again, one of the Will Lees stirred in his sleep. He sat up, looked around, and massaged his eyes. Pyg dropped down flat on his stomach. All the others went to ground, too. The boy waited and waited and waited until he couldn't stand it any longer. He had to know what was going on. Rising up ever so slowly, Pyg peeked over the gently north-south waving tips of the tall grass. He was surprised—actually alarmed—to see this Lee on his feet. What was he up to? Had he heard something? Sensed something? Pyg ducked down flat once again, but before long he was back up again. Kneeling in the grass, he watched Lee stagger away from the campfire. He was coming right at them. He knew! Still wiping his eyes, the old man stumbled unsteadily into the tall grass. What was wrong? What was going on? The boy heard nearby guns being cocked. He reached for his own silver six-shooter. Then suddenly Pyg knew what was happening.

"Don't shoot," the boy whispered. "He's just going to the bathroom. This is our chance to get him."

Too Short motioned the others to get down lower. They all hunched low in the grass like rabbits watching a coyote. Then the littlest cowboy crawled over to Little Dogie and whispered something in his ear.

The boy watched as Little Dogie nodded and then crawled off through the grass heading in the direction of Lee. The Lee he had sworn was Will. The giant soon disappeared from view and even from hearing. Somehow, when he really needed to, the giant could glide silently. What a surprise.

Lee kept coming. When he was only about fifteen yards away, he stopped and unbuttoned his fly. Pyg looked away, embarrassed. But he soon looked back, in spite of himself, because he wanted to see what Little Dogie was up. Staring at an old man peeing right at him, Pyg felt uncomfortable but this time didn't look away. He actually strained to see better in the thin moonlight. Discovering that he had stopped breathing, he took a shallow breath. Where was Little Dogie? Didn't he realize that Lee had almost finished doing his business? Now was the time to strike! He might have known that the giant would fail—

There he was! Rising up behind Lee. Drawing back his huge right arm. Clutching his six-shooter in his right hand. Holding it by the barrel. Ready to deliver a knockout blow with the blunt butt of the gun. His arm poised, loaded, cocked, a hammer about to come crushing down. Good. Pyg silently apologized to Little Dogie for having doubted him.

No! Little Dogie collapsed back into the grass as if he were the one who had been knocked out. What was going on? Had the giant lost his nerve? Probably. Had he had a heart attack? Pyg hoped so. Damn him. Pyg glanced around at Too Short, who shrugged and then shook his head. The boy looked at the others, who were all shaking their heads, mystified.

Lee buttoned up his fly, turned around, and stumbled back toward his bedroll. He was getting away. He had gotten away. Pyg was furious and got angrier with each step the old man took. The boy was actually shaking.

As Lee was rolling himself up in his bedroll once again, Little Dogie could be heard crawling noisily through the grass. Soon he reappeared on hands and knees and looking about as sheepish as a giant can look.

"It waddn't him," Little Dogie whispered hoarsely. "It was Mason."

"You sure?" whispered Too Short.

"Hell, yeah, I'm sure. He's missin' an ear. Last time I seen Will, he had two."

Ivan the Terrible started laughing. As the news was whispered around, the farmers began to chuckle, too.

"Shhhhhhhhh!" ordered Too Short.

"Sorry," the giant whispered in a tiny voice.

CHAPTER 47

"Now what?" whispered a discouraged Too Short. He waited. "Don't ever'body whisper at once."

Still nobody made a sound. Now they were finally quiet. Now they were behaving as stalkers should, silent as shadows.

"They're brothers," Jesse finally disturbed the silence. They all looked at the Harvey Girl. "They sorta look alike. Maybe they act alike." She lapsed back into silence. They all kept staring. "Will's prob'ly gonna need to piss, too. Trust me. I know a thing're two about old men. Less wait."

"Waitin' ain't no plan," Little Dogie whispered. "Waitin's just waitin'."

"Lemme tell ya somethin', Pygmy," whispered Too Short. "We're gonna wait. That means you too, Little Man."

The Comanche moon rode across a sky that looked as flat as the Staked Plain, but had more landmarks. The Big Dipper drifted. The North Star stayed put, just like Will Lee.

"Look," Pyg's lips moved almost silently.

Jesse stirred beside him, leaned forward, and froze, like a bird dog. Will Lee rose clumsily from his camp bed and looked around. He rubbed his eyes and began an unsteady stagger toward relief. He was coming straight toward them, then veered off to his right.

"You," Too Short mouthed silently, pointing at Ivan the Terrible. "Go."

While the Russian crawled off into the tall grass and vanished, Will Lee continued his search for the perfect place to take a leak. He waded through grass that came up to his crotch. He was a little shorter than his brother and had two ears. About fifteen yards from the smoldering campfire, the rancher stopped and started unbuttoning.

"You shouldn't watch this," Pyg whispered in Jesse's ear.

"Yeah, right," the Harvey Girl whispered, rising up a little more.

Will stood there with his legs splayed. They waited. Ivan the Terrible did not appear. Will held his pose. No Terrible. Will must be almost finished by now. Still no Russian.

"What's wrong?" Pyg whispered, even though he knew he shouldn't. "Will can't pee forever. Where's—?"

"He ain't pissed a drop yet," whispered Jesse. "Sometimes old men're like that."

"Oh."

Relaxing slightly, Pyg felt an urge to pee himself. He blamed all this talk of urinating. He ordered himself to wait. Then he felt Jesse nudging him. While he was distracted by his body's needs, she had noticed something. Impolitely, she pointed.

Clutching a dark stone, Ivan rose up behind Will Lee and did something terrible to the back of his head. The rancher sank soundlessly beneath the surface of a gently waving ocean of grass.

Crouching as low as they could, they carried Will Lee as if he were a fallen comrade. Blood trickled from the back of his head and stained the tall grass. He was as heavy, as motionless, as death, but he was still breathing. Terrible carried Lee's feet. Little Dogie had him under the armpits. Too Short hung on to his belt, and Jesse clung to a handful of shirt but didn't really seem to be helping much. Not knowing what else to do, Pyg followed along behind, looking back often to see if anybody was coming. He told himself that he was the rearguard, but he felt more like the boy not chosen to play on the team. Pyg wished he had more to do, but he wasn't unhappy. And with every crouching step, he felt better. They were going to make it. They were getting away with it. No cries in the night. No shots fired. Just a little farther now . . .

Hearing a horse whinny, an alarmed Pyg whipped his head around and stared into the moonlight. He saw a blur resolve into a rearing horse. The boy thought: Shhhh! Then he noticed more movement that turned into more horses, milling, stamping, excited. They had stumbled upon and roused the trail drive's remuda. Would anyone hear?

"Hurry," whispered Too Short.

They quickened their pace, which seemed to excite the horses even more. Now several were rearing and whinnying to spread the alarm. The horses were mounting each other as if danger made them crave copulation. (Pyg had always liked that word.) The animals crowded a rope fence but didn't try to break through it, which they easily could have done. It was just a single strand of rope tied to a row of slender poles stuck in the ground, but where had the wood come from? The drivers must have brought the poles with them: They had crossed this treeless plain before.

"They're stealin' the horses!" came a cry in the night.

"Run," whispered Too Short.

The posse stood up a little straighter and moved much faster. Pyg ran to keep up.

"There they are!" yelled a distant voice.

The trail drivers were soon running, too. Since they weren't trying to hide in the grass—and weren't carrying anybody—they ran faster than the posse. Afraid to look back, Pyg heard them stumbling and cursing, getting closer, gaining fast. Then he heard gunshots. He thought: It would serve them right if they killed their own Will. He ducked lower and tried to run faster, but low and fast canceled each other out. He felt slow and awkward and all too exposed. A bullet swished through the tall grass just to his left. Pyg dove, sprawled, and got grass in his mouth. Then it took all his will power to get up and run again.

"Vaquero!" yelled Too Short. "Vaquero, come on!" Then more quietly: "Little Dogie, git down lower. You're too—"

"Awww," screamed the giant.

Little Dogie dropped Will Lee and pitched forward on his face. It took both Too Short and Jesse to take Little Dogie's place carrying the prisoner. The small cowboy grabbed Will Lee under one pit, the Harvey Girl lifted the other, and they stumbled on.

"Pyg, help Little Dogie!" Too Short yelled. "Git him up and goin'."

Oh, great! Just the assignment the boy was longing for. Help his enemy, help his tormentor, help the man who had never helped him. Help his would-be killer? Well, he had wanted more to do. Now he had more than enough.

"I'll help you up," Pyg told the prostrate giant. Reaching down, he added: "Take my hand."

But the big man just went on clutching his stomach and writhing. Pyg saw blood seeping between his huge fingers. The boy tried to feel sorry for the giant, but was having a hard time. Curiously he felt sorry for himself for not being able to feel sorry for the huge man.

"We've got to move," Pyg said urgently. "They're coming."

"Cain't," hissed Little Dogie.

The boy had always thought the giant was unstoppable. Maybe they all had. But now he could see how wrong he had been. Getting behind the giant, he tried to lift him, but it was like trying to lift a fallen tree. A big tree.

"Too Short!" the boy yelled. "I need some help!"

But Too Short, who was already shrinking in the distance, evidently didn't hear. None of them heard. The battle was too noisy and they were too busy. Or maybe nobody cared enough about Little Dogie to risk getting shot in order to help him. Pyg could well understand such feelings. He wanted to abandon the giant, too, but he couldn't make himself do it.

"Help!" Pyg screamed. "He's really hurt! Help! Help!"

At last someone heard. At last somebody paid attention. At last someone was coming to help, but it was the last person Pyg expected.

"Hold on, we're acomin'," yelled Kenny Cozby. "He'd leave us, but we ain't gonna leave him."

Taking charge, Kenny assigned farmers to various parts of Little Dogie's anatomy. One nester was given his right arm, another to his left, and a third supported his great head. The others grabbed his legs. They were all big, strong farmboys, and so managed to lift and carry the giant.

"Pyg, you gotta slow 'em down, or we ain't got no chance," Kenny puffed. "Kill some few and that'll discourage t'others."

The boy stopped, turned, and drew his silver gun. He was trying to decide which of the scrambling trail drivers to kill first, but he didn't want to kill any of them. He hated their boss but not them. He was a hell of a gunfighter, huh? Then he remembered the horses. Turning his Tiffany gun on the remuda, Pyg took careful aim. Holding his breath, he pulled the trigger.

One of the slim posts holding up the rope fence snapped in two. Pyg aimed again, near the bottom on the next post, and fired once more. It snapped, too. He aimed low again, in order to avoid hitting the horses, and broke a third post. Part of the rope fence collapsed. The horses came thundering out through the gap. Pyg shot over the horses' heads to scatter them.

Then he heard horses' hooves bearing down on him from another direction. Turning to confront this new danger, Pyg saw Vaquero riding to the rescue. With renewed heart and hope, the posse put on an unexpected burst of speed. Running a little too fast, the sodbusters managed to drop Little Dogie. Then they hesitated a moment as if undecided.

"Pick him up!" yelled Kenny Cozby.

The farmers dutifully bent to their work while bullets whizzed over their heads. Swearing, they lifted the giant off the ground and struggled on. They moved with all the speed and grace of a ten-legged turtle.

Pyg reloaded as he ran, turned, and fired over the heads of the pursuing trail drivers. Maybe the shots would slow them down. They not only kept coming, they shot back. A bullet whirred through the tall grass a foot away. Pyg could smell his own body. It smelled like sweat and grime and no baths and something else. He knew he was smelling his own fear.

Then he tripped and fell and was lucky not to shoot himself. He lost his silver gun and started crawling around wildly looking for it.

"Whoa!" yelled Vaquero. "Whoa, whoa."

They all scrambled for mounts except Pyg who was still looking for his gun. It was like a game of musical chairs but any losers would die. None of the players cared whether it was the horse he or she had ridden in on or not. The farmers carrying the giant dropped him in their haste to mount up and get away.

"No!" screamed Kenny Cozby. "Put him on a horse. Right now!"

The clodhoppers returned to their burden. Grunting and groaning, huffing and puffing, they lifted Little Dogie up and pushed him onto the back of a dark horse. He lay stomach down across the saddle. Then they scrambled to save themselves, anxious to join the general flight, already well underway.

But where was the Tiffany six-shooter? It was obviously lost somewhere in the tall black grass, but it couldn't have gone far. Was Pyg really willing to die for that gun? He wanted to leave it and run for his life, but he kept searching.

Glancing up, Pyg saw Too Short ride off with Will Lee slung across his saddle. Good. They had gotten what they came for and were getting away. All except Pyg. But then Little Dogie slid off his horse.

"Pick him up!" bellowed Kenny Cozby. "Tie him on."

Shaking their heads, the farmers turned back to their enormous albatross. They lifted. They pushed and pulled. They wrestled the giant back onto the horse. Then they started tying him onboard. It seemed to take forever and the trail drivers were coming on fast.

"Oww!" yelled one of the put-upon farmers.

He grabbed at his chest and sank into the grass.

"Pick him up, too," ordered Kenny.

As the poor farmers were obeying, Pyg found his gun. Not with his hands but with his knee. He crawled over it. Ouch.

Glancing back, he saw a trail driver kneeling in the grass only twenty yards away. He had a rifle at his shoulder and was taking dead aim. The boy knew he had to do something. If he didn't, people on his side were going to start dying. His side? What did he think this was? A game in the park? Hating himself, Pyg aimed the silver gun and fired. He knew he had killed an innocent man. He wanted to vomit but decided to wait and do it later.

Catching a farmer's lame plowhorse, Pyg jumped aboard, kicked it in its exposed ribs, and limped off into the night. The trail drivers couldn't give chase because their horses were running wild across the dark prairie. The wind had come up, and the black grass looked like the devil's own roiling sea. Pyg began to feel sea sick and then threw up on poor Dobbins' neck.

"You hit?" yelled Jessie.

"No," Pyg mumbled through his unclean mouth. To himself he added: but I hit somebody else.

CHAPTER 48

"I ain't never been too good at 'rithmetic," mumbled Little Dogie. He paused and looked uncomfortable as if his wound were hurting him. Taking a deep and evidently painful breath, he went on: "Guess I never had 'nough schoolin'." He made more huge faces. "Guess thass how come I miscounted how many men we got 'round here." Another grimace. "Now I know we got plenty. 'Pologize."

The cowboys and the sodbusters were eating around the same campfire. The cowhands supplied the beans and dried beef. The farmers added potatoes and carrots from their gardens. It was the best meal Pyg had eaten in some time.

"Well, I know one thing," Kenny Cozby said. "Fer better or worse, you're a man and a half."

"Ummm," said the giant.

"Ummm," agreed the farmer.

Little Dogie lay beside the fire wrapped in a blanket. It was a warm night, but the giant kept shivering. The wounded sodbuster, whose name was Clyde White, lay beside him. He kept shivering, too. It was as if the two of them were living in a different season. It was winter where they were, summer for the rest of them. The sick seemed always to live in their own world.

Looking around the campfire, Pyg missed Ivan the Terrible. The Russian had been dispatched to ferry Will Lee to the jail in Tascosa. A farmer named Rozzle O'Day—where did farmers get their names anyway?—had gone along to help out. Too Short wanted to get the official forces of law and order involved as soon as possible. He wanted bars and a formal charge of murder. Too Short said killing Custer had been Lee's big mistake, because he would now have to fight not just the Home Ranch but the West's new sense of civ'lization. Somehow it all went back to Old Goodnight's Code. The Code of the West. Would Goodnight finally have his revenge?

"You know they're gonna come lookin' for us, for *him*," Kenny Cozby said. "I been thinkin' mebbe we oughta keep movin'. Mebbe ride all night."

"Them two're too worse off to move," said Too Short. "But you're right. They'll come. Mebbe tonight."

"Thass what I been figurin' on," said the farmer. "So if'n we're stayin', mebbe we oughta try to fool 'em?"

"How you figure?"

"We're farmers. We know farm things."

"Uh-huh?"

"We know how to protect our crops."

"Yeah."

"Scarecrows. I been thinkin' 'bout scarecrows. They look like men but they ain't."

"I know 'bout scarecrows."

"What if'n we put scarecrows in our bedrolls. Not real scarecrows but somethin' like. We bed 'em all down around the fire. Nice and snug. Then we go off in the dark and wait. When them trail drivers come, since there're so many of 'em, they'll just storm right on in. Figure they got us outnumbered and us dumb enough to be sound asleep. Then we got 'em good. They's in the light and we's in the dark."

"Ummm."

"Ummm."

Fortunately, clouds had rubbed out the moon and the stars.

The scarecrows were made of tall prairie grass and didn't have arms or legs. They were grass logs—wrapped in bedrolls—with grass balls for heads. Hats covered their grass faces. From a distance, Pyg thought the camp looked quite convincing. He wished the scarecrows would snore, but otherwise they were fine. They waited. Was the fire a little too big? They waited. Was the fire now too small? They waited. If the fire went out, they would lose their advantage.

"I'll go put some more chips on the fire," Pyg whispered.

"Okay," Too Short whispered.

Crouching low, Pyg run-waddled the fifty yards to the campfire. More cow chips were stacked nearby. He picked up about half of them and tossed them on the fire. Then he worried that he had used too many.

Returning, Pyg settled down, half sitting, half lying, with his Winchester 76 draped over his thighs. The bright fire grew fainter. Pyg's consciousness was beginning to burn with a low flame, too. When his chin hit his chest, it woke him up with a start. He looked around warily but nothing had changed except the fire burned more dimly than ever. The boy started to doze off again.

"Shhh," Too Short cautioned.

Rousing, Pyg saw dark shapes rising up out of the black grass. They looked less like men than did the sleeping scarecrows. The boy tried to count the lumps of darkness, but they blended together. The figures grew more human as they drew nearer the fire. They began to look like hittable targets. Pyg raised his rifle, sighted, and waited some more. The shadow men approached the scarecrows with drawn weapons, keeping them carefully covered. One of the shadows kicked a straw man and his hat fell off his grass face. Then all the trail drivers attacked the sleepers in a kicking frenzy. They wanted to kick the scarecrows to death. Grass flew.

"Drop your guns!" screamed Too Short. "We don't wanna kill you!"

The trail drivers stopped kicking, turned, and stared into the darkness. Some of their mouths were open, making black holes.

"Pyg, shoot somethin'," Too Short ordered. "Show 'em we're serious."

Right, but shoot what? Pyg looked for a target. He spotted a trail driver wearing eyeglasses and aimed. Could he shoot them off? Possibly but not certainly. Then he noticed the white grip of a six-shooter. It was stuffed in a holster because the cowboy who wore it also carried a rifle. Pyg liked the white grip because it was easy to see in the dim light. Drawing a serious bead, he squeezed the trigger. The white-handled six-shooter jumped backward out of its holster and dove into the dust.

"Good, that's the idea," yelled Too Short. "Now the rest of you drop your guns before we stop playin' around. You're surrounded. Make up your minds right now!"

The trail drivers couldn't tell if they were surrounded or not, could they? They hesitated, not sure what to do, but they didn't drop their guns.

"Shoot one of 'em in the foot," Too Short said.

Pyg started to protest, but changed his mind. He looked for the biggest foot, aimed at the instep, and squeezed off a painful bullet. The trail driver collapsed and twisted on the ground in agony.

"Next time we're gonna git more fatal," yelled Too Short. "Drop your guns right now or you're all dead men." He turned to Pyg. "Shoot one in the kneecap."

If he shot someone in the kneecap, Pyg knew the man would limp badly for the rest of his life. He decided to shoot a trail driver in the shin. But then the boy recognized a target he hadn't even been looking for: Mason Lee staring right at him across the black grass. Pyg aimed, not at the shin, but at the kneecap. He squeezed and Mason Lee jumped. He would have a hard time ever jumping again.

"Thass Mason," squealed Jesse. "He shot Mason Lee. Look."

All the cowboys stared hard to see if the Harvey Girl was right.

"Nice shootin'," said Too Short. Then he yelled: "Mason, the next one's gonna be in your gut. You tell your men to drop their guns, or you're gonna die, and they're gonna die, too. And nona us is gonna have a Merry Christmas."

Pyg couldn't hear what Mason said, but the trail drivers started dropping their guns. The weapons bounced on the dark earth.

The boy felt guilty for having aimed at the kneecap. The shin would have done just as well. Was he becoming too much of a cowboy?

The trail drivers knelt in the dust on the south side of the fire with smoke blowing in their eyes. Their boss, Mason Lee, didn't kneel with them because he couldn't. He was missing a kneecap. Pyg still felt bad about that. Mason Lee lay on his side in obvious pain, writhing in slow motion.

"All y'all, take off your boots," ordered Too Short. He stood on the other side of the fire away from the smoke with his rifle pointed in the general direction of the prisoners. "And be quick about it."

Grumbling, the trail drivers sat in the dust and started tugging at their boots. Some knee-high hightops, some midcalf, some with blunt toes, some pointed. Nobody minded that Mason wasn't taking off his boots. He wasn't going to run anywhere.

"Jesse, go git 'em," Too Short ordered.

She hesitated.

"Please," Pyg said.

The Harvey Girl crossed to the smoky side of the fire and started collecting the well-worn footgear. One boot was ventilated by a bullet hole and dripped blood. When her arms were overloaded, she crossed back to the good side of the fire and dumped the boots. Then she returned for a second load. Dumped them. And went back for a third and final load. When she was finished, she stood there wiping smoke tears out of her eyes.

"Now throw 'em on the fire, all of 'em," Too Short ordered.

She hesitated.

"Please," said Pyg.

Jesse started tossing boots into the fire, and the trail drivers started complaining, but she paid no attention. She just kept feeding boots into the cow-chip flames. The leather didn't burn like kindling, but it burned. The trail drivers, who were kneeling again, looked as if they were losing old friends.

"Now you got a choice to make," Too Short told his prisoners. "You know Will Lee done murdered one of our cowboys in cold blood. That makes all of you accomplices and just as guilty as he is. He's on his way to the Tascosa jail where he's gonna be tried for his crime. And then hung. Now you can join him if'n you want to. Thass one choice. Or you can swear to turn around and go on home and not have nothin' more to do with this here business. Thass your other choice. Up to you."

Fed by the boots, the fire got smokier, increasing the discomfort of the men kneeling in the smoke's path.

"Don't ever'body speak at once."

Nobody spoke.

"Okay, less do it this here way. Ever'body who wants to go up to jail in Tascosa, keep on kneelin' down. Ever'body who don't, ever'body who swears to git the hell outta here and not come back, git up and run like hell. You got horses out there somewheres. All you gotta do is find 'em, round up your sick cows, and head on back home. But if'n you ever show up here ag'in, we're gonna hang you. Swear to God almighty."

They waited.

"Don't take all night."

A tall cowboy with holes in his socks got up and sprinted like hell into the darkness. Then another cowboy with holey socks ran for it. Actually they all had holes in their socks, and before long they were all fleeing. Some fast, some slow, one limping badly. All were on their way home but Mason Lee.

"Ouch!" yelled a trail driver who had stepped on a sticker or a thorn or a scorpion or maybe even a snake. "Owwww!"

The next cry came from farther away: "Shit!"

Pyg realized that he could track the progress of the fleeing trail drivers by the diminishing volume of their cries of pain. The Staked Plains were no place for tender feet.

The wind changed, which rarely happened out here, and blew smoke in the boy's face. He felt the rebuke.

CHAPTER 49

Revelie woke up to frost on the grass and immediately worried about Percy and the sick cows. Walking up and down in the big living room, she kept asking herself: What can I do for him? What can I do for them? Over and over. It did not take her long to realize that she couldn't do anything for her son. Not right now. But perhaps she could do something for the sick cattle. Without help, the winter would surely kill all of them. They couldn't cope during warm days: How would they possibly survive cold ones? She needed a plan, not that any plan would work, but some plan should be tried. Revelie considered asking Loving what she should do, but decided: no. He would be too worried about her safety. With her husband dead, her lover gravely ill, and her son away, she would have to decide for herself what she herself should do. But what? But how? She paced faster, hoping that moving her body would help turn her mind, but the faster her feet moved, the slower her mind seemed to tumble.

Then, in midstride, Revelie had an idea, a modest one. Of course, she knew it might not work, realized it might mean considerable effort for no reward, but she was secretly proud of herself for fashioning any plan at all. She was no longer relying upon strong men, not out of choice, but because there weren't any strong men around. It felt good. Realizing she couldn't save all the sick cattle, Revelie determined to try to rescue a few. And while she was ministering to them, she would also be studying them, trying to understand the fever, hoping to defeat it.

After dressing warmly, Revelie headed for the stable.

Riding sidesaddle through a herd drinking from the red river, Revelie kept looking for cows that were sick but not too sick to move. She carried something in her right hand that frightened her: a lariat. She had no idea how to rope anything, but she was going to rope a sick cow anyway—if she could only find a suitable one.

Then she did. Revelie saw a cow stumble as it left the water's edge. Regaining its balance, it walked slowly, stiff-legged, up the bank. Then it stopped and peed a stream much redder than the river. Revelie nudged Boston in the direction of the fevered but mobile animal. She was irrationally afraid it might run away. Holding the hondo, she shook out a loop as she had seen the cowboys do. When she was close enough, she whirled the loop over her head and got a surprise. Her horse jumped sideways as if the lariat were a flying snake, and she almost fell off. So she hadn't quite mastered roping.

Regrouping, Revelie walked her horse in a small circle and approached the sick cow once again. This time she rode right up to it and didn't so much rope it as drop a loop over its long horns from about a foot away. Thrilled by her accomplishment, she began leading—sometimes dragging—the cow back to the barn.

"Get along, little dogie," she sang, since singing was supposed to calm cattle, but that was as much of the song as she knew. "Get along, little dogie," she repeated and then made up the lyrics as she went along: "This is for your own good . . . you'll chew your cud . . . where it's warm and dry. Oh, my, oh, my. Get along little dogie . . ."

But the cow did not appear to be a music lover, at least not in its present condition. Or else it had perfect pitch and realized Revelie was massacring a revered cowboy standard. The weird song did not calm the cow—it continued to fight the rope—but it did seem to relax the "cowboy." Which was almost how Revelie saw herself at the moment. In the end, the cow made it to the barn alive, which seemed an achievement.

Over the next several days, Revelie kept repeating this operation—her plan—until there was no more room in the barn. Her small roundup had produced an indoor herd of a dozen suffering cattle. The circumstances had been deplorable, but the work itself was enjoyable. She was so happily surprised she could do it.

CHAPTER 50

Revelie watched the first snow drift down into the red canyon. It was an unseasonably early snow, falling two weeks before Thanksgiving. Thank Whatever, she had gotten her sick cows indoors before it started. The white gently covered the red of the earth and the deep green of the cedars. The snow also piled up on cottonwood branches, white on white. She knew a north wind would be blowing hard and cold up on the plains where her boy was. Watching through the window of the sickroom, she shivered on his behalf.

"He'll be comin' back soon," Loving said from his sickbed.

"How soon?" asked Revelie.

"I don't rightly know, but won't be long now. Once the snow flies, thass usually the end of the trail drives. Thass prob'ly the end of the fever, too. Won't be back till spring most likely. So your baby boy'll be comin' home any day now, waggin' his tail behind him."

"I hope you're right. I hate to think of him out there in that blizzard."

"It ain't no blizzard."

"It could be building up to one."

"Would you read to me?" He waited. "Please."

"You just want to distract me."

"No, the story's just now gittin' good. I cain't wait to see who gits hisself killt and who don't."

"You're bloodthirsty." She sighed. "Well, all right, but I dislike this book more and more." Reluctantly, she left the window, picked up the thick volume, and sat in a rocking chair. "I thought it was going to be a funny story about knights and ladies and chivalry, but it's turned so bloodthirsty, like you. All those guns!"

"I thought you was better 'bout guns."

"Well, perhaps I am, but I certainly never expected guns in a story about King Arthur."

"Well, I like it."

"All right, all right." She opened the substantial work at the flimsy gold bookmark. "Let's see." Her finger moved down the page until she found her place. She lowered her voice to sound more like a man: "*'Stand to your guns, men! Open fire!'*"

"Aye, aye," said Loving.

"'The thirteen gatlings began to vomit death into the fated ten thousand.'" Revelie went on to describe a raging battle where swords and spears fought machine guns. The modern world was in a one-sided, life-and-death struggle with the Middle Ages. "'Within ten short minutes after we had opened fire, armed resistance was totally annihilated, the campaign was ended, we fifty-four were masters of England. Twenty-five thousand men lay dead around us.'"

Revelie slammed the book closed.

"Is that the end?" asked Loving.

"It's the end as far as I'm concerned," she said.

Getting up, she placed the murderous book on a table and retreated to the window. Her breath made the cold window fog up. Trying to calm down, she used her finger to write her son's name in the mist, telling herself that it was a kind of spell to bring Percy home. And it worked. She saw riders moving down the canyon's red-and-white wall. What a miracle! She had special powers! But she reminded herself that she had been writing Percy's name over and over for weeks, in the sand, on paper, even—carving it—on a cottonwood trunk, and it hadn't done any good. Well, she was getting better at the dark arts, that was all. Now it had worked, hadn't it? Who else could be winding down the wall? She tried to pick out which rider was Percy, but she couldn't tell. It made her feel like a failure as a mother.

"I think he's coming now," Revelie said quietly, reining in her excitement, hoping not to jinx it.

"Told ya," said Loving.

Wiping the fog off the window, Revelie stared hard at the indistinct figures descending like the snow. Counting them, she grew concerned.

"There are only five riders," Revelie said. "Perhaps it's not them after all." She paused for a moment thinking, worrying. "Or perhaps something terrible has happened to them. They set off from here with a much larger armada and now–"

"Is that some kinda army?" asked Loving.

"And it's all my fault," she continued, ignoring his question. "Me and my silly ideas. Me and my quarantine. I'll never forgive myself if–"

"Don't worry. He'll be–"

"I'll be right back."

"No, you won't. Go."

Revelie hurried out of the sickroom, down the hall, across the big living room, and out onto the long front porch. Shivering, she ducked back inside and grabbed a coat off the cow-horn coatrack by the door. Going out to the very edge of the porch, she looked up at the descending file of riders.

To her disgust, Revelie recognized not her son but the Harvey Girl. She could see Jesse's dirty, oily hair bouncing off her shoulders. But if it really was the girl, then her boy would surely be nearby. Unless . . . no, don't think such thoughts. The mother studied the Harvey Girl's nearest neighbors. Yes! There he was riding just ahead of Jesse. But where were all the others?

Then Revelie thought: Unless the news is really bad, we must celebrate. We must "kill the fat calf," as my husband used to say. It is a great day. We will celebrate Thanksgiving early. We will start our own tradition.

Revelie grew colder and colder as she watched the riders zigzag to the bottom of the canyon wall. Then they disappeared. She hurried inside and warmed herself at the blaze in the mammoth fireplace. Glancing up at the stags who had died with their horns locked in combat, she thought: males! Then she hurried back out to search for her son. She brushed away flakes that had drifted onto the porch and found another porch, her lashes.

Revelie had time to grow thoroughly cold before she saw snow-blurred riders heading in her direction. But they were still a half mile away. She ran out through the white air to meet them–him. She ran and ran. They were still so far away. Their horses were just walking. Why weren't they galloping? Why wasn't her son as eager to get to her as she was to get to him? She was gasping for air now and swallowing lots of snowflakes. She felt as if she were going to drown. She waved.

The horses were still walking. She waved harder, but nobody seemed to care. She was freezing. Couldn't they see that she was freezing to death? Her feet were wet and frozen. She wanted to stop running, catch her breath, but love made her keep going. Even though that love did not seem to be reciprocated.

Tripping over something hidden under the snow, Revelie pitched forward. She felt a burst of pain in her right knee and her left wrist. Could she get up? She had to. Struggling, she raised herself to her hands and knees. Looking ahead, she saw walking horses. Gathering herself, she managed to stand. She walked a few steps. Then she was running again. But now she was wet and much colder and starting to be afraid.

"Percy!" she screamed into the snow-wet wind.

The snow was falling much harder now, blinding her. The world of the red canyon was all white. Clawing at the snow in her eyes, Revelie saw a snow-white horse jump forward. It raced toward her. Yes, yes, her son would rescue her from the blizzard.

The white horse charged past her. Oh, no, he hadn't seen her. He was racing for the big house where he expected to find her. She was freezing, abandoned, lost. But the horse wheeled. Percy was coming back for her. She relaxed and let out a visible sigh. Her son slowed his horse as he drew nearer. He leaned down. His arm was out. He wanted to pull her up onto the horse with him. But was she strong enough and limber enough to do her part? Even with his help, could she really vault up onto the back of his tall horse? To please him, she made up her mind to try. Gritting her teeth, she reached up and embraced him. He swept her up off the snowy ground and deposited her on the saddle behind him. Thank God. Trying to hang on, Revelie reached around Percy and felt the distinct bulge of so-soft breasts.

Ouch, it was as if Revelie had touched two very hot pots: She was fondling a female. No, her son hadn't rescued her. No, no, it was the Harvey Girl. Revelie quickly moved her hands lower. She didn't want to know this woman at all, much less this intimately.

"Thass better," the Harvey Girl yelled into the howling storm.

"I'm sorry," Revelie screamed into the snow. "Excuse me."

"Fergit it."

But Revelie doubted she would ever be able to forget it no matter how hard she tried. Glancing back, she saw another horse gaining on them. That must be Percy. She hoped she wasn't wrong again.

"Hi, Mom," she heard her son yell. "Are you okay?"

"I'm cold," Revelie called back.

Percy pulled even with his mother. She reached out her hand, and so did he, but they were too far apart to touch.

"You should've stayed inside."

"I couldn't wait to see you. To find out how you are. How are you?"

"I'm fine."

"He hurt his arm," Jesse yelled her way into the conversation. "Horse bucked him off a coupla days back." She laughed. "Thass how come he asked me to come git you. Case you was wonderin'."

"How bad is it?" asked the concerned mother. "Percy, talk to me. Is it broken?"

"No, it ain't broke," bellowed the Harvey Girl. "If it was broke, it'd git all swolled up. He wouldn't be able to move his fingers or nothin'. It's just sprained and all."

"Percy, you must see a doctor," Revelie said.

"Fat chance before the spring thaw," Jesse shouted.

"You don't have to shout."

"I like to shout. Cleans out my pipes, if'n you know what I mean."

"I don't but I can imagine."

"Mom, be nice, she rescued you."

Damn, damn, damn.

R evelie sat on the bed holding Loving's hand. Too Short lounged in the big, comfortable rocker, his feet not touching the floor. Percy and the Harvey Girl sat side by side in cane-bottomed chairs. They were a little too close.

"Them sodbusters hightailed it for home as soon as they come across a familiar trail," Too Short said. "Some of 'em's still got crops to git in. They weren't a bad lot. They was your idea, Miz Revelie, and I gotta hand it to you."

"Thass right," said Jesse. "They done saved Little Dogie's life."

"Of course, that was a mixed blessing," said Percy.

"He's kidding," said the Harvey Girl.

"Not entirely."

Another silence descended upon the sickroom. Revelie found herself playing with Loving's hand, stroking it, tickling it. She stopped.

"Thass too bad about Custer," said Loving. "I cain't hardly believe it. Custer's dead."

Revelie laughed and then saw everybody staring at her. She felt herself blush.

"I'm sorry," she almost whispered. "It's just that Custer has been dead for a long time. I mean the real Custer."

"Our Custer was real to us," said Jesse.

"I said I was sorry."

"Fergit it."

Revelie needed to send the conversation off in another direction, so she announced: "The fever hasn't been as bad since you started the quarantine."

"Good," said her son. "Loving, how're you doing? You're looking better."

"Your mama saved my life," said the still-handsome cowboy.

Revelie squeezed Loving's hand, then noticed Percy and Jesse noticing. So she dropped his hand as if she had accidentally grabbed the hot end of a branding iron. Jesse and Percy noticed that, too. Her son wasn't smiling and there were quotation-mark lines between his eyes. Or were they exclamation points? Or question marks?

"Was my father really a good shot?" Percy asked unexpectedly. "Was he one of the best ever?"

"Yes!" Loving and Revelie said together, which was too bad.

"Who was better?" The boy stared at the sick man. "My father or you?"

The silence in the room was the quiet of the tomb, a guilty tomb.

"Your father done won their only shootout," said Too Short. "I mean it was just a shootin' match. They weren't shootin' at each other. See?"

"But–" Revelie began and then stopped abruptly.

She stopped talking because she realized she shouldn't tell the story she had been about to blurt out. It was a family secret—her husband's secret, Loving's secret, and hers—with many implications. Loving had actually won that long-ago shooting match, but he had fooled Goodnight into believing he had won. Now the best policy was surely to fool the son, too.

"What?" asked Percy

"Nothing," lied his mother.

"You've got a secret," guessed Jesse.

"Hush!" Revelie said sharply.

"You don't have to shout," said the Harvey Girl. "Less'n you're just cleanin' out your pipes."

Revelie stood up, went to the window, and looked out at a white and innocent world. Reflected in the glass, she saw Jesse whispering to Percy. What did those two have to whisper about? What secrets did *they* have?

CHAPTER 51

"Less git outta here," Jesse whispered to Pyg. "This room keeps git-tin' smaller 'n' smaller." She thought a moment. "I know, you can teach me how to shoot better. Somethin' a girl out here oughta know. Come on, please."

"But it's snowing," Pyg protested.

"It's almost stopped," Jesse whispered. "Besides, we been snowed on before. Won't rust us none. Please, please."

"All right."

Jesse jumped up out of the cane-bottomed chair. Pyg got up more slowly. He was still puzzled about something, but he wasn't sure just what.

"Where are you going?" asked his mother.

"Jesse wants me to give her a shooting lesson," he said, and saw a hurt look spread across his mom's face.

"But it's snowing," Revelie protested.

"It's stopping," said Pyg. "We might get a little damp, but I don't think we'll rust. We'll be back."

"I hate shooting," said Revelie.

"I love it," said Jesse.

"It's the one thing I'm good at," said Pyg.

Leaving the pressurized sickroom, the boy and girl hurried down the hall, crossed the living room, and grabbed coats off the cow-horn coatrack.

"I cain't wait," Jesse said, as if expecting a sexual charge from shoot-ing. Her chance to be a man.

. . .

The snow continued to thin. In a box canyon about a mile from the big house, they dismounted and reconnoitered. Pyg liked the little dead-end canyon because any ricochets would have a hard time escaping its confines. With any luck, they wouldn't accidentally kill any people or cows. At the far end of the box, he saw a prickly pear outlined with snow.

"Let's kill the cactus," Pyg said, pointing, even though he knew his mother wouldn't approve.

It was about thirty feet away.

"Yeah, yeah," said Jesse.

"Aim at that top—uh, I don't know what to call it—the top lobe."

"Go for the head, right? Sure, but tell me what to do."

Pyg wasn't sure he could put his technique into words because it was instinctive, but he would try. "Well, uh, you aim the pistol as if you were pointing your index finger." Noticing her looking puzzled, he added: "This one."

"Okay," she said. "Then what?"

"Well, you aim and then you wait a split second for everything to slow down and for the target to get bigger. That's when you shoot."

"The target gits bigger?"

"Yes."

"Okay, here goes."

Jesse pulled the six-gun out of her belt, pointed, waited a long time, and pulled the trigger. There was a terrible boom as the box canyon trapped not only the bullet but the sound. Her lead kicked up snow six feet in front of the cactus.

"Close," encouraged Pyg.

"No, it waddn't," Jesse said. "I missed it by a Texas mile."

"Did you wait for the slowness and for the magnification of the—?"

"Yeah, but nothin' got slower and nothin' got bigger. The longer I looked, the smaller it got."

"Really? Try again. Wait a little longer this time. And relax. You know you're going to hit the target so there's nothing to worry about."

"But I *don't* know."

"Try to know. Now once again."

Jesse leveled her six-shooter, pointed . . .

"Wait . . . wait . . . wait . . ."

"Nothin's happenin'. Nothin' good."

"Concentrate."

"I'm concentratin'."

Jesse pulled the trigger and hit the sandstone wall some four feet above the prickly pear's head.

"I'm tellin' you," she said, "nothin' got bigger, no way, not atall."

"Are you sure?" asked Pyg.

"Course I'm sure. Sure and sure some more. Pyg, you ain't normal."

For the first time, the boy began to think that maybe she was right. But to whom did he owe his abnormality, which father?

"Less rest a minute," Jesse said. "I ain't never gonna git the hang of this, not like you do." Her stare made him uncomfortable. "Look, I been thinkin': You see some things better'n what I do, but mebbe I see some other things clearer'n what you do. Mebbe they look bigger to me than what they do to you. See what I mean?"

"No."

"Your mama and Loving."

"No!"

Pyg drew his gun and killed the cactus right through the middle of its head.

"Nice shootin'."

"Thank you. Now be quiet."

But he knew she wouldn't.

"They cain't keep their hands off each other."

"You're imagining things."

"No, I ain't. Cain't you see it?"

"No, I don't see anything of the kind."

"You just don't wanna see it."

"Please, let's talk about something else."

"Look, I done listened to you rattlin' on about shootin'. Why? 'Cause you know a heap about shootin', and I don't. Now you gotta listen to me 'cause I know about this stuff, and you don't. Trust me."

"Shut up!"

"That ain't nice. I'm just tryin' to help out. You gotta open your eyes and—"

Pyg tackled her. He surprised not only her but himself. Such behavior was so unlike him. Or so he thought. They rolled over and over in the wet snow.

"Hell!"

"Just shut up!"

As they struggled together, he tried to cover her mouth. She bit his hand.

"Ow!"

Oh, no, she was going for his balls. She really wanted to hurt him. Hurt him bad. Anticipating the pain, he felt weak.

"No!"

"Yes."

But she wasn't hurting him. Anyway not much. And it hurt in a good way. A very good way. He relaxed for a moment and gave in to the feeling.

"Wanna make up?" she asked, out of breath.

Oh, yes, he was tempted. Yes, he wanted to go on feeling this feeling. Yes, he wanted whatever was to come next. Yes, he wanted it more than anything. No, he was mad at her. No, she had insulted his mother. No, he didn't want to think about what she wanted to talk about. No, she wouldn't shut up. No, no, no, no, no!

Rolling away from her, pulling away, Pyg managed to sit up. Feeling dizzy, he stumbled to his feet. Then he lost his balance and almost fell on top of her. He staggered backward and then ran for the horses as if pursued by wild Indians. He had a vision of Jesse chasing him, riding him down, never shutting up, going on and on about his mother and . . .

Out of dread, out of confusion, out of spite, Pyg unhitched Jesse's horse, Boy Howdy, from a cedar tree and whacked it on the ass.

"Hey!" screamed Jesse. "You pig!"

He wasn't entirely sure how she was spelling the word in her head, but he could make an educated guess. He rode off at a gallop, kicking snow back at her. It served her right.

CHAPTER 52

Revelie was pleased: It was obvious that her son and the Harvey Girl weren't getting along. Whenever he entered a room, she left it. When meals were served, leaving was out of the question, but they sat at opposite ends of the table. They were sitting at opposite ends now. The table was the long whitewashed one in the cook shack. It was dinnertime, but out here they called it supper. When Percy looked in Jesse's direction, she looked away. Neither said anything. They just ate their steaks sprinkled with chili powder and their red beans sprinkled with chili powder. The silence was music to the mother. She wondered what had happened, not that she particularly cared, so long as it had happened.

"'Scuse me, Miz Revelie," said a recuperating Little Dogie, his voice tight and hoarse. "It ain't my place to suggest somethin' like this here." He waited as if for someone to stop him. "But I'm gonna suggest anyhow." He waited again. "If'n you don't mind too much."

"I don't mind," said Revelie. "At least I don't think I do. It's hard to know without knowing what you have in mind. It isn't some kind of bacchanal, is it?" As soon as she said it, she knew she shouldn't have. He wouldn't know what it meant. What was she trying to prove? That she was better educated than these unschooled cowboys? She recognized her "bacchanal" as a form of snobbism and disliked herself for it.

"I'm afraid it sorta is," said Little Dogie. "But I ain't suggestin' barrels of wine 'cause I dunno where we'd git 'em."

"Oh," said Revelie. "Go on."

"Well, I been thinkin'—and this is kinda hard to say, ya know—but I been figurin' mebbe we oughta do somethin' to thank them damn farmers." He paused for a long time as if this cud deserved a long chew. "How I see it is they pretty much saved my skin." He chewed more cud.

"And if'n you think about it, they done saved the quarantine, too. Without 'em, well, you know." More cud chewing. "And here we got Thanksgivin' comin' up." He stopped talking and stayed stopped.

"Please, go on," prompted Revelie.

"Thass about all I got to say," said the giant. "More'n I shoulda said in these here surroundin's."

Revelie began to like the idea. Yes, Thanksgiving would be an ideal time to give thanks to the farmers. She was sorry she hadn't thought of it herself. She just wished she did have barrels of wine at her disposal.

"I like it," Revelie said at last. "We will invite the farmers for a Thanksgiving feast. Yes. Good. Thank you for the suggestion."

She saw that her son was looking at her with an approving smile. She also noticed Jesse smiling at her. At least they weren't looking and smiling at each other. Another reason for thanksgiving.

Then Revelie saw Percy throw a red bean at Jesse. Oh, no. It bounced off her cheek and landed in her plate.

"Nice shot," said Vaquero.

But the Harvey Girl disdained to notice. Thank you, thank you.

Revelie felt good. The room smelled good. The huge round table looked good, loaded down with three wild turkeys plus a turkey pie with minced hard-boiled eggs. The trimmings included green chili hominy, grilled corn on the cob, black-eyed peas with okra, and corn pudding. She had helped Coffee with the cooking and was proud of the results. She had also decreed: no beans. She was sick of beans.

"Please pass the beans," said Tin Soldier, who hadn't studied the table very carefully. Why should he? There were always beans.

"I'm sorry," said Revelie, who was amused rather than upset. She felt too good to be upset. She smiled benevolently. "We're all out of beans today. Actually, I'm not all that sorry, to tell the truth."

"I'm sicka beans, too," said Opry. "Thank you very much."

"Thank *you* for being my ally."

Revelie wished Loving had felt well enough to come to the table, but otherwise everything was almost perfect. More than most years, she really did feel thankful today. Thankful to the farmers who had manned her quarantine line. And thankful to the farmers' wives for accepting her invitation, since she so rarely saw other women out here. (Except Jesse, who didn't count.) She was thankful to God or Whomever or Whatever that her son had come back to her whole. She was even thankful to have big jobs to do out here in wild West Texas: running this ranch and fighting the fever. Now she realized she had been wasting away in Boston. It all felt good.

And yes, the mother was also thankful her Percy and that Harvey girl had chosen seats as far apart as possible at a round table with no ends. Revelie noticed that Jesse seemed to be cozying up to the young farmer sitting next to her: Kenny Cozby. Good. Let her pick on somebody besides her son for a change. The girl was whispering secrets in the farm boy's ear. Thank you God or Whomever or Whatever. Wasn't Thanksgiving a great holiday? Her heart purred instead of beating.

"You sure look a lot like your daddy," Kenny Cozby announced, staring at Percy.

"Oh, did you know my father?" asked Revelie's boy.

"I was just talkin' to him."

No. Revelie cringed. Shut up. Please, not here. Not now when everything was going so well. Not with all the guests listening. And they were. All other conversation had suddenly ceased.

"Where did this talk take place?" demanded Percy.

"You know," said Kenny, "in the back bedroom there."

"You are talking about the sickroom, right?"

Shut up! Please, shut up!

"Uh, right."

"Wrong! He's not my father."

"He ain't?"

Revelie could feel all her guests staring at her, then at her son, then back at her again. The farmers—who probably considered ranchers an immoral class anyway—looked disapproving. Especially the wives. She hated being embarrassed in front of sodbusters. Was this snobbism?

"No, he isn't!" Percy declared. "Who told you he was my father? Was it her, Jesse, your new best friend?"

"No, I swear I didn't tell him nothin'," said Jesse.

"You're a liar!" accused Percy.

"No, I ain't."

Percy turned angrily to the dumbfounded farmer. "She put you up to this, didn't she?"

"No, she didn't. I swear. She's tellin' you the truth."

"You're lying, just like her."

"I ain't no liar," sputtered Kenny. "You lookin' for a fight or somethin'? I thought we was all gonna be friends. What—?"

"Shut up!" Percy ordered. "I hate liars."

"Now, now, calm down, everyone," Revelie said, her voice tight but controlled. "Let's all take a deep breath."

"I don't need a breath," said her son. "I need answers."

"Shut up!"

"Don't raise your voice to me, young man."

She regretted it as soon as she said it. *Young man.* She sounded like her mother.

"Tell me, Mother," Percy demanded, staring hard at her, "do I look like that man in the back bedroom? Do I or not?"

The dining room fell even more silent. They were all looking at her, farmers, farmers' wives, cowboys.

"This is not the time or the place."

"What time would be the right time? I mean for you to tell me the truth." He waited. "Mother?"

"Don't talk to your mother like that," said Kenny.

"Shut up!" yelled Percy. "Mother, tell me the truth right now!"

"You know the truth. I've always told you the truth. You know who you are."

And yet, at the moment, she felt she hardly knew him—or who he was.

"No, I don't. Tell me who I am. What's my last name?"

"It's Goodnight, of course."

"I don't believe you."

"Pyg, please stop," Jesse jumped in.

"Don't call him Pyg," ordered Revelie.

"What should she call me? Jack Loving Junior?"

"Pyg," pleaded the Harvey Girl.

"I can't stand it here. Nobody tells me the truth."

Percy got up from the round table and walked rapidly out of the dining room. His mother followed him, and Jesse followed her. They made a small parade as they crossed a corner of the living room and headed down the corridor.

"Wait," Revelie called in the hallway. "Please, wait."

"Get away from me," Percy said.

Entering his room, he slammed the door behind him with a bang. His mother paused at the closed door, then opened it and walked in, followed closely by the Harvey Girl.

"Wait, listen—" Revelie began.

"I didn't—" Jesse interrupted.

"Shut up!" the mother interrupted the interruption. "Get out of here! We don't need your interference."

"Both of you get out," Percy raised his voice.

"No."

"No."

"Then I'm getting out."

"Percy, you're embarrassing me, and we have guests."

"I don't care."

CHAPTER 53

Pyg knew what he had to do: He had been thinking about it a lot lately. Partly because of Jesse's accusations. Partly due to his own observations. He had to find out who he really was. And the only way he could think of to discover the truth—after turning it over and over in his tumbling mind—was to find the ax and the headstone.

Pyg started stuffing clothing into saddlebags. Angry, he shoved in shirts without folding them properly, just wadded them up. With his mother looking on, he was a real packing rebel.

"What are you doing?" stammered Revelie. "You're wrinkling—"

"I'm going to go find my father," Pyg said, panting as if packing were hard work.

"I'm coming with you," said Jesse.

"What are you talking about?" asked his mother. "Your father is dead. He's under the ground. Do you want to dig him up again?"

"I'm not so sure he is dead," said Pyg, feeling his lungs collapsing. "I've got to know."

"He's as dead as a stone, a clod. I'm sorry. I'm really sorry."

"I'm going to find out if you're telling the truth or lying to me."

"You would accuse your own mother of lying?"

Pyg stopped packing and looked out a window, anywhere but at his mother. He didn't want to hurt her, but he had to find out who he really was. Couldn't she see that? No, of course not, especially if . . .

"I'm going," Pyg said flatly.

"What do you expect to find out there?" demanded his mother. "What's there that isn't here? Right here?"

"The ax."

He thought she shivered.

"And what would that tell you?" asked his mother.

"I don't know. That's why I want to find it."

"And what will you do"—she really did shiver—"if you do?"

"Try to pull it out."

"You aren't that superstitious, are you? I thought I taught you better than that."

"I have to know." He stared at her. "If you won't tell me, maybe it will."

"Really that's superstitious nonsense."

"Then why are you so worried I might find the ax?"

Slinging his saddlebags over his shoulder, Pyg pushed past his mother—actually shoving her, gently—and ran down the hall.

"Wait!" screamed his mother, who never screamed.

"I'm coming with you," shouted Jesse.

"No!" yelled Revelie.

Pyg stopped and turned around to face the Harvey Girl, who was chasing him down the corridor.

"Don't you dare try it," yelled the soft-spoken boy. "If you come anyplace near me, I'll shoot you. And you know I can shoot."

"Aim at my damned heart," Jesse yelled defiantly.

"Percy, if you're really going," shouted his mother, "at least take a coat."

Looking back, he saw her holding one, rushing down the steps. He halted, waited, took the coat, and rushed off without a word.

CHAPTER 54

Pyg was lonesome. He had insisted on going alone, but now he was lonely. He looked ahead of him and saw nothing but flat nothing. This landscape of rippling grass reminded him of Boston's rippling ocean, but this sea bore no ships. Lonesome. Once this land would have offered herds of buffalo to keep Pyg company, but no more. This sea was fished out. Anyway all the big fish were gone. The only life left was small and creeping and hidden from sight. He couldn't even find a prairie dog or a horned frog to keep him company. Lonely.

Pyg saw a dust devil jump up nearby. It couldn't be a companion, but perhaps it would serve as a playmate. Seeing whirlwinds so often in this country, he had long wondered what it would be like to ride into the middle of one. He imagined that it would be fun. Kicking Smoke in the ribs, Pyg charged. As he bore down on the pint-sized tornado, he happened to remember his mother telling him the story of a crazy would-be knight who tried to fight a spinning windmill. Laughing out loud, he kicked again and raced faster. He felt great, not lonesome anymore, not plagued by questions, but simply riding all out toward fun.

When he hit the devil, Pyg felt that he was in a hailstorm. A blizzard of rocks and sand and small animals. Heavy flakes hit him in the face, bouncing off his cheeks, his forehead, his tightly closed eyelids. His whole body was pelted. He felt as if he were being stoned to death like an unfaithful wife in the Old Testament, but he had never committed any sexual sins, much to his sudden regret. He couldn't breathe with so much dirt in his nose. It was as if he were being buried alive beneath the dust of the plains. Pyg didn't know which way to turn, which way was up, which way down, which way whatever. But Smoke had the sense for which horses were well known. He galloped straight through the tornado and out the other side. Pulling up, Pyg sat in the

saddle gasping. Then he used his index finger to try to claw the dirt out
of his nose and mouth.

Pyg took a vow: He swore off dust devils forever.

Having escaped the whirlwind, the lone rider felt content for an
hour or so. Then he was lonely again. Lonesome. His only companion
seemed to be the ever-sinking sun, which drew him on toward the New
Mexico Territory where Big Sal and his gang were supposed to be hiding out. The boy got lonelier and lonelier, especially with the sun low
and night approaching.

Then Pyg saw another whirlwind. This dust devil was approaching
from behind, bearing down on him, chasing him. He congratulated
himself on being too smart to tangle with even a small twister ever
again. Once burned, once pelted, once with dirt up your nose . . .

He didn't want to joust with another devil, but this devil seemed
determined to joust with him. It was taking dead aim and charging
right at him. Pyg reined his horse to the right and spurred, but the
whirlwind turned, too. It was still coming after him. This devil was
chasing him! No, that was crazy. But it kept on coming. Dust devils
couldn't see, could they? Rocks and sand and wind didn't have eyes.
As the small storm rode him down, he hated to admit it, but he was
scared. He didn't believe in the supernatural, but he spurred hard and
he wasn't a hard spurrer.

"Hold up!" yelled the whirlwind.

Recognizing the voice, Pyg was embarrassed at having been afraid
of the dust storm which—he now realized—was man-made. But soon
embarrassment turned to irritation building into anger. Why was he
being followed? Hadn't he made it very clear to everyone that he
wanted to go alone? He raised his feet to kick his mount, but stopped
in midstroke. He tugged back gently on the reins.

Too Short materialized out of the dust, but he wasn't the only one.
He was accompanied by two other riders. One was big: Little Dogie.
Damn, damn, damn, and all those words the cowboys knew but he
wasn't comfortable with, not yet. The other was normal-sized: Opry,
the songster. As the boy watched them draw closer, he was again
tempted to kick his horse into action, but again he didn't.

When they reached him, Pyg complained: "I told you not to come
with me."

"I know," Too Short said. "But your mama done told us we had to or else. And we're more ascared of your mama than you."

"But I'm a killer," Pyg said with a laugh.

"So's your mama." Little Dogie laughed. "Between the two of you, we figured you was the less dangerous murderer."

Opry laughed out of the side of his mouth, the right side, where his smiling scar was.

"What are you talking about?" Pyg demanded. "Did you just call my mother a murderer?"

"Course not," Too Short jumped in.

"He was just funnin' you," said Opry, and he laughed his crooked laugh again.

"No, he wasn't," Pyg declared. "What did he mean?"

"I didn't mean nothin'," Little Dogie chuckled. "I was just funnin', like he said."

"I don't believe you."

"Suit yourself," said the giant. "I figured you could take a joke, but looks like I reckoned wrong."

"It didn't sound like a joke."

"So I ain't a very good comedian. 'Scuse me for not makin' you laugh. I'm powerful sorry, I am."

It seemed to Pyg that Little Dogie was like someone with a chronic disease. The sickness got better from time to time but it always came back with a vengeance. The boy wasn't sure meanness really qualified as a disease, but he considered it one. After the farmers saved his life, the giant had gotten better for a while, but now he was suffering a relapse and was as mean as ever. If meanness was a sickness, was there any treatment that could cure it permanently? Any drug? Well, the boy could think of one medicine that would surely work: a lead pill.

But just because Little Dogie was mean didn't mean that he didn't know secrets about Pyg's mother. Surely he knew a lot about what went on—and what had gone on—around the Home Ranch. His insinuations couldn't be automatically dismissed. So Pyg couldn't help wondering: Whom could his mother have killed? No one, of course not, impossible, unthinkable. But . . .

"That's about enough jokin' around," Too Short said. "It's time we headed on back."

"Back!" exclaimed the startled boy.

"Sure," explained Little Dogie. "Your mama said her little boy done run off—as little boys will—and she wanted us to find you and bring you back home ag'in."

"Like Little Bo Peep's sheep," added Opry.

"Well, I'm not going back," Pyg said.

"Thass what all the little boys say," said Little Dogie. "But in the end, they come along peaceful like if'n they don't wanna git a spankin'."

The silver gun seemed to jump of its own accord into Pyg's hand. He pointed it at the giant's broad middle.

"Do you think you can spank me?" the boy asked. "Come ahead and try it. The first thing I'll do is shoot off your ears, and I'll try real hard not to miss." He took a breath. "Then I'll shoot your arms off. You won't be a very good spanker without hands, will you? Come on."

"But your mama done made us promise to bring you back," Opry said. "If you're so hot to shoot somebody, come back with us and shoot her." He laughed.

Turning the gun on Opry, Pyg said: "How about I shoot that grin off your face. Do you want to bet me I can't?" He studied the last-nameless cowboy, who was mopping his brow with his leather cuff. "You've got a freckle right between your eyes. I'll bet you twenty dollars I can hit it. Get your money ready."

Pyg raised the silver gun, took careful aim, and softly squeezed. The lonely explosion did not disturb the vast flatness. Opry fell backward off his horse and lay motionless on the ground.

The boy turned his gun on Little Dogie, who dropped the reins of his horse and held both hands in front of his face. Pyg fired again. The horse bolted and Little Dogie fell to the earth.

Too Short just shook his head.

"You shot 'em, you bury 'em," said the little cowboy. "Gonna take a while to dig a hole big enough for Little Dogie. Better git started."

CHAPTER 55

"Not so damn fast," grumbled Little Dogie, sitting up. "I'm sorry to disappoint you, but Mr. Cain't Miss done missed."

"Are you sure?" asked Pyg. "Take a look at your belt buckle."

The big cowboy's equally huge buckle—it would have been a shield on a smaller man—looked like it had been stepped on by a giant. Where it had been convex, it was now concave. And twisted.

"You take chances," said Too Short.

"Sometimes," Pyg said.

Opry was stirring now, too. Sitting up, he reached up and touched his right ear. It was bleeding. Just a trickle. Just nicked.

"Lemme git this straight," said Too Short. "You two tough ol' cowboys figured Pyg couldn't miss. So you reckoned you was done dead. So you just went ahead and did what dead men do: fell off'n yore horses and laid down in the damn dust. I'm surprised you didn't stiffen up, too, while you was at it." He laughed at his own wit. "You let this here boy bluff you into believin' you was corpses." He laughed some more.

"Pyg, yore buyin' me a new buckle," Little Dogie huffed.

"We'll discuss that later," Pyg said, "when I get back from where I'm going. Do say hello to my mother for me. So long."

"No, wait," Too Short said. "If you ain't acomin' with us, we're agoin' with you."

"No," said the boy.

"You're gonna have to shoot me for real if you wanna git ridda me. I'm stickin'. And they're stickin', too, if'n they know what's good for 'em. I cain't tell your mama I let you go off alone to chase outlaws. I'd be lookin' for another job, and in these parts that's worse'n bein' dead. Sorta."

"No."

"Ya know, you might need a little help. Them outlaws may not be pushovers like our friends here."

"How many times do I have to say it? No, no, no . . ."

As they rode west, Pyg was still in a foul, killing mood.

"Relax, we're here to help," said Too Short. "We're on your side."

"Sure," said Pyg.

"Opry, why doncha cheer Pyg up by singin' him one of your funny songs," Little Dogie said. "I'm sure he'd appreciate it."

"Don't feel like singin'," Opry grumbled.

He evidently needed cheering up, too.

CHAPTER 56

Pyg was sometimes afraid to go to sleep. Wrapped in his blanket, his head propped on his saddle, the boy was terrified of losing consciousness. Because sleep was like death. You weren't there. You weren't anybody. While you were asleep, you were about as alive as the bleached-white skull of a cow. You were alive but you didn't know you were alive, which was the same as being dead. Sleep was a little death that was a rehearsal for the big death. Lying on the hard ground, his hip bone nestled in a shallow hole that he had dug, Pyg was desperately afraid of ceasing to exist. Even for a few hours. It wasn't that he didn't think he would wake up. It was that he would be dead until he woke up. Dead, gone, nobody, nothing. He told himself that dreams should be a comfort, but they sometimes turned scary, or they didn't come at all. Every night, he met an executioner when he closed his eyes, so he tried to keep them open as long as he could.

Fighting heavy lids, Pyg sensed movement out there in the black grass. Was he dreaming? Half dreaming? He couldn't tell. He closed his eyes, but they popped open again. Another dark ripple in the grass. He realized that he was frightened, but didn't know what to do. What if he raised an alarm and the intruder turned out to be the wind or an armadillo? Now he bit the inside of his cheek to try to stay awake. He stared, more or less unblinking, at the ghostly black grass. He saw nothing, nothing, still nothing, blink, nothing nothing nothing nothing, blink blink, nothing at all, nothing, nothing . . .

A black specter crawled out of the black grass and called him back to life. Pyg's hand reached under his saddle-pillow and found his bright gun. The solid silver butt was cool in his hand. It made his palm itch. Moving slowly, he lifted the Tiffany six-shooter and took careful aim at the dark silhouette. He pulled back the hammer and must have made more noise than he intended.

"Aim at my damn heart," Jesse challenged once again.

His finger was too tight on the trigger to stop: Pyg fired. But he missed. He never missed. The shot clipped the grass just over her head.

"Thanks," she said.

"Don't thank me," Pyg said. "I was trying to kill you."

"No, you waddn't."

"Yes, I was."

"No, you ain't like that. You wouldn't shoot no woman. See, we girls got the damn advantage."

Too Short, Opry, and Little Dogie had been jolted awake by the gunshot and were grumbling, cursing, reaching for weapons with sleep-slowed hands.

"I wouldn't count too much on that," Pyg said. "I killed a girl once before."

"Yeah, but that was to save a girl," Jesse said. "Me."

"Shut up about my mother or I will shoot you, girl or no girl."

"Both of you shut up," bellowed Little Dogie, "or I'll kill the pair of you. With my bare hands. Wring your necks and watch you flop."

Soon the camp was quiet again, except for the snoring, but Pyg was not asleep. Once again, he kept his eyes open to ward off his great terror. Not another specter crawling out of the black grass to attack him, but his old goblin: sleep itself. This dread had first descended on him when he was a boy of eight or nine. Back then, time passed even more slowly than it did now. Then an hour seemed an eternity and a whole night was forever. Drifting off to sleep was drifting into dead and gone. He would awaken in the morning with a surge of joy: He was Lazarus come back from the dead. But as soon as the exhilaration wore off, he would start worrying about the approach of night and sleep. And his fears had not changed much as he had grown older and wiser. Well, there was one difference: These spells came less often, but when they recurred, they were as bad as ever. He kept telling himself that if he didn't sleep he would surely die a real and permanent death from which there would be no waking. Which made sense but didn't help.

Lying on his back, eyes still open, Pyg found himself imagining

Jesse in his arms. He shuddered but couldn't get the picture out of his head. In spite of himself, he liked the idea. He imagined what they would do next . . . and then . . . and . . . and . . . No, he had almost fallen asleep. It was as if he had been counting wooly Harvey Girls instead of . . .

No, he had almost dropped off again. He had to get her out of his head or he would never be able to stay awake. Think about the ax. Think about Big Sal. Think about the cave. Think about Jesse's lips on his . . .

No! Don't think about her. Stay awake. Stay . . .

Pyg woke up, a happy Lazarus, but with sticky pants.

After another hard day in the saddle, a day that ate up another forty-five miles, the impromptu posse bedded down again. But still fearing sleep, Pyg kept his eyes open. Glancing in the direction of Jesse's bedroll, a dozen feet away, he saw her dead to the world. Or was she only pretending? Was she—as the cowboys said—playing possum? If he watched long enough, would he see her roll slowly out of her blanket and come creeping toward him? She had followed him out here. She must have something in mind, right? Watching her, he willed her to move. To come to him. To keep him awake and make his dreams come true. But she remained motionless, oblivious to him and the whole universe. Was she too dumb to be afraid of sleep?

Well, if she was too enamored of death to come to him, perhaps he should go to her. At least going to her, coupling with her, would keep him awake. Ever so slowly, he untwined from his bedroll. Then he studied Too Short, Opry, and especially Little Dogie to make sure they weren't restless in their sleep. He didn't see any movement, and the giant's snores continued as usual. Good, he rose to his hands and knees and started crawling. Little Dogie snorted. Pyg crouched like a frightened rabbit and waited . . . and waited . . . and started to get drowsy. Shake it off. Time to move. Pyg continued his crawl and could not help noticing that he had an erection.

When he finally reached Jesse, Pyg didn't know what to do. Watching her sleep—*dead* to the world—he thought the matter over. Should he touch her shoulder while simultaneously placing his hand over her mouth so she wouldn't wake the others? Or tap her nose? Or just wait until his presence woke her up? He decided to wait, but his proximity did not even cause her eyelids to flutter. Tired of waiting, Pyg decided to kiss Jesse as she slept. His lips drew closer to hers . . . and closer . . . and . . .

"Uggggg!" sputtered Jesse, coming back to life. "Git offa me."

"Shhh," whispered Pyg. "It's me."

"I know who," she said in a loud whisper. "Leave me alone."

"I want to talk to you," he lied in a soft whisper. "Come with me, please."

"You don't wanna talk to me. You wanna fuck me. Well, thass just too bad because I don't wanna fuck you. Not no more. You had your chance and you blew it. Excuse the damn expression."

"But I thought—"

"Stop your damn thinkin'. I didn't come out here to be with you. I come out here to git away from your mama. Go back to sleep."

Hearing Little Dogie laughing, Pyg's hard penis shrank to a soft thumb.

CHAPTER 57

P yg squinted at the setting sun, which hurt his eyes. He told himself again—as he had been telling himself for a week now—that the afternoon glare was the price you paid for amazing sunsets unlike anything he had ever seen back east. He was looking forward to another one now. The sky was already pink, and other colors were surely on the way. Yes, here they came. Violet. Purple. Gold. Orange.

Black?

Widening his eyes now, Pyg saw a black cloud rising up from the ground, swallowing the setting sun. Was a storm coming? But bad weather generally blew in from the north. And storms generally descended rather than ascended. Of course, it was probably an optical illusion. Maybe he had been looking at the sun too long.

"Looks like rain," announced Too Short.

"Damn," said Jesse.

"Rain's a good thing," said Opry.

"Rain's a good thing," she said, "if'n you're in a house lookin' at it through a winder."

"So you really are a girl, after all?" Little Dogie chided.

"Them's fightin' words."

The black cloud kept rising and getting bigger. It covered the setting sun and cast a vast shadow over the land. But there were small holes in the cloud where bits of the expanding sun peeked through. These were irregular—wiggly actually—holes. It was as if the fading sun were seen through the fluttering leaves of a tree as big as a county.

"Funny storm," said Pyg.

"I ain't laughin'," said Jesse.

Then the sun sank out of sight, and the black cloud was absorbed by the night, but no thunder rolled and not a drop of rain fell.

. . .

Thrilled to find himself alive again, Pyg opened his eyes with a bang in the half light of early morning. The sun wasn't up yet, but it was happily on its way. Just as it was sneaking over the horizon, Pyg saw the black cloud again. This time it was descending. The black cloud molded itself into a funnel.

"Wake up!" Pyg yelled.

Little Dogie cursed. Too Short snorted. Opry woke up coughing. Jesse slept on as if really dead and not just gone.

"Twister!" Pyg shouted.

"Hell!" yelled Little Dogie, getting it about right.

"What?" asked Jesse, finally rousing.

Opry, a smoker, just kept on coughing.

"What are we supposed to do?" asked Pyg.

"Run down in the cellar," said Little Dogie.

"What?" asked Jesse, rousing and rousing some more.

"Yeah, it's twister season," Opry said between coughs. "Mebbe we oughta turn back. Twisters just skip right over that there red canyon. It's like a huge ol' storm cellar. Which is just what we ain't got here."

"Mebbe we oughta," agreed Little Dogie. "Me, I never liked twisters."

"Don't worry," Pyg said. "That twister could pick up a house, but I doubt it could budge your ass."

"Suck my corncob," said Little Dogie.

"It's a charming proposal, but thanks anyway."

Pyg noticed that the funnel cloud was getting smaller rather than larger. Was it moving away from them, thank God? No, it didn't seem to be. Rather it appeared to be imitating water draining out of a bathtub: funneling itself down into the ground.

"Funny twister," said Pyg.

"Shut up with your funnies," said Little Dogie.

Opry just coughed.

"Least it's shrivelin'," said Too Short.

"Like it's losin' its hardon," said the giant.

"What's goin' on?" asked Jesse.

"We'd better find out," Pyg said. "Let's go."

"No," cautioned Opry.

"If you're scared, you can go on home," the boy said.

"No, he cain't," Too Short said with authority. "If we catch up to them grave robbers, we're gonna need ever' man we can git ahold of. We all go, or we all turn back. Thass final."

They rode toward the shrinking black cloud, but before they had ridden a mile, it was almost gone. As it was disappearing, Pyg picked out a rocky butte as a landmark to aim at. They rode toward that pile of rocks for hours, almost all day, and reached it in the afternoon. Dismounting, they looked around for answers to their mystery, but found nothing suspicious or even interesting. They were in rough, broken country, dry, brown, rocky, and unwelcoming. Ugly prickly pear cacti, monsters with thorny green mittens, reached for them at every step.

"Nice place you found," said Little Dogie.

"Ain't it," said Jesse. "Maybe it was just a cloud."

"Perhaps," said Pyg. "But I never saw a cloud behave that way."

"You an expert on the comin's and goin's of clouds all of a sudden?" asked the giant.

"I can tell a cirrus from a cumulus," the boy said, "and this one wasn't either one."

"Don't talk your damn Greek at me," Little Dogie sputtered. "Whadda we do now?"

They all looked at the boy as if he might know the answer to that question. Which surprised him, disturbed him, and gave him the slightest twinge of pleasure.

"I think we should wait here for a while," Pyg said at last. "The cloud might come back at sunset. The way it did last night."

"I dunno," grumbled Little Dogie. "How come it'd come back, huh? Clouds is clouds, ain't no two of 'em alike. We could wait here forever."

"Yeah, thass right," interrupted Opry. "I say we just go on home. We're just wastin' time here, if'n you ask me."

"The horses could use a rest," decided Too Short.

While they relaxed, Pyg kept trying to imagine what could have caused the cloud. Perhaps a sudden dust storm. Or some sort of mirage. Or a huge flock of birds. Black birds. Crows. Ravens. Buzzards. What if he had managed to locate the world's largest congregation of skin-headed vultures? The other cowboys would never stop kidding him.

Since he had purposely kept himself awake for much of the night, Pyg began to get drowsy as he reclined on the rocky ground. He yawned. He yawned again. And he seemed to feel the earth spinning beneath him. Reluctantly he closed his eyes . . .

When he opened them again, the sun was much lower in the sky. The harsh, dry landscape looked better in the softer light. As the red sun touched the black horizon, Pyg felt the chill of a vast shadow. Looking up, he saw the black cloud overhead right on schedule. He not only saw the cloud but he heard it. This cloud didn't thunder, it squeaked. It sounded like a million mice squealing their way across the heavens. Mice on the wing. A plague of flying mice. Perhaps he was still asleep, dreaming, nightmaring.

"Bats!" yelled Jesse. "I hate bats."

"Very girlish of you." Little Dogie laughed.

"I'll kill you."

"Don't you want me to protect you from the big, bad, blood-suckin' bats?"

"Go suck yourself."

"Girlish, but she ain't too ladylike."

Pyg stared up at the black, squeaking bat cloud. What did it mean? His mouth gaped open, then twisted into a big smile, because now he was pretty sure he did know what it meant. Thank goodness for science class.

"Where do bats live?" yelled Pyg. Nobody answered. "They live in caves." He looked around to see if the others were impressed. They didn't seem to be. "And a million billion bats would need a really big cave. And a big cave is where Big Sal is supposed to have his hide-out." Now they were paying attention. "We have to find the bats' home."

Pyg was already running up the butte in search of high ground. At the top, he paused, breathless, and looked around. The others were stumbling after him. Up here, bats flapped and squealed about his head. Trying to brush them away, to keep them off his face, his hand grazed their soft, short fur. Pyg shuddered because it felt like petting rats. Turning this way and that to try to get away from them, he grew dizzy. He noticed that the others were swatting away, too. Especially Little Dogie. For some reason, big often feared small. Pyg wanted to run, but he remembered that he had climbed up here for a purpose and fought down the urge to flee. Deliberately calming himself, he tried to track the bats back to their source. At first, they all seemed to be flapping in circles around his head, but he slowly began to discern a pattern. He thought most of them were flying in a generally northeasterly direction, which of course meant that they had come from the southwest. So he looked southwest and saw what appeared to be a black stem supporting the dark squeaky cloud.

"Look!" he shouted, pointing. "See where the cloud touches the ground? It looks like a black pillar. Or a tail. Look!"

The others shaded their eyes to keep off the bats and stared.

"I see it," yelped Jesse. Now she was pointing, too. "Right there."

Soon the others saw it as well. It was perhaps a mile and a half away.

"Let's go," yelled Pyg. "Hurry."

"Mount up," said Too Short.

They went running and skidding down the steep side of the butte. Pyg's boots started rocks rolling and tumbling, and something in his chest was tumbling, too. Little Dogie dislodged even bigger rocks and caused a landslide.

Mounting up, they rode southwest toward the biggest bat city on earth. Pyg kicked Smoke into a gallop. The dark stem began to fade as fewer and fewer bats emerged from the cave. Would it disappear completely before they ran it to ground? He spurred Smoke, which was something he rarely did.

"I see it!" Pyg yelled. "It's a big black mouth. Right there. See it?"

"Yes!" shouted Jesse.

The boy spurred his horse again even though there was no special hurry now. The cave wasn't going to get away.

CHAPTER 58

S till mounted, they surveyed the mammoth mouth from the rim of a rocky canyon. It appeared to be a formidable fortress. Pyg realized they couldn't attack it, day or night, without a way to light its dark bowels. And all they had were the long-stemmed matches they had brought along to start campfires. In the fast-dimming daylight, the vast black mouth looked like night incarnate.

"Whadda we do now, Boss?" Little Dogie asked Pyg, giving the last word a special, sarcastic emphasis. "Got any bright ideas?"

"Maybe they ain't even here," Opry said, applying his leather cuff to his brow.

Pyg just kept staring at the black hole. It was at least a hundred feet high, maybe more, and three hundred feet wide, maybe much more. It was a giant ulcer in the face of the earth. It hurt the boy like an ulcer because he had no earthly idea what to do.

"They'll come riding in any minute now," Pyg bluffed. "We'll wait for them. They'll be like the bats, only in reverse."

"What the hell's that s'posed to mean?" demanded Opry.

The boy took his time: "Maybe the outlaws hunt during the day the way the bats hunt at night."

"Good thinkin'," said Jesse, which pleased Pyg.

"You're crazy," said Opry.

"No, he ain't," said the Harvey Girl. "I mean he usually is. Crazy as locoweed. But this time—"

Jesse stopped talking and stared.

"Shhh," hissed Pyg.

Like Jesse, Pyg had seen several riders walking their horses down the undulating floor of the canyon. He counted them quickly: one, two, three, four, five, six. So they were outnumbered: six men to four, plus a girl. Studying these riders more carefully, he saw a very big man, a very fat man.

"That's him," Pyg said softly. "Anyway it could be. He probably is."

"I'm not so sure," said Opry. "There's lotsa fatties in this world. That ain't no crime, is it, bein' a tubba lard?"

The boy noted with both pleasure and alarm that the outlaw was even bigger than Little Dogie. Even at a distance, his fat seemed to include a lot of muscle. Inadvertently Pyg squeezed his legs together. His horse bolted forward. He had to pull up sharply on the reins to keep from going over the lip of the canyon.

"Yeah, *Boss*," scoffed Little Dogie, "what now?"

Pyg tried to think fast, but he was too busy staring at the rider he assumed was Big Sal.

"*Boss*, what now?" Little Dogie repeated with a chuckle.

What to say? What to do? What in the world—?

"If we ride in shooting," Pyg said, "they'll just take cover in the cave. And then where will we be? They know the cave better than we do." He paused. "I say we wait."

"Thass what you always say," said Little Dogie. "Wait, wait, wait."

"We wait," repeated Pyg. "They'll make camp in the cave. They'll start a campfire and that will light up the place. We have to have light. All we have are matches. So we wait until they light their fire. That will give everybody light, them and us, too. Understood?"

Nobody complained. Pyg was beginning to realize that Little Dogie's calling him "Boss," however sarcastic, might be a good thing. Since he had more or less met the challenge, they were all starting to look to him as Boss. He hoped Too Short didn't mind too much. Pyg began to feel like his father's son, whoever that father might happen to be. The foreman or the boss? They had both been leaders of men.

The outlaws' campfire lit up the mouth of the cave so it showed its great limestone teeth: big jagged rocks. Pyg thought: poor Jonah. Was this place the whale that would swallow them all?

"Ain't we done waited long enough, Boss?" asked Little Dogie.

"Not yet," said Pyg, sitting on a rock. "We'll wait until they get started eating. Then we'll go. I want them to have their hands full when they see us."

They waited sitting on the rocks.

Pyg watched as giant shadows marched up and down along the walls of the cave. Among them was a shadow that looked three times bigger than the other giants. He was a colossus who dwarfed all the other demigods. He might have been Cyclops in his cave. Pyg recalled that Odysseus—his favorite from Greek class—had stabbed his giant in the eye with a sharp post. But then he hadn't had a gun. Pyg hoped never to get within eye-stabbing distance of Big Sal. Watching, the boy was waiting for the huge shadows to stop walking about, to settle down, to begin eating their shadow suppers. Waiting, he had time to wonder who the outlaws had robbed today. Who had they killed?

"Boss, how about it?" asked Little Dogie.

"Wait," said Pyg.

"I hate waitin'."

"Wait."

While they waited, Pyg saw the mammoth shadows give in to equally large hungers. Soon the shadow men were squatting and shoveling it in.

"Let's go," Pyg said. "Leave the horses."

With the boy leading the way—to his own surprise—they quickly but quietly descended the wall of the shallow canyon. Well, more or less quietly. Opry turned out to be surprisingly noisy, and Little Dogie's giant feet never moved soundlessly. But the giants inside the cave did not seem to notice because they had food on their shadowy minds. When they reached the canyon floor, Pyg halted his posse with a raised hand. He looked around. Then he motioned them to continue, to follow him. Little Dogie's big feet made so much noise that Pyg considered leaving him behind, but then he reminded himself that he could use all the help he could get, especially if this war came down to giant against giant. The big mouth kept getting bigger and more whalelike. Poor Jonah. Poor Jonahs.

When they reached the lip of the cave—evidently unheard—they hid behind a huge, sharp-pointed limestone canine. Pyg peeked over the edge of this immense tooth and studied the outlaws' camp on a stone floor about fifteen feet below where he stood. He could see them plainly because, besides making a fire, they had also lit several torches. A couple of outlaws had finished eating–damn!–and put down their tin plates, but Big Sal was still chowing with gusto.

What to do now? How to attack? What would General Grant do? He would just attack full out and who gave a damn who got killed. What about General Lee? Pyg recalled one battle–what was its name?– where Lee had defied convention, divided his forces, and attacked from two sides. The boy boss couldn't even remember if Lee had won the battle–God, he wished he could–but he liked the concept anyway because it might convince the enemy that he had more men than he really had.

"We'll split up," he whispered. "You three"–he pointed up at Little Dogie, down at Too Short, then at Opry in the middle–"go in hugging the north wall of the cave." He nodded at the Harvey Girl. "Jesse and I'll creep in along the south wall. When we get close enough, I'll yell out that we have them surrounded." He took a breath. "Right after I yell, the three of you"–he pointed up, down, and in the middle once again–"start yelling your heads off, from your side of the cave. That should impress them. Make them think we're a multitude."

Why had he used that word? What a silly word to use when his leadership was so fragile.

"Sounds good to me," whispered Too Short.

Thank you. Thank you.

"What about me?" whispered Jesse. "Ain't I s'posed to yell, too?"

"No," Pyg whispered as firmly as he could.

He didn't want the badmen to hear that one-fifth of his army was female, but he didn't explain his reasoning to the Harvey Girl. He told himself an explanation might be overheard, especially if she argued, which was entirely possible.

"Oh, and take off your boots," Pyg whisper-ordered. "They make too much noise."

"I ain't takin' off my boots," whispered Little Dogie.

"Me neither," Opry said too loudly.

Their refusals hung in the nervous night air.

"Yes, you are," said Too Short.

CHAPTER 59

As he entered the giant cave mouth, Pyg's heart was a scared rabbit thrashing in the jaws of a coyote. Couldn't the outlaws hear it banging? He ordered himself to calm down, but his pulse disobeyed. He might be learning to give orders to others, but he still couldn't give them to himself. Wearing only socks, he stepped on a sharp-edged rock and wanted to cry out, but managed to subdue himself. They were halfway to the outlaws and all seemed to be going well. Then Pyg heard a crash. Rocks skittering. Opry's voice swearing. And Pyg had been worried his heart was too noisy. Damn that cowboy. Who had asked him to come along anyway? Now the outlaws were looking around, putting down plates, picking up guns.

"Surrender!" Pyg yelled. "You're surrounded."

The bandits answered by shooting in the direction of his voice. Bullets bounced off the cave wall over his head. Pyg remembered that in low light shooters fortunately tended to shoot high.

"Give up!" shouted Too Short from the other side of the cave. "We gotcha!"

The outlaws turned their fire on the little cowboy's voice. Pyg hoped they were still shooting high.

"HANDS UP, DAMMIT!" bellowed Little Dogie.

More shooting. It occurred to Pyg that a high shot might actually hit the giant. The thought did not entirely displease him.

"We got you covered," Jesse sang out, soprano.

"Shhhhh!" Pyg shushed. Then he yelled in his best alto: "Drop your guns!"

Evidently convinced they were outnumbered—that part of the plan had worked, anyway—the outlaws ran. Deeper into the cave. Down into the bowels of mother earth. Just where Pyg did not want to go. He aimed at a huge target, Big Sal's back, pulled the trigger, and killed some limestone at the outlaw's feet. Sometimes lessons are learned too well: In the dim light, he had overcompensated and shot too low.

Carrying torches, the outlaws disappeared down a black hole. Pyg chased them, not entirely sure what he would do if he caught them. The others ran after him, following his leadership, and he still wasn't entirely sure why. Especially since there was bat shit everywhere, which he had learned in Andover science class to call guano. But fortunately the outlaws had excavated a path.

Running into the great blackness, Pyg entered another world, unlike any he had ever known or even suspected. The light thrown off by the outlaw torches revealed shadowy columns running from floor to roof, thick at the top, thick at the bottom, but narrow in the middle, like great rock women. Remembering science class, he realized that these shapely pillars had been formed when stalactites, growing down from the cave's roof, had joined with stalagmites, growing up from the floor. From the great vaulted ceiling hung huge limestone chandeliers, covered with thousands of rock candles which somebody had forgotten to light. And he heard dripping coming from somewhere, everywhere. The boy kept expecting the cave to collapse, trapping him and his party seeming miles underground where they would never be found.

Trying to make this great cavity seem less strange, Pyg's mind cast about for anything he could compare it to. Anything at all. He thought of Alice falling down the rabbit hole, but Wonderland was made up. He thought of the Greeks' Hades, but it seemed made up, too. Anyway, thinking of Hades was not particularly comforting. And he was looking for comfort. He thought of train tunnels (smaller) and mine shafts (much smaller). Then he thought of Jesse and his mother and all the other women in the world: They all had a hole in them, a cave, a deep and mysterious cavern. To him, it was a strange and unknown world. What was in there?

The outlaws' light was getting fainter because they were moving faster than Pyg and his cautious cowboys. He started to yell out to hurry up, but realized he was the one setting the pace. The rocks hurt his bootless feet.

"Ouch!" yelled Little Dogie.

The cavern began a steep descent into the middle of the earth, and the boy and his men slowed down even more. With the outlaws' torches receding even faster, the world of the cave kept getting stranger. It reminded Pyg of the inside of a long train, a very fancy train, a train in which only kings and queens could ride. He thought some of the rocks looked like fingers. Were they closing around him? They were wet fingers. Where did the water come from? Everything was dripping. Drop, drop, drop, drop. But the interiors of trains weren't wet. What was wet? Women were wet. Their tunnels were sopping, weren't they? But now was not the time for such thoughts. He was supposed to be a leader of men, not a sex-mad boy.

"We're losing them," he said and heard his voice echo. "Come on, hurry up. The light's getting away."

Pyg scurried faster but couldn't quite bring himself to break into a run. The incline was so steep, the dark obstacles so many, the uncertainty so great.

Pyg held up his hand to stop the others: The tunnel had narrowed and a black hole—a huge pothole—barred their way. Fortunately a plank lay across the abyss. The outlaws had evidently been in too much of a hurry—or too dumb—to kick it into the hole. After a moment's hesitation, Pyg walked across it, but Little Dogie just stood there staring down into the void and blocking the way. He seemed paralyzed. What a fraud. What a coward. The giant picked up a rock the size of a baseball and dropped it into the hole. Pyg listened. They all listened. The boy did not hear the rock hit anything. Nobody did. Not a bang, not a thump. Nothing at all. Deep silence. Little Dogie crawled across the plank. Too Short and Opry crawled, too. Even Jesse, who always wanted to appear more fearless than any man, crawled. Pyg almost wished he had crawled. Now they moved even more slowly.

Descending the earth's own birth canal, Pyg could not get his mother out of his mind. He was embarrassed by his own thoughts, his own suspicions. But it was as if the deeper he went, the deeper he went. He wondered how many men had entered her cave. And who upon leaving had left him behind? What confusion, with tunnels and possibilities leading off on every side. Descending, Pyg could not decide whom he hated more: Goodnight or Loving? He felt they were both culpable in compromising his mother and him. Now he needed the ax the way he needed the guilty sperm, to tell him who was his real father.

He had to know, but how far would he have to wind down into the earth to find out? If he ever did? And survived?

Falling farther and farther behind the fleeing outlaws—and their bright torches—Pyg found it harder and harder to see the path in front of him. The light was escaping. The boy and the "men" he led were slowly going blind. The outlaw torches were little more than a will-o'-the-wisp now, leading them down to their destruction. Stubbing his bootless toe on a rock he hadn't seen, he thought: Damn!

Almost groping his way now, Pyg did not feel like much of a leader, much of a boss. He wondered if he would be a better leader now if he had had a father when he was growing up. Maybe leadership was the sort of thing that fathers taught their sons. He couldn't help asking himself: What had not having a father done to him? What price had he paid? How would he have been different? Who would he have been? If he had had a father, would he still be a virgin? Would his dad have told him things about sex that a boy needed to know? And about lots of other things, too? He felt he had never needed a father more than right now.

Pyg struck a long-stemmed match. The tunnel flared up before him, and he tried to turn his mind into a camera to photograph it all before the match went out, memorizing every twist, every stone, every pitfall. He saw huge boulders leaning against each other over his head and felt uncomfortably like Chicken Little, but he held his tongue. Fortunately. Maybe being a leader had something to do with keeping your mouth shut. What he didn't see, again fortunately, was bat shit. Evidently the winged rats didn't penetrate to this depth. Maybe they were right. When the flame reached his fingers, Pyg dropped the match and watched it gutter out on the cave floor. He shook his hand. Ouch.

Then he groped his way forward, guided by the fuzzy photograph in his memory. He felt as lost as if he were feeling his way down the corridors of his own brain, if his brain had corridors. After he had gone another thirty yards, he was totally lost again. He couldn't remember the terrain, and he kept bumping into something sharp. Something armed with tiny thorns. What? How?

Pyg was still trying to figure it out when he heard a titter. Then a laugh. His men were laughing at him. Hurt by the laughter, he thought: The idiots, don't they know they are giving away their position? Then Pyg himself started to laugh. He didn't want to, but he couldn't help it. Evidently there was something about being trapped in utter, complete, unforgiving darkness that was funny. He couldn't explain it. He just laughed and laughed.

A gunshot stopped the laughter.

The bullet ricocheted off a column above Pyg's head. Luckily, the outlaws were still shooting high. The cave amplified the sound of the shot, making it deafening. The absolute darkness magnified the boy's fears. He wanted to turn and run out of the cave and back to his mother's arms. But bosses—even boy bosses—weren't supposed to be runners, were they? He dropped to the ground and crawled behind a boulder. He felt an urge to laugh again but was afraid it would draw another shot. He didn't want to die laughing in the dark.

Then Pyg heard laughter boiling up from below, from the depths. It must be outlaw laughter. Bandit giggles. They were laughing, too. Which tickled the cowboys, who started laughing all over again. This was one happy shootout. But if the outlaws were laughing, then they must also be in the dark. Which meant their torches had either burned out—which seemed unlikely to have happened so quickly—or they had put them out deliberately. What were they up to? Were they digging in to make a stand? Why here? Why now? What did they know about this cave that he didn't know?

Pyg wondered if perhaps he should pull his men back to the entrance and just wait there. The outlaws would have to come out eventually. They would get them then. But what if there was another way out of the cave? Now that he had finally found Big Sal and his men, perhaps he should stick to them.

The boy was shaken by another reverberating gunshot. What if all this noise shook loose the stones overhead? Pyg felt as if the roof of the cave was going to fall right down on him, but this time he not only heard the shot but also saw it. The muzzle flash gave away the location of the shooter. Pyg drew out his silver gun, aimed from memory into the black, and squeezed the trigger.

"Oww!" came the cry.

In perfect darkness, Pyg had gotten his aim back. He expected return fire, but it didn't come. Maybe they had learned that shooting could be dangerous to the shooter. He heard someone crawling toward him.

"Nice shootin'," whispered an invisible Jesse. "But what're we gonna do now?"

"I don't know," Pyg admitted. "Got any ideas?"

"Mebbe we oughta strike a match. See where the hell we are."

It was the last thing Pyg wanted to do. A lit match would be an invitation to shoot. It would say: Here I am, kill me.

"Right," Pyg said. He considered carefully. "You stay behind this rock and strike the match. I'll move over behind another rock, if I can find one in the dark. You keep your head down because they'll be shooting at the light. I'll stick up where they don't expect and look around. See if I can figure out a plan. Okay?"

"You stole them words right outta my mind," Jesse said.

"Really?"

"No."

"But you'll do it?"

"Course."

"Wait till I say now."

Pyg squeezed her arm in the dark and then crawled away in search of another rock. Feeling his way, he found a stone that was too small. Feeling again, he touched a boulder.

"Now," he whispered.

Nothing happened.

"Now!" he repeated, a little louder and with more urgency.

The match flared and the cavern sounded as if it were exploding. All the outlaws were shooting. Their bullets glanced harmlessly off the big rock that protected Jesse. The shots were louder than the loudest thunderstorm. Surely the cave would collapse now.

Peeking over his boulder, Pyg saw the tumbleweeds right away. Dead, dry, brown tumbleweeds with millions of tiny thorns. Now he knew what had been sticking him in the dark. The cave must have been acting as a huge funnel sucking down whatever came its way, and lots of tumbleweeds evidently did. Windblown, hundreds of them had tumbled across the arid landscape until they reached the cave's great stone mouth and tumbled in. Gobbled up, the tumbleweeds rolled down the cavern's throat until they lodged against columns or rocks or whatever else stopped them. Several dozen were now piled up in this steep, narrow corridor.

As Jesse's match started to gutter out, an idea began to flicker in the dark recesses of Pyg's head. The enemy was not only outlaws but darkness. What if he could light up the cave? How? By using these very mobile, very volatile weeds. What if he set these tumbleweeds on fire and rolled them down onto the outlaws? They would be tumbling wheels of light, wouldn't they?

Pyg crawled around—on all fours like a bacon pig—to tell his army his new plan. Jesse was game, which was the good thing about her. Too Short didn't have a better idea. Little Dogie was skeptical. Opry complained it was the worst notion he had ever heard in his life.

In the utter absence of light—or alternatives—they all groped at the tumbleweeds, hurting their hands on the tiny spikes, maneuvering them into a line like big marbles all in a row. Now they were ready to play a game of fire marbles that could easily get out of hand and turn into a disaster. Holding his breath and lying flat, Pyg struck a match and held it beneath the first tumbleweed. A bullet smashed the wall over his head. The tumbler was reluctant to burn. He hadn't counted on that. But then it flared up. Little Dogie picked up the burning ball and threw it down the corridor toward the outlaws. Then he ducked. More bullets killed rocks. The great flaming marble bounced once and then rolled fast down the steep slope, maybe thirty degrees or even more.

Pyg was already lighting the second tumbleweed in line, helped out by game Jesse, who struck her own match. This ball blazed up twice as fast. Little Dogie gave it a kick and it started rolling, picking up speed. Too Short joined in lighting a third ball of flame, and it went bounding off after the others. Follow the leader. They launched a parade of a dozen roaring tumbleweeds in quick succession. Then they all hunkered down and watched.

As the blazing balls approached the outlaws, they turned and ran from the fire and light. Pyg and his army fired after them, but hit nothing. The boy marksman wondered: Was there too much light now?

The burning marbles chased the outlaws down the steep stone corridor—and Pyg's army raced after them—into a vast underground ballroom. A womb? It seemed to cover a dozen subterranean acres at the very least. The badmen ran for cover. The burning tumbleweeds bumped into other tumblers that had collected in the great hall over the years, and set them on fire, too. It made a hell of a blaze. Would the great cavern burn down?

"Look at this place," said Jesse, suddenly stopping. "My God, it's beautiful."

"What?" asked Pyg, out of breath.

"It's amazing. Really, look."

Pyg looked. He saw great stone curtains with elaborate folds. He saw even more elaborate chandeliers. He saw stone forests. He saw a stone throne. He even saw something that looked like a longhorn's tail with a tuft of stone fur at the end. He saw an enchanted world. Jesse was right: It was beautiful. In the middle of a gunfight, she had noticed. He liked her more and more, perhaps in part because she didn't like him. He even thought: She's beautiful, too, like the room. She had met every test, albeit tests usually reserved for men, and yet remained lovely. Her beauty was dark where his mother's was light, which was perhaps why he had overlooked its power. But he didn't want another mother, did he? Especially with all he didn't know about her? He just hoped he wasn't going to get Jesse killed. A bullet cracked off a curtain and he closed his eyes and ducked.

Reminding himself that the tumbleweeds would not burn forever, he knew he had to somehow outflank his enemy while they still had the light. He felt as if the Sword of Damocles were suspended over his head, not metaphorically but literally, for looking up, he saw a sharp-pointed stone sword hanging directly above him. It was too big for any mortal knight. This sword needed a giant like Big Sal or Little Dogie or Goliath.

Peeking over a boulder, Pyg saw what looked like a row of huge stone ice cream cones—and an outlaw taking careful aim at him. My God, the man really wanted to kill him. Kill him dead! And they didn't even know each other. Pyg fired first. The outlaw's left eye exploded. Now Pyg regretted that he had aimed at the eye. It seemed too cruel, too theatrical. He looked around to see if Jesse had noticed. She was frowning. He felt doubly bad. But now with one less outlaw to worry about, the score was evening: It stood at five of us (including a girl) to five of them (including the one who had cried out in the dark and must be wounded).

Bullets were bouncing everywhere. The chance of getting killed by a ricochet was almost as good as being hit by a good shot. Which gave Pyg an idea. He decided to try a ricochet shot on purpose, like in billiards, a game in which he excelled at school. The obvious bull's-eye was Big Sal, whom he had seen ducking behind a stone column. The giant outlaw was not only the biggest but the most important target. If Pyg could wound or kill Big Sal, the others might give up. He planned his bank shot carefully. Hit the face of that column . . . at that angle . . . then the bullet would veer off just so . . . Pyg squeezed the trigger. The cave shook. He hit the spot he was aiming at, but he had misjudged the ricochet: His bullet smashed into the wall behind Big Sal.

"Nice shootin', Boss," laughed Little Dogie. "You missed by a bow-legged mile. They're over there."

Pyg recalculated his bank shot, trying to learn from his miss. Then he aimed, squeezed, and shook the cave once again. Big Sal, who must have been feeling safe behind his rock, yelped in pain.

"I think you just put one in the corner pocket," said Jesse. A woman who understood.

"Give up!" Pyg yelled, adopting the language of his men. "Or you'll all get shot."

The outlaws answered like a firing squad. They executed stalactites and stalagmites. Bang, bang, bang, drip, drip, drip, bang, bang, bang. They mowed down rows of stony icicles no bigger than drinking straws. Some of the straws dropped into a green lake, making small green splashes and green ripples.

It was getting darker and darker in the big room as the tumbleweed flames burned lower. Pyg knew he had to act while he could still see. Now, he decided, would be a good time to talk to Too Short. The littlest cowboy was hunkered down a dozen feet away behind a huge stone tooth with its roots exposed. Crouching low, Pyg ran and then dove behind the big molar as bullets bounced off its crown.

"Hi," said Too Short.

"I've got sort of a plan," Pyg said. "We still want to make them think there are more us than there are of them. Here's what I was thinking."

CHAPTER 60

P yg and Too Short both punched a handful of bullets out of their gun belts. They whispered together one last time. Then Pyg bolted left and Too Short took off to the right. The outlaws fired but missed. Close though, too damn close. Rolling, Pyg came to rest behind a camel-shaped rock—two humps—just a few feet from one of the fading tumbleweed bonfires. Looking back, he glimpsed Too Short behind a rock that looked like a duck or maybe a ship. He, too, was near a pile of smoldering tumbleweeds.

"Now!" yelled Pyg.

More or less simultaneously, the boy boss and the little cowboy tossed handfuls of cartridges into the two dying conflagrations. Almost immediately the bullets in the fire started going off. Frightened he might shoot himself, Pyg dove flat behind his camel. Lead ricocheted of its limestone humps. Hearing Too Short's bullets firing fifty feet away, he hoped the little cowboy had gotten behind something, too.

"Everybody shoot!" Pyg yelled.

Rising up as far as he dared, he started firing in the general direction of the outlaws. He was not concerned about picking out individual targets. He just wanted to demonstrate firepower. The others responded as well. Game as ever, Jesse was up shooting her old wired-together gun. Too Short and Little Dogie were firing, too. But where was Opry? Was his gun empty? Still it sounded like the cavalry had just ridden into this vast cavern, but louder. Much louder. Much too loud. The earth seemed to quake. The cavern writhed. The ceiling thought about falling.

"Give up!" Pyg shouted again.

"Or we'll shoot you up one side and down the other!" yelled the suddenly aggressive Little Dogie. "You hear me?"

Evidently believing they were outflanked and outnumbered once again, the outlaws turned tail and ran once more. They sprinted as if they thought they were pursued by an army. Pyg fired and heard another scream, but none of the bandits fell. The boy blamed the fast-descending darkness for his "miss," which hurt but didn't stop anybody. Then he noticed a large, slow, inviting target: Big Sal was just struggling up from behind his stalagmite. Evidently not too badly wounded, he started lumbering after his men. Weighed down by his fat and a bullet, the massive outlaw ran like a dying buffalo bull. Reminding himself not to hurry, Pyg aimed more carefully this time: He stared down the barrel of his silver gun at the outlaw's left shoulder blade. The boy was going to put this wounded buffalo out of his misery. Squeezing the trigger, being sure to make it smooth, Pyg heard an impotent click. When was he going to learn how to count to six?

The outlaws—with Big Sal bringing up the rear—ran down a dark tunnel at the back of the vast room. Pyg and his "army" jumped from cover and raced after the fleeing badmen. While he struggled to reload on the run, the others exercised their weapons and only hurt the cave. By the time they reached the big room's back-door tunnel, the outlaws had already disappeared into utter obscurity. The boy and his army stopped suddenly as if the darkness were a wall. He started to strike another match but changed his mind.

"How many matches do we have left?" Pyg asked.

Making a hurried blind count, they found they had twenty-one. Working by feel in the dark, Pyg distributed the matches equally, four apiece.

Then Pyg lit the twenty-first and saw the tunnel make a sharp, steep, downhill turn to the right. He attempted to run with the flaming match in his hand, but it soon fluttered out. Trying to light another, he managed to drop all four of his matches. He bent to pick them up, but couldn't find them in the dark, not without getting down on his hands and knees and feeling everywhere. He didn't want to ask for help because he felt too foolish. What was he going to do now? No matches. No light. And what lay beyond the turn in the tunnel was a complete mystery to him. He started running again anyway as if he knew what he was doing and where he was going. He heard the others right behind him, bitching and moaning as their sock feet tread on unseen obstacles.

Turning the doubly blind corner, feeling his way on the run, secretly terrified of what he would find on the other side, Pyg stopped suddenly because he heard a terrible scream. He almost felt he had bellowed it himself since it expressed how he was feeling. Then another scream overlapped the first scream, which echoed weirdly, an echo within an echo. In the dark, Jesse ran into Pyg from behind. In spite of the dire circumstances, he took a moment to enjoy the feel of her breasts on his back. He was still enjoying it when a third scream echoed back down the tunnel. The screams sounded like the cries of the damned, which, Pyg supposed, they probably were. But what had the outlaws run into? A dragon? No, don't be silly. A dragon would have provided some much-needed light in this darkness. But what was it? Pyg did not want to lead his men into the jaws of the same catastrophe. Up ahead, he thought he heard whimpering.

"Anybody got a match?" asked an embarrassed Pyg, but nobody asked where his had gone to.

Jesse struck a match on the limestone wall and the flame revealed the deadly trap the outlaws had run into. Another huge hole—an open trap door to hell—yawned in the middle of this tunnel. The fastest outlaws hadn't been able to stop in time to keep from falling in. Three slower bandits—fortunately hobbled by their wounds—now cowered on the slippery edge of the black hole. Their leaky bullet holes had saved them from running headlong into the mouth of sudden screaming death. Pyg recalled that he hadn't heard the falling men hit the bottom of the pit. Like the stone Little Dogie had dropped into an earlier hole, they seemed to have descended into something bottomless.

"Drop your guns!" Pyg yelled.

But just then Jesse yelped "Ouch" and dropped her match. Fortunately, Too Short lit another one immediately. The outlaws dropped their guns.

"And get on your bellies."

They sank facedown onto the cave floor.

"Jesse, throw their guns in the pit."

The Harvey Girl hurried forward and started kicking the outlaw's artillery into the bottomless pit, where they were never heard from again.

"Aw, you're just a buncha girls," grumbled Big Sal.

Jesse kicked him in the mouth. Pyg hoped the big man would spit out a giant tooth, but he didn't.

"That waddn't nice," mumbled Big Sal. "I'm hurt."

What was it about big men that turned them into little boys at the first twinge of pain?

"Shut up!" said Pyg. It felt good.

Big Sal shut up. The boy stared at the fat man's hands: Did he have flattened thumbs? Thumbs busted by Pyg's "father"? Thumbs busted using his famous ax? Thumbs busted because the outlaws had hung Pyg's mother up by her thumbs? Unfortunately, at this distance in this light, he couldn't tell if Big Sal's thumbs had been busted or not.

"Ow," yelped Too Short and dropped his lighted match.

But Little Dogie quickly lit another.

"Quick, while we've still got matches left, tie them up," Pyg issued another order. It felt good, too. "Use their belts. Bandanas. Anything you can find. I'll keep them covered. Little Dogie, you take Big Sal. Too Short, you take the little guy." He pointed at the runt of the litter; then he worried that assigning the smallest outlaw to the littlest cowboy might have been insensitive. Oh, well. He pointed to a middle-sized outlaw and said: "Jesse, you help Opry with that one."

"Me help Opry?" flared the Harvey Girl. "How 'bout Opry helpin' me?"

"Okay," said Too Short, with no miff in his voice.

"Pleasure," said Little Dogie, sounding almost good-natured.

The Home Ranch cowboys—and one cowgirl—descended on the prostrate outlaws like hunters eager to skin buffalo. They jumped on their backs and went to work. Pyg watched Little Dogie especially closely to be sure he did the job right. Holding a lit match between his teeth, the big man stripped off his own bandana and started tying the bigger man's elbows together behind his back. Pyg opened his mouth to tell the giant he was doing it all wrong—tie his hands, not his elbows—but shut up just in time. Because he realized Big Sal would never be able to untie these knots. The outlaw's hands couldn't reach his bound elbows, and his elbows didn't have fingers.

"Hey, everyone, look at Little Dogie," Pyg raised his voice. "That's good. Tie their elbows."

The Home Ranch giant spit out his match. It fluttered through the air like a bright dying butterfly and landed on Big Sal's back. He screamed and bucked. It was Too Short's turn to light another match. Clamping it between his teeth, he went back to work. Several long-stemmed matches later, all the outlaws were good and tied, their elbows pinned together behind their backs, their feet bound together, too, with bandanas, belts, torn strips of shirts, and even smelly socks. Their boots had been thrown into the pit where they made no sound.

"Jesse, while we've still got some matches," Pyg said, "go back and look for their torches."

"I'll go," volunteered Opry.

But Pyg was beginning to enjoy giving orders and resented having one countermanded.

"No, Jesse, you go," said the boss. "Opry, you stay here in case they give us any trouble."

But the Harvey Girl didn't move. Evidently he wasn't *her* boss.

"Jesse, get going, hurry up."

She just stared at him.

"Please."

"You didn't never ask *me* please," protested Little Dogie.

"You ain't got tits," Too Short explained.

"Good point," laughed the giant.

Taking three matches with her, Jesse headed back up the tunnel to look for the outlaw torches. Pyg knew these flaming brands might have burned themselves out, but he doubted it. He believed the bandits had extinguished them because they knew lighted torches made them well-lit targets. Nothing was well lit now as the latest match tumbled toward the cave's old floor.

"Don't light any more," the boy said. "We'll need the rest if she can't find the torches. And they aren't going anywhere anyway."

The cave went utterly dark, and the boy started laughing. He couldn't help it. There was just something funny about the human condition in a state of complete darkness. Other laughing voices joined in. Even the outlaws laughed in spite of their plight. Big Sal giggled.

Time passed slowly in the utter dark. Had Jesse gotten lost or fallen into another infinite crater? What was taking the girl so long? Pyg listened hard to try to hear if the outlaws were up to any mischief, but all he heard was the incessant drip, dripping. If he counted the drips, perhaps he could calculate the time as it passed . . . ten, eleven, twelve . . . forty-nine, fifty, fifty-one, fifty-two . . . one hundred forty-nine, one hundred fifty . . .

Pyg saw a dim light approaching like a train in a tunnel.

L it by the torches Jesse had found, Pyg began to question the prison- ers. The others had wanted to hold the interrogation up on top. They had seen enough of this cavern and couldn't wait to get out. But Pyg had been pigheaded and insisted they do it down here. He had his reasons. He had an idea.

The outlaws were sitting up now with their backs against the wall of the tunnel. Pyg held a torch—a stick tipped with a wad of cloth dipped in bacon fat—in Big Sal's face as he began asking his questions. He told himself he wouldn't mind too much if the monster's moustache caught on fire and burned up. He smiled: It would be a brush fire.

"Where is it?" demanded Pyg.

"Where's what?" asked the very uncomfortable fat outlaw.

"I'm sorry. Please, let me introduce myself. I am the son"—there was an involuntary catch in his voice—"of Jimmy Goodnight. You stole my father's"—another brief catch—"tombstone and ax."

"No, I didn't," protested the helpless outlaw leader. "What're you talkin' about? Why'd I do somethin' crazy like that? What'd I do with a tombstone? And what was that about a ax?"

"You know very well," Pyg said with certainty. "You are quite famil- iar with my father's ax."

"No, I ain't."

"Yes, you are. My father's ax is the reason your thumbs look like soup spoons. That's why you stole the ax. Because my father crushed your thumbs with it."

"No, no, we ain't took no ax. Why make up such lies?"

"You're the one who's lying," Pyg said. "And you're the one who's going to pay the consequences."

"What're you sayin', Boss?"

"You'll see." Pyg turned to his cowboys: "Pull them over to the edge of the pit. Then get them on their feet."

Obeying orders, they grabbed the outlaws by their feet and dragged them to the very brink of the abyss. Too Short and Little Dogie had no trouble with the second phase of the operation, the standing-them-up part, but Jesse and Opry struggled. They got their man partway up, but then he collapsed again. What was wrong with them? Well, Jesse wasn't as strong as a man, but Opry didn't have that excuse.

"Do you two need any help?" asked Pyg.

"No, stop treatin' me like a girl," Jesse flared again. "Just shut up and let us work."

Pyg couldn't understand it: The madder she got at him, the more he liked her. The more she pushed him away, the closer he wanted to get. It didn't make any sense.

"I wasn't treating you like a girl," said Pyg. "I was treating Opry like a girl."

While he looked on, the troublesome twosome changed strategies. They had been trying to pull their outlaw up by grabbing the front of his shirt. Now they sat him up, got behind him, grabbed him—one under each armpit—and lifted. They got the outlaw's butt off the ground, but then dropped him. They readjusted their grip, took a deep breath, and grunted as they strained. They got him halfway up, paused, took another deep breath, then grunted again. Now they were too strong and overdid it. They lifted him past vertical and the bandit was in danger of toppling forward into the pit. Opry just threw up his hands and accepted the inevitable, but Jesse frantically reached out and grabbed the back of the outlaw's shirt. She hung on and barely managed to pull him back from the brink.

"Nice work, Jesse," said Pyg.

"Shut up," said an out-of-breath Jesse. "Don't make fun of me. I don't like it."

"But—"

"I told you to shut up."

Just as he was getting used to giving orders, Pyg could see that he was going to have to take a few from this girl if he really liked her. He shut up. Little Dogie laughed. Too Short smiled. Pyg couldn't really blame them. Well, if he couldn't praise, perhaps he could criticize.

"Opry, what's wrong with you?" Pyg asked.

"I dunno," muttered the singing cowboy. "I don't like caves."

"Yeah," muttered the cowboys and the outlaws together.

"Well, steady him, okay?" Pyg told the songster. "We don't want him falling in. Not yet anyway. Not until we get good and ready."

"What's that supposed to mean?" asked Big Sal.

"You'll find out. Take a good look, gentlemen. That hole looks pretty deep." By the light of his torch, the hole yawned like a grave dug for giants. "I wonder how deep it is. Let's see, shall we?"

Bending down, Pyg tried to pick up a small boulder, but it was too heavy.

"Now look who's a weakling," chided Jesse.

But there was more than one way to move a rock: Pyg got down behind it and rolled it into the black hole. Then he watched the outlaws as they listened. And listened. And listened. But they were never rewarded for their listening. The outlaws looked unhappier and unhappier.

"I didn't hear anything," Pyg said, "did you?"

None of the outlaws said anything, but their faces said a lot.

"I wonder what would go through your mind as you were falling all that way. It would be a real chance to reflect upon your life, wouldn't it? There's no telling how long you would tumble. Maybe there's no bottom at all. I certainly didn't hear anything, did you?"

The outlaws only spoke with their distorted expressions.

"Perhaps you would fall forever. Or maybe this is the entrance to hell. Maybe you'd fall right into fire and brimstone. What do you think?"

Their faces said they didn't like the idea. Pyg was surprised he could be so cold-blooded. Pleasantly surprised.

"All we have to do is give you a gentle push, and you're going into that hole. But you could save yourselves from a long fall and a fast trip to hell by telling me what I want to know. Where is my father's ax? What did you do with it? I certainly hope, for your sakes, you didn't destroy it."

"No, no, no," the three outlaws all said at the same time.

"Then if you didn't destroy it, where is it?"

"We don't know," blubbered one of the flat-thumbed badmen.

"We don't know nothin'," whimpered a second flat thumb.

"They're tellin' God's truth," said Big Sal with slightly more dignity. "We didn't have nothin' to do with this." He paused. "Swear on my mother's life."

"I don't believe you had a mother," said Pyg. "You would have killed her coming out."

"I had a mother. Course, I had a mother. What're you talkin' about?"

"Then she will be sad to hear how you died. Blindfold them. Nobody should have to witness his own death. Blindfold them as if they were on the scaffold. Which they are, but it's a longer drop."

Pyg tossed another, smaller stone into the pit. Of course, nobody heard it hit. Then nervously another.

"Hurry up with those blindfolds," Pyg said. "These torches won't last forever." He paused. "Hurry up, please."

Tearing off strips from the helpless outlaws' shirttails, Pyg's men went to work blinding the badmen. Big Sal didn't resist, but the other two tried to duck their heads out of the way. They didn't succeed.

"Okay, good," Pyg told his cowboys. "I'll take over from here."

His men retreated a few steps.

"The time has come to talk or try your best to fly," Pyg said, approaching the littlest outlaw. He tapped this runt of a bandit on the shoulder. "What's your name? I'd hate for you to die nameless." He waited. "Come on, tell me your name or I'll push you in the pit right now."

The outlaw swayed on his bound feet. Pyg had to prop him up to keep him from falling into hell by accident.

"I won't catch you next time," Pyg threatened. "Speak."

"I'm Oyster."

"This ain't no time fer jokin'," said Too Short. "Does that damn hole seem funny to you?"

"No, I ain't jokin'." His voice was trembling. "It's a nickname." He paused. "My last name, it's Schell with a 'c.'"

All the cowboys laughed.

"Okay, Oyster Schell," said Pyg, "can you tell me where to find my father's ax? If not, I'm afraid you're on your way." Pyg paused. "Out of fairness, I'll give you a moment to think it over."

Stepping back from Oyster, Pyg motioned for his cowpokes to join him. They huddled while the teenage boss issued instructions.

"All right, time's up," Pyg said. "What have you decided?"

"I really don't know nothin'," protested Oyster. "I'd sure tell you if I did. I really would. I—"

"Say your prayers," said Pyg.

Moving behind the outlaw, the boy smashed him on the back of the skull with the butt of his silver gun. Damn, the runt's head was hard. Pyg hoped he hadn't hurt his fancy six-shooter. Outlaw Oyster slumped forward.

"OOUUAAAWWWOOOUUUAAAWWWoouuuuuu!"

Pyg studied the remaining outlaws to see if they were impressed. Big Sal frowned, his whole face twisting downward. It was grotesque. The other robber wasn't happy either, but on a smaller scale.

"Where is my father's ax?" Pyg shouted in the giant outlaw's ear.

"I really dunno," whimpered Big Sal. "Swear to God."

"That's unfortunate. Because you're going to meet your God very soon."

Leaving Big Sal for the moment, Pyg moved on to the Mama-Bear-sized outlaw. The boy tapped the frightened badman on the shoulder.

"How about you, Mr. Busted Thumbs? What's your name?"

"Adam," the outlaw said immediately. "Adam Munter."

"Well, Adam Munter, can you help me find my father's ax?"

"I would if'n I could but—"

"Then you're going in right now! Flap your wings."

"I sure wish I could. I do. I wish—"

"Happy landing."

Pyg hit Adam hard on the back of his head, and he crumpled.

"OOUUUAAAWWWWWWoooouuuuuu!"

Hearing the scream, Big Sal's huge knees buckled and he almost fell into oblivion. Urine soaked through his crotch and ran down his pant leg.

"You're the only one left," Pyg said. "I guess you're next. Got anything to say for yourself?"

Big Sal was whimpering softly, but didn't say anything.

"Will you give me back my father's ax?" Pyg asked angrily. "I've got to get it back." He added to himself: It's the only way I'll ever know who I am. "I'm serious about this. I really am. Do you really believe that you can defy all laws including the law of gravity?"

"I'd give it back to you if'n I had it," Big Sal blubbered, "but I didn't take it. I only seen it that one time, and I never wanted to see it ag'in. And I ain't seen it ag'in neither."

"You're lying. You destroyed it. Tell me where the pieces are."

"They ain't no pieces. Not s'far's I know. I ain't never touched that ax, though it did once touch me. Don't you think I wanna live? I'd tell you anything I know to stay alive, but I don't know nothin', honest."

"Honest?"

Pyg and his cowboys laughed.

"This ain't funny," protested Big Sal. "You ain't bein' fair. Don't you wanna be fair?"

"I want the ax."

"Yore daddy was a fair man. Mean but fair. He coulda hung us all that day, but he didn't. He just beat on our thumbs 'cause it was the fair thing to do. We heard tell he had some kinda code. I sure wisht you was more like yore daddy."

This talk of his "father" just made Pyg madder. Who was this outlaw to tell him what his supposed daddy was like? Who was he to tell him he didn't resemble his pop? Big Sal deserved to die. The boy walked around behind the fat bandit and put both hands on his back. He could feel both the badman's shoulder blades: They were quivering.

"Do you have any last words?" asked Pyg, the executioner.

"Yeah, this ain't fair."

"I don't know why, but it seems that ax means more to you than your life. I'm not sure it means that much even to me. I'm pretty sure I'd tell. But you've decided not to, so here goes. Say hello to hell."

"Opry!" Big Sal cried in a loud, trembling voice. "Help me. Don't let 'im—"

Pyg tried to hold up, but too late: the butt of his gun struck the back of the giant head.

"EEEEOOOOWWWaaauuuuooooohhh!"

Then the boy heard sock-muffled feet, running feet, scrambling backward up the tunnel, trying to get away.

"Stop him!" the boy boss yelled.

Then Pyg just stood there under tons of earth—under *the* earth—trying to understand. He had never suspected Opry. Never wondered about him. Never watched him at all. Now of course he remembered how Opry had always said they should give up this hunt. They should turn back. Nor had he been particularly helpful in the cave. Thinking it over, Pyg couldn't remember Opry striking any matches during their

subterranean chase. Or firing any shots. Telling himself to stop thinking, the torch-bearing Pyg started to run up the tunnel after the Home
Ranch outlaw.

"OOOOAAAAWWWaaauuuuooooohhh!" Opry's scream carried
back to him.

Pyg stopped running and listened hard, but he never heard the
impact of the body. In the dark, Opry must have taken a wrong turn up
the wrong tunnel—there were so many branching off every which way—
and come upon another black pothole. Maybe he would pop out in
China. Pyg tried to smile but couldn't.

The boy was still puzzling over questions: Who the hell had Opry
been anyway? If he was a member of the outlaw gang, why didn't he
have busted thumbs? He must have joined the gang later or simply not
come along that day. Maybe he was sick that afternoon and so saved
his thumbs. Well, everything was busted now.

"Poor Opry," said Jesse, perched on the lip of the seemingly bottomless pit, seemingly one of many. "Oh, I know he musta been a bad
un, but I liked him. I did. I'll miss his contrary ass and his songs. I sure
will. Is that wrong?"

Pyg didn't know what to say. He was still trying to get used to the
idea of Opry-the-traitor. Had Opry tried to drown him during the
flood? Had he tried to burn him alive in the whorehouse? Death by
fire, death by water.

"No, that ain't wrong," Too Short told the Harvey Girl.

"Mebbe we oughta say some words over him," Jesse said. "Anybody
know any Bible?"

Pyg knew lots of Bible, but he didn't speak up. Nobody else did
either.

"Okay," said the Harvey Girl, "God fergive me 'cause I'm gonna git
this kinda wrong, but here goes: There's a time to sprout up and a time
to git cut down. A time fer sunshine and a time fer rain."

"We could use more rain time," said Little Dogie.

"A time fer speakin', and a time fer shuttin' up," she said pointedly.
"A time fer better, a time fer worse. A time fer remembrin', and a time
fer fergittin'. A time fer sinnin', and a time fer forgivin'. Opry waddn't
all bad."

Pyg was tongue-tied.

"Amen," said Too Short.

"Lemme say somethin'," said Little Dogie. "It's somethin' he used to sing, and I sing even worse'n he used to but I'm gonna try. I'm sure they's better songs, but it's the only one that come to me offhand. It's prob'ly more'n the lyin' sunuvabitch deserves, anyhow, so here goes:

> *"And the cowboy riz up sadly*
> *And mounted his cayuse,*
> *Sayin', 'The time'll come when longhorns*
> *And cowboys ain't no use.'*
> *And while gazin' sadly backward*
> *Upon the dead bovine*
> *His bronc stepped in a doghole*
> *And fell and broke his spine."*

"Mebbe it ain't just right, but Opry loved that there song."

Pyg turned and they followed him back down the tunnel.

CHAPTER 61

Pyg studied the three outlaws who lay at his feet at the very edge of a round black hell. All alive and not so well. Two of them had been knocked out by a blow from the silver six-gun. The third, Big Sal, who hadn't been hit that hard, had probably just fainted dead away. None of them had gone into the bottomless pit. None of them had screamed. Too Short had belted out all the screams—except for Opry's—and he had made a good job of it, too. The little cowboy had screamed for Oyster Schell, scaring the two others. He had screamed for Adam Munter, scaring the piss out of a fat man. And the pint-sized puncher with the ten-gallon voice had even gotten carried away and screamed for Big Sal as well. Of course, that last scream hadn't really been necessary, since none of the bandits were awake to hear and be scared by it. Pyg's plan had all been a trick, which the unconscious outlaws would come to appreciate when they woke up.

"I swear," said Jesse, "they don't know nothin' 'bout that ax atall. Did you see that big guy piss hisself? He woulda told if he'd a known. They all woulda. Tell me I'm wrong."

"No, you aren't wrong, unfortunately," Pyg admitted. "I was sure they'd give up what they knew. And I suppose they did. Nothing. Now where does that leave us? I still have to find that ax. It's who I am."

"I know," Jesse said.

Pyg glared at her, but then he smiled. She looked so good in the light of these torches. She reminded him of the beauty of the candlelit girls back home in Boston drawing rooms. But he decided not to tell her so. That would be treating her like a girl.

"What're we gonna do with our friends here?" Jesse asked.

"Push 'em in the hole anyhow," said Little Dogie. "That's a lot eas-ier'n hangin' 'em, and it's what they got comin'.'"

"No," grumbled Big Sal groggily as he woke up. "No, that ain't fair."

"Shut up about fair," said Pyg. "You never cared about fair before."

But Pyg realized he didn't want to push them into the hole. He didn't so much care about what it would do to them as what it might do to him. If he really was Goodnight's son, then maybe he really did need some kind of code. And he couldn't imagine a code that would countenance chucking men into pits with no bottoms without any pretense of a trial. Damn Big Sal for pointing out to him that his "dad" had a code. His heritage seemed always to be making his life more complicated than it should have been.

"Let's get out of here before we run out of light," Pyg said. "We'll take them with us. Untie their feet but leave the blindfolds." He paused to think. "Jesse, you take a torch and lead the way. Little Dogie, you take Big Sal. Too Short, grab Adam. I'll take the runt." He grabbed Oyster's arm. "Keep them going and keep them from falling into any holes."

"Poor Opry," Jesse said again.

"Yeah," said Pyg without much feeling.

The climb up out of the cavern was much harder than the descent, not only because of the incline, but also because the chase was over. The chase had energized them. Walking out again didn't. Pyg was breathing hard while Little Dogie huffed and puffed like a dying locomotive. And Big Sal was even louder. They took a break when they reached the big ballroom, but a short one. Soon they were climbing once again. The sightless outlaws kept stumbling and falling. They dirtied themselves and skinned themselves.

"This ain't fair," Big Sal kept mumbling. "This ain't atall fair."

Pyg considered gagging him, but didn't want to waste the time. He had a horror that total darkness might return. Then the trip up out of the cave would really be the darkest nightmare.

"Hurry," said Pyg. "Keep up."

"I'm goin' as fast as I can," said Little Dogie.

The giant cowboy and the immense outlaw brought up the rear, ten yards behind the others and almost lost in darkness. The boy reminded himself that huge bodies were harder to move than small bodies.

"Hold up," Pyg said. "We'll wait for them."

He expected Little Dogie to defend himself with some insult or other, but the big man was too out of breath to talk. The two giants caught up, but immediately the others, who had had their rest, started out again. No rest for the weary giants. Their breath thundered through the cavern. Pyg looked up to make sure the stone sky wasn't falling. It seemed to be wobbling. Again the giants were falling behind.

"Hold up," Pyg said once again.

While they were waiting, he decided he should check on the health of Jesse's lead torch. Pyg released his tight grip on Oyster's arm and moved uphill a few steps.

"Jesse, how's the light?" he asked.

"It's startin' to flicker," she said.

Not waiting any longer for the giants, Pyg ordered: "Keep going. Hurry, hurry."

While the others passed him, Pyg stood waiting for his outlaw to catch up with him. But Oyster had other ideas. He turned around and ran back down into the cavern, pushing past Little Dogie and Big Sal. Grabbing Jesse's torch, Pyg ran after Oyster, but the outlaw soon disappeared into the black.

"OOOOEEEAAAuuuuaaahhhwwwhhheeee!" he screamed.

Oh, no, not again! Pyg had killed another human being. Where was his code now? What use was it? He felt infinite guilt. The bodies were building up on one side of the scale and his good deeds were pretty light on the other side. He feared for his immortal soul without quite believing it existed. Then he saw the cringing outlaw.

"Nice try, Oyster. But couldn't you be more original?"

When they emerged into the moon and starlight, Pyg called a halt. They were all tired and out of breath. The last three hundred yards had been especially steep and taxing. The big men seemed to have suffered the most, Jesse the least.

"What's the matter with you guys?" she chided, barely breathing hard. "I thought you were s'posed to be tough."

"Shut up!" gasped Little Dogie.

Jesse took his advice. He might be weak as a baby right now, but once he recovered, he would be Goliath again. Why get on a giant's bad side if you didn't have to?

Little Dogie and Big Sal sat on limestone boulders and huffed and puffed as if they were trying to flatten the Little Pigs' house. Or maybe

Pyg's house. He laughed to himself at his private joke. But he had to admit that he was huffing and puffing, too. Like a bunch of locomotives pulling into a station, their loud breaths came slower and slower and slower until the train almost stopped.

"Tell me, Oyster," Pyg said in a relatively normal voice, "where's the nearest town?"

"I dunno," mumbled the blindfolded outlaw.

"Oyster, Oyster, I don't believe you," the boy said. "So let's try it again."

"I dunno."

"You really aren't very original, are you, Oyster? So let me make your predicament a little clearer to you. As I see it, we have two choices. We can hang you all right here and right now, and save everybody a lot of bother. Or we can take you to the nearest town and turn you over to the sheriff. You still might end up getting hanged, but it'll take longer. So take your pick, for certain now or probably later. With those two choices clearly in mind, let me ask my question again: Where's the nearest town?"

"Carlsbad," said Big Sal. "'Bout fifteen miles west of here."

"You'll show us?"

Big Sal nodded his huge, blindfolded, boulder head.

"Good. We'll wait until the sun comes up, and the bats come home. Tie their feet till then."

"That ain't fair," said Big Sal.

They tied their feet.

Jesse's last torch was flickering out, but they still had the moon and starlight. Pyg kept finding himself staring at the Harvey Girl. Was it the soft dim light that made her look so pretty now? Was this effect the reason romance tended to be a night flower? Or did he just know her better, like her more, and so believe she was turning into a beauty? Or was it because she had pushed him away, rejected his advances? How could anyone ever figure out what they really felt?

"We should try to get some sleep," Pyg decided. "I'll take the first watch. Too Short, I'll wake you in a couple of hours."

As Pyg kept watch, they all seemed to fall asleep almost immediately, even the outlaws. The sleeping giants were even noisier than they had been awake, but the racket didn't rouse anyone. Pyg found himself watching the gentle heave of Jesse's chest, and felt a little guilty. He was intruding on something private, spying, but he didn't stop. He noticed that her reddish-brown hair looked black in the night. He admired the way it framed her peaceful face. One lock fell across and partially obscured her mouth. The boy knew his mother would say the girl's hair was dirty, but he thought it was beautiful. It looked like spun obsidian. So what if the gleam owed some of its brightness to grease? She stirred. He looked guiltily away, not wanting to get caught. When he risked a glance, she was scratching her nose, but her eyes were still closed. She had brushed back the loose strand. He looked away again, but soon glanced back. Good, she seemed to be settling down again. He went back to staring.

Pyg had to remind himself occasionally to peek at the outlaws to make sure they weren't up to any mischief. They all seemed to be sound asleep. Could any of them be faking? He doubted it, but he couldn't see their eyes because they were all still blindfolded. Three blind outlaws.

Jesse turned over. Now she had her back to him. Had she somehow sensed his eyes and turned away? Was he disturbing her sleep? The boy missed her face but liked the outline of her body as seen from behind, the small shoulders, the narrower waist, the swell of the hips. A slumbering guitar. He was so engrossed in his clandestine admiration that he did not notice anything amiss until he heard running feet.

Startled, turning his head, Pyg saw Big Sal getting away. Agile for a man of his size, he had somehow managed to work his feet free of the belt that bound them. He had even succeeded in scraping off his blindfold. Only his elbows were still pinned behind his back. And he was surprisingly fast for a fat man.

Feeling guilty for his lack of vigilance, Pyg drew his silver gun and took aim at the middle of the big man's broad back. His finger tightened on the trigger, but the shot was too easy. He was ashamed of himself. Lowering his aim, Pyg shot the giant outlaw in his right ankle, which was the size of a tree trunk.

"AAAAOOOOEEEeeeoowwweee!" he screamed, for real this time, and fell, shaking the earth.

Pyg knew what Big Sal was thinking: It ain't fair.

CHAPTER 62

"This ain't fair," complained Big Sal. "My leg's killin' me. You're killin' me."

"Then you had better be showing us the fastest possible way to Carlsbad," Pyg said. "It looks like your foot is getting bigger every minute. The sooner we get there, the sooner we'll find a doctor."

All morning, as they rode northeast, Pyg had watched the giant outlaw's bare right foot swell until now it was the size of an anvil. And the swelling was spreading up his leg. His calf was already bigger than his pants leg, which had been ripped open at the seam to make room.

"We can gallop if'n you want." Little Dogie laughed. "Wanna gallop?"

"No, no, I couldn't stand it," protested the alarmed outlaw. "That'd kill me for sure."

Pyg was thankful that Little Dogie had someone to pick on besides him. At the same time, he felt a little sorry for the butt of the big cowboy's jokes. He knew what it felt like.

Like Big Sal's foot, a worry kept growing inside Pyg. It started out as nagging doubt but swelled into a fear. What if the sheriff in Carlsbad told them he didn't need their help? What if he said these men hadn't broken any New Mexico Territory laws and he didn't give a damn what they had done in Texas? What would Pyg do then?

"Cain't you untie our elbows?" begged Oyster. "My shoulders're achin'."

"Fergit it," said Little Dogie.

They kept riding, Big Sal kept complaining, and his foot kept growing. Now it was the size of his horse's head . . . now it was as large as a toddler . . . when it looked as big as a bear cub, the town of Carlsbad appeared in the distance.

. . .

In the early afternoon, Pyg's little procession rode down the dusty Main Street of a slow-moving adobe town. There were only a few citizens, mostly Mexican, wandering about. The posse found the sheriff's office directly across the street from the saloon, which seemed a good idea. They pulled up in front and the cowboys dismounted. The outlaws couldn't because their feet were tied to their stirrups. Big Sal was of course the exception. His feet weren't tied because he wasn't going to try to run away. The sheriff emerged from his headquarters.

"What can I do for you fellers?" asked the lawman behind the metal star.

Pyg approached him. "Good afternoon," said the boy. "My name's, uh–" He paused, because he didn't want to introduce himself as, well, a pig, but neither did he want to remind anyone that his real name was Percy. After an awkward moment, he said: "My name's Goodnight. We're from the Home Ranch over in Texas. And we've got some outlaws for you."

"What?" asked the sheriff. "Who are they? Oh, I'm Sheriff Sherman, no relation. You better tell me more."

The lawman had black hair and a white beard.

"This ain't right," wailed Big Sal. "I'm dyin'."

"They're what's left of the old Robbers' Roost gang," Pyg said. "Did you ever hear of them?"

The sheriff looked offended. "Robbers' Roost? Of course. Whaddaya take me fer?"

"He didn't mean nothin'," said Little Dogie.

Pyg was surprised: Was the giant actually trying to help him?

"Where'd you find 'em?" asked Sheriff Sherman.

"In a cave about fifteen miles east of here," Pyg said.

"Fulla bats and outlaws," said Little Dogie.

"I don't know if they're wanted here or not," said the boy, "but we thought we should find out."

"Wanted?" said Sheriff Sherman. "Not hardly. They's a damn reward is all."

"Good," said Jesse, "then mebbe we can afford to buy some more matches. I prefer my victuals cooked. Call me picky."

. . .

Pyg placed five hundred dollars in gold coins in the middle of the table where the money shared space with a whiskey bottle and four glasses. The Pecos River Saloon was empty, so the boy didn't mind flashing the gold. It was more hard money than any of the cowboys, Pyg included, had ever seen in one place at one time. They all stared at the gold as if it were the most beautiful sunrise they had ever seen in their lives. And maybe it was. Who knew? Perhaps these small, golden suns were heralding a new day for all of them.

"We'll divide this three ways," Pyg said.

"Cain't you count?" asked Jesse. "They's four of us."

Pyg had considered long and hard about this decision. And always he had come to the same conclusion: A leader wouldn't take any of the money. He owned the ranch, the land, the responsibilities. Weren't these enough?

"I'm not taking a share," Pyg said. "If anybody disagrees, we'll go out in the street and shoot it out. Any takers?"

"Uncle," Jesse said.

"You're givin' a share to the girl?" asked Little Dogie. "An equal share?"

"Yes, I am," said the boy.

"That ain't fair," said the giant, reverting to form. Evidently all giants thought and spoke alike.

"She's a better cowboy than you are," Pyg said. "Shut up or you're out. Nothing for you at all. We'll divide it two ways. Got anything else to say?"

Little Dogie just shrugged his mountain shoulders. Pyg counted out the lucre, one for Jesse, one for Too Short, one for Little Dogie. He went around and around, dealing twenty-dollar gold pieces as if they were cards. Round and round eight times. He had dispensed $480 and now there was a single gold piece left. Whom should he give it to? Or should he ask for silver from the bartender? Making up his mind, Pyg handed the one remaining coin to Jesse.

"That ain't fair," complained Little Dogie once again.

"No, no way," Jesse protested her good fortune. "Pyg, you take it. You oughta git somethin'. Even if you are a son of a bitch, literally."

He was surprised she knew a word with so many syllables. "No, I couldn't."

"If you give it to me," she said, "I'm handin' it over to Little Dogie. Think about it."

"Okay, you win," said Pyg. "Thank you very much. If nobody has any objections, I'll buy the drinks."

Nobody objected. The Harvey Girl poured out drinks for everybody. Pyg thought about offering a toast but decided against it.

"Sand in your eye," said Too Short. "We ain't had enough rain fer mud."

They all drank.

"Here's to the damnedest wild goose chase that ever was," Little Dogie said.

They all drank again.

"But this here wild goose done laid a buncha gold eggs," said Jesse.

"Yeah, but we didn't find what we come for, did we? Course I never figured we would, Pyg here bein' a feller who couldn't locate his socks inside his boots." Little Dogie laughed at his own wit.

"Count your money and stop complainin'," said Too Short. "Them fellers needed catchin' and we caught 'em. Now we'll go catch that there ax."

"I waddn't complainin'," said the giant. "You ain't got no sense a humor is all."

"It has been something of a wild goose chase," Pyg said slowly. He sipped his whiskey and made a face. "But for me it isn't over. You've already done enough. More than enough. You should go home now. With my thanks."

Pyg indulged a fantasy: Little Dogie and Too Short would return to the Home Ranch, but Jesse would insist on staying to finish the job. It would just be the two of them on the trail of the ax. And little by little, she would become more friendly until . . .

"I ain't quittin' in the middle of a job of work," announced Too Short. "I'm stickin'."

"Me, too," said Little Dogie. "You cain't git ridda me that easy."

Jesse didn't say anything. Pyg saw his fantasy turning into a nightmare: The other two would stay and she would leave. He stared at her. She looked away, up at the rafters, down at her gold, then up again and down again.

"I s'pose your mama's still back at the ranch nursin' on Loving," Jesse said. "And so long as she's there, I'd rather be here."

Pyg was angry at the Harvey Girl for once again implying that his mother and Loving were more than friends. But at the same time he was glad she was staying. He was afraid he was beginning to like her a lot.

"Well, then," Pyg said at last. "Let's talk about the ax. If Big Sal didn't take it, who did? Anybody got any ideas?"

Pyg already had a possible—maybe even a probable—ax thief in mind, but he wanted to hear what the others thought. Would they name the same suspect, or would they suggest names he had over-looked? They evidently didn't suspect anyone because they didn't say anything.

"Please," said Pyg, "try to help me out here."

More silence.

"Well, it coulda been Will Lee," Jesse blurted out.

CHAPTER 63

Tascosa rose up like a mirage. The tops of buildings—exaggerated by false fronts—seemed to float on an inland sea that wasn't there. As they drew nearer, the sea evaporated. A flood had been averted.

The Home Ranch posse trotted into town the way Pyg's "father" had in that antediluvian time before the boy was born. He studied the blacksmith shop where all those outlaw thumbs had been crushed. Moving on, he surveyed the hotel where his mother had been hanged by her thumbs until his father rescued her. When they reached the general store, they turned their horses left for one block, then right again. Arriving at the jail, they dismounted. They all crowded into the sheriff's small office.

"What can I do for you?" the sheriff asked, squinting at them.

"How do you do?" Pyg said. "My name's Goodnight. I need to speak to a prisoner named Will Lee. It's very important. Whether he wants to talk to me or not."

"Yes, of course," said the lawman. "Uh, I'm Stan Bower. Sheriff." He paused for what seemed a long time. "I'd be happy to let ya jabber at him all you want, but his cowboys done broke him outta my jail. I tried to stop 'em. Really, I did. But there was some few of 'em and I was outnumbered. They was gonna kill me."

"Let's ride," Pyg said.

"Hold up," said Sheriff Bower. "I won't have no vigilantes in my territory. If your name's really Goodnight, then you know your daddy was all for law and order and justice and stuff."

"Then deputize us," said the boy.

The sheriff looked down at his scuffed boots while he thought the matter over.

"That ain't a bad idea at that," he said at last. "Hold up yore right hands."

They all dutifully raised their hands.

"You're all deputies. Her, too."

"Why do they call this here river the Canadian?" asked Jesse.

"Dunno," said Too Short.

"I mean this damn river's done lost its damn way."

The four deputies splashed into the lost river that flowed just south of town. Pyg's calves got cold, then his thighs, then his crotch. Feeling himself shrinking inside his pants, he glanced over at Jesse, as if she could see the shrinkage. Her crotch was wet, too, which started his mind spinning. Now he was unshrinking inside his pants. He kept staring at the Harvey Girl imagining all sorts of things.

"AAAAOOOOEEEeeeooowwweee!" Pyg screamed.

While he hadn't been paying attention to business, a water moccasin had bitten him on the leg and was still hanging on. He drew his silver gun because his first instinct was to shoot the snake, but he was afraid he might also shoot himself. Turning the gun around, he gripped it by the barrel and used it as a club. He hit the moccasin on the head as hard as he could. It let go.

"What's wrong?" yelled Too Short.

"A snake bit me!" Pyg shouted back.

"Not ag'in," complained Little Dogie.

"Turn around, we're going back," said Too Short.

Feeling a pathetic failure, Pyg was afraid he was going to die. He blamed himself for daydreaming when he should have been watching out for trouble. Then it occurred to him that he was dying a virgin, and he hated death even more. The horses splashed up onto the north bank of the misnamed river.

"Git him off his horse," Too Short shouted.

Little Dogie reached up and plucked the boy from the saddle as if he were a doll. Then he laid him gently on the sand.

"You know, gittin' bit oncet is bad luck," the giant said, "but gittin' bit twicet is just plain careless."

"Cut off his pants leg," Too Short ordered.

Little Dogie produced a knife and split Pyg's fancy jodhpurs vertically up the seam. It seemed he was going all the way to the boy's balls.

Pyg flinched. The giant laughed and stopped a few inches short. Then he tore the material horizontally and tossed the leg away.

"Move," said Too Short.

When Little Dogie stood and backed up, the little cowboy swooped down. He had a knife in his hand, too.

"Grit your teeth," Too Short said. "I'm gonna cut you."

Gritting, Pyg lifted his head and watched as the little cowboy cut an *X* on top of what looked like quotation marks. Blood flowed.

"Somebody's gotta suck out the poison," Too Short said. "I cain't. I got cavities. My teeth're killin' me. If I sucked on poison, they'd really kill me fer sure. I'm sorry, Pyg. Come on, somebody."

Nobody moved.

"Where's Custer when you need him?" Little Dogie said. "Damn, what we wants another Injun. They don't give a damn if'n they git poisoned to death 'cause they're goin' to the Happy Huntin' Ground, wherever the hell that is."

"Shut up about Injuns," Jesse said. "Custer was twice the man you are."

"You an Injun lover all of a sudden?" said the giant. "I thought you waddn't too partial to—"

"Shut up!" said Too Short. "Ever'body just shut up." They all did. "Pyg's gonna die if'n we don't get that there poison outta him."

Still nobody moved.

"Now who's got the best teeth?"

Nobody said anything. No volunteers.

"I cain't believe this."

Pyg knew he was going to die without ever having a chance to enter a woman or pull the ax out of the stone.

"Okay, I'll do it," Jesse said peevishly. "But if this kills me, I ain't never gonna forgive nona you. Especially you, Pyg." She shook her head. "I'll haunt you all your damn life. I'll haunt and haunt some more. Count on it."

Gradually, reluctantly, the Harvey Girl sank to her knees. Pyg sighed with new hope. She took her time about pressing her lips to his flesh. Slowly she began to suck. Pyg had never loved anybody more in his life. Not only was she beautiful, at least in his eyes, but she was trying to save his life. Risking her own life to ransom his. But what if he died anyway? That would be so unfair. Realizing he was thinking like

Big Sal, he tried to be optimistic, but he felt his life slipping away. Jesse spit out a mouthful of blood and pressed her lips to his leg once again.

"You're real good at suckin'," said Little Dogie. "I reckon you had a lotta practice, huh?"

"Shut up!" Pyg yelled in a fog. "She's braver than you are."

Too Short hit Little Dogie right on the belly button.

"Uuuuff," said the giant.

He clenched his cannonball fists to punch back, then dropped his hands to his side.

"I meant it as a compliment," said Little Dogie. "Look, she's doin' a good job."

Too Short hit him again.

"Uuuff."

Little Dogie carried Pyg back into town. The others rode, but the giant walked, cradling the boy.

Pyg caught himself thinking: The big man's not so bad. But then he thought again: Yes, he is.

CHAPTER 64

Revelie was staring out the window again. Snow had started to fall once more in the red-walled canyon. She felt cold and trapped. She shivered.

"I hope he doesn't find it," she said as if to the window.

"He probably won't," said Loving, propped up in bed. "It's probably busted up or at the bottom of some damn river by now. Whoever stole it just did it out of meanness. Not 'cause they needed a damn ax to keep around the house. Believe me, it's long gone."

"I hope so, but what if it's not?" She didn't look at him but kept staring out the window. "What will happen if he finds it? What then?"

"But he won't."

"Do you think he'll try to pull the ax out of the stone?" she asked the window.

"No."

"Of course he will." She pressed her nose against the glass and shivered again because it was so cold. "You know he will."

"No."

"Don't lie to me," she said sharply. "He'll try to pull it out. He'll try very hard. And what if he can't? What if he fails? What will he think then?"

"Don't worry yourself over somethin' that's never gonna happen."

"I'll tell you what will happen if the ax stays stuck in that stone. He will think he isn't his father's son. He will believe he has proof."

"No, he won't. That's no kinda proof. Lotsa sons cain't do what their fathers did. Lots. It don't prove nothin'."

"No, but he'll think it does. He'll think he isn't his father's son and his mother is a whore. That's what he'll think. I don't think I could stand that. I really don't."

Revelie's shoulders hunched and she started to cry softly, facing the cold window. Her whole body shuddered.

"Don't cry," Loving said. "I cain't stand it when you cry."

"I know this is unfair to you," Revelie sobbed, her back still turned. "Why shouldn't you be able to embrace your son as your son?"

"We don't know that for sure."

"We're almost sure. As good as sure. Mr. Goodnight and I tried for years and nothing happened. Then we . . . well, we . . . well . . . and presto there was Percy. He is your son, and you should be able to tell him so. I know that. But I have lived with this lie so long, I'm afraid of what will happen if I tell the truth."

"I know."

"I don't want to lose his respect. His love. I don't want him to think his mother is a whore."

"I know."

"I know it's unfair to you. And unfair to him, too, really. But somehow I can't help wanting to preserve my son's esteem. I know it's selfish, but does that make sense?"

"Sort of."

"Only sort of?"

"It makes sense," he said and waited in vain for her to say something. "Turn around, please." She took her time making up her mind, then turned slowly. "Come here."

Revelie walked awkwardly to the bed, like an old woman with arthritis. She sat down on the covers and they stared at each other, neither knowing what to say. Leaning over, she kissed him. The kiss lasted a long time and she felt it in her nipples and down below. Revelie didn't feel so old anymore. She wanted to make love, but she knew he couldn't. He was too sick, too weak. Peeling back the blankets, Revelie descended upon Loving. He was too ill to be an active participant, but he could be a passive one. Her guilt fueled the frenzy.

She thought: What if Percy walked in on them now?

Revelie headed for the barn to do penance. Having just "sinned" with Loving, she now wanted to make it up to God or the universe or whoever or whatever. It seemed to her that she was also doing penance for another, older, larger sin, one that again involved Loving. As she marched along, she found herself once more reliving that terrible night when Mr. Goodnight had discovered her in bed with his best friend. Again she "saw" the drawn revolver and the angry eyes. Again she grabbed a gun and fired. And again she only winged her husband but killed a cowboy named Simon who was standing behind him. Yes, she had a lot to atone for. She doubted saving cattle would weigh enough in justice's scales to overcome the weight of killing another human being. But she did what she could, and right now the cows needed saving, needed healing.

The barn, like almost all of the other buildings on the Home Ranch, was built of blocks of red sandstone. They had had one devastating fire at the ranch and did not intend to have another. They would have constructed a stone dome for the barn if they had known how. Since they didn't, they built the roof out of cedar with slate shingles on top.

Entering the barn, Revelie was revolted. The sight of the grotesquely sick cows nauseated her. This was penance indeed. If she had never paid for her crimes, she was paying now. Moving from cow to cow, like a doctor making rounds, Revelie checked on the condition of each patient. This one was worse. That one was a lot worse. The next one was about the same. None were ever better. In just a few weeks, her hapless herd had shrunk from twelve to five.

"How are you doing today, Jane Eyre?" Revelie asked a mottled red-and-white cow.

She put her hand on Jane's back to check her temperature. As usual, the hide was hot to the touch. Then she scratched behind the cow's huge ears, but got no response. No twitch of an ear. No flick of a tail. Since Revelie hoped not only to help the animal but also to study the disease, she tried to make mental notes. But she didn't know what to look for and probably wouldn't recognize it if she found it. A sense of hopelessness drifted down on her like killing snow.

Revelie moved wearily on to the only bull in the barn. She would never have dared approach a healthy longhorn stud—they were much too dangerous—but a sick bull was as helpless as a calf. His heavy horns, almost six feet across, weighed down his head. He no longer had the strength to hold up his crowning glory.

"Mr. Darcy, are you feeling better today?" Revelie asked, touching his hot back, trying to sound cheerful.

Mr. Darcy answered by urinating blood, which splattered on Revelie's highbutton shoes. She moved on to a cow that was white all over.

"Emma, how are you?"

It seemed that rigor mortis had set in while Emma was still standing up. After a brief pat—the skin was dry and hot—Revelie moved on to a cow that was mostly brown.

"Evangeline, are you feeling any better?" she asked with fake optimism. "No? I'm sorry. I really don't know what to do for you. I wish I did."

This cow seemed hotter than ever, but she couldn't be sure. Her shoulders sagging, Revelie slouched to the last of her chargers, a cow with what looked like big red freckles all over.

"How about you, Hester Prynne?" she asked. "Having a red-letter day?"

Once again, the cow didn't laugh. The disease must have sapped her sense of humor. Of course, Revelie wasn't laughing either. What had she been thinking when she brought the sick cattle into the barn? She was only prolonging their misery. Stooping, Revelie scratched the cow's flaccid belly. Were cows ever ticklish? Not this one. Revelie scratched harder and felt a bump. Did this disease cause nodules? Her hands explored carefully. Her fingers recognized the feel. Revelie pinched and pulled.

Another tick.

"Jesse!"

Silence.

"Jesse! Jesse!"

Nothing.

"JesseJesseJesse!"

In his delirium, Pyg kept calling out her name. But she didn't respond. Was she dead? Had the poison entered her body through a hole in one of her teeth? Had he killed the girl he thought he loved?

"Jesse, I'm sorry."

Silence.

"Sorry, sorry."

Nothing.

"Sorrysorrysorry."

She was dead. She must be dead. And he was her executioner. He wanted to die, too. Like that play they read in school.

"Jesse, I love you."

Silence.

"Jesse, I'm sorry love sorry love love sorry you."

Then even his voice—which seemed to be the last voice in the world—was stilled as he drifted into unconsciousness.

"Percy," Revelie called out in her sleep.

She was awakened by the sound of her own voice. She woke Loving, too.

"You're dreamin' ag'in," he said sleepily.

"I'm sorry," she apologized. "I know you need your rest."

"I don't git nothin' but rest," he said. "I don't mind."

They drifted off to sleep again, but she slept restlessly, turning one way, then the other, trying to escape from something.

"No, Percy! No! No!"

She woke up wet with sweat.

When he woke up, Pyg saw Jesse sitting beside his bed. She was frowning. He felt embarrassed.

"I've been babbling," he said hoarsely.

"So it was just babble?" asked Jesse.

"I don't know." Then he braced himself to tell a lie. "I don't remember what I said."

"Thass what I figgered," she said.

And she got up and walked out of the room. He tried to get up and follow her but fell back in the bed. He hated himself for not admitting what he felt.

CHAPTER 65

After so many days in bed, Pyg felt unsteady as he reviewed his troops. They were gathered in the street in front of the livery stable. Since his jodhpurs had been ruined to save his life, he now wore a brand-new pair of Strausses bought at the Wright & Farnsworth General Store. But they weren't broken in yet and made the boy feel conspicuous and uncomfortable. Standing there wanting to scratch, Pyg couldn't help wondering if his "men" would take orders from a weakened leader. Well, there was only one way to find out.

"We'll ride due east," Pyg said shyly. "We'll pass to the north of the LS spread, and come around behind them." He paused because he knew he shouldn't say what he was about to say. He would just be showing off. "Like Hannibal did," he said under his breath.

"What?" asked Jesse. "I didn't hear you."

"Nothing," Pyg said.

"Come on," she said, "no secrets. Not fair. You gotta tell."

Embarrassed, Pyg wondered if he was blushing. He saw them all looking at him and decided it would be less trouble just to tell.

"We'll go around and attack them from behind the way Hannibal did," he said.

"Who the hell is Hanna Whatsit?" Jesse asked.

"Hannibal," he repeated. "Well, if you must know, he was a general from Carthage who crossed the Alps with a cavalry of elephants and attacked the Romans from the rear."

"You're just tryin' to show off, aincha? Tryin' to make the rest of us feel ignorant, huh?"

They all scowled at him.

"No, I wasn't," Pyg protested. "I didn't want to tell you. You made me."

"Now it's my fault that you're a snob! Come on."

. . .

As the cold water worked its way up his calf, Pyg shivered externally and internally. He kept staring at the fast water, looking so hard it hurt his eyes, trying to see snakes. Hoping not to see them. He wished the water weren't so dirty, so red. He could feel fear shrinking his penis. When the cold water finally reached his crotch, Pyg was sure it couldn't shrink any more, but he was wrong. He just hoped it wouldn't disappear entirely. Feeling his horse's hooves losing contact with the bottom, he was more uneasy than ever because nothing was solid, nothing was sure. Life itself bobbed on gentle but uncertain waves.

Then Pyg saw the snake—as he seemed to have always known he would see it—swimming toward him again. It was happening again. He was paralyzed by fear and embarrassed by fear at the same time. Perhaps the paralysis was part embarrassment.

Was this how the New Hannibal died?

Trying to take careful aim—with the river rising and falling, his horse thrashing in fright—Pyg squeezed the trigger. He killed some water near the snake. He cocked and aimed again and squeezed and saw a red explosion where the snake's head had been. Red ripples spread out from where the bullet had entered the water. Redder than the red river.

"Nice shootin'," said Little Dogie. "You killed a damn turtle."

"No, I didn't," Pyg protested. But suddenly he wasn't sure because all he had seen was a head sticking up out of the water. "Did I, Jesse?"

"Sorry, Pyg," she said. "Turtle heads look lots like snake heads. Anyhow it looked to me like a real vicious turtle."

Well, that one might not have been a snake, but he knew very well that there were snakes out there. The boy didn't begin to relax until Smoke's hooves scraped solid ground. He didn't relax completely until his boots cleared the surface. Coming dripping and living out of the red water, he breathed a deep sigh, as if he had swum the river under water.

"Pyg, where we gonna git them there elephants?" chided Little Dogie. "You ain't told us that parta yore plan yet. I'm countin' on them elephants. They oughta come in mighty handy."

Pyg found himself wishing the farmers hadn't saved the giant back there on the prairie. Little Dogie felt like what the preachers back in

Boston had called original sin: always on the boy's back, weighing him down, making decisions much more difficult. Elephantless, Pyg and his very small army rode toward the morning sun.

"This is sure gonna be the long way 'round," Little Dogie complained.

"Exactly," said Pyg. Staring at the unremitting flatness, he added: "But look on the bright side: no Alps."

The unchanging landscape encouraged his mind to wander and question: What should he do if he failed to pull the ax from the stone? Embrace Loving as his long-lost father? Forgive, forget, forbear? No, he couldn't. Surely he would hate his father for betraying his "father." The two men were supposed to have been best friends.

But what about his mother? If he couldn't forgive his father, could he at least forgive her? He wanted to. He tried to. But so far he was unable to. He doubted he would ever be able to absolve her if she had indeed betrayed his godlike "father." But why did he seem godlike? This man whom Pyg had never met? Wasn't it because of the stories his mother had told him about his "father"? She had made him a hero, and you weren't supposed to cheat on heroes. Was it fair? Probably not, but it was a feeling, and feelings didn't have to be fair or make sense, did they?

"What're you woolgatherin' about?" asked Jesse.

"Nothing," Pyg lied.

"But you been lookin' so serious."

"The sun's in my eyes."

"Well, if you didn't wanna talk about it, why didn't you just say so?"

Maybe he shouldn't even try to pull out the ax. Then nobody would have to know anything one way or another. He could say his father's headstone was sacred, and he didn't want to deface it by removing the ax. Then they could all continue to live in peace together. He wished he could ask Jesse's advice, but she had been so abrasive lately. Besides, leaders were supposed to be decisive, to know their own minds . . .

"Somethin's botherin' you," she said.

"The sun," he lied. "I'll be glad when it's behind us."

. . .

Their shadows stretched before them. Pyg watched his getting taller and taller.

"You don't seem no happier now the sun's not in your eyes," Jesse said. "Whass wrong?"

"Nothing," he lied again.

"Nothin'," she said, "nothin', nothin', nothin'. Cain't you say nothin' but nothin'?"

"That's not what I said. I said 'nothing' with a 'g.'"

"Then you oughta learn how to talk right. You really oughta. That may be how they talk in Boston, but it ain't how folks talk out here. And yore out here now, if'n you hadn't noticed."

"So when in Rome . . ."

"Whass that s'posed to mean?"

"When in Rome, do as the Romans do."

"We ain't in Rome. What're you talkin' about anyhow?"

"It's just an old saying. Never mind."

"Okay, don't tell me what it means. I prob'ly wouldn't understand nohow. I'm just a poor ignorant Harvey Girl, as you well know."

"I don't think that at all. I assure you. Anyway it means you should act the way the natives act. In Rome you should try to conform to Italian customs."

"Next time I'm in Rome," she said haughtily, "I'll bear that in mind."

Pyg took his time responding, thinking over all she had said and he had said. He realized, more clearly than before, that he was in a new Rome, a new western empire. His first instinct was to write a class paper about his new insight. His next thought was: When in the New Rome, do as the New Romans do.

"You're right," Pyg said. "It's my fault." He paused. "Could you teach me?"

"Teach you what?" she hissed. "You don't need no teachin'. Thass your problem."

"Teach me to talk the way you do?"

"You're makin' funna me. Stoppit."

Jesse kicked her horse and spurted ahead. Pyg kicked his and raced after her.

"I'm not making fun, I assure you," he yelled. When he caught up, he added: "I should have said: I'm not *makin'* fun, right? Please help me."

She looked at him skeptically, then frowned: "Fergit it."

It took him a while but he finally convinced her, more or less. They rode a little ahead of the others so they wouldn't be disturbed—or kidded.

"I already know about dropping *g*'s," said Pyg, ever the good student. "'Nothing' becomes 'nothin',' right?

"Right," Jesse said with a suspicious smile. "Very good."

"And 'anything' becomes 'anythin'.'"

"Wrong."

"What?"

"See, it ain't as easy as you thought, is it? You're right about 'nothin',' but 'anything' ain't nothin' like 'nothin'.' 'Anything' just stays 'anything.'"

"Now who's showin' off?" Pyg said.

Jesse gave him a smile so bright it almost made him sneeze. It made her look even prettier. He told himself not to think such thoughts. What was wrong with him? He should keep his mind on his lessons. He shouldn't be wanting to fuck the schoolmarm.

"You got your 'goin'' and 'comin','" Jesse said. "You got your 'ridin'' and 'ropin'.' You got your 'fightin'' and 'clawin'' and 'shootin'.' You got your 'murderin'.' But at the same time, sittin' right over there and laughin' at you, is 'anything.' Keeps you humble, don't it?"

"Yes, it does."

"No, no, no, not 'yes.' It's 'yeah' or 'yeow.' I don't never wanna hear no more 'yeses.' You got that?"

"Yes."

"No!"

"*Yeah.* I was just kiddin'."

"Good."

A smiling Pyg felt a curious schoolroom pride, and he had a crush on the teacher.

"And you employ the double negative whenever possible."

"What?"

"Never mind."

"Don't you never-mind me. I mean don't you never never-mind me. I went to school. I know the rules, some of 'em anyhow. I just fergot about that there double thing fer a minute there. Don't try to show me up if you want me to help ya."

"I'm sorry. I really am. Please go on."

They rode in silence for a while. He felt she was trying to decide if he was serious about trying to learn her language.

"I'm serious about this," Pyg said.

"I'm serious about this *here*," Jesse said.

"This *here*," he repeated.

"You got your 'this here.' You got your 'them there.' It's always better to use too many words insteada too few. It's friendlier like."

"Yeah, that's very well said, very smart."

"You're funnin' me ag'in."

"No, I ain't."

"Very good. But can you say 'cain't'?"

At the campfire that night, Jesse and Pyg sat together a little farther from the fire than the others. The cowboys may have thought that they were engaged in some sort of romantic dialogue, but they were actually discussing grammar.

"*T*'s seem to be a casualty of your new language," Pyg observed. "For instance 'wanna' and 'gonna.' What have you got against the poor letter *T*?"

"Not so fast," Jesse said softly. "I *betcha* cain't think of a buncha others."

"Well, there's—" he began but then paused.

"Don't be in such a hurry to figure out how we talk," she said. "It ain't all that easy. Ain't all that simple. Ain't atall. There's your *T*, Mister Smarty."

"Ain't I tryin' to learn, huh? Go pick on someone else."

"And you better say 'somebody' insteada 'someone,' okay?"

"Really? 'Somebody.' All right."

"And 'okay' insteada 'all right,' okay?"

"All right." He paused. "Okay."

CHAPTER 66

A light snow peppered and salted their breakfast of beef jerky and coffee (which had also been their dinner). As the day progressed, the storm progressed, too. The flakes got bigger and thicker. Pyg knew the country could use all the moisture it could get—or rather git—but he still hated each and every flake. He was cold and wet and still weak from the snakebite. He pulled his hat lower, as if that would do any good. By afternoon, the snow was so thick that it erased the sun. Now Pyg no longer knew east from west, north from south, up from down, almost.

"Too Short," the boy said, "would you mind takin' the lead?"

He didn't say why he wanted the little cowboy to point the way. He didn't have to. They all knew: He was lost. He braced for a cutting remark from Little Dogie, but it didn't come. Too Short, whose sense of direction wasn't perfect but was a lot better than Pyg's, turned his horse a few degrees to the left. And they all followed him. The boy thought they were riding due north toward the Oklahoma Territory, but he didn't say anything.

The wind picked up and the temperature dropped. Having packed so hurriedly, Pyg had forgotten to bring gloves. His thumbs felt as if they were going to crack wide open. He started alternating hands, first holding the reins with his right while his left retreated to his jacket pocket. Then he reversed, steering with his left hand while his right burrowed in the coat that his mother had insisted he bring along. Then the wind really started to howl, making it much colder. The snowflakes attacked them horizontally. Then it started to hail.

Pyg thought: like stones at a stoning. Evoking the biblical punishment his mother might have once received. The boy kept changing hands, the cold one for the warm one, almost as fast as he changed how he felt about his mother. She was good because she had reared him so well, a least in his opinion. She was bad because she had fornicated out of wedlock, which was exactly what he hoped to do with Jesse. But she was his mother and should be held to a higher standard. His fantasies had nothing to do with her sex life.

"This hurts!" Jesse yelled at the storm.

They sat around a sputtering campfire freezing. The hail had stopped but the snow was heavier than ever. There seemed to be no space between flakes. Snow fell as a thousand whistling curtains.

"This here's more'n a norther," observed Too Short.

"We're all sleepin' together tonight," said Pyg, still self-conscious about dropping his *g*'s. "We'll keep each other warm."

"Well, *I* ain't sleepin' nexta *you*," said Little Dogie. "I can tell you that right now."

Pyg waited for Too Short to take control, then remembered he was supposed to be the leader. He took a deep, cold breath, inhaling snowflakes. He coughed.

"Okay, Little Dogie, you're the biggest," Pyg said. "You'll give off the most body heat, like a big fireplace. You'll be in the middle. Jesse, you'll be on the back side of him. Too Short, you'll be on the front side. I'll be behind Jesse."

Pyg was a little surprised to discover that they all bedded down according to his orders. All the bedrolls were stacked on the collective pile. Soon the boy was dozing off. The mental strain of leadership had worn him out.

Pyg dreamed that he was in bed with Jesse and fondling her breasts. She was so tough, and yet her chest was so soft, unbelievably, amazingly soft. He couldn't understand how she could combine such opposites in the same being. Beneath his touch, her soft nipples grew harder and harder. He loved this dream and hoped he wouldn't wake up for a long, long time. He didn't get his wish. He dreamed he had a sharp pain in his right side and it woke him up. Jesse was driving her elbow into his ribs. His hands were still on her breasts. No wonder he had enjoyed his dream so much.

"Just 'cause you learned how to say 'ain't,'" she whispered, "don't mean you can paw me."

She elbowed him again.

. . .

Whithen he woke the next morning, Pyg found himself buried alive. Alarmed, he thrashed about. Then he realized he was covered over by snow rather than dirt and relaxed a little. After all, he could breathe and he was surprisingly warm. Pushing the snow away, Pyg saw that he lay beneath a foot of white.

"Be still," Jesse said. "I'm still sleepin'."

"You're lying," Pyg said.

"'Lyin','" she said. "Now shut up."

The snow was still tumbling down on them. Pyg wondered if they would be able to go on. Perhaps they should turn back and wait out the blizzard in Tascosa. But maybe there was shelter closer at hand. Sure, but where? And how could they ever hope to find it? In a blinding snowstorm, they could ride right past salvation and never see it.

"Maybe we oughta turn back," Jesse whispered.

"I thought you were sleepin'," said Pyg, proud of dropping a *g*.

"Correction," she said. "'I thought you *was* sleepin'. Anyhow maybe we oughta. It's gonna be tough on the horses."

"You're readin' my mind," he said, "but I dunno."

"Very good. But whaddaya think?"

"Shut up," grouched Little Dogie, "or I'll strangle the botha ya."

In a snow-blanketed world, there was no hope of finding wood or even grass to burn. They ate a cold breakfast of jerky and no coffee. Snow blew in their mouths as they bit into the dried and now-frozen beef.

"We cain't go on," said Little Dogie. "We gotta turn back."

Having the giant frame the argument helped Pyg make up his mind.

"It's a two-day ride back," the boy said. "And in this storm, it's more than two days. I think if we keep going—goin'—we have a better chance of findin' shelter. I'm willing"—he thought about changing it to "willin'" but rejected the idea—"to bet that we'll find a ranch or farm or something."

"'Somethin','" Jesse muttered under her breath.

"So less go," said Pyg, feeling he was forcing it. "Less stop killin' time."

A few minutes later, they rode—or rather wallowed—out of camp. The snow was well over their horses' knees. They rode in single file and took turns leading. Of course, the lead horse had the toughest job: breaking the trail. But none of the animals had easy going.

Pyg knew the horses were suffering, but so was he. His gloveless hands got colder and colder. Again his thumbs suffered the most and made him mad. Since his thumbs hurt so much, he wanted to wreak vengeance on thumbs. His "father" had busted them. Maybe he would shoot them off. He knew he could.

The noonday sun was barely visible above the thrashing men and animals. The horses were exhausted. Pyg was now riding with both hands in his pockets, letting his mount follow the others, except when it was his turn to lead.

"Jesse, I'm sorry," Pyg almost shouted to make himself heard. "We shoulda gone back."

"No, look," she yelled. "Ain't that smoke?"

"No, that's just—"

But then he saw the smoke, too. Taking both hands out of his pockets, he spurred his horse. It bounded forward but soon bogged down again.

"This way!" he called through chapped lips.

The frozen riders slowly descended upon a farm. The only building was made out of sod, half in and half out of the ground. It blended perfectly with the landscape except for the faint trace of black smoke. If Jesse hadn't seen it . . . He would thank her later.

Jesse dismounted first and the others soon followed. Pyg stumbled down three buried steps to the dugout's front door and knocked, but his hand was so cold he hardly made any noise. The door didn't open. Little Dogie stepped up and made the door rattle.

It opened.

"Pyg," said a voice from the dark interior, "what're you doin' here?" Then a man stepped out into the storm and embraced the boy. It took Pyg a moment to place this farmer in his memory.

"Betcha," he said. "Betcha White." How had he gotten that nickname? "What are you doing here?"

"'Doin'' here," corrected Jesse.

"I live here is all," said Betcha.

"I'm stranded," said Pyg.

"Not no more. Come on in. What're you waitin' fer?"

The four frozen travelers tramped into the tiny sod house and stamped their snow-covered feet on the dirt floor, making mud.

"I'm sorry," said Pyg. "I'm afraid we're makin' a mess."

"Don't worry 'bout it," said Betcha. "It's just dirt anyway. Cain't hurt dirt."

They all recognized the farmer now. He had been one of the sodbusters who joined the quarantine. They had met him at Home Ranch headquarters when they all started out together. When their posse began to divide, Betcha went off with one of the other groups, but they all remembered him. There were handshakes all around, backslaps, smiles. Betcha stood well over six feet tall and must have weighed 250 pounds. He had black hair and a full black beard. When his teeth peeked through, they were as white as the blizzard.

"How'd you find me?" Betcha asked.

"Jesse found you," Pyg said. "She saw your smoke."

"That's our peach pits."

"What?"

"Our peach pits. They burn better'n coal. And they make the blackest smoke."

"Peach pits? Really?"

"Yeah, we got an orchard. You prob'ly didn't notice, what with the snow and all, but we do and we're kinda proud of it. Last spring, a peddler come through here, and he said he'd buy our pits if'n we'd save 'em for him. He thought he could sell 'em down the line to start new orchards. So we figured, you know, ever' peach pit in the cellar was a penny in the bank."

"Good for you."

"Not so fast. This fall the same peddler come back by. And we showed him our mountain of pits. And he said he'd take two dozen. That was all! We was real put out until we found out how good they burn."

"Thank God for peach pits," Jesse said.

"Alba, come on out here and meet these folks," the sodbuster said.

A curtain screening off the bottom of the room stirred and then was pushed aside. The farmer's wife emerged, followed closely by a boy of about six and a girl of perhaps four. Alba was as small as Betcha was big. Her hair was a droopy red. The kids were blonds. Pyg found himself wondering if Betcha had ever asked himself if they were really his. No, of course not. He was letting his own suspicions cloud everything else. Introductions were made all around.

"We'll kill a chicken," said Alba.

"Not unless you keep them indoors," Pyg laughed. "It's terrible out there."

"We'll kill a chicken," she repeated.

Pyg might be a developing leader in some circles, but not in all. This woman was clearly having none of his leadership. She was going to kill that chicken come hell or high snowdrifts.

"I'll come with you," Betcha said.

"No, your family needs you," Jesse said.

"It won't take more'n a coupla days. And there ain't nothin' I can do around here till spring plantin'."

"Nothin' 'cept start on the new house," said Alba.

"Besides, it's the least I can do. We ain't had no more fever since your mama did that thing."

"But what if somethin' happens to you?" asked the Harvey Girl.

"Nothin's gonna happen," said Betcha.

They tried to dissuade him, but they actually welcomed another body, another gun, since they knew they were going to be seriously outgunned.

The blizzard blew for two more days and then slowly lost its will to live.

CHAPTER 67

Under cover of a cold night, approaching from the east, from the rear, Pyg's "army" descended upon the LS headquarters. Like the elephants of Carthage. They saw a large snow-covered, white-washed house with wings. But what caught their attention was the cook shack: They could see the cowboys sitting down to dinner. It was good to find them all together in one place, wasn't it? All accounted for?

"Now whut?" muttered Little Dogie.

Pyg studied what he thought of as the battlefield. What were the strong points for his army? What were the weaknesses of the enemy? Remembering the importance of the high ground at Gettysburg, he looked for elevation. All he saw was an old-fashioned wooden wind-mill. It had not only a wooden frame but also a wooden flywheel. Metal was coming in but the LS clung to the old ways. He kept staring up at it as something of a plan began to take shape.

"Perhaps we should attempt to set the windmill wheel on fire," Pyg said at last.

"Percy! Stop that," said Jesse.

"Right. Less light up that wheel. They'll all come runnin' out, and we'll git the drop on them, ''em.' And I'll be up there on the high ground, just under the wheel, with an intimidating angle of fire. I mean 'intimidatin'.'"

"Good, but I'm lightin' the windmill," said Too Short.

"No, you *ain't*," said Pyg. "I'm gonna do it. This here damn thing is my damn plan and I'm damn gonna—"

"Don't overdo it," Jesse said.

"I'll light the fire," he said with what he hoped was authority.

"Okay," Too Short backed off, surprising the boy.

"When I get to the top, stop the wheel. Once it catches fire, let it go again."

As Pyg climbed the tower, his bare hands brushed aside the thick snow on the rungs. His fingers felt brittle and his palms seemed to be burning. Each handhold felt colder and colder. As he neared the top, Pyg couldn't feel his hands anymore. What was he going to do now? He was the one who had insisted that he climb the tower, but what if he couldn't even strike a match? He pulled himself up onto the small wooden stage beneath the flywheel, which was really flying, spinning so fast it threatened to launch itself into the air. Waving down at the others, he watched as Little Dogie pulled a four-foot lever that braked the wheel. The great fan shuddered, complained, and stopped.

Pyg brushed the snow off the platform. Then he reached inside his coat and pulled out straw and kindling borrowed from the White family, along with the man of the family. It was supposed to be for campfires, but came in very handy now. The boy numbly put the straw down first, then the smaller twigs, then the larger. Now it was time to light it. Trying to grip with fingers that couldn't feel anything except cold, he struck a match but then dropped it. A tiny firework sailed down to earth.

Embarrassed, Pyg pulled out another match, gripped it tightly, and struck it with his thumbnail. It flared up brightly but was snuffed out almost instantly by the wind. Pyg had only one match left, and he couldn't feel the tips of his fingers. Why hadn't he brought gloves? Why hadn't he brought more matches? How embarrassing would it be if he had to climb down and borrow more?

Below he could see that his troops had taken cover, prepared for the ambush. Jesse huddled behind a pile of firewood. Too Short and Betcha White crouched behind the stone cistern. Little Dogie hid behind a wagon. Turning his back to the wind to protect his one remaining match, the boy started to strike it and then hesitated. Maybe he should have let Too Short light the fire. He was dependable. He wouldn't drop a match or let it blow out. He wouldn't even hesitate. Screwing up his courage, Pyg struck his last hope. He cupped his hands over it to protect the flame. Moving ever so slowly, he lowered the match to the dry straw. The flame flickered, fluttered, and caught.

But would the wheel itself catch fire? In conjuring up his plan, he had just assumed that it would, but now he wondered. The straw burned hot but would soon consume itself. What if the kindling didn't catch? And his matches were gone. The kindling caught. The smaller twigs burned first, then the larger. Then something he hadn't anticipated happened: The platform itself caught fire. The boy beat a hasty retreat down the rungs of the ladder. Scrambling ten feet lower, he paused to see if the wheel was burning.

It was. Once it was blazing merrily, Pyg waved at those below to release the flywheel. Then he worried that the spinning fan might blow out the flames, but it did just the reverse: It fanned them. The wheel was made of dozens and dozens of thin wooden strips. It had many more blades than a metal mill. These laths were not much different from kindling. They made a mighty whirling firestorm. The night was lighted by a new spinning sun.

The fire was spreading down the wooden tower. Before it had been too cold, now it was too hot. Forced to retreat from the flames, Pyg descended slowly, hand under hand. All the while, he kept watching for the LS cowboys to come rushing out of the cook shack to see what was wrong. But they were too intent on dinner. They didn't notice a thing. This amazing show had been defeated by appetite. It had all been for nothing. At last, Pyg gave up on his idea of shooting at Will Lee from above and scrambled on down the tower.

By the time he reached the ground, Pyg had formulated an alternative plan. Sloshing through the snow, he approached the cookhouse. Creeping up on one of the windows, he pulled his silver gun and aimed at the kerosene lamp on a long white table. He squeezed off a shot and the lamp exploded, spraying fire and fuel everywhere. Burning cowboys came racing out of the cook shack. The smart ones rolled in the snow to put out the flames. The dumb ones tried to outrun the fire, which rode them off into the night.

"Ever'body, you better give up!" shouted Too Short. "We got you surrounded," he lied. "Put your hands behind your heads."

The working cowboys did, but Will Lee, the object of the attack, ran for it. With his hair smoking, he raced directly under the burning windmill. Pyg had Lee in his sights and was about to pull the trigger when he paused: He suddenly realized he didn't want to shoot a man in the back. Maybe he had a code, after all. Besides, it had occurred to him that he might need the rancher alive to find his father's ax. Lowering his aim, Pyg shot out Will Lee's right knee. Will collapsed screaming on the ground, where his good leg continued to try to run, turning the sudden cripple in a slow circle like the hands of a clock.

Pyg's shot started a chain of other shots. He couldn't tell who was shooting at whom. Or who at *who*. He just hoped nobody would get hurt. Now he regretted having pulled the trigger. Surely he could have run the mean old man down without ruining his leg. And who knew what other tragedies he had unleashed?

Holstering his gun, the boy raced toward Lee, but he stopped instinctively when he heard a terrible wrenching of metal couplings and wood. Frozen, he saw a giant flaming sunflower, a whirlwind of fire, a destructive sun, a burning moon, fall on Will Lee. It engulfed him in hell. He was shouting something, but the boy couldn't hear what it was. Maybe he wasn't saying words at all. The stench was immediate and revolting. The fire seemed happy.

B ig, friendly Betcha White lay beside the cistern with a hole in his forehead. Pyg threw up into the well, contaminating the water. He was so sorry. He felt as if he had killed the helpful farmer himself. There were also five dead LS cowboys. He hadn't meant for them to die either. He hated himself. Then he was suddenly terrified.

"Where's Jesse?" Pyg called. He couldn't believe he hadn't noticed she was missing. "Jesse! Jesse!" Where had he last seen her? Oh, yes, she had taken cover behind the woodpile. He started running. "Jesse!"

Rounding the stacked wood, Pyg saw her lying on her back. He dropped to his knees beside her. Blood oozed from her mouth and there were bubbles in it. He doubted the bubbles were a good sign. She had been shot in the right side of the chest.

"Jesse, are you okay?" Pyg asked foolishly.

"Not 'specially," she whispered through the blood.

Had Pyg killed her, too? The woman he loved? Or thought he loved? Anyway this girl he couldn't get out of his mind? Whom—*who*—he might have married if she had lived. No, don't think that way. He felt Too Short beside him.

"Looks like it punctured her lung," said the little cowpoke.

"No!" gasped Pyg. "Will she—?"

"I dunno."

Then Pyg noticed the fire. Stray sparks had evidently ignited the barn. What if his ax was in there? The world was burning down, the maybe love of his life was dying, and the boy didn't know what to do. Some leader he was.

Kneeling over her, Pyg was a man at war with himself. A personal civil war. One self wanted to rush Jesse to a doctor as soon as possible while the other self still wanted to find Jimmy Goodnight's stolen ax. One self knew there was no time to question prisoners, but the other self had to interrogate them. He should be searching for medicine, not a glorified hatchet, but he hesitated. The man in him wanted to love and protect and heal the woman, but the boy still wanted his toy, his magic blade. Which was he? Boy or man? Son of Goodnight idealism or son of Loving grace? He squeezed Jesse's hand and stood up.

"Hitch up a wagon," Pyg ordered. "Get a mattress from the house and load it in the back. Put Jesse on it. Hurry." He took a breath and internally changed directions. "Is the foreman still alive?"

"Think so," said Too Short.

"I wanna talk to him."

"I'll git 'im."

"Right now!"

While he waited for Too Short to return from his errand, Pyg tried to think of some ruse to trick answers out of the ramrod of the LS. Unfortunately, he couldn't threaten the foreman with a bottomless pit. He looked around for a substitute but found it a hard order to fill.

Seeing Too Short approaching with his prisoner, Pyg started shouting while the foreman was still a dozen feet away: "I'm in a hurry! Where's the ax! You talk or I'll—"

The foreman yelled back: "In the barn."

Pyg was bitterly divided again. He was burning inside because the barn wasn't burning fast enough. He couldn't even try to put out the fire because all the water on the ranch was frozen. He wanted to rush into the hot flames, pull the ax out of the tombstone, race back out into the cold snow, roll over a couple of times, jump up and then drive Jesse to the doctor's. So much for the boy in him.

"We're gonna need to hitch up another wagon," Pyg decided out loud. "I'll go now and drive Jesse to Tascosa. Too Short, you stay here. When the barn finishes burning down, see if you can find the ax in the ashes. The ax and the tombstone. Load them in your wagon along with Betcha. Take him home and then meet us in town." He wanted to ask Too Short: Is that all right with you? But he didn't think a leader of men would.

"Okay," said Too Short. "What'll we do with them cowboys who give up?"

"Let them go," said Pyg, forgetting to say "'em." "We got the one we wanted."

When the wagon pulled out of LS Ranch headquarters, Pyg shook the reins and popped the whip, but the horses didn't run. They couldn't, not in deep snow. Little Dogie, riding escort, led two unmounted horses. In the wagon bed, Jesse kept moaning and the boy-man kept wanting to try to comfort her. He promised her she was going to be all right, told her not to worry, said they would be there soon, felt like a liar.

"Little Dogie, let's change places," Pyg called out.

"You bet," said the giant.

They didn't precisely exchange positions. Little Dogie took over the reins and sat in the driver's seat. Pyg crawled in the back to keep Jesse company. Three saddle horses were tied to the back of the wagon. Pyg tried to hold Jesse's hand, but she pushed him away. Did she blame him for what had happened to her? Well, why wouldn't she?

"Faster!" Pyg yelled at Little Dogie.

"We cain't go no faster in this snow," Goliath said. "We're lucky to be movin' atall."

"We ain't lucky atall," Pyg said. "Not atall."

"Very good," said Jesse, the first words she had uttered in hours. Then she started coughing.

"I'm sorry," said the boy.

"Shut up," coughed the girl.

"I love you," he said.

"I said shut up," she said.

Four days later—slowed by the snow and the mud—they pulled into Tascosa. Jesse was still alive, but barely. She hadn't said a word for two days now. Pyg was driving the wagon. Little Dogie was lying down in the bed next to Jesse. They were both asleep.

"Whoa," Pyg commanded, pulling back on the reins.

The wagon stopped in front of Dr. Sam Jefferson's office. Jumping down from the wagon, Pyg hurried inside. The doctor was taking a bath in a tin tub at the back of his shop. He was a combination physician and bathhouse operator.

"Doctor, get out of the tub," Pyg ordered, not trying to talk Texan now. "We've got a girl outside who may be dying."

The doc looked irritated.

"Please hurry."

An hour later, Jesse lay on clean white sheets in the doctor's office. Pyg thought she looked paler than the bedding. She was still silent and still breathing.

"Can you save her?" Pyg asked.

"To tell you the truth, I don't know," said Dr. Jefferson. "Her right lung has collapsed."

"Collapsed? That sounds so . . ."

"The wound has already started to heal. That's good but it's also bad. Bad because I don't dare try to remove the bullet. That would only reopen a healing wound and cause more damage."

"So what do we do?"

"Wait another day or two. Then try to reinflate the lung."

"How?"

"Be patient. Would you like a bath?"

CHAPTER 68

Waiting, but not patiently, Pyg divided his time between watching Jesse's unconscious form on the bed and watching out the window for the ax. He felt guilty when he looked at the Harvey Girl because he had almost gotten her killed, and she might die yet. He also felt guilty when he looked out the window, because he was neglecting Jesse. Back and forth, guilty here, guilty there, at fault everywhere he turned his eyes. Jesse was unconscious but not unmoving. She often stirred restlessly as if she were in pain at some deep level. Outside, it had started to rain on top of the fallen snow. Watching drops rolling down the window, Pyg heard Jesse moan as if she were calling his attention back to her. Maybe she was waking up.

"Jesse," he called.

She didn't answer, didn't even moan again.

"Jesse."

Nothing.

Tired almost to death of sitting, Pyg stood up and walked slowly, stiffly to the wet window. He looked east and saw a gray lump approaching through the rain. Could it be the ax coming to him at last? Or was it Too Short coming without the ax? Or was it just a load of hay? Straining to recognize Too Short, Pyg couldn't even be sure the lump was a wagon.

"It might be comin'," he told the unconscious girl, careful to drop his *g*. "I ain't sure." Bad grammar still felt wrong, felt bad, but he would keep trying for her. Talking to her, attempting to include her in his ax vigil, made him feel a little less guilty. "I still cain't tell. Course that foreman was probably lyin'. There probably wasn't anything in that barn at all." Could the ax have eluded him again? Where else could he look?

Slowly the lump resolved into a silhouette, taking shape against the murky, messy sky. Pyg could make out a cowboy hat but not the face beneath it. He wiped the breath fog off the window in an attempt to see better.

"The driver ain't too big," Pyg reported. "Still I cain't tell if it's Too Short or some other dwarf." He wiped the window again. "I think it's Too Short."

He wanted to run out of the room, race down the street in the mud and rain, and jump into the back of the wagon. But he told himself he shouldn't desert Jesse even though she didn't know he was there. He felt guilty just wanting to leave.

"Yeah, it's him."

Jesse moaned.

Pressing his face closer to the glass, Pyg stared hard as if his eyes were magnets pulling the ax toward him. If there was an ax to pull. Come on, come on. Oh, no!

Lightning bolted out of the sky and hit the ax. Breaking out of his prison cell, Pyg ran into the storm without even his hat. The cold rain felt like hail pounding his skin while fears pounded below the surface. Had the ax survived? After all this trouble and pain, had lightning melted the blade before he got a chance to try his luck with it? And what about Too Short? Had he killed his favorite cowboy just as he had virtually killed his favorite girl?

"Too Short!" he yelled into the soaking gale, but it was as useless as trying to talk to Jesse.

At least Too Short was still upright on the wagon seat. If the white-hot finger hadn't tapped the cowboy on the top of his head, it must have come down on the blade. Would being hit by lightning make the ax even more special or reduce it to nothing?

"Too Short! Too Short!"

The little cowboy started waving, and Pyg ran even faster. As he met the wagon, Too Short halted the weary, hoof-heavy team. Pyg climbed the spoked wheel, squeezed the little cowboy's shoulder, and jumped into the bed of the wagon. Stubbing his toe on the tombstone, he sprawled on top of the granite slab. The stone lay flat on its back and the boy lay flat on his stomach. Rest in peace, Pyg Goodnight.

But he couldn't rest. Squirming, he got to his hands and knees and read the inscription upside down:

CATTLEMAN
1849–1883
JAMES GOODNIGHT

He was relieved to see the ax blade still embedded in the tombstone's hard left shoulder. He was also glad he hadn't fallen on it. Moving closer, he examined the steel for heat damage, but didn't see any. This must be some tough ax.

"The lightning didn't hurt it," Pyg announced.

"What?" asked Too Short.

"The lightning didn't hurt the ax," the boy yelled.

"No, but it come purdy close."

"What?"

"That damn sizzler didn't miss by much."

"It missed?"

"Course it missed. You see any smoke comin' outa my hat?"

"It missed the ax, too."

"Course."

"You sure?"

"Touch it."

The ax blade wasn't just cold but freezing.

"Oh."

CHAPTER 69

The next day, Pyg ran into Dr. Jefferson at the long bar of the Exchange Saloon, which did not give the boy a lot of faith in this man of medicine. The boy told himself that he would kill the doctor if he failed to save Jesse.

"I have a novel idea," said Dr. Jefferson. "Really, as far as I know, it has never been tried before."

"Then why try it now?" Pyg asked. "Jesse isn't a laboratory rat."

The doctor stared at the boy for a long time. "Because I don't know what else to do."

"Tell me about the idea."

"I wanna hear this, too," said Little Dogie, abandoning a card game and coming over to the bar.

"The lungs are like two balloons. If one is punctured, it collapses. You know that. But if the balloon could be repaired, it could be reinflated, right?"

"I think so" said Pyg. "Right."

"So what would you do with a repaired balloon?"

"Blow it up again."

"Precisely. That is exactly what I intend to do. I will blow into her mouth and inflate her collapsed lung."

"Not while I'm alive."

"What are you talking about? It gives her a chance."

"If any lips touch her lips, they'll be mine."

"Wonder what she'd say about that," said Little Dogie. "Last I heard, she waddn't too partial to your lips or any other part of your anatomy."

"I'll do it," Pyg said. "Just tell me what to do."

"All right, have it your own way," said Dr. Jefferson. "But you're now responsible for whether she lives or dies."

. . .

Pyg prepared to kiss an unconscious Jesse back to life. He took a deep breath, started to bend over her, then stopped and stood up again. He drew in another deep breath, held it, and let it out once more.

"Too bashful to kiss her?" Little Dogie asked. "Then I'd be tickled to take your place."

"I'd kill you."

"Temper, temper."

Taking in a third deep breath, the deepest of all, Pyg lowered his lips to Jesse's. And he blew. And blew. And *blew*. The doctor had told him it was important to inflate the lungs with one blow. Otherwise the air would escape from her while he was taking another breath. But something was wrong. He could feel a rush of air—a draft—blowing on his cheek. He stopped and took a breath.

"I'm blowing in her mouth," Pyg gasped, "and it's coming out her nose."

"I should have thought of that," said Dr. Jefferson. He took a breath. "Hold her nose."

Bending over, touching his toes, Pyg inhaled as he stood up, determined to set a record for deep breaths. Then he hurriedly bent over Jesse, pinched her nose, and kissed her. He blew. He blew from his chest. And when that was empty, he blew from his diaphragm. And when that was empty, too, he blew from his toes. His whole body hurt. His head felt as if it were going to cave in. Feeling he was letting Jesse down, Pyg stopped blowing and started breathing again. Then he watched the doctor place his ear on the girl's chest, listening.

"I think you made some progress," Dr. Jefferson said, straightening up, "but her lung has collapsed again. I would be happy to take over."

"No, thanks," said Pyg.

"I got the biggest lungs," said Little Dogie. "Mebbe I oughta try."

"No!"

Pyg took several deep breaths in a row, then a final, record, bottomless one. He kissed Jesse again and blew as hard as he could for as long as he could. The harder he blew, the harder he squeezed her nose. When he realized what he was doing, he wondered if he was hurting her. Was she conscious enough at some level to feel anything? Relaxing his grip slightly, he kept on blowing. Beginning to feel faint, Pyg refused to give up. He saw spots in front of his eyes and the spots were getting bigger. He could feel himself falling into one of those spots, then nothing.

When he regained consciousness, lying on the floor, Pyg saw Little Dogie kissing Jesse. It was his worst nightmare. Or almost the worst. Her dying would be the worst. The giant kept blowing and blowing and blowing out of his oceanic lungs. Pyg was angry, jealous, amazed, disheartened, and furious.

"Stop!" he ordered.

Too Short put his hand over the boy's mouth. He kept trying to yell "stop" but it came out "stmp." Little Dogie did not obey. Evidently passing out did not increase your stock as a leader. Having a hand over your mouth didn't either. Pyg tried to bite Too Short's fingers, but he couldn't even do that right.

While the giant continued to blow, Dr. Jefferson put his ear to Jesse's chest. Pyg was jealous of him, too, with his ear too near Jesse's right nipple. He tried to tell the doctor to stop, but it again came out "stmp." Too Short's hand ate all vowels.

"Good, good," the doctor said. "Keep going. I can hear her lung filling with air."

And unbelievably, Goliath did go on and on. He blew like the north wind, which never stopped blowing in these parts. (Whenever it did, all the chickens fell over, as the boy had been told many times.) Little Dogie blew like the storms of their good dreams that brought rain. He blew like the storms of their bad dreams that loosed tornadoes. He blew like Gabriel on Judgment Day.

"Good," said Dr. Jefferson.

Little Dogie blew like the bugles at Gettysburg. Like the bugles of the cavalry coming to the rescue.

"Don't stop," the doctor said. "You're getting there."

Like a child blowing up a balloon.

"Thanks," Jesse said.

She wasn't talking to Pyg. She was thanking Little Dogie. The boy burned. She kissed the giant—who had kissed her so long on the mouth—on the cheek. Pyg recoiled, but at least she was alive again, at least talking again. She smiled shakily.

"It waddn't your fault, Pyg," Jesse said.

But the exoneration seemed an accusation to the boy. He had literally fallen down on the job. And now he had to be grateful to Little Dogie, of all the people on this earth.

CHAPTER 70

Revelie was looking out the bedroom window again. Was she hoping she would see him coming or afraid she might? The thought was quickly followed by a shiver.

"What's wrong?" asked Loving from his sickbed.

"Nothing," Revelie snapped, turning from the window to glare at him.

"Now I know there's somethin' the matter," he said. "And you're losin' weight."

"All women want to lose weight." She drew herself up. "That's a good thing."

"Not that much weight."

"Mr. Loving"—softening, she smiled—"are you complaining about my figure?"

"Not hardly. You know better'n that. I'm worried about you."

"Don't worry about me." She wasn't smiling anymore. "Worry about yourself."

"Revelie! What's wrong?"

She turned back to the window and almost pressed her still-pretty nose against the glass. What should she tell him? What could she tell him? She wasn't really concealing anything, she told herself, because she didn't know the answer herself.

"I'm fine, really."

Shivering again, she tried to hide it.

"No, you ain't," Loving told her back. "Please don't lock the door and keep me on the other side."

Revelie recognized a turning of the tables that disturbed her: She had always accused her late husband, Mr. Goodnight, of locking her out. Sometimes he did it literally. Had she turned into him?

"I don't know what's wrong," she admitted, at last.

"But somethin' is," he said. "Thass a beginnin'."

Revelie turned to face Loving. She took several deep breaths as if she were going to swim underwater.

"I can't eat. When I smell food, I feel as if I am going to throw up. When I put food in my mouth, I sometimes do throw up." She paused. "I must be worrying too much about Percy." Pause. "I never should have come back to Texas."

He looked hurt.

"I'm sorry. Of course, I should've come. I couldn't help coming. Nothing on earth—"

"What else?" asked Loving, brushing his hurt aside. "What other symptoms you got?"

Revelie didn't say anything.

"Tell me, please."

"I can't," Revelie blurted out.

"Why not?" Loving asked, with a don't-bar-the-door expression.

"It's too personal."

She turned back to the window.

"Personal?" said Loving accusingly. "We ain't been personal? You don't know me, I don't know you? Whut?"

"It's *too* personal," she told the window, fogging it. "Really."

"Between us, nothin' is. Nothin' atall."

She couldn't make up her mind.

"We're somethin' or we ain't."

She thought and thought, hesitated and hesitated, seemed to understand *Hamlet* better than before.

"When I, uh, well, when I, uh, urinate . . ." She stopped, paralyzed by the word.

"Please, go on. You've seen me—"

"I know, I know." She couldn't say it. Then she summoned her courage. "It's pink." She waited but he didn't say anything. "It's red," she confessed.

"How red?"

"Red."

"Bloodred?"

She waited and waited. "Yes."

"We have to get you help. Go to Tascosa. Go tomorrow. No, go today. Are you listenin'?"

"I have to wait for Percy."

"No."

"Yes."

"I have to."

Still looking for her son, she saw a cold rain beginning to fall. Anyway it looked cold. She shivered again. Was she sick or had she seen something? The rain was washing away what was left of the snow. A dark, wet red was emerging.

"Look at me," Loving demanded. "You're spendin' your whole life lookin' out that there winder."

Revelie noticed that his voice was stronger. He finally seemed to be getting a little better. Just as she was getting worse. Was there some kind of law of nature at work here, one going down as the other went up? Or was it moral retribution?

"I'm sorry," Revelie said, peering over her shoulder at him. "I just can't seem to stop looking. It's . . . I don't know."

"I know."

"No, you don't know," she flared. "How could you? You've never had a—" She stopped herself. "I'm sorry. I'm really sorry."

Loving just smiled at her. Then she went back to looking out the window. The rain looked very cold. No one would arrive in weather like this. She flinched again. Something was moving on the face of the red cliff. Maybe it was a landslide caused by the rain. That had happened before. Focusing with all her strength, the mother saw a wagon—yes, it was certainly something with wheels—maneuvering down the trace of a road. She flinched again, a bigger flinch. Were they expecting the delivery of supplies? Who or what could it be?

Of course, if Percy had found the tombstone and the ax, he would need a wagon to carry it in, wouldn't he? Revelie stared hard and saw ghostly riders begin to emerge. Who were they? Try as she might she didn't recognize her son. Was she happy or sad? She was both. But she still wasn't sure. She tried to stare even harder.

"See somethin'?" asked Loving.

"A wagon is coming down the cliff," Revelie said. "But I don't see Percy. Where are those binoculars?"

"What? Oh, the field glasses. They're right where they always are when you ask, on top of the chest of drawers."

"Of course."

Revelie hurried to the bureau and retrieved the binoculars. Returning to the window, she held them to her eyes and focused. The wagon with its accompanying riders jumped closer, but faces were still a blur. Straining her eyes, she did manage to recognize an indistinct Little Dogie, not by his features but by his size. And there was a vague Too Short, marked by his shortness, driving the wagon. She looked for Jesse's long, dirty hair and didn't see it. Which was not entirely bad news. But most of all she looked for her son and didn't see him either. She looked again and again.

"What's wrong?" asked Loving, who knew her very well.

"Nothing," Revelie said, afraid to pronounce the truth.

"Not that ag'in."

"I don't see Percy."

"Don't worry—"

"Be quiet now."

Then she felt guilty. How could she scold an invalid? But he was getting better, wasn't he? Still . . .

She kept raking the riders with her binoculars. Yes, that was definitely Little Dogie. Yes, that was certainly Too Short. But that was all—except for three horses hitched behind the wagon. Riderless horses. The mother tried to stop thinking—imagining tragedies—but she couldn't. What did the wagon mean? Perhaps it held not the ax and stone, but her son. Was he just gravely wounded? Or was it his body?

"I'm sorry," Revelie said. "I didn't mean that. I'm just so . . ."

She flinched because she was expecting him to say that he knew once again.

"I'm worried, too," Loving said.

"If he'll just come back to me," Revelie said, "I don't care what he finds out."

But she didn't even convince herself. She braced herself for another *I know.*

"I don't neither," said the handsome cowboy.

Well, of course, he didn't care what Pyg found out. What would be bad news to her would be good news to Loving. He probably wanted a son, an acknowledged son, a sliver of immortality. Realizing their hopes and fears were at odds, she flinched again. It was a big flinch.

"I'm on your side," Loving said.

She flinched bigger.

"Oh, there's someone in the back of the wagon," Revelie said. "It could be Percy. I'm not sure." She refocused the binoculars. "The hair is longer than Percy's."

"He ain't been near no barbers," Loving said.

"Or it could be Jesse."

They endured a silence.

"If it ain't Jesse, I mean if it's him," Loving said, "well, maybe we oughta just tell him the truth. Before he . . ."

"Percy may have already tried to pull out that damnable ax. It may be too late to be the first ones to tell him the truth."

Revelie flinched the biggest flinch of all.

CHAPTER 71

Revelie could see Percy plainly now: He was sitting in the back of the wagon, for some reason. He must have been injured, wounded so badly he couldn't ride. She told herself she never should have let him go, although she didn't know how she could have stopped him. Focusing her binoculars on his face, the mother tried to read his expression. Was he different from the son who had parted from her a month ago? Was he resentful? Was he angry? What had he found out? He was frowning, but couldn't that just be fatigue? Or perhaps pain? Or just the ice-cold rain? That scowling face wasn't necessarily an accusation.

Or was it?

"I'm going to meet him," Revelie announced.

"Don't go out in that freezing rain," Loving cautioned. "You'll git even sicker, and then where'll we be. A house fulla invalids."

Revelie hurried out of the sickroom, ran down the hall and across the vast living room, slammed through the front door, and pulled herself up short on the front porch. That rain really did look wicked, and the wagon was still several hundred yards away. She longed to run out anyway, but then she had a thought that embarrassed her. She didn't want to welcome her son back with wet hair. She hesitated on the big porch.

Through sheets of rain, Revelie saw Too Short flap his reins and start the horses running. The little cowboy was obviously anxious to get home, but was her son? Having left the binoculars behind because she had intended to run out into the storm, the mother couldn't see her Percy's face very distinctly. But she still looked for clues of what he knew or didn't know. Yes, he knew. No, he didn't. Yes, he hated her. No, he loved her. Yes, he knew but had forgiven. No, he could never forgive. They were now only fifty yards away and she still couldn't tell.

To hell with her hair. To hell with whatever illness was wasting her.

Too hell with common sense. Revelie bolted from the porch and ran toward the oncoming wagon. She had to embrace her son. She had to hold him. Then whatever happened would happen. He might reject her. He might accuse her. She might be making matters worse. In which case, she only hoped she might die of pneumonia. She kept running.

Percy vaulted out of the wagon—he was all right—and came striding toward her. Her hair flat and dripping, Revelie ran faster. Freezing rain soaked her clothing. When she reached him, she jumped and he caught her. She wrapped her arms around his neck and her legs around his body. Then she was embarrassed and let go with her legs.

"Are you all right?" she said into the storm.

"I'm fine," he said.

She hugged him tight for a long time, probably too long. She could feel him growing impatient.

"Then why were you riding in the wagon?"

"Jesse's been shot. I was riding with her."

"Oh, no." Revelie was surprised to find herself actually sympathetic. "How is she?"

"She had a collapsed lung, but we managed to fix it up," he said. "I think she's gonna be all right."

"*Gonna?*" asked Revelie.

"I talk different now," he said. "Differ'nt. I guess I should be sorry, but I ain't. Not really. Jesse saved my life. Risked her own. I owe her."

Oh, no, thought Revelie. But if Jesse had really saved her son . . .

"I suppose I owe her, too," said the mom. "What happened?"

"I'll tell you later," he brushed aside her question.

He was growing up.

"Did you find your father's headstone?" she asked.

"Yeah," he said.

His mother waited for him to say more. Where had he found it? What had he done then? Had he tried to pull the ax out of the stone? What happened when he couldn't? He was staring hard at her. Very hard.

"Did you—?" his shivering mother asked.

"No."

"You didn't even—?"

"No!"

CHAPTER 72

Revelie woke up hot in a pool of water. She couldn't understand where she was. In a river? In a lake? In a flood? In the ocean that bathed the shores of her beloved Boston? Not only did she not know where she was, she didn't know when. What time was it? What month? What year? She was so disoriented that she was dizzy, queasy.

"Good morning," said an unfamiliar voice.

"What?" she muttered, trying to shake off the dizziness.

"I said good morning," repeated Loving.

Now she recognized his voice. Slowly the sickroom came into focus. But why was she so hot? Why was she swimming in water?

"You had a restless night," said the now-familiar voice. "How do you feel?"

"I'm burning up," Revelie said through parched lips. "I need a glass of water."

She tried to get up, but fell back into the wet pool. Now she realized: It was a pool of her own fevered sweat. She could not believe how weak she was. She shivered.

"You're sick," Loving said.

"No, I'll be all right," Revelie said.

She tried to sit up and failed.

"Lie still," he said. "Let me take your temperature."

She lay back and tried to relax. He put his hand on her forehead.

"You're burning up," he said.

"I said that," she said.

"You're really burning."

"I know."

Revelie waited for Loving to say he had told her so, had warned her she was getting sick, but he didn't. That was the good part about being in love with a laconic cowboy. What was she supposed to do now?

"I've got to get up," she said at last.

"Lie still," he said.

"No, I have too much to do."

"No, you don't."

"Yes."

"No. Listen to me."

Revelie lay still and tried to think. Was she just having a bad morning or was she really sick? Well, she couldn't stand up. She couldn't even sit up. She was lying in a lake of her own perspiration. Perhaps something was the matter with her. She took deep breaths while she tried to consider her situation. Considering only made it worse.

"I might be contagious," Revelie said.

"Mebbe," Loving said. "I dunno."

"But I have to get up." She shuddered. "I have to move to another bedroom."

"No! Why?"

"You might catch what I have."

"I don't give a damn."

"Well, I do! I haven't nursed you all this time so that you—in your weakened condition—can catch something from me and die. I won't have it."

Now Loving was taking deep breaths. Revelie could hear him but wouldn't look at him.

"Revelie, you've taken care of me for weeks," Loving finally said. "Now I'm feeling better. Now I'm stronger. Now it is my turn to take care of you. It's only fair."

"But—"

"You hafta be fair. You ain't goin' nowhere. I'm the nurse now."

"No—"

Trying to get up, she felt weaker than ever and fell back onto the sweat-soaked bed. Since she didn't have the strength to move to another bedroom, she decided to stay where she was. Of course, she could have called some of the cowboys to carry her to another room, but that would be embarrassing. And then her son would know how sick she was. She didn't want to burden him. At the same time, she worried: What would he think when he found his mother actually lying in the same bed with Loving?

"Mother," said a strange voice.

Revelie could feel herself drowning in her own sweat again. Resentfully, she tried to swim to the surface, but it was hard going.

"Mother, Mother," said Percy. "How do you feel?"

"Fine," she lied. "Leave ax." She knew she was incoherent but couldn't stop herself: "Don't touch . . . Leave alone . . . Leave in stone . . . Ax stuck in stone so amazing . . . Don't separate . . . Shame separate . . . Leave together . . . Lovers . . ."

"Mother."

"Shame . . . Shame . . ."

CHAPTER 73

When his mother fell asleep—or lost consciousness—Pyg went to check on Jesse. She too was sleeping or unconscious. He told himself he just wanted to comfort her when he lay down on the bed beside her.

"Whaddaya think you're doin'?" Jesse protested.

"I thought you were asleep," Pyg said.

"So you could take advantage, huh?" she accused.

"No," he attempted to defend himself.

"Who do you think you are, anyhow? Lemme tell you somethin': You ain't Loving and I ain't your mama, okay? Just 'cause they do it don't mean we're gonna do it. Git outta my bed right now."

"But—"

"Git out!"

Pyg sheepishly withdrew.

After a long, cold walk by the river, Pyg returned to the sickroom that his mother and Loving now shared. His opening the door awakened her. She stared at him with glassy eyes and seemed not to recognize him.

"It's me, Pyg," he said.

"Pyg?" she asked. "Oh, yes, Percy. I'm sorry I got sick."

"I'm sorry I woke you."

"I reckon I should be sorry, too," said Loving sleepily, "since ever'-body else is, but I don't know what about."

"Mom, I'll let you rest," Pyg said, backing up.

"No, don't go," his mother said. "There's something I want to ask you. Something important."

But then she closed her eyes and seemed to go back to sleep. Pyg turned to go.

"No, stay," his mother said, her eyes fluttering open. "I was planning for us to have a long talk and then I would ask you something. But I'm too tired."

"Then you should rest," Pyg said.

"I'll rest as soon as I ask you." She paused. "It's a favor. I need you to do me a favor."

"Anything."

"Don't say that until you hear what it is." She took a breath and collected her strength. "I want you to promise me . . ." Then she seemed to run out of strength.

"We'll talk about it when you're stronger," Pyg said.

"No, please," she said. "I want you to promise that you won't try to pull the ax out of the tombstone."

"What?" he asked, although he had heard her perfectly well.

"Not now, not ever. Do you promise?"

Pyg didn't want to. He had chased that ax for months and many many miles. Now that he had finally brought it home, was he to be denied an answer to the riddle? He told himself his mother wasn't playing fair: exploiting his sympathy when she was sick. No, he wouldn't do it. He wouldn't refuse in so many words but would turn and walk out the door. He turned.

"Promise!" called his mother.

"I promise," he said.

CHAPTER 74

"You ain't so hot," Loving said.

"Well, I like that," said Revelie.

"I mean your temperature."

"I know."

"Good, got your sense of humor back."

Loving rolled toward her and kissed her. Something was different about his kiss. Was it more energy? More feeling? More conviction? Was it passion? Evidently they were both recovering.

"You're getting pretty frisky," Revelie said.

"You ain't seen nothin' yet," Loving laughed.

He unbuttoned her sweat-stained bodice. She was still wearing the same clothes she had gotten sick in. His mouth descended from her lips to her hard nipples.

"Do you feel up to frisky?" he asked between sucks.

"I seem to be all right," she said. "How about you?"

His answer was to descend once again. Pulling up her skirt and down her underclothing, he buried his face in her pubic hair. She began moaning. What a way to celebrate! And she had so much to celebrate. She was better. Loving was better. And Percy wasn't going to try to pull out the ax.

Loving was coughing. Oh, no, had he swallowed one of her pubic hairs? The very idea embarrassed her. What if he survived a bullet only to be killed by . . .?

"What's wrong?" she asked in spite of herself.

"Nothin'," he said.

But she could see him digging something out of his mouth. Was it a corkscrew hair? Or something worse? She was more embarrassed than ever.

"What is it?" she demanded, although she wasn't sure she wanted to know.

"Nothin'," he said again.

"Show me. You took something out of your mouth."

"No, I didn't."

"Don't lie to me! Show me! Show me!" She knew she was becoming hysterical, but she couldn't stop. "Show me! Right now! Show me!"

Revelie grabbed Loving's hand—the hand that had removed whatever it was from his mouth—and held on tight.

"Let me see."

When he opened his hand, Revelie had to fight against vomit. Between his index finger and his thumb, Loving held a gray blob.

"What is it?"

"Just some lint."

"Hold it closer."

"No."

"Hold it closer!"

"Oh, all right."

Like the tumblers in a safe, Revelie saw not numbers but images aligned: The tick on her was the same as the tick on those dying long-horns. And implications landslided. If cows had a tick and the fever, and she had a tick and the fever, then there was probably a connection. Evidently she was a lot like a cow.

"Revelie?" said Loving.

"Give me a moment," she said.

Her mind was spinning but no longer from illness. She remembered that the fever never struck during the winter. Of course ticks were killed off during cold weather. But they always returned when the fever returned, in the spring, as the world warmed up again. In trying to save her barn cows, was she prolonging not only their lives but also the lives of the fever-carrying ticks who were sucking their blood?

Her low-fevered mind raced: The enemy was the ticks. What to do? She wasn't a doctor. She didn't know. But she tried to think like a doctor. No use. She tried common sense. Could they examine all the cows and remove the ticks one at a time? Sure, walk up to a healthy long-horn bull and ask him politely if you can pull a tick from beneath his tail. Better think of something else. Maybe they could burn them out: set prairie fires that would cremate the ticks and their eggs hiding in the grass. But how would they control the flames? What if they ended up burning down Texas? Think more.

No, yes, well, maybe. Could they dip all the cows in some sort of tick poison? But what if that poison killed the cows, too? Still there must be something that would work. Some poison that would kill ticks but not cows. She promised herself she would find it. Strangely enough, she knew she could.

"I'm sorry," Loving said.

"No, that was great."

"What?"

"Just great. Thank you."

"Tell me, ma'am, are you losin' your mind?"

CHAPTER 75

A week later, Revelie was up, around, and busy again. On a trip to the barn early one morning, she found a dead cow. It must have died overnight. Expecting to throw up at any moment, Revelie searched the carcass, running her fingers here, there, every disgusting place. She found a tick deep inside its left ear, where she had never thought to look before. The parasite was still attempting to suck the dead blood of the dead cow. Touching it should have turned her stomach, but she didn't vomit. She was growing less squeamish as she grew more determined. Where else had she never looked? Pulling hard, Revelie raised the dead tail. Exploring with her fingers, she discovered a second tick in a very intimate place. Her own intimate place quivered sympathetically. She continued to search with disgusting thoroughness—including all orifices—but found nothing more.

Leaving the barn, she plotted the demise of her two ticks. She decided to try carbolic acid since it was the only disinfectant that the ranch happened to have on hand. Visiting the cook shack, she dumped her two suspects into a pan. Carrying her bloodsuckers as if they were a meal, Revelie headed for Loving's sickroom, because she knew a big bottle of carbolic acid waited for her on his night table.

Revelie half expected to find Loving sleeping—the sick man often slept late—but he was wide awake. He was actually sitting up with his legs over the side of the bed. She hadn't seen him in such a pose for a very long time. He seemed on the verge of getting out of bed.

"Be careful," Revelie said without thinking. "You're still very weak. Don't hurt yourself." She knew she sounded more like a mother than a lover, but she couldn't help herself. "But it's good to see you sitting up," she said by way of apology.

"I think I'm strong enough to git up," Loving said. "And they's only one way to find out."

Revelie wondered why she accepted bad grammar from Loving but not from her son. In Loving, it was endearing. In Percy, what was it? A sinking into the lower classes? Was she really so snobbish? Or did she just hate to hear her son talking the way that Harvey Girl talked? Was that snobbishness, too?

"I'll help you," Revelie said.

"Thanks," Loving said.

Hurrying to his side, she hooked her arm under his.

"Here goes not a damn thing," he said.

Revelie lifted and Loving struggled to stand. But he only got halfway up before he sank back onto the bed.

"Sorry," he said.

"That's all right," she said. "You almost made it. You'll make it next time. Tell me when you're ready."

"I dunno," said Loving. "Mebbe I oughta wait till tomorrow."

"All right, we'll try again tomorrow. You're getting stronger every day."

"No, don't wait," said Percy. "Try again right now. I'll help."

Focused on Loving, Revelie hadn't noticed her son come into the room. Which she could hardly believe. Her eyes normally spotted him and followed him everywhere.

"Okay," agreed Loving.

With Revelie gripping him under his heart-side arm, with Percy holding him on his right, Loving tried to stand once again. Once more, he hesitated halfway up, but this time he regrouped, with help, and managed to stand up on his own feet.

Revelie almost said: "I love you." But she checked herself just in time. "You did it," she said. "I really admire you."

"Nice goin'," said Percy.

Loving took a step, but one was all he could muster. He sank back onto the bed. Then he lay down and close his eyes.

"That was great," Revelie said. "Very encouraging."

. . .

Revelie remembered her ticks. Withdrawing to the privacy of the bath-room at the end of the hall, she sat down on the commode. She placed the pan of ticks on the floor in front of her. With shaky fingers, she poured carbolic acid into the bottle cap. Then she rained—drop by drop—death on the ticks. Anyway she hoped they would die. The blood-engorged blobs twisted and turned in apparent agony. She didn't feel sorry for them even though she thought she should. After a few minutes, the ticks stopped writhing. The carbolic acid had killed them.

Revelie did a little bloodthirsty dance. Now all she had to do was find a way to baptize thousands of cattle with this lethal lifesaving elixir.

Seeing his mother heading for the barn, Pyg decided it was a good time to talk to Loving alone. As he approached the sickroom, the boy was working up the courage to ask *the* question: Are you my father? But wasn't there some way to soften what might sound like an accusation? Couldn't he creep up on the question somehow? Well, he couldn't think of how. He would just have to do his best once they were face to face. Determined, he opened the sickroom door.

"Hi," said Loving. "You think you could help me git up ag'in?"

Pyg hesitated. Should he confront him now or afterward? "Of course," he said at last.

The boy grasped Loving's hand—as if shaking hands—and pulled him upright. Then, to support him, he hugged him. Pyg felt a warmth, like a pleasant fever, spreading through his chest. Was he at last embracing his father?

"I'm gonna walk to that there winder and look out," Loving said. "Help me but don't help me too much."

Pyg released Loving and then hovered behind him, ready to catch him: one step, another step, a third, a fourth, and then a rest stop. The wounded cowboy just stood there swaying from side to side.

"I been on cattle drives," Loving said, out of breath, "that was short-er'n this here walk."

He started again and stumbled. Pyg grabbed his left arm and held him upright.

"It's like you was the daddy now," Loving said, "and I'm the damn baby, gittin' taught how to walk."

"Tell me about my 'father,'" Pyg said, which wasn't at all what he had intended to say. What was happening to his determination to have some sort of showdown? "Please."

"He was the best friend I ever had," Loving said, leaning on Pyg. "But I waddn't to him."

With the boy supporting him, the healing cowboy took half a dozen learner steps and then almost collapsed. Pyg caught him just in time.

"I waddn't to him," Loving repeated. "I cain't make it up to him no more, but I'd like to make it up to you, if'n I can. Next best thing. Course I gotta git better first. But, you know, I been feelin' better ever since you brought that damn ax back. It's good to have the botha you home. Sure as shootin', it's a load off my mind. You know, I'm afraid I'm finally gonna git well."

"Then tell me how you got shot," Pyg said, feeling a little braver. "Why? What happened?"

"Just got in an argument in a saloon," Loving said. "Stay outta them saloons."

"What was the argument about?"

"Nothin' important. Just saloon shenanigans."

"I don't believe you."

"You'd accuse a sick man of lyin'?"

"You've been so mysterious. I'm sorry, but I can't help but wonder why. Did it have anything to do with my mother?"

"No!" Loving said too sharply.

Anyway Pyg thought it was too sharp. Which convinced the boy of the contrary.

"Maybe you were defending her honor," he said.

"No!!" Loving said too fiercely.

To end this talk, Loving took another couple of steps, staggered again, and was caught again. To keep him from falling, Pyg hugged him tightly.

Revelie opened the door and stared.

"I didn't know you two were so close," she said.

Pyg tried to decode her attitude, but failed. Was she pleased? Displeased? Feeling betrayed? Feeling affirmed? Guilty? Innocent? Jealous? His mother was as much a mystery as ever.

CHAPTER 76

"He walked," Pyg said.

"Well, he didn't walk on water, did he?" asked Jesse.

"Almost."

They shared a branch of a cottonwood tree that grew on the bank of the red river that had sculpted the canyon. The river rolled by some dozen feet beneath their dangling legs. Pyg had noticed the tomboy up in the tree and had climbed up to tell her the news. He loved it that she climbed trees. Well, was it the climbing he loved or the girl doing it? He wasn't sure.

"I done climbed up here to git away from ever'body," Jesse said.

The more she pushed him away—the more she climbed trees to be alone—the more he liked her. He wanted to put his arm around her, but he was afraid she might push him right out of the tree. The river was a long way down, it was wet, and it might have snakes in it. He decided he would verbally embrace her, and she wouldn't even know he was doing it, because he would do it in a foreign language. If she asked what it meant, he could always lie to her.

"*Na-su-yake,*" Pyg said innocently.

Jesse turned and stared at him. "What?"

"It's just something Custer taught me."

"Don't talk Injun talk at me. I don't like it."

"Why not?"

"I just don't."

"It means—"

"I don't care what it means." Her eyes were angry. "Just leave me alone."

Why was she so upset? He couldn't understand it. Was she still angry at Custer for some reason? He thought the Comanche's death had put all that behind them.

"*Na-su-yake,*" Pyg repeated mischievously.

"Shut up," Jesse scolded. "Don't say that no more."

Something in her tone made Pyg suspect that she might know the meaning of the words. Which meant she wasn't angry at Custer but at Pyg. She didn't want him telling her that he loved her in any language.

"You know, don't you?" he asked.

"Know what?" she asked.

"What it means?"

"No."

"Yes, you do. You know it means: 'My mind cries for you.' Don't you? Custer taught you the same way he taught me."

"No."

"You're pretending you don't understand because you can't say it back. I mean cain't. You cain't say it back."

"No, that ain't it."

"Then what is it?"

"I cain't tell you."

"Yes, you can. My mind cries for you. That means I love you and you can tell me everything. Anything at all."

"No, I cain't."

"Why not?"

They dangled their feet over the river for a long time. He was getting irritated, which he didn't want to do. He thought about climbing back down the tree or diving into the river.

"Because I been a hypocrite," Jesse said at last.

"That's a big word," said Pyg.

"I ain't no idyot," she bristled. "Anyhow it's in the Bible. Least I think it is."

"How have you been hypocritical?" he asked.

"Thass an even bigger word. Anyhow I been tellin' you that you ain't really who you say you are—"

"What?"

"That you ain't Mr. Goodnight's son."

"Are you tryin' to start another fight?"

"No, no, I ain't. I'm tryin' to tell you: I ain't who I claim to be neither."

"You aren't? I mean ain't?"

She inched away from him on the branch and stared down at the slow-moving clay-red water.

"No, I ain't," Jesse said at long last. "My grandma was a Comanche Indian. She used to say *na-su-yake* to me all the time." Jesse paused. "You hate me now, doncha?"

"No."

"Well, I hate myself."

"Don't say that."

"'Cause I been denyin' it right-'n'-left. I denied it to Custer. I been denyin' it over and over fer years. One way and another. My parents was so damned ashamed of the taint of Indian blood. Thass how come I wanted to be a damn Harvey Girl. They's . . . they's . . . well, they ain't Injuns. They's real Americans."

Pyg was surprised to see her wipe a tear off her cheek. Jesse wasn't a crier.

"Indians are the realest Americans," he said. "They—you—were here before the rest of us came stragglin' in."

"You're just sayin' that."

"No, I'm not. *Na-su-yake.*"

Jesse started crying harder than ever. He hugged her to him. They both lost their balance and fell backward off their branch into the red water, the canyon's aorta, which connected directly to its ever-bleeding heart.

CHAPTER 77

Shortly after the new year, the ranch readied itself for a solemn funeral. Actually it was a second funeral for the same man, Jimmy Goodnight, one-time king of the ranchers. The second ceremony was Revelie's idea, since she had missed the first. She had been far away in Boston hiding from the law. They weren't going to dig up Goodnight's bones and bury him again. They were simply going to reinstall his tombstone now that it had been recovered. A preacher was coming from Tascosa, which now had a church. And Revelie was putting on widow's weeds.

Around three o'clock in the afternoon, the cowboys all gathered in the vast living room. Supposedly all of them had bathed. Revelie wondered how many really had. None of the cowhands owned a suit, but their shirts and pants were fairly clean. A few of the boots had even been polished. They all wore strips of black cloth tied around their arms.

The widow remembered a happier time when the cowboys had gathered at a much smaller house, just a log cabin with a dog run, to celebrate her marriage to Mr. Goodnight. Those cowboys also wore cloths, white ones, tied around their arms, or rather half of them did. The cowpokes with the white armbands had been designated females for the purposes of dancing. The bride had been the only actual woman at her wilderness wedding ball. Weddings and funerals, so different, so much alike. Now she wore a long black dress instead of a long white one. Back then, she cried tears of joy. Now she laughed at the slightest provocation because life was too sad not to.

Surveying the figures scattered about the big room, Revelie saw Percy and Jesse standing together near the fireplace. She wore a part of her Harvey Girl uniform: a black shirtwaist dress. Percy was the only man in the room wearing a suit. He had once tried to throw away his frock coat, but his mother had saved it for him. Revelie thought her son looked too good for the Harvey Girl, but she had to admit Jesse looked respectable for a change. The girl said something to the boy and then they found seats on a wide sofa in front of the fire. Revelie knew Jesse was still weak from her wound; she must have needed to sit down to rest. He was attentive; she seemed cool. Revelie felt slighted on her son's behalf.

Loving sat on another couch because he also needed to rest, but he was much stronger than he had been even a fortnight ago. His face looked ruddy rather than sickly pale. He wore a dark blue shirt, which was as close to black as his wardrobe went. He seemed lost in memories. Revelie stared at him, trying to make him look at her. He did, and smiled wanly. Then he readjusted the black cloth on his arm.

Deciding it was time, Revelie went to fetch the preacher. He was waiting in the master bedroom where Loving had been sick for so very long. His name was Brother Chance Magruder, which seemed a strange name for a man of his calling. He was a Baptist preacher but welcomed all faiths since his was the only game in town. Unfortunately, he hadn't known Goodnight, but Revelie had told him what she could in half an hour over dinner, which was what they called the midday meal out here in the wild. Brother Chance wore a threadbare black suit and a black tie. He carried a black Bible. His face was flushed. Was he experiencing stage fright or had he brought a flask? Or both?

"I think we're about ready," Revelie said gravely. "If you are."

The reverend cleared his throat loudly. She waited. He cleared his throat again. She was betting on the flask.

"Of course," he croaked.

Revelie led the tipsy reverend down the hall and into the great room. Murmuring stopped. She guided him to a place just to the right of the fireplace. Everybody instinctively stood up, even Loving. The preacher wobbled ever so slightly. Revelie sat down beside Loving on the couch.

"If you ask me," he whispered, "that there preacher ain't got the sense of a shepherd."

Revelie tried unsuccessfully to repress a laugh. Then the tumblers in her mind lined up again and she stopped laughing. Maybe shepherds weren't so dumb, after all. For Revelie had just remembered that sheep-men fought disease with something called a sheep dip, which was just a bathtub for woollies. She had seen and smelled these dips back home in Massachusetts, a state where sheep were more popular than they were out here in Texas. If you could dip a sheep in disinfectant, why couldn't you dip a cow? You just needed a bigger bathtub. Perhaps these smart cattlemen could actually learn something from those dumb sheepherders. Revelie smiled broadly, but then remembered that she was at a service for the dead. She tried to make her mouth frown but smiled in her mind. Funny where ideas came from.

"Brothers and sisters," the preacher began, sonorous and shaky at the same time, "we are gathered here today to mourn the passing of Brother Goodman . . ."

Focused on the service now, Revelie no longer felt like smiling: She hated this man of God. She wanted to strangle him. She wished she could crucify him. She had to get hold of herself.

Attempting to get back to smiling inside, Revelie saw herself—and her cowboys—dipping the cows the way Brother Chance baptized the faithful: total immersion. She made a bet with herself that she could save more cows than he saved souls.

"I mean Brother Goodnight," the preacher corrected himself. "I'm sorry. I think one thing and my tongue says another. I thought I might quote a poem to you. I only hope my tongue doesn't revolt against my mind again."

He took a deep breath. Revelie hoped he would choke on it.

> "He whose glory was redressing human wrong;
> Who spake no slander, no, nor listened to it;
> Who loved one only and who clave to her—"

The preacher cleared his throat again.

"'Clave,' that means *clung to*. So Mr. Goodnight was a good, a just, a faithful man."

Revelie shivered.

> "The shadow of his loss drew like an eclipse,
> Darkening the world. We have lost him: he is gone:

We know him now: all narrow jealousies
Are silent; and we see him as he moved,
How modest, kindly, all-accomplished, wise,
With what sublime repression of himself . . .
Wearing the white flower of a blameless life."

Revelie, who knew that her husband's life was not entirely blame-less, found herself crying. She recognized the poem and even realized the preacher had taken a few liberties, but she didn't mind. She wiped her eyes on her black sleeve even though she knew Boston would not approve. She wanted to hug that damned drunk preacher.

CHAPTER 78

The minister marched through the flock and out the front door. They all followed, even Loving, steadied by Revelie.

"Are you sure this is a good idea?" she asked. "You don't want to get overtired."

"It ain't far," Loving said. "I can make it."

They all descended the porch stairs and set foot on the red earth. Looking around, Revelie saw her son at the side of the Harvey Girl. He seemed poised to catch her if she collapsed. Which was how his mother felt as she walked beside Loving. They were both in love with invalids. But she hoped her boy wasn't as committed as she was. It occurred to her that she was judging Jesse differently from the way she judged Loving. The Harvey Girl and the handsome cowboy were both from the same class, weren't they? Her Boston friends would hardly approve of her liaison with the handsome cowboy any more than they would endorse Jesse. But there was an obvious difference. Or was there?

When the mourners arrived at the thorny grove where Jimmy Goodnight was buried, they formed a circle around the grave. A pregnant hump in the ground revealed where the body was buried. The headstone had already been replaced at the top of the grave. But Revelie was dismayed to discover—

"There's a handle," she said, trying to keep her voice down. "Where did that come from?"

She tried to control her face so it wouldn't show alarm. Someone had taken it on himself to install a new handle to replace the one that had burned up. Surely he had been trying to help out. But she knew immediately that an ax with a handle was much more of a temptation than an ax blade without one. It was much more dangerous.

· · ·

Pyg was surprised by the ax handle, too. He had supposed that the ax and stone would be in the same condition they had been when he turned them over to the ranch. But here was this newly installed handle practically inviting somebody to try his luck. Come one, come all, step right up and try to pull the ax out of the rock.

"Dust unto dust," said the preacher. "Ashes to ashes. Jesus went before him to prepare a place for him. In His house are many mansions even more wonderful than the home we have just left. Fear not for He is with him and He is with you.

"Let us pray. Our Father who art in heaven, hallowed be Thy Name. Thy Kingdom come, Thy will be done on earth as it is–"

"No!" Revelie gasped. "You promised."

Pyg glanced back at her, but kept walking toward the ax. He knew he had promised. He knew it was a sin–anyway a betrayal–to break a promise. He didn't stop.

"On earth as it is in Heaven," the preacher tried again. "Forgive us our trespasses as we forgive those who trespass–"

"Stop!" Revelie ordered.

Pyg paused and looked back once again, but his mother's very opposition meant he had to do it. She wouldn't be so upset if she didn't have a secret, would she? He kept going.

"No, Percy, don't," implored his mother. "You gave me your word."

"As we forgive those who trespass against us," Preacher Chance tried to keep going. "Lead us not into temptation–"

"Stop! Stop! You mustn't. You are being disrespectful to Brother Chance, to me, to everyone here, including your father."

"But deliver us from evil," the preacher kept going.

"Whoever that is?" Pyg said in a soft voice.

"You are ruining the service," his mother said.

"For Thine is the Kingdom," said Reverend Chance.

"I'm sorry," Pyg said, keeping his voice low. "I really am. But I have to do this."

"And the power."

"No, you don't."

"Yes, I do."

"And the glory forever."

Pyg placed his trembling right hand on the handle. Then he

brought up his left, which was even more anxious. Was he making a mistake? Very likely. He hated causing his mother so much pain, but that very pain drove him on. It was an admission of guilt, wasn't it? He told himself that he had to find out, promise or no promise, sin or no sin, bad taste or . . .

"Amen," said Brother Chance.

"Please," said Revelie.

"I hafta," said Pyg.

"Why?"

"You know."

Revelie turned to her enemy, Jesse, and begged her: "Tell him not to do it! Tell him before it's too late. He's ruining the ceremony and everything."

Pyg expected Jesse to shrug and turn her back, but she didn't.

"Pyg," said the Harvey Girl, "you sure this is a good idea? Think."

Pyg bent at the knees, took a deep breath, and pulled. The ax didn't move.

"Anybody else wanna try," asked Little Dogie, "before I pull it out?"

No one spoke.

"Well, here goes."

Striding forward, Little Dogie shouldered Pyg aside and grabbed the handle. He pulled and pulled and pulled, and then screamed.

"Owwwaaahh."

He collapsed. Something had given way inside that giant body. Something had torn. He lay on the ground while Pyg took another turn.

The boy pulled a little harder, but it didn't feel right, so he tugged more gently. He imagined that he had asked Jesse to dance, and she was nice for a change, and so he took her by the hand and led her onto the dance floor.

"Come with me," he said softly to the blade. "I'll take care of you."

Pyg felt the stone loosening its stony grip, felt the ax surrendering itself to him. He wanted to hurry, but he told himself to be patient. Slowly, easy now, gently. He gave the slightest tug and drew the ax from the stone.

Pyg smiled and raised the ax high over his head. The crowd fell utterly quiet and everybody started backing up to give him room. Then

Loving cheered. Too Short yelled. And the other cowboys joined in. Revelie screamed.

Horses whinnied. Roosters crowed. Bulls snorted and kicked up red dirt. A donkey brayed. A redtailed hawk screamed high overhead. Mice squeaked, grasshoppers leaped high in the air, spiders stopped their weaving and looked around. Prairie dogs came up out of their burrows to see what had disturbed the universe. A turtle hurried. An old diamondback rattled its tail. A single drop of rain fell out of the pale-blue sky and hit Pyg right between his blue and brown eyes.

Blinking, Pyg stared up at the ax in his hand, at the sky, at the sun. He let out a scream that began as a war cry but ended in laughter. He shook his new weapon at the heavens. And bees buzzed loud about his head.

"Well done," said his breathless mother. Then she added: "Pyg."

CHAPTER 79

They lay down in the moon-cast shadow of his father's tombstone. They lay beside the swell of earth that covered his father's bones. Beside them lay his father's ax. The boy, the girl, and the scepter.

"I ain't so sure 'bout you," said Jesse. "You're gittin' real strange and strange some more. How come you wanna come out chere to the graveyard?"

"Sorry, I just wanted to be close to my dad," Pyg said. "It's like I'm tryin' to get to know him. Do you want to go back to the house?"

"No, siree," she said. "It's still your mama's house. I reckon I wouldn't mind gittin' to know your daddy a little bit better myself."

They lay on their backs looking for pictures in the stars. No matter where he looked in the heavens, Pyg saw nipples. Big ones. Small ones. Bright ones. Dim ones. A million, billion twinkling nipples beckoning to him.

When Pyg rolled onto his side and reached for a real, living breast, Jesse did not pull away. He caressed the cloth over her right nipple. He reached inside her shirt and felt puckering skin. He unbuttoned and exposed dark moonlit nipples more beautiful than the myriad bright nipples in the sky. Galileo was no more excited when he first saw the rings of Saturn. Pyg started to hurry, ripping at her clothing. She slowed him down.

"Cowboy, this ain't no gunfight," Jesse said. "Drawin' fast and shootin' quick ain't the best policy when it comes to this kinda work. Trust me. Take a deep breath and relax."

Pyg took a deep breath, but he did not relax. Jesse kicked off her boots and helped him pull off her Strausses. She guided him into her. And then . . . almost . . . almost . . . almost . . .

A rooster crowed in the night. Coyotes took up the howl. A screech-owl screamed overhead. Beneath the earth, moles and earthworms stopped burrowing, wondering what had happened up there in the vast spinning world. Nighthawks dived and moths clapped their wings.

Pyg bellowed a scream that began as a war cry but ended in unqualified delight.

"I done love you and love you some more," he said softly.

"No, don't say it like that," she said. "Say it like *you* talk, so you mean it."

"I love you."

Pyg realized his heart had lost its virginity, too.